THE WINNERS

WITHDRAWN

P9-ASI-262

Gramley Library
Salem College
Winston-Salem, NC 27108

ALSO BY JULIO CORTAZAR

Hopscotch

End of the Game

Cronopios and Famas

62: A Model Kit

All Fires the Fire and Other Stories

A Manual for Manuel

A Change of Light

We Love Glenda So Much

WITHDRAWN

PQ
7797
.C7145
P72
1965

JULIO CORTÁZAR

. . . .

THE WINNERS

TRANSLATED FROM THE SPANISH
BY ELAINE KERRIGAN

PANTHEON BOOKS, NEW YORK

Salem Academy and College
Gramley Library
Winston-Salem, N.C. 27108

Copyright © 1965 by Random House, Inc.

All rights reserved under International and Pan-American Copyright Conventions. Published in New York by Pantheon Books, a division of Random House, Inc. Hardcover edition published by Pantheon Books, a division of Random House, Inc., in 1965. Originally published in Argentina as *Los Premios* by Editorial Sudamericana, Buenos Aires. Copyright © 1960 by Editorial Sudamericana Sociedad Anónima.

Library of Congress catalog card number: 64–18305
ISBN: 0-394-72301-5

Manufactured in the United States of America

First Pantheon Paperback Edition

What is an author to do with ordinary people, absolutely "ordinary," and how can he put them before his readers so as to make them at all interesting? It is impossible to leave them out of fiction altogether, for commonplace people are at every moment the chief and essential links in the chain of human affairs; if we leave them out, we lose all semblance of truth.

DOSTOYEVSKY, *The Idiot* IV,1

PROLOGUE

I

"The marquise left at five," Carlos Lopez thought. "Where the devil did I read that?"

He was at the London Café on Peru and Avenida; it was five-ten. Did the marquise leave at five? Lopez shook his head to push away the incomplete recollection, and tried his Quilmes Cristal beer. It wasn't cold enough.

"Take a person away from his routine, he's like a fish out of water," Dr. Restelli said, staring at his glass. "I'm used to my sweet maté tea at four, you know. Look at that woman coming out of the subway; I don't know if you can see her, there are so many people. There she goes, the blonde. Do you think we'll run into such free and easy blondes on our cruise?"

"I doubt it," said Lopez. "The most beautiful women always travel on another ship. That's how it is."

"Ah, skeptical youth," said Dr. Restelli. "I'm well past the dangerous age, though naturally I go on an occasional fling. I'm optimistic, however; I've packed three bottles of brandy in my suitcase, and I'm almost sure we'll have the company of lovely young ladies."

"We'll see, if we ever leave at all," said Lopez. "Speaking of women, here comes one worth turning your head about seventy degrees toward Florida. There . . . stop. The one talking to the long-haired guy. They look like the types who'd be going on this trip with us, although I'll be damned if I know how anyone has to look to go on this trip. Let's have another beer."

Dr. Restelli agreed. Lopez thought that Restelli, with his stiff collar, and blue silk, purple-dotted tie, looked most amazingly like a turtle. He used a pince-nez, which jeopardized discipline at the public school where he taught Argentine history (Lopez taught Spanish), and between his looks and his teaching he earned himself several nicknames, ranging from "Black Cat" to "Derby." "And what nicknames have they given me?" Lopez thought hypocritically; he was sure that the boys had settled for Lopez*-the-one-from-the-phone-book or something like that.

"A gorgeous creature," Dr. Restelli decided. "I wouldn't mind a bit if she joined the cruise. It must be the prospect of sea air and nights in the tropics, for I must confess, I feel remarkably exhilarated. Your health, my friend and colleague!"

"Yours, Doctor and fellow prizewinner," Lopez said, lowering the level in his stein appreciably.

Dr. Restelli had a good opinion (with certain reservations) of his friend and colleague. At faculty meetings he usually differed with the lenient grades proposed by Lopez, who insisted on defending stolid drifters and other less derelict types, who were nevertheless given to copying during tests or reading the newspaper in the middle of a discussion of Vilcapugio (and it was difficult enough to find an honorable explanation of the beatings General Belgrano took from the Spaniards). But apart from being somewhat bohemian, Lopez was an excellent colleague, always ready to recognize that it was Dr. Restelli who should deliver the Ninth of July speeches. And Dr. Restelli, in the end, always yielded modestly to Dr. Guglielmetti's solicitations and the extremely cordial, even though unmerited, pressure at the faculty meetings. After all, it was lucky that Lopez had won the Tourist Lottery and not Gomez, the Negro, or that female who taught third-year English. It was possible to get along with Lopez, even if he sometimes indulged in an excessive liberalism, an almost reprehensible leftism, and *that* Restelli could tolerate in no one. But, on the other hand, he did like girls and the horses.

"*When you were fourteen, just fourteen Aprils ago, you gave yourself up to revelries and the delights of the tango,*" Lopez hummed. "Why did you buy a ticket, Doctor?"

* Spanish equivalent of Smith, or other common surname.

"I simply surrendered in the face of Señora Rébora's insistence. You know how that woman gets when she makes up her mind about something. Did she pester you too? Of course now we're grateful, and it's only fair to say so."

"She chewed my ear for about eight recesses," Lopez said. "Impossible to get very far in the racing section with a horsefly like that buzzing around. But the curious thing is that her connection with it wasn't too clear. Basically, it's just another lottery."

"Ah, not so. Pardon me, but this was something very special and completely different."

"But why was Madame Rébora selling tickets?"

"We may assume," Dr. Restelli said mysteriously, "that the sale of this particular lottery was destined for a certain public, a select public, as they say. And probably for this undertaking, the State appealed to our women for aid, as they have on historic occasions. It might have been embarrassing if the winner had to mix with people of, let's say, low quality."

"All right," Lopez agreed. "But you forget that the winners have the right to drag as many as three members of their family to the dance."

"My dear colleague, if my deceased wife and my daughter, the wife of young Robirosa, could have come along with me—"

"Of course, of course," said Lopez. "You're a particular case. But look, why beat around the bush: if I suddenly went mad and invited my sister, for example, you'd see how the quality would lower, to use your own words."

"I don't think your sister—"

"Neither would she," said Lopez. "But I assure you she's one of those women who say 'Huh?' and think 'vomit' is a bad word."

"Actually, the term is a little strong. I prefer 'regurgitate.' "

"She, on the other hand, rather favors 'throw up' or 'give back.' And what do you say about our lucky student?"

Dr. Restelli passed from his beer to the most obvious annoyance. He'd never understand how Señora Rébora, a bore but not at all a fool, and who, after all, boasted a family name of some ancestry, could have allowed herself to be carried away by a mania to sell all her tickets, lowering herself to the extent of offering chances to pupils in the upper grades. A sad result of a stroke of luck of the kind recorded only in certain chronicles, perhaps apocryphal, of the Casino at Monte Carlo, was that the student Felipe Trejo, as well as Lopez and Restelli, held a winning number. And Trejo was the worst in his class, and the most likely source of certain muffled noises too often heard in Argentine history period.

"Believe me, Lopez, they shouldn't let vermin like that on the boat. Among other things, he's a minor."

"Not only is he going on the trip, but he's bringing the family," Lopez said. "I found that out from a reporter I know who was going around doing stories on the few winners he could manage to get in touch with."

Poor Restelli, poor revered Black Cat. School would cast its shadow over his entire trip, that is, if there was a trip, and Felipe Trejo's metallic laugh would spoil his attempted flirtations, the Line-Crossing ceremony when he would be changed from a Pollywog to a Shellback, and even his chocolate ice cream, not to mention the lifeboat drills, which were always amusing. "If he only knew I've drunk beer with Trejo and his gang in Plaza Eleven, and thanks to them, I know about Black Cat and Derby . . . Poor guy, he makes such a big deal out of being a teacher."

"That might be all to the good," Dr. Restelli said hopefully. "The family might tone him down. Don't you think so? Of course, you can't help but think so."

"Take a look," said Lopez, "at those twins or almost-twins coming down Peru. They're crossing the Avenida. See them?"

"I'm not sure," said Dr. Restelli. "One in white and the other in green?"

"That's it. Especially the one in white."

"She's very nice. Yes, the one in white. Hm, good calves. Perhaps a little hurried in the walk. Do you think they'll be joining the group?"

"No, Doctor, it's obvious they're going on without stopping."

"A pity. I must say, I once had a young lady like that. Striking resemblance."

"To the one in white?"

"No, the one in green. I'll never forget . . . but that can't possibly interest you. It does? Then another little beer; we still have half an hour before the group convenes. You see, this girl came from a good family and knew I was married. However, to make a long story short, she literally threw herself into my arms. The nights, my friend . . ."

"I never doubted you knew your Kama Sutra," Lopez said. "More beer, Roberto."

"The gentlemen are thirsty today," Roberto remarked. "You can tell it's humid. It says so in the paper."

"If it's in the paper, it must be true," said Lopez. "I'm beginning to figure out who our traveling companions are going to be. They have the same expression on their faces as we do, somewhere between amused and distrustful. Just look around, Doctor, you'll see for yourself."

"Why distrustful?" asked Dr. Restelli. "Those rumors are absolutely unfounded. You'll see, we'll sail exactly as stated on the back of the ticket. The lottery depends upon the endorsement of the State; it's not just a fly-by-night raffle. It has been sold in the best circles, and it would be odd to suspect any sort of irregularity."

"I admire your confidence in the bureaucratic order," said Lopez. "Clearly it corresponds to your inner order, as they say. I, on the other hand, am like a Turk's trunk, and I'm never sure of anything. It's not exactly that I distrust the lottery, though I've asked myself more than once if it might not end up like the Gelria swindle."

"The Gelria was an agency-run thing, probably Jews involved," said Dr. Restelli. "Even the name, come to think of it . . . It's not that I'm anti-Semitic, far from it, but for years I've observed the infiltration of that race, quite meritorious, if you like, for other reasons. To your health."

"To yours," said Lopez, holding back his laughter. The marquise . . . would she really leave at five? The same people as always came in and went out through the door leading to the Avenida de Mayo. Lopez took advantage of his interlocutor's meditation, probably ethnic in nature, to look around the café carefully. Nearly all of the tables were occupied, but only at a few was an atmosphere of likely travelers prevalent. A group of girls left, with the usual confusion: laughter, scuffling, and glances at possible admirers or critics. A woman came in armed with several children and entered the little salon set with reassuring tablecloths, where other women and peaceful couples sat over cold drinks, pastries, or at most a glass of beer. A young fellow (but yes, that one yes) came in with a very good-looking girl (I hope she's coming) and sat down close to Lopez' table. They were nervous and looked at one another with a false naturalness, which their hands, fumbling with purses and cigarettes, contradicted. Outside, the Avenida de Mayo was insisting on its usual disorder: the five-o'clock edition of the newspaper was being hawked, and a loudspeaker was extolling some product or other. There was the furious summer light of five-thirty (a false hour, like so many other things which come too early or too late), and the smell of a mixture of gasoline, hot asphalt, eau de cologne, and damp sawdust filled the air. Lopez suddenly found it strange that the Tourist Lottery should ever have seemed unreasonable to him. Only because of his long observance of Buenos Aires—not to say more than that, to get metaphysical— was he able to accept as reasonable the spectacle that surrounded and included him. The most chaotic hypothesis of chaos paled before this confusion: ninety-two degrees in the shade, arrivals and departures, marches and countermarches, hats and briefcases, policemen and five-o'clock editions, buses and beers, all crammed into every fraction of every second and vertiginously transforming the following fraction of a second. Now the woman in the red skirt and the man in the checked jacket were about to pass one another, they were two pavement squares apart, at that same moment Dr. Restelli was bringing his beer to his mouth, and the lovely (she really was) girl was taking out her lipstick. Now the two pedestrians were back to back, the glass was slowly lowered, and the lipstick was writing the eternal curved word. Who would have the nerve to think the lottery was strange?

II

"Two coffees," Lucio ordered.
"And a glass of water, please," Nora added.
"They always bring water with the coffee," said Lucio.
"That's true."
"Besides, you never drink it."

"But I'm thirsty today," said Nora.

"Yes, it's hot in here," said Lucio, changing his tone. He leaned across the table. "You look tired."

"Well, between the luggage and the taxis . . ."

"The taxis and the luggage, it all sounds so odd," Lucio said.

"Yes."

"You're tired, aren't you?"

"Yes."

"You'll sleep well tonight."

"I hope so," said Nora. As usual, Lucio said the most innocent things in a tone of voice she had learned to understand. She probably wouldn't sleep well tonight, since this would be her first night with Lucio. Her second first night.

"Sweetie," said Lucio, stroking her hand. "Sweetie pie."

Nora thought of the Hotel Belgrano, of the first night with Lucio, but it wasn't so much recalling as forgetting about it a little less.

"Dope," said Nora. Her lipstick refill . . . would it be in her overnight bag?

"Good coffee," said Lucio. "Do you think they've figured anything out yet at your house? Not that it matters, but just to avoid problems."

"Mama thinks I'm going to the movies with Mocha."

"They'll raise the roof tomorrow."

"They can't do anything now," said Nora. "No kidding, they celebrated my birthday . . . I'm mostly worried about Dad. Dad isn't bad, but Mama does what she wants with him and with everyone else."

"It's getting hotter in here by the minute."

"You're nervous," said Nora.

"No, but I'd like to be on board once and for all. Doesn't it seem funny they'd make us come here first? I guess they'll take us to the docks in a car."

"Who do you think the others are?" said Nora. "That woman in black . . . do you think?"

"No. That woman wouldn't be traveling. Maybe those two talking at that table."

"There'll have to be a lot more, at least twenty."

"You're a little pale," said Lucio.

"It's the heat."

"Just as well we'll be able to rest until we're tired of it," Lucio said. "I hope we get a good cabin."

"With hot water," said Nora.

"Yes, and fan and porthole. An outside cabin."

"Why do you say cabin instead of stateroom?"

"I don't know. Stateroom . . . actually cabin sounds better. Stateroom is like traveling in state or something like that. Did I tell you the boys in the office wanted to come and see us off?"

"See *us* off?" said Nora. "But how? Then they know about us?"

"Well, to see *me* off," said Lucio. "They don't know anything. The only one I spoke to was Medrano, at the Club. And he's okay. Remember, he's going too, so it's better I told him beforehand."

"Just think, he won, too," said Nora. "Isn't that incredible?"

"Señora Apelbaum offered us the whole block of tickets. I guess the rest was divided up around La Boca, I don't know. Why are you so pretty?"

"Because," said Nora, letting Lucio hold her hand and squeeze it. As usual, when he talked to her intimately, inquiringly, Nora would withdraw politely, yielding just enough not to hurt his feelings. Lucio looked at her smiling mouth, which opened perfectly around a set of very white, small teeth (further back there was one gold-filled tooth). If only we do get a good cabin tonight, and if Nora does get a good rest . . . There was so much to blot out (but really there was nothing; what had to be blotted out was that foolish nothing in which she persisted). He saw Medrano come through the door on the Florida side in the middle of a bunch of rough-looking characters, and a lady in a lace blouse. He raised his arm, almost in relief. Medrano recognized him and came over to their table.

III

The subway isn't so bad during dog days. It takes about ten minutes between Loria and Peru, and it's time enough to cool off and look through the newspaper. The problem had been to pack and change without Bettina asking too many questions, but Medrano had invented a reunion of the class of '35, a dinner at Loprete's, preceded by a drink some place or other. He had done so much lying since the lottery drawing that the final and almost businesslike lie was hardly worth mentioning.

Bettina had stayed in bed, naked, the fan turned on, reading Proust in Menasché's translation. They had been making love all morning, stopping only to sleep or to have a whisky or a coke. After eating a cold chicken they had discussed the value of Marcel Aymé's work, Emilio Ballagas' poems, and the current fluctuation of Mexican currency. At four Medrano took a shower and Bettina opened the Proust book (they had made love once more). In the subway, as he compassionately watched a schoolboy trying to look like a tough hood, Medrano traced a mental line from the beginning of the day's activities and found them satisfactory. Now Saturday could begin.

He was looking at the paper but thinking of Bettina, a little surprised to find he was still thinking of her. The farewell letter (he liked to think of it as the posthumous letter) had been written the night before, while Bettina was sleeping with one foot outside the sheet and her hair in her eyes. Everything was explained (except, of course, she'd see everything from an opposite point of view), the personal matters favorably liquidated. He had broken with Susana Daneri the same way, without even leaving the country as he was now; every time since when he'd run into Susana (usually at openings at galleries, inevitable in Buenos Aires) she'd smile like an old friend, without a hint of resentment or nostalgia. He imagined himself going into Pizarro's and running into Bettina, a smiling, friendly Bettina. Well, even if she were only smiling. But undoubtedly Bettina would go back to Rauch, where her impeccable family awaited her in total innocence, and two courses in Spanish to teach.

"Doctor Livingstone, I presume," said Medrano.

"I'd like you to meet Gabriel Medrano," Lucio said. "Well, sit down and have something."

He shook Nora's slightly timid hand and ordered a dry Martini. Nora found him older than what she would have expected of one of Lucio's friends. He must have been at least forty, but he wore

Salem Academy and College
Gramley Library
Winston-Salem, N.C. 27108

his Italian silk suit and white shirt with a lot of style. Lucio would
never learn to dress like that even if he had the money.

"What do you think of all these people?" Lucio asked. "We
were trying to figure out who we'll be going with. I think a list was
published in the papers, but I didn't see it."

"Luckily, the list wasn't very reliable," Medrano said. "Aside
from me, they left out the names of a few others who wanted to
avoid publicity or family catastrophes."

"Besides, there're the guests of the winners."

"Ah, yes," said Medrano, and he thought of Bettina asleep.
"Well, at the moment I see Carlos Lopez over there with a very
respectable-looking gentleman. You know them?"

"No."

"Lopez quit the Club three years ago; I know him from
those days. It must have been a little before you joined. I'm going
to find out if he's going."

Lopez was one of the winners, and they were happy to see one
another again, especially under the present circumstances. Lopez
introduced Dr. Restelli, who said that Medrano's face was familiar. Medrano took advantage of the fact that the adjoining table
had been vacated to call over Nora and Lucio. All this took time,
because it wasn't easy at the London to get up and change places
without provoking the staff's notorious moods. Lopez called Roberto, who grumbled, but helped with the table change and pock-
eted a peso tip without a word of thanks. The noisy, rough-looking
group began to rumble ominously and demanded a second beer. It
wasn't easy to talk at this time of day, when everyone was thirsty
and squeezed into the London like sardines, sacrificing the last
breath of air for the dubious compensation of a beer or tonic.
There was hardly much difference any more between the bar
and the street; a compact crowd of people carrying packages, papers, and briefcases, especially briefcases of various colors and sizes,
were going up and down the Avenida now.

"In short," said Dr. Restelli, "if I've understood correctly, all
of us present will have the pleasure of being together on this agreeable cruise."

"We shall," said Medrano. "I fear, however, that part of that noisy symposium over there to the left will also be joining our happy group."

"You think so, old man?" said Lopez, pretending horror.

"They look shady," said Lucio. "It's one thing going to a football game with them, but on a ship . . ."

"Who knows," said Nora, who felt called upon to add a touch of modernity. "They may be very nice."

"Right now," said Lopez, "a modest young girl seems to want to join their group. Yes, there she goes. Accompanied by a woman dressed in black, reeking of virtue."

"Mother and daughter," said Nora, infallible when it came to such things. "Lord, look at their clothes."

"That finishes the speculation," said Lopez. "They're sailing with us and also landing with us, that is, if we actually get off and actually get there."

"Democracy . . ." said Dr. Restelli, but his voice trailed off into a noisy outburst from the mouth of the subway. The loud types seemed to recognize certain tribal signs, since two of them responded immediately: one with a whooping yell pitched an octave higher than the signal and another by putting two fingers in his mouth and letting out a terrifying whistle.

". . . unfortunately having to mingle with one's social inferiors," Dr. Restelli concluded.

"Exactly," Medrano replied politely. "Furthermore, I wonder why we're going at all."

"Pardon?"

"Why should we go at all?"

"Well," said Lopez, "I suppose it's always more amusing than staying home. Personally, I like the idea of having won a trip for ten pesos. Don't forget, a paid vacation is already a considerable prize. Can't pass up something like that."

"I realize it's not to be put down," said Medrano. "For instance, the prize has given me an excuse to close my office and not look at decayed teeth for a while. But you'll have to admit that this whole business . . . I've had the feeling more than once that this is going to end up in a way . . . Well, you opt the adjective, that's always the most optional part of speech."

Nora looked at Lucio.

"I think you're exaggerating," said Lucio. "If everyone turned down prizes for fear of being swindled . . ."

"I don't think Medrano was thinking of a swindle," said Lopez. "It's more like something in the air, a kind of grand-scale practical joke. Look at that woman who just came in wearing . . . probably she's going too . . . And there, Doctor, is our Trejo who has just sat down, surrounded by his loving family. This café is beginning to look more and more transatlantic every minute."

"I'll never understand how Señora Rébora could sell tickets to students, and especially to that one," said Dr. Restelli.

"It's hotter than ever," said Nora. "Please order me a cold drink."

"We'll be all right once we're on board, you'll see," said Lucio, waving his arm to attract the attention of Roberto, who was busy with the growing table of enthusiastic young men, as they ordered such extravangancies as *cappucino*, bock beer, *chorizo* sandwiches —items generally ignored at the café or at least considered a bit unusual at that time of day.

"Yes, I imagine it will be cooler," said Nora, looking hesitantly at Medrano. She was still nervous about what he had said, or perhaps it was a way of concentrating her nervousness on something conversational and communicable. Her stomach was hurting a bit; maybe she'd have to go to the ladies' room. How unpleasant to have to get up in front of all these men. But maybe she'd be able to hold it. Yes, she could. It was more of a muscular pain. What would the cabin be like? Two tiny beds, one on top of the other . . . She'd like the upper one, but Lucio would get into his pajamas and climb into the upper berth, too.

"Have you ever been to sea, Nora?" Medrano asked. It was just like him to call her by her first name right away. You could see he wasn't shy with women. No, she hadn't, except for an excursion along the Delta, but that, of course . . . And had he? Yes, a little, as a young man (as if he were old). To Europe and the United States, dentists' conventions and tourism . . . When the franc was worth ten centavos, just imagine.

"Fortunately, everything here will be paid for," said Nora, and she immediately felt like swallowing her tongue. Medrano was watching her compassionately, protecting her at once. Lopez was

also looking at her sympathetically, but thére was an admixture of
Buenos Aires admiration in his look too, which consisted in not
missing a good thing. If everyone were as nice as these two, the
trip would be worth the trouble. Nora sipped a little grenadine and
sneezed. Medrano and Lopez were still smiling, shielding her, and
Lucio was looking almost as if he wanted to protect her from so
much sympathy. A white dove perched for a moment on the railing
at the subway entrance. It remained indifferent and detached, surrounded by the crowd that went surging up and down the Avenida,
then flew off with the same apparent lack of motive that had inspired it to alight. At the corner door a woman, holding a child by
the hand, came in. "More children," thought Lopez. "And this
one is surely going on the trip, that is, if we ever get moving. It's
almost six, time for last-minute instructions. Something always happens at six."

IV

"I bet they have delicious ice cream here," said Jorge.
"Do you think so?" said Claudia, looking at her son conspira-
torially.
"Of course I do. Lemon and chocolate."
"That's an awful combination, but if you like it . . ."
The chairs at the London were particularly uncomfortable; they
tried to hold the body in an implacably upright position. Claudia
was tired from packing, and at the last minute she had discovered
she was missing a number of things, and Persio had had to run and
buy them. Luckily, the poor fellow hadn't much work with his own
luggage; he packed as if he were going on a picnic. Meanwhile, she
finished closing the apartment and wrote one of those last-minute
letters, for which she was suddenly completely empty of ideas and
even emotions . . . But now she'd rest until she was tired of resting. She'd needed a rest for a long time. "For a long time I've
needed to get tired in order to rest," she corrected herself, toying
indifferently with the words. Persio would be along any minute;
at the very end he had remembered some item he had forgotten to
lock up in his mysterious room in Chacarita, where he accumu-

lated books on occultism and manuscripts of his own which would probably never be published. Poor Persio, he was the one who really needed a rest; it was lucky that the authorities had permitted Claudia (with the help of a telephone call from Dr. Leon Lewbaum to the engineer So-and-So) to present Persio as a distant relative and to take him along, practically as contraband. But if anyone deserved taking advantage of the lottery it was Persio, the untiring corrector of proofs at Kraft Publishing, a roomer at vague establishments on the west side of the city, and a nocturnal stroller along the waterfront and streets around the Flores section. "He'll get more out of this nonsensical trip than I will," Claudia thought, looking at her nails. "Poor Persio."

She felt better after having some coffee. And so she was going on a trip with her son, and while she was at it, smuggling in her old friend transformed into a false relative. She was going because she had won a prize, because the salt air would do Jorge good, because it would be even better for Persio. She again thought out the same sentences, repeating: "And so . . ." She sipped her coffee, distractedly, and began again. It wasn't easy to fall in step with what was happening, what was going to happen. There wasn't that much difference if it were for three months or for the rest of her life. What was the difference? She wasn't happy, or miserable either; neither of those extremes which withstand violent changes. Her husband would go on paying Jorge's keep anywhere in the world. That's what his income was for, and so was the black market, handy in a pinch, and the traveler's checks.

"Are all of these people going?" asked Jorge, gradually returning to reality from his ice cream.

"No. We could guess, if you want to. I think that lady in pink is going."

"You think so? She's very ugly."

"Well, we won't take her. Now you guess."

"Those men at that table with the girl."

"Could be. They seem nice. Did you bring a handkerchief?"

"Yes, Mama. Mama, is the boat big?"

"I suppose so. It seems it's a special ship."

"Hasn't anyone seen it?"

"Perhaps, but it isn't a famous ship."

"It'll be ugly then," Jorge said sadly. "Everyone knows the beautiful ones. Persio, Persio! Mama, there's Persio."

"Persio on time," said Claudia. "It makes me think the lottery has corrupted his old ways."

"Persio, here we are! What did you bring me, Persio?"

"News from the star," said Persio, and Jorge looked up at him happily, and waited.

V

The student Felipe Trejo was very much absorbed in what was happening at the next table.

"You'll see," he said to his father, who was mopping his sweaty brow with the greatest possible elegance. "I'm sure some of those bums are boarding with us."

"Can't you speak properly, Felipe?" Señora Trejo complained. "This boy, when will he learn some manners?"

Beba Trejo was discussing make-up problems with her small hand mirror, which she also employed, at the moment, as a periscope.

"Well, those characters," Felipe condescended. "You'll see. They're probably from the Market district."

"I don't think they're all going," said Señora Trejo. "Probably the couple at the head of the table and that lady, the one who must be the girl's mother."

"They're terribly common," said Beba.

"Terribly common," Felipe mocked.

"Don't be stupid."

"Look at her, the Duchess of Windsor. The same face even."

"Children," said Señora Trejo.

Felipe was elated with the awareness of his sudden importance, and he was using it carefully so as not to burn it all up at once. He had to put his sister, especially her, in her place and get back at her for all the tricks she had pulled on him before he'd won the prize.

"There are people at the other tables who seem quite nice," said Señora Trejo.

"Well-dressed people," said Señor Trejo.

"They're here at my invitation," Felipe thought, and he could
have shouted with happiness. "The old man, the old lady, and that
turd. I'll do what I want now." He turned toward the people at
the other table and waited until one of them looked at him.

"By any chance, are you going on the trip?" he asked a strong-
looking fellow in a striped shirt.

"Not me, kid," said the strong-looking type. "Only the young
guy here with his old lady, and the young lady with her old lady,
too."

"Oh! You came to see them off."

"That's right. You going?"

"Yes, with my family."

"Well, ain't you got it made, buddy boy."

"That's the way it crumbles," said Felipe. "Say, maybe you'll
tie the next one up."

"Sure. Why not?"

"Right, why not?"

VI

"Besides, I have news of the octopat," said Persio.

Jorge leaned forward, his elbows on the table.

"Did you find it under the bed or in the tub?" he asked.

"Climbing around in the typewriter," said Persio. "What do
you think it was doing?"

"Typing."

"What a smart boy," said Persio to Claudia. "Of course it was
typing. I have the note, I'll read you part of it. It says: 'You're
going on a trip and leaving me behind like an old shoe. The poor
octopat will be anxiously waiting for you.' Signed: 'The octopat,
with a hug and a reproach.' "

"Poor octopat," said Jorge. "What's it going to eat while you're
away?"

"Matches, lead from pencils, telegrams, and a can of sardines."

"He won't be able to open it," said Claudia.

"Oh, yes, the octopat knows how," said Jorge. "And the star,
Persio?"

"It seems to have rained on the star," said Persio.

"If it did rain," Jorge calculated, "the antmen are going to have to climb onto rafts. Will it be like the Flood or a little less?"

Persio wasn't too sure, but he figured the antmen would know how to get out of the affair.

"You didn't bring the telescope," said Jorge. "What are we going to do if we want to look at the star?"

"Star telepathy," said Persio, winking. "Claudia, you're tired."

"That woman in white," said Claudia, "would say it's the humidity. Well, Persio, here we are. What's going to happen?"

"Ah, that . . . I haven't had much time to study the question, but I'm already preparing the offensive."

"The offensive?"

"Yes. A thing or a fact has to be attacked in many ways. People usually select one tactic and only get halfway results. I always prepare my offensive and afterwards synchronize the results."

"I understand," said Claudia in a tone of voice which revealed her lack of understanding.

"A kind of push-pull has to be in operation," said Persio. "I don't know if I'm making myself clear. Occasionally, it's as if there were things blocking the way, then they have to be pushed aside for one to make out what's happening further on. Women, for instance, and pardon my mentioning them in front of a child. But there are other things you have to grab by the handle and pull. That chap Dali knows what he's doing (maybe he doesn't, but it's all the same) when he paints a body full of drawers. It seems to me many things have handles. For example, poetic images. If one sees them from the outside, only the outer and obvious meaning can be grasped, even if it's sometimes well concealed. Are you satisfied with the exterior, the obvious meaning? No, you're not. You have to pull the handle and fall into the drawer. To pull is to appropriate, to approach, and even to go too far."

"Ah," said Claudia, making a discreet sign for Jorge to blow his nose.

"This place, for instance, is thick with significant elements: every table, every necktie. I see an underlying order within this awful disorder. I wonder what the outcome will be."

"So do I. But it's amusing."

"Amusement is always a spectacle: but let's not delve too deeply, for some foul trap is bound to come open at our feet. It's not that I'm against amusement, but every time I want to enjoy myself I must first lock up the laboratory and throw out all the acids and alkalines. I mean that I must surrender and give in to the appearance of things. You know very well how dramatic the humorous can be . . ."

"Recite the verse about Garrick for Persio," said Claudia to Jorge. "A good illustration of your theory."

"*When the public saw Mr. Garrick, an actor from England . . .*" Jorge declaimed at a shout. Persio listened attentively and then applauded. There was applause from other tables, and Jorge blushed.

"*Quod erat demonstrandum,*" Persio said. "Of course, I was alluding to a more ontological plane, to the fact that all amusement is like the consciousness of a mask, which animates and finally supplants the real face. Why does man laugh? There's nothing to laugh about, if it's not for the sake of laughter alone. You've noticed that children who laugh a great deal usually end up crying."

"They're dopes," said Jorge. "Should I say the one about the fisherman and the pearl?"

"You'll be able to recite what you like under an audience of stars," Persio said. "Now I'd like to find out something about this semigastronomical setup surrounding us. And those accordions . . . what are they supposed to signify?"

"Wow," said Jorge, his mouth wide open.

VII

A black Lincoln, a black suit, a black tie. All the rest was blurred. What was most in evidence around Don Galo Porriño was his chauffeur, with his imposing shoulders, and Don Galo's wheelchair, a battle of rubber and chrome. A crowd stopped to see the chauffeur and nurse lift Don Galo out of the car and lower him to the chair on the sidewalk. A certain pity could be detected on the faces in the crowd, a pity tempered by the obvious signs of wealth surrounding the old gentleman. And besides, Don Galo looked like a chicken with a plucked neck, and he had such a nasty, sly glance that it gave you the urge to sing the International right in his face, something that never had happened—according to Medrano—in spite of the fact that Argentina was a free country and music an art encouraged in the best circles.

"I forgot that Don Galo was one of the prizewinners. How could he help winning a prize? That goes without saying, but I never imagined that he would *make* the trip. It's unbelievable."

"Do you know that gentleman?" asked Nora.

"The person who doesn't know Don Galo Porriño in the town of Junín deserves to be stoned to death in that handsome plaza with the wide walks," said Medrano. "The vicissitudes of being a dentist took me to that progressive city until about five years ago, a happy point when I could again return to Buenos Aires. And Don Galo was one of the first outstanding personages I met there."

"He looks like a respectable gentleman," said Dr. Restelli. "The truth is that with a car like that it seems somewhat strange . . ."

"With a car like that," said Lopez, "he could throw the captain in the water and use the ship as an ashtray."

"With a car like that," said Medrano, "one can go very far. As far as Junín and as far as the London, as all of you can see. One of my weaknesses is gossipology, although I'd add in my defense that only certain superior forms of gossip, such as history, hold any interest for me. What shall I tell you about Don Galo? (This is just how certain writers begin when they know very well what they're going to say.) I'd say that he would be better named Gaius, and you'll soon see why. One of the most famous of Junín's department stores is the 'Blue and Gold,' a predestined name. But if you've ever been a tourist in the provincial area, which I doubt, you'll know that in the city of Veinticinco de Mayo there is another 'Blue and Gold' department store, and that in practically every outlying town and village of our vast province there are 'Blue and Gold' stores situated on the most strategic corners. In short, all this means millions of pesos in the pockets of Don Galo, industrious Spanish Galician that he is, who, I suppose, reached this country penniless like all his compatriots and worked with the characteristic Galician efficiency in our siesta-disposed pampas. Don Galo, paralyzed and almost without family, lives in a palace

in Palermo. A well-organized bureaucracy watches over the chain
of 'Blue and Gold' stores: attendants who are all eyes and ears
for the king, who stand guard, reform, inform, and sanction. But
I have here . . . Am I boring you?"

"Oh, no," said Nora, drinking in his words.

"Well, then," Medrano went on ironically, careful of his style,
which he was sure only Lopez really appreciated, "five years ago
Don Galo wanted to celebrate the diamond wedding anni-
versary of his business in materials, tailoring, and all its subdivisions.
The local sales managers were officially informed that the boss was
looking forward to a homage from his employees, and that he in-
tended to hold an inspection of all his stores. At that time I was
very friendly with Peña, the manager of the Junín branch, who
was worrying himself sick over Don Galo's visit. Peña found out
that the visit would be highly technical and that Don Galo was
prepared to look over the last dozen buttons in the button box.
Undoubtedly the result of secret information. As all the managers
were equally worried, a kind of armament race began among the
affiliates. It was absolutely hilarious at the Club because of the
stories about Peña and how he had bribed two traveling salesmen
to bring him news about the store which was preparing the celebration in the neighboring town or what the employees were going
to do at the Pehuajó store. He himself was preparing as much as
possible, and everyone at the store was working unbelievably late
hours. The employees were both furious and frightened.

"Don Galo began his self-homage tour through Lobos, I believe, visited three or four of his stores, and on one sunny Saturday
he showed up in Junín. In those days he had a blue Buick, but
Peña had ordered an open car, the kind Alexander might have
used to enter Persepolis. Don Galo was quite impressed when Peña
and a committee met him at the entrance of the town and invited
him to come into the open car. The entourage made a majestic
appearance on the main street. I, so as not to miss a thing, had
situated myself at the edge of the sidewalk, not far from the store.
When the automobile approached, the employees, strategically
distributed, began to applaud. The girls threw white flowers, and
the men, a good many just plain mercenaries, waved little flags
with the blue and gold insignia. A kind of triumphal arch which

read: WELCOME DON GALO, had been suspended from one side of
the street to the other. This bit of familiarity in using only the first
name had cost Peña a night's sleep, but the old man liked the
courage of his subjects. The automobile stopped in front of the
store, the applause quickened (forgive the hateful phrase), and
Don Galo, like a marmoset on the edge of his chair, waved his
right hand occasionally in order to return the salutes. I assure you
that he could have very well saluted with both hands, but I had
already realized what kind of fellow Don Galo was, and I could
see that Peña had not exaggerated. The feudal lord was visiting
his serfs, soliciting and weighing the homage with an air somewhere between amiability and distrust. I was beating my brains
trying to remember when I had seen a sight like this before. Not
the same scene, because in itself it was like any other official re-
ception—flags, posters, and bouquets of flowers. But it was what
was concealed (and for me what was revealing) in the scene:
something that encompassed the terrified clerks, poor Peña, and
even the expression, somewhere between greed and boredom, on
Don Galo's face. When Peña mounted a little bench to read the
welcome speech (and I confess that I had a finger in it because
things like that are practically the only amusement one is offered
in small towns), Don Galo bristled in his chair, nodding his head
from time to time and accepting, courteously cold, the thundering
salvos of applause which the employees launched exactly at
the moments Peña had indicated in rehearsal the night before. At
the most moving and emotional moment (we had already described Don Galo's activities in detail: self-made man, self-edu-
cated, etcetera), I saw the object of adoration make a signal to
his gorilla of a chauffeur. The gorilla came out of the automobile
and spoke to someone at the edge of the sidewalk, who blushed
and then spoke to his neighbor, who hesitated and looked in every
direction, as if expecting an apparition of salvation . . . I realized
that I was getting nearer the solution, that I was about to realize
why all this seemed so familiar to me. 'He's requested the silver
urinal,' I thought. 'Gaius Trimaltion. Good Lord, events repeat
themselves as best they can . . .' But it was not a urinal, of
course, scarcely a glass of water, just a well-calculated glass to
smash against Peña, to break up the pathos of the speech and to

recoup the advantage which he had lost by accepting the open car . . ."

Nora had not understood the end of the story, but she let herself be carried away by Lopez' contagious laugh. Roberto had just finished installing Don Galo near a window, and was bringing him an orange juice. The chauffeur had retired now and was waiting at the doorway, chatting with the nurse. Don Galo's wheelchair was in everyone's way and a great nuisance, but this seemed to cause Don Galo enormous satisfaction. Lopez was fascinated.

"It doesn't seem possible," he repeated. "With that kind of health and all that money he's going to make this trip only because it's free?"

"Not quite, not exactly free," said Medrano. "The ticket cost him ten pesos."

"Men of action are often, in their old age, given to these adolescent caprices," said Dr. Restelli. "I, too, luck aside, ask myself if I really should—"

"Here come some fellows with accordions," said Lucio. "Is it in honor of us?"

VIII

It was clear the café was strictly for squares, with its ministerial chairs and its waiters whose teeth began to bother them as soon as you asked them for a pint of draft, no foam. No atmosphere—that was the worst part.

Atilio Presutti, better known as Pelusa, pushed his right hand through his tightly curled, carrot-colored hair and then pulled it out at the nape of his neck after the laborious trajectory. He stroked his chestnut-colored mustache and looked with satisfaction at his freckled face in the wall mirror. Apparently not entirely satisfied, he drew out a blue comb from the upper pocket of his jacket and began to comb his hair with helpful little jabs delivered with his free hand to mark the rounded line for his bangs. Taken by his elegance, two of his friends also began to slick up their hairdos.

"This place is for squares," Pelusa repeated. "Who'd think of coming here for a send-off?"

"The ice cream's good," said Nelly, shaking Pelusa's lapel so
the dandruff would blow off. "Why did you wear your blue suit,
Atilio? I swear, just looking at you makes me sweat."

"If I'd have left it in the suitcase, it would get wrinkled," said
Pelusa. "I'd take off my jacket but this place makes me feel funny."

"Oh keep quiet, Atilio," said Nelly's mother. "Don't talk to
me about send-offs after the one on Sunday. My God, every time
I think of it . . ."

"That wasn't much of anything, Doña Pepa," said Pelusa.
Señora Presutti looked sternly at her son.

"What do you mean, it wasn't much? Ah, Doña Pepa, these
children . . . He says it wasn't much of anything. And your father
in bed with his shoulder blade dislocated and his ankle in a cast!"

"And so what?" said Pelusa. "The old boy's stronger than a
locomotive."

"But what happened?" asked one of his friends.

"Weren't you there on Sunday?"

"You don't remember I wasn't there? I had to get ready for the
fight. And no parties for me when I'm in training. I told you, remember?"

"Yeah, I remember," said Pelusa. "You missed something, Rusito!"

"No kidding, was there an accident?"

"Great. The old man fell off the terrace into the courtyard and
almost killed himself. God, what a mess!"

"A serious accident, you know," said Señora Presutti. "Tell him
about it, Atilio. I shudder just thinking about it."

"Poor Doña Rosita," said Nelly.

"Poor dear," said Nelly's mother.

"It wasn't nothing," said Pelusa. "Well, you know the whole
gang got together to give Nelly and me a send-off. The old lady
here made a tremendous ravioli dish, and the guys brought beer
and cake. We were all just fine on the terrace; we put up the awning and brought out the record player. Everything was just right.
How many of us were there? Thirty, at least."

"More," said Nelly. "I counted almost forty. There was just
enough stew, I remember."

"Okay, we were all just fine and dandy, not like here in this

furniture store. The old man was at the head of the table and Don
Rapa sitting next to him—you know, the one from the shipyards?
You know how the old man likes his booze. Look! Look at the
face on the old lady! It's not true, maybe? What's so wrong with
it? All I know is we were smashed by the time the bananas were
served, but my old man was way out. Wow, was he singing, *mamma
mia!* Just then it struck him he should toast the voyage. Up he gets,
the pint in his hand, and when he starts to talk he takes a coughing fit and falls over backwards, right into the courtyard. The noise
scared the hell out of me. Poor guy, he sounded like he was a sack
of potatoes landing, I swear."

"Poor Don Pipo," said Rusito, while Señora Presutti took a
handkerchief out of her purse.

"Do you see, Atilio? Now you made your mother cry," said
Nelly's mother. "Don't cry, Doña Rosita. After all, nothing happened."

"Of course not," said Pelusa. "But what a mess. We all went
downstairs. I was sure the old man'd broke his head in two. The
women were crying and screaming, what a riot! You couldn't hear
a thing. I told Nelly to turn off the record player, and Doña Pepa
here had to take care of the old lady, who was having a fit, doubled
over and twisting around."

"And Don Pipo?" asked Rusito, anxious for gore.

"The old man is a phenomenon," said Pelusa. "Now when I
saw him stretched out like a stiff on the tiles I thought: 'You're
an orphan.' We sent the kid out to call an ambulance and while
he was gone we lifted up the old man's shirt to see if he was still
breathing. The first thing he did when he opened his eyes was to
put his hand in his pocket to see if anybody had lifted his wallet.
The old man's like that. Then he said his back was hurting, but
not bad. He said we should go on with the party. Do you remember, Ma? When we brought you around to let you know it wasn't
anything? What a riot! Instead of calming down, you went into
an even worse fit."

"That reminds me," said Nelly's mother. "Once, in my
house . . ."

"All in all, when the ambulance got there the old man was sitting up on the floor already, and we were all laughing like crazy. It's

a shame the interns wouldn't let him stay home. Finally they carried him away, poor guy. Meanwhile, when one of them asked me to sign some sort of paper, while I was at it, I asked him to look at my ear—you know, it gets stopped up with wax."

"Fantastic," said Rusito, who was really impressed. "Look what I missed. And that day I had to be in training."

Another friend, who seemed stuffed into an enormous hard collar, suddenly stood up.

"Look who's coming! Boy, this is really something."

The accordion players of Asdrúbal Crésida's typical Argentine orchestra made their way between the ever-growing masses of tables. They were impeccably dressed in checked suits, their hair slicked down, and to the manner born. Coming in behind them was a young man wearing a pearl-grey suit, a black shirt, and a cream-colored tie fastened with a tie pin in the shape of a football shield.

"My brother," said Pelusa, even though no one had overlooked that important detail. "He came to surprise us!"

The well-known crooner Humberto Roland reached the table and shook everyone's hand except his mother's, effusively.

"Crazy, baby," said Pelusa. "Did you get someone to sub for you at the radio station?"

"I told them I had a toothache," said Humberto Roland. "That way they can't dock me. These are some buddies of mine from the orchestra who wanted to come and see you off, too."

Threateningly, Roberto brought over another table and four chairs. The star ordered an iced coffee and the musicians joined him, ordering beer.

IX

Paula and Raul came in through the door leading from the Calle Florida and sat down at a table next to the window. Paula hardly glanced at the inside of the café, but Raul amused himself by trying to guess who, among all these sweating citizens of Buenos Aires, might be their fellow voyagers.

"If I didn't have the announcement in my pocket, I'd think

someone was playing a joke," said Raul. "Isn't it unbelievable?"

"Right now it's rather stuffy and hot. But I admit that the letter alone is worth the trip."

Raul unfolded a piece of cream-colored paper and summed up its contents:

" 'At six o'clock in this café. The baggage will be picked up in the morning at your home. It is requested that you come unaccompanied. The Office of Municipal Affairs will cover all expenses.' As lotteries go, you have to admit this one's extraordinary! Can you imagine why we're meeting here?"

"I gave up trying to understand this whole thing some time ago," said Paula. "I only know that you won a prize and invited me, thereby disqualifying me forever from *Who's Who in Argentina.*"

"Quite the contrary, this enigmatic trip will give you enormous prestige. You'll be able to talk of a spiritual retreat, to say you're working on a monograph about Dylan Thomas. As far as I'm concerned, the greatest attraction of all this madness is that it always ends badly."

"Yes, that can be an attraction sometimes," said Paula. "*Le besoin de la fatalité* they talk about."

"At the very worst it will be a cruise like any other cruise, except that we won't exactly know where we're going. A cruise that will last three or four months. I admit that this final piece of information is what convinced me. Where in the world can they take us in so much time? To China, maybe?"

"To which China?"

"To both of them, to honor Argentina's traditional neutrality."

"Wishful thinking. But you'll see, they'll take us as far as Genoa and from there, in a bus through Europe, and then they'll leave us, and we'll be complete wrecks."

"That I doubt," said Raul. "If that were it, they would have proclaimed it loud and long. I suspect they met unexpected difficulties at the last minute."

"All the same," said Paula, "something has been said about the itinerary."

"Nothing definite. Vague terms in the contract that I don't remember any more, insinuations designed to arouse the spirit of adventure. In short, a free trip limited only by the international situation. In other words, they're not going to take us to Algeria, or Vladivostok, or Las Vegas. The smartest thing was giving us paid vacations. What bureaucrat could resist that? And the checkbook full of traveler's checks, that counts too. Dollars, just think of it, dollars."

"And you were able to invite me."

"Of course. Just so you could see if salt air and exotic ports can cure lovesickness."

"It will certainly be better than Nembutal," said Paula, looking at him. Raul returned her look. They remained awhile that way, motionless, almost defiant.

"All right," said Raul, "stop the nonsense. You promised me."

"Okay," said Paula.

"You always say 'okay' when everything is at its vaguest."

"Will you kindly note that I only said: 'It will certainly be better than Nembutal'?"

"All right then, let it drop."

"Okay," Paula repeated. "Don't get mad, handsome. I'm very grateful, believe me. You're getting me out of a difficult situation by inviting me, even if I do lose what remains of my reputation. Raul, I think the trip will be good for me. Especially if we get into something completely absurd. At least we can laugh!"

"At least it will be a change," said Raul. "I've had enough of making up plans of chalets for people like your family or mine. I realize that this cruise is idiotic, and that it's really no solution at all, but only a postponement. We'll come back, after all, and everything will be like it always was. Maybe it'll be a little different."

"I'll never understand why you didn't take advantage of this trip and invite another fellow, someone closer to you than I am."

"Maybe exactly for that reason, milady. Just so I could break all my ties with this great capital city of the south. Besides, to be really close to someone, you know . . ."

"I think," said Paula, looking into his eyes, "that you're a marvelous person."

"Thank you. It's really not true, but when you say so it does take on a certain air of authenticity."

"I also think the trip is going to be very amusing."

"Very."

Paula took a deep breath. She suddenly felt something like a wave of happiness come over her.

"Did you bring the seasick pills?" she asked.

But Raul was looking over at a crowd of noisy young men.

"Good God," he said. "One of them looks like he's going to sing."

A

Taking advantage of the mother-son dialogue, Persio looks around him thoughtfully, and to each presence he applies the logos or he extracts the thread from the logos, and then he probes into the depths for the delicate, subtle path which will reveal the spectacle to him, or which ought—at least he'd like it that way—to open up a passage toward a synthesis. Without any effort at all, Persio gives up the secondary images of the central action, and instead calculates and concentrates on the essential detail, examining and stripping the circumstantial atmosphere around him, separating and analyzing, sorting and weighing. His view of things around him takes on a relief which a cold fever might produce, a cold fever or a hallucination without tigers or coleoptera, and an ardor with which a hunter might pursue his prey without monkey leaps or swans' verbiage. The retinue of people accompanying the voyagers, those people attending the sailing (or game), are already outside the café, unaware of the bet he has placed. Persio is fully enjoying the game of isolating, under a microscope, the brief constellation of those who remain, of those who are really making the trip. He does not know any more about the rules of the game than they do, but he feels that they are in the process of being born from every one of the players, as on an infinite chessboard between mute opponents, where bishops and queens turn into dolphins and toy satyrs. Every move is a battle at sea, every step a river of words or tears, every square on the chessboard a grain of sand, a sea of blood, a comedy of squirrels, or a farce given by buffoons who wander through fields of bells and applause.

Thus, a municipal concern of good intentions incited by a spirit of beneficence, and perhaps (without being absolutely certain) an obscure science in which luck deals the cards, and also the fate of the winners, has made this gathering at the London possible, this small army of which Persio invents the chiefs, the quartermasters, the deserters, and maybe even the heroes. He scrutinizes the distances from the aquarium to the belvedere, and the ices of time which separate a virile stare from a smile dressed in its lipstick, and the incalculable distance of the destinies which suddenly turn into a gavel on schedule. He observes this mixture, verging on the dreadful, of lonely creatures who find themselves stepping out of taxis, leaving stations, lovers, and offices, this mixture which is already a single body, a body that still does not recognize itself and is incapable of knowing the strange pretext of a confused legend. A legend which is, perhaps, told or not told in vain.

X

"And so," said Persio sighing, "we suddenly are, perhaps, just a single thing that no one sees, or someone sees, or someone doesn't see."

"It sounds as if you've just come to the surface of the water," said Claudia, "and you expect me to understand you. At least tell me what the intervening ideas were. Or is your offensive unavoidably concealed?"

"No, quite the contrary," said Persio. "It's simply easier to see than to tell what one has seen. I'm terribly happy that you've given me the opportunity to take this trip, Claudia. I'm going to feel so well with you and Jorge. I'll be on the deck doing gymnastics and singing, if it's permitted."

"Haven't you ever been on a ship?" asked Jorge.

"No, but I've read novels by Conrad and Pio Baroja, authors that you'll admire before long. Doesn't it seem to you, Claudia, that the act of undertaking any activity at all is something of a renunciation of some part of what we are in order to integrate ourselves into some kind of unknown machine, a centipede in which we would hardly be more than an annulus or a couple of feet?"

"I think, Persio, that without the thing you call renunciation we wouldn't be very much. We're already too passive, we accept

our fate too easily. At best, we're stylites, or we're like those stone
saints with birds' nests on their heads."

"My remark was not meant to be axiomatic, and even less normative," said Persio in his most petulant manner. "In fact, what
I do is fall into outmoded unanimism, but I search for the return
through the other side. It's well known that the whole is more, and
at the same time, less, than the sum of all its parts. What I'd like
to find out, if I could place myself inside and outside the whole
—and I think it can be done—is if the human centipede responds,
in its constitution and its dissolution, to something more than
chance events; if it is a figure, in the magical sense of the word,
and if that figure is capable of moving, under certain circumstances,
on more essential planes than those of its isolated members. Uf!"

"More essential?" said Claudia. "Let's examine that dubious
vocabulary, first."

"When we look at a constellation," said Persio, "we can see
something like an assurance that the harmony and the rhythm
uniting its stars (a rhythm which we impose, of course, but
which we impose because something also happens there which
determines this harmony) is more profound, more substantial
than the isolated existence of any one of its stars. Haven't you ever
noticed that stars by themselves, those poor isolated stars that
don't integrate into any constellation, seem insignificant next
to the indecipherable writing? The sacred character of constellations isn't entirely explained by astrological reasons and mnemo-
technics. Man must have felt from the very beginning that each
one of them was like a clan, a society, a race: something actively
different, perhaps even antagonistic. On certain nights I've lived
through the war of the stars, an unbearable game of tensions.
Though on the terrace of my boarding house you can't see too
well, as there's always smoke in the air."

"Do you look at the stars through a telescope, Persio?" Jorge
asked.

"Oh, no," said Persio. "You know, there are certain things one
has to look at with the naked eye. Not that I'm opposed to science,
but I think that only a poetic vision can encompass the meaning of
the figures which the angels design and bring together. Tonight,
right here in this poor café, perhaps, there is one of these figures."

"Where is it, Persio?" asked Jorge, looking all around him.

"It begins with the lottery," said Persio, seriously. "A kind of bowling game of a lottery has selected a number of men and women out of several hundred thousand. Then, in their turn, the winners have selected their traveling companions, something which I personally appreciate a great deal. Just think, Claudia, there is nothing pragmatic nor functional in the tracing of the figure. We are not the enormous rose window of the Gothic cathedral but rather the sudden and ephemeral petrification of the rose in the kaleidoscope. But before surrendering and disintegrating at the point of a new and capricious change in the kaleidoscope, what games will we all play? How should we combine the warm colors and the cool colors, the lunatics and the mercurial fellows, the humors and the temperaments?"

"What kaleidoscope are you talking about, Persio?" asked Jorge.

You could hear someone singing a tango.

XI

Felipe Trejo's mother, as well as his father and sister, were of the opinion that it would not be unwise to order tea and cake. Who knows what time they would eat on the ship, and besides it wasn't good to go aboard with an empty stomach (ice cream was not really food; it melted). It would be sensible to eat dry foods at first, and to sleep on one's back. The very worst thing for seasickness was the mere suggestion of it. Aunt Felisa would become seasick by just going down to the waterfront, or by going to a film which showed a moving submarine. Felipe was listening to phrases he knew by heart and he was overwhelmingly bored. Now his mother would say that when she was young she had gotten seasick on the Delta. Then Señor Trejo would remark that he had warned her not to eat so much melon that day. Then Señora Trejo would say that the melon was not to blame since she had eaten it with salt, and melon with salt never hurt anyone. Felipe, however, would have liked to know what they were talking about at the table where the Black Cat and Lopez were sitting; probably about school. What else were teachers going to talk about? Actually, he should have gone and said hello to them. But for what? Anyway, he would see them on the ship. Lopez didn't bother him, just the opposite, he was a good guy, but the Black Cat, he was exactly dull enough to win a prize, the crumb.

In spite of himself, his thoughts returned to the Negrita, who had stayed home with an expression that wasn't really sad, but a little sad all the same. Not because of him, of course. What bothered her, the little tramp, was not to be able to travel with her bosses. Actually, he had been a fool. If he had insisted that the Negrita come, his mother would have had to weaken. Either the Negrita or nobody. "But Felipe . . ." "What do you want now? Wouldn't it be convenient for you to have a servant aboard?" But they would have guessed his intentions. And they were capable of spoiling his time by bringing up the fact that he was a minor, and then with a little complaint to the judge, he'd have to forget the trip, damn it all. He asked himself if his parents really would have sacrificed the trip for that. Undoubtedly not. Bah, after all, what did the Negrita matter to him? Up until the very end she hadn't wanted him to come up to her room, and she only allowed him a tussle in the hallway, and even then he had to bribe her with talk about giving her a watch as soon as he got some money out of his old man. The little tease, and to think that with those legs . . . Felipe began to feel that sweet softening of his body which heralded an entirely opposite phenomenon, and he sat straight up in the chair. He chose the pastry with the most chocolate, just a fraction of a second before Beba would have swooped down on it.

"Always the greedy pig, aren't you?"

"Go on and take it, lady of the camellias."

"Children . . ." said Señora Trejo.

Who knows if there were going to be girls to play around with on board? He remembered—not willingly, but inevitably—his conversation with Ordóñez, the ringleader of the fifth-year class, and his advice one summer night on a bench in the Congress Garden. "Pull yourself together, kid, and get a girl, you're too big now to be using your fist." To his disdainful but somewhat troubled protests, Ordóñez had answered with a friendly slap on the knees. "Come on, don't pull the tough-guy act with me. I'm two years older than you and I know what I'm talking about. At your age it's pin-ups and plenty of wrist action. There's nothing wrong with it, but now you're going to the ball and you can't get along with just that. Look, the first girl that shows it to you, drag her off to go rowing at Tigre Park, and you can do it anywhere there. And if you don't have enough money, let me know; I'll tell my brother, the accountant, to lend you his room in town for an afternoon. It's always better in bed, you can imagine . . ." And then a series of details, recollections, and friendly counsels. In spite of all his shame and fury, Felipe had been grateful to Ordoñez. Very different from Alfieri, for example. Of course, Alfieri . . .

"It looks like we're going to have music here," said Señora Trejo.

"How inappropriate" said Beba. "They shouldn't allow it."

Yielding to the gentle requests of relatives and friends, the popular crooner Humberto Roland stood up, while Pelusa and Rusito, pushing, shoving, and arguing, made room for the three accordionists to install themselves comfortably and take out their instruments. People were laughing and joking around them, and others outside the café were pressing against the windows which looked onto the Avenida. A policeman on Florida looked across with obvious confusion.

"Oh great, man, a gas!" screamed Rusito. "Pelusa, your brother's a gasser!"

Pelusa was sitting next to Nelly again, making gestures to silence the people around them.

"Let's see if they'll pay a little attention now! *Mamma mia*, this place is the end."

Humberto Roland coughed and smoothed his hair back.

"You'll have to excuse me for not bringing the rhythm section," he said. "We'll do the best we can."

"Very good, kid, very good."

"In honor of my dear brother and his wonderful girl, on the day of their departure, I'm going to sing the famous Visca y Cadícamo tango, 'Muñeca brava.' "

"Go, man!" said Rusito.

The accordionists wound out the introduction and Humberto Roland, after putting his left hand in his pants pocket and his right one in the air, sang:

Che madám que parlás en francés
y tirás ventolín a dos manos,
que cenás con champán bien frapé
y en el tango enredás tu ilusión . . .

A sudden and surprising acoustical inversion took place in the
London. No sooner was Pelusa's table plunged into a deathly
silence than the conversations at the surrounding tables took on
an exaggerated volume. Pelusa and Rusito looked furiously around
them, while Humberto Roland's voice swelled:

Tenés un camba que te acamala
y veinte abriles que son diqueros . . .

Carlos Lopez felt perfectly cheerful, and grinned at Medrano.
Dr. Restelli was visibly annoyed "by the turn of events," as he put
it.

"These people have an enviable freedom," said Lopez. "There is
almost a kind of perfection in the way they act, within certain
limits, of course. And they haven't the slightest suspicion that the
world has gone beyond tangos and racing."

"Look at Don Galo," said Medrano. "It looks like the old man is
having a stroke."

Don Galo had gone from absolute stupefaction to gesturing
threateningly at the chauffeur, who came into the café at a run,
listened to his boss, and left again. They could see him talking to
the policeman who was watching the scene from the window on
Florida. And they could see the policeman's gesture, which consisted of bringing his fingers together tight in an upward flight
and then waving the hand in a vertical seesaw movement.

"Of course," Medrano said. "After all, what's so bad about it?"

Te llaman todos muñeca brava
porque a los giles mareás sin grupo . . .

Paula and Raul were enjoying the whole scene enormously,
much more than Lucio and Nora, who were noticeably disconcerted.
Felipe's family was suddenly overcome by an icy warning of things
to come, but Felipe watched the flashing movements of the accordionists' fingers with fascination. A little further on, Jorge was

starting his second ice cream, and Claudia and Persio were lost in a metaphysical discussion. And above all of them, above their indifference or even their gaiety, Humberto Roland came to the melancholy conclusion:

> *Pa mi sos siempre la que no supo*
> *guardar un cacho de amor y juventú* . . .

Amid screams, applause, and the sound of spoons clinking against the table, Pelusa, who was very moved, stood up and hugged his brother. Then he shook hands with the accordionists, hit his chest, and took out an enormous handkerchief to blow his nose. Humberto Roland bowed condescendingly, while Nelly and the ladies initiated a chorus of praise which the singer acknowledged with his indefatigable smile. At that moment, a child, invisible until then, let out a kind of roar as a result of choking on a whipped-cream pastry. There was a tremendous upheaval at the table, climaxed by a universal shout directed toward Roberto, who was ordered to bring a glass of water.

"You were great," Pelusa said tenderly.

"No better than usual," Humberto Roland answered.

"You sing with such feeling," Nelly's mother ventured.

"He was always like that," said Señora Presutti. "You couldn't talk to him about studying or anything else. Nothing but art."

"Just like me," said Rusito. "You think I could put in time on the books? No. Just fighting. All the time."

Nelly finished extracting the pieces of cake from the child's throat. The crowds of people at the windows began to leave, and Dr. Restelli ran his finger around his starched collar, considerably relieved.

"Well," said Lopez, "it looks like it's time."

Two men in dark blue suits had just stationed themselves in the middle of the café. One of them clapped his hands abruptly, and the other signaled for everyone to be silent. He spoke with a voice that would have made that precaution unnecessary:

"Any guests not here by written appointment, including the people who have come to see the passengers off, are kindly requested to leave the establishment!"

"The what?" asked Nelly.

"We have to beat it," said one of Pelusa's friends. "And just when we were beginning to have a good time."

Once the surprise was over, shouts and protests rose up on all sides. The man who had spoken raised a hand, his palm turned toward the customers, and said:

"I am Inspector of the Office of Municipal Affairs and am following the orders of my superiors. I want all the people gathered here by written appointment to remain seated and the rest to leave as soon as possible."

"Look," said Lucio to Nora. "There's a ring of policemen on the Avenida. This looks more like a roundup than anything else."

The personnel of the London, as surprised as the customers, did not have time to make checks for all the drinks and other items on a moment's notice, and extraordinary complications ensued concerning the proper change, the returning of pastries, and other technical difficulties. At Pelusa's table they were shouting. Señora Presutti and Nelly's mother were in the throes of saying goodbye to the relatives who were staying behind. Nelly was consoling her mother and future mother-in-law. Pelusa hugged Humberto Roland again and slapped all his friends on the back.

"Good luck, good luck!" they all shouted. "Write, Pelusa!"

"I'll send you a card, man!"

"Don't forget the gang!"

"How can I forget! Good luck!"

"Yaaay team! Go La Boca!" screamed Rusito, looking defiantly at the other tables.

Two distinguished-looking men had approached the Inspector of Municipal Affairs and were looking at him as if he had fallen from another planet.

"You might be obeying the orders of your superiors," said one of them, "but I've never seen such abuse of power in all my life."

"Move on, move on," said the Inspector, without looking at them.

"I am Dr. Lastra," said Dr. Lastra, "and I know my rights and my responsibilities as well as you do. This is a public restaurant, and nobody can make me leave without a written order."

The Inspector took out a paper and showed it to him.

"And so what?" said the other man. "This is nothing more than legalized crime. We wouldn't be, by any chance, in a state of siege?"

"You can register your complaint at the proper place," said the Inspector. "Go on, Viñas, get those ladies out of the little salon. If you don't, they'll go on powdering their noses until tomorrow."

So many people were pushing against the police cordon in the Avenida to see what was happening, that there was a traffic jam. The customers, with indignant, scandalized expressions, were rushing out through the door leading to the Calle Florida, where there was less of a mob. The Inspector and the man called Viñas went from table to table to ask the lottery winners for the written announcement of the meeting and to register the names of the invited guests. A policeman, leaning up against the bar, chatted with the waiters and the cashier, who were ordered not to move from where they were. Almost deserted, the London looked like a café at eight in the morning, which contrasted strangely with the light of early nightfall and the uproar on the street.

"Good," said the Inspector. "You can lower the iron shutters now."

B

Why does a spider web or a Picasso painting have to be what it is? Why doesn't the painting have to explain the web and why doesn't the spider have to give us the reason for the painting? To be that way, what does it mean? What one sees in the tiniest particle of chalk depends on the cloud which passes on the other side of the windowpane or even on the inner hopes of the person contemplating it. Things are more meaningful when they are observed, eight and eight are sixteen plus the person doing the addition. Thus, to be that way may also mean not to be that way, or can scarcely be worth anything that way, or to proclaim that way or deceive that way. Seen like this, a group of people who must embark does not guarantee their embarking, insomuch as the circumstances may vary and there will not be an embarkation, or not vary, in which case the spider web or the Picasso painting or the group of embarked people will crystallize, and one will no longer be able to conceive of the latter's former state as a group of people who must embark. In any case, the desire, so sad and at the same time so rhetorical, that something at last might be, might happen, passes from table to table at the London like unseizable drops of mercury, the miracle of childhood.

It is that which brings one nearer to something, which induces and leads one to—something. It is like the other side of a thing, the mystery which drew it (yes, it seems as if it were drawn, one cannot say brought) to be what it is. All historians walk through a gallery of Hans Arp shapes, which cannot be turned around, and these same historians must be satisfied to see them from the front, at either side of the gallery, to see Hans Arp shapes as if they were canvases hung on the walls. The historian knows the causes of the Battle of Zama perfectly well, only right that he should, but the causes which he knows are only other shapes of Hans Arp in other galleries, and the causes of these causes or the effects of the causes of these causes are brilliantly illuminated on the front surface, as the Hans Arp shapes in every gallery.

In this way and without the helpful analogy which brings lovely alternatives to the present in which we are and shall be, it is possible that at ground level we might find the London; at a height of thirty feet there might be a heavy checkerboard covered with pieces badly arranged on the squares, lacking in all harmony as concerns the chiaroscuro and established custom; at ten inches Atilio Presutti's ruddy face might be seen; at the height of an eighth of an inch there might be a shining nickel surface (a button, a mirror?); and at fifty yards, Picasso's guitarist, painted in 1918, belonging to Apollinaire. If the distance which makes one thing what it is were measured by our certitude of knowing the thing such as it is, it would be useless to continue this monologue, to work cheerfully weaving its fabric. And it would be of much less use to look for reasons to explain the congregation, reasons already sufficiently explicit in the letters written on official letterhead paper and signed with a legalized signature. The development in time (an inevitable point of view, an aberrant causality) conceives of itself only through the work of an impoverished Eleatic set of pigeon-holes—before, now, and afterward—which sometimes conceal a Gallic duration or an extratemporal influence of vague hypnotic suggestion. The mere now of what is happening (the police have lowered the shutters) reflects and smashes time into innumerable facets; from some of these facets one could perhaps again mount the hyaline ray, to go back, thus in Paula Lavalle's life a garden of Acasusso might bloom again, or Gabriel Medrano might then be able to half-close the colored glass door of his childhood in Lomas de Zamora. Nothing more than that, and that is less than nothing in the jungle of casual leaves which have blown together at this meeting. The history of the world shines forth from any bronze button on the uniform of any of the policemen who break up the mob. At the same moment in which interest is concentrated in this button (the second counting from the collar), the relations which encompass and bring it to be what it is are as aspired toward the horror of a vast offensive in which not even falling face down on the ground makes any sense. The vortex at the center of the button that threatens to absorb the person looking at it, if he dares to do anything more than look at it, is the crushing vision of the deadly play of mirrors which rises from the effects to the causes. Each time the misguided readers of novels insist on the necessity of verisimilitude they assume irremediably the attitude of the imbecile who, after a twenty-day trip aboard the Claude Bernard, asks pointing to the prow: "C'est-par-là-qu'on-va-en-avant?"

XII

When they left the café it was almost night, and threatening reddish heat clouds were crushed against the sky. The Inspector deferentially commissioned two policemen to help the chauffeur transport Don Galo as far as a bus waiting for them further on, near the old town hall. The distance and the street-crossing inexplicably complicated the moving of Don Galo, and another policeman was needed to stop traffic on the corner of Bolivar. Contrary to what Medrano and Lopez had supposed, not many curious pedestrians remained in the street; people looked for a moment at the strange spectacle of the London with its iron shutters lowered, exchanged some words, and kept walking.

"Why the devil don't they bring the bus to the café?" Raul asked one of the policemen.

"Orders, sir," said the policeman.

The reciprocal introductions, initiated by the amiable Inspector and then continued spontaneously by the travelers themselves, introductions which were both tense and amused, permitted the passengers to form a compact group which followed Don Galo's wheelchair like a cortege. The bus must have belonged to the police, even though no inscription was in evidence on the shiny black surface. The high windows were tiny and narrow, and getting Don Galo settled inside was particularly complicated by the momentary confusion and everybody's good will, especially Pelusa's, who busied himself on the running board, shouting orders and counterorders to the silent chauffeur. As soon as Don Galo was installed in the first seat, and the wheelchair folded like a gigantic accordion between the chauffeur's hands, the travelers climbed in and sat down almost like blind people in the gloomy vehicle. Lucio and Nora, who had crossed the Avenida with their arms tightly enlaced, looked for a place in the back and remained very quiet. They were watching the other passengers, as well as the police scattered along the street, with some hesitation. Medrano and Lopez had already struck up a conversation with Raul and Paula, and Dr. Restelli exchanged some conventional remarks with Persio. Claudia and Jorge were enjoying themselves enormously, each in his own way; everyone else was too involved in shouting to notice what was happening.

The noise of the metal shutters of the London, which Roberto and the rest of the staff were lifting again now, reached Lopez' ears like a final chord, the closing of a piece which was to stay definitively in the past. Medrano, who sat beside Lopez, lit another cigarette and looked out at the illegible posters pasted on the newsstands. Then a horn sounded and the bus pulled out very slowly. The opinion of Pelusa's sorrowful entourage was that partings were always sad because some leave and others stay, but while there was health . . . to which someone responded that trips were always the same, the pleasure of some and the grief of the rest, mainly because there are those who leave . . . but it was necessary to also think of those who remain behind. The world was badly organized, and it was always the same—for some there was everything and for others, nothing.

"What did you think of the Inspector's speech?" asked Medrano.

"Well, something happened that very often happens to me," said Lopez. "While he was making explanations, I had no objections, and I even began to feel perfectly at home in his weird new framework. Now, I'm not so sure."

"There's a kind of luxury of detail that amuses me," said Medrano. "It would have been much simpler to have had us meet at the customs office or on the dock, don't you think? But that would have deprived someone, perhaps, of the secret pleasure of watching us from one of those windows in the Municipal Building. As in certain chess games, in which the moves are complicated for reasons of pure extravagance."

"Sometimes," said Lopez, "the moves are complicated so as to mask them. There seems to be a kind of hidden doom in all this, as if they were at the point of swindling us out of the trip, as if they didn't know quite what to do with us."

"It would be a pity," said Medrano, reminding himself of Bettina. "I wouldn't like it one bit if we were left standing on the pier at the last minute."

It was already night and they were approaching the north dock. The Inspector picked up a microphone and addressed the passengers as if he were a Cook's guide. Raul and Paula, seated in front, noticed that the bus driver was going very slowly to give the Inspector time to explain everything.

"Have you had a good look at our traveling companions?" asked Raul, close to Paula's ear. "The country is more than well represented. From the highest to the lowest elements in their most obvious forms . . . I wonder what the devil we're doing here."

"I think I'm going to enjoy myself," said Paula. "Listen to the explanations our Virgil is giving. The word 'difficulties' pops up in every sentence."

"For ten pesos," said Raul, "one can't expect miracles. What do you think of the woman with the little boy? I like her face. There's a delicate quality about her cheekbones and mouth."

"The most incredible person is the cripple. He looks like an enormous tick."

"What do you think of the boy with his family?"

"I'd say the family's with the boy."

"The family is less distinct than he is," said Raul.

"Everything depends on the color of the glass through which you look," recited Paula.

The Inspector insisted most especially on the necessity of conserving, at all costs, the equanimity-characteristic-of-cultivated-people, and not becoming upset by minor details and organizational difficulties ("difficulties" again).

"But if everything is in good order . . ." Dr. Restelli said to Persio. "Everything seems perfectly fine, don't you think?"

"Slightly confused, I'd say, just to say something."

"No sir, nothing of the sort. I suppose the authorities had their own reasons for organizing everything just as they have. Personally, I would have altered some details, I won't conceal that; above all I would have changed the definitive passenger list, taking into consideration the fact that not everyone present is really on the same cultural level as the others. There's a young fellow, you can see him sitting on the other side . . ."

"We still don't know one another," said Persio. "Maybe we'll never know one another."

"It may be that you won't ever meet him, sir. As for me, my pedagogic functions . . ."

"Well," said Persio, waving his hand in a majestic gesture. "During shipwrecks the worst scoundrels usually turn out to be the heroes. You remember what happened on the *Andrea Doria*."

"I don't remember," said Dr. Restelli, a bit peevishly.

"Well, there was the case of the monk who saved a sailor. You see, you never can tell. Don't the Inspector's words seem terribly disheartening?"

"He's still talking. Perhaps we ought to listen."

"The worst part is that he always repeats the same thing," said Persio. "And we're already here at the docks."

Jorge suddenly remembered his rubber ball and bilboquet set with the gilded nails, and wondered what he had done with them. In what suitcase had they been packed? And the Davy Crockett novel?

"We'll find everything in the cabin," said Claudia.

"How wonderful, a cabin for the two of us. Do you get seasick, Mama?"

"No. Almost no one will get seasick, except for Persio, I'm

afraid, and some of those ladies who were at the table where they sang tangos. It's always that way, you know."

Felipe shuffled an imaginary list of ports of call in his mind ("unless some unforeseen contretemps arises that will force us to modify our plans at the last minute," the Inspector was saying). Señor and Señora Trejo were looking out at the street, observing each lamppost as if they would never see another one, and as if the loss would be overwhelming.

"It's always sad to leave one's country," said Señor Trejo.

"You act as if we were never coming back," said Beba.

"Of course, my dear," said Señora Trejo. "One always goes back to the corner where one began life, as they say in that poem."

Felipe chose names of ports as if they were fruits, he savored them in his mouth, and bit into them little by little: Rio, Dakar, Capetown, Yokohama. "No one from the gang will ever see so many things at once," he thought. "I'll send them picture postcards . . ." He closed his eyes and stretched out in his seat. The Inspector was referring to the unavoidable necessity of taking certain precautions.

"I must warn you of the unavoidable necessity of taking certain precautions," said the Inspector. "The Office of Municipal Affairs has taken care of all the details, but last-minute difficulties might force us to modify certain aspects of the trip."

A completely unexpected clucking sound made by Don Galo Porriño was hurled into a double silence: the pause in the Inspector's sentence and the sudden dead stop of the bus.

"What ship are we going on?" clucked Don Galo. "Why all this poppycock about not knowing the ship we're going on . . ."

XIII

"That is the question," thought Paula. "That's exactly the sad question that may spoil the game. Now they'll answer: 'On the—' "

"Señor Porriño," said the Inspector, "the ship itself constitutes one of the technical difficulties to which I was referring. An hour ago, when I had the pleasure of joining you, the Office was in the process of making last-minute decisions, but in the interim unsuspected difficulties could have arisen, which would alter the situation. I believe, then, that it is preferable to wait a few moments longer, so that there will be no doubts at all."

"An individual cabin," said Don Galo curtly, "with a private bath. That's the agreement."

"Agreed," the Inspector said amiably. "That is not exactly in the terms of the contract, but I don't think, Señor Porriño, that in this sense there will be any difficulties."

"It isn't like a dream. That would be too easy," thought Paula. "Raul would say it's rather like a drawing, a sketch . . ."

"A drawing like what?" she asked.

"What do you mean a drawing like what?" Raul asked.

"You'd say that all this is rather like a drawing . . ."

"Anamorphic, you silly ass. Yes, it is a little like that. So we don't even know what ship they're putting us on."

They both burst into laughter because it really didn't matter to either of them. The same could not be said for Dr. Restelli, who, for the first time in his life, was beginning to doubt the established order. As far as Lopez and Medrano were concerned, Don Galo's interruption had inspired them to smoke another Fontanares. They were enjoying themselves enormously, too.

"It's like the phantom train," said Jorge, who understood everything that was going on very well. "You get inside and all sorts of things happen: a hairy spider creeps across your face, dancing skeletons dangle in front of you . . ."

"We spend our lives complaining that nothing interesting ever happens to us," said Claudia. "But when something finally does happen (and only something like this can be interesting) the majority of people begin to worry. I don't know what you think, but as far as I'm concerned, phantom trains amuse me far more than the General Roca Railroad."

"Of course," said Medrano. "What really worries Don Galo and a few others is that we're living a kind of postponement of the future. That's why they're uneasy and insist on knowing the name of the ship. What does the name of the ship mean? It's only a guarantee for what we still call tomorrow, that monster with a veiled face, invisible and savage."

"Meanwhile," Lopez said, "they're beginning to draw, little by little, the ominous outlines of a warship and a cargo ship in light colors. Probably Swedish, like all ships with a clean look."

"It's quite all right to talk about the postponement of the future," Claudia said. "But it's also an adventure, very commonplace, but nevertheless an adventure, and the future naturally becomes the most important factor. If the present moment has a special savor for us, it's because the future serves as condiment, to use a culinary metaphor."

"But what happens is that not everybody likes hot sauces," Medrano said. "Maybe there are two radically opposed ways to intensify the sensation of the present. In this case the Office of Municipal Affairs chooses to suppress all concrete reference to the future, by inventing a mysterious negative. The farsighted person gets frightened, naturally. I, on the other hand, find the present ridiculous situation tenser, more interesting."

"I do too," said Claudia. "Partly because I don't believe in the future. What's hidden from us is no more than the causes of the present. Probably even they themselves don't know how much magic the bureaucratic mysteries create for us."

"Of course they don't," said Lopez. "Magic, come on—you'd be closer to the truth if you said it was a monumental mess of red tape, pretexts, and hierarchies."

"It doesn't matter," said Claudia. "As long as it amuses us tonight."

The bus had stopped next to one of the customs sheds. The port was plunged in darkness, except for a couple of dim streetlights and the glow of the policemen's cigarettes near the half-closed gate. Everything disappeared into the shadows a few feet further on, and the thick odor of the port in summer crushed heavily against the puzzled or joyous faces of those who began to get off the bus. Don Galo was already settled in his wheelchair; the chauffeur was wheeling it toward the inner door, where the Inspector was leading the group. It was not by chance, thought Raul, that everybody walked together in a tightly knit group. It did not seem very prudent, nor even safe, to lag behind.

One of the police officers came forward, politely.

"Good evening, ladies and gentlemen."

The Inspector took out some cards from his pocket and turned

them over to another officer. He shone a flashlight on them, and
the light coincided with the far-off honk of a horn and a cough
from someone who could not be seen.

"Through here, if you don't mind," said the officer.

The flashlight dragged a yellow eye of light across the cement
floor, which was covered with straw, broken metal packing bands,
and crumpled paper. The voices of the few people who were talking suddenly rose in volume and reverberated in the vast empty
shed. The yellow eye revealed the long bench of the customs building and halted to show the way to the cautiously approaching
group. Pelusa's voice could be heard saying: "What a scene they're
putting on! It's like a Boris Karloff movie." As Felipe Trejo lit a
cigarette (his astonished mother watched him smoke for the first
time in her presence), the light from the match momentarily
made the whole insecure procession sway back and forth in the
glimmering shadows of the night. Nora was hanging on Lucio's
arm, closing her eyes because she did not want to open them until
they were at the other side, under a starless sky, but where the air
at least smelled fresh. They were the first to see the ship, but when
Nora excitedly turned around to tell the others, the police and the
Inspector had already surrounded the group; the flashlight was
turned off and in its place was the weak glow of a lamppost, il-
luminating the foot of a wooden gangplank. The Inspector
clapped his hands sharply, and from the back of the shed the sound
was repeated, even sharper and more mechanical, like a frightening
joke.

"I very much appreciate your spirit of co-operation," said the Inspector, "and it only remains for me to wish you a pleasant voyage.
The ship's officers will take charge of you on the bridge and will
accompany you to your respective cabins. The ship will leave
within an hour."

Medrano suddenly thought that the passivity and irony had
lasted long enough, and he stepped away from the group. As usual,
when things like this happened, he felt like bursting into laughter,
but he controlled himself.

"Tell me, Inspector, do you know the name of the ship?"

The Inspector bent his head politely. A bald spot was clearly
outlined on the crown of his head, even in the dark.

"Yes, sir," he said. "The officer, who has just received a tele-phone call from the Office, tells me it is the *Malcolm*, and belongs to the Magenta Star Lines."

"A freighter, judging by its outline," said Lopez.

"A mixed ship, sir. The best, believe me. A ship perfectly suited to receive a small group of select passengers, which is exactly what we have. I have had some experience in this sort of thing, even though I have spent the greater part of my career in branch offi-ces."

"They'll be perfectly all right," said a police officer. "I've gone aboard and I can vouch for the ship. There was a strike by the crew but everything is being worked out. You know what communism is—well, the staff ends up by being contaminated even in the most respectable companies. Fortunately, we live in a country where there's law and order. Even if they speak English, they get around to understanding that and lay down their clubs."

"Please come aboard, ladies and gentlemen," said the Inspector, moving to one side. "It has been a great pleasure meeting you, and I'm sorry that I won't be able to accompany you until the very end."

He let out a giggle, which seemed forced to Medrano. The group hurried to the foot of the gangplank; some waved to the police officers and Inspector, and Pelusa turned to help with the trans-port of Don Galo, who looked as if he had fallen asleep. The women clutched nervously at the railing, and the rest of the group walked quickly up the gangplank in silence. Then it occurred to Raul to turn around, just before setting foot on the deck, and he saw the Inspector and officers in the shadows below, talking in low voices. Everything still muted: the light, the voices, the sheds, even the lapping of the river against the hull of the ship and the dock. And neither was it very well lit on the bridge of the *Malcolm*.

C

Now, once again, Persio is going to think, to wield his thought as if it were a short, sharp dagger, aiming it against the muffled com-motion which reaches his cabin like a battle fought on innumerable pieces of felt, a cavalcade in a forest of cork trees. Impossible to know at exactly what moment the great lobster starts to move the piston, then the great flywheel where velocity has been asleep for days now rises up, irritated, rubbing its eyes, checks its wings, tail, and claws for attack against the sea and air, checks out the hoarseness by a blast from the stack, and the dark-lighted binnacle in the wheelhouse, the compass-housing, both a routine and inconstant. Easily swayed. Not leaving his cabin, Persio already knows what the ship is like, that it is surrounded at this azimuthal moment by two stubborn, dirty tugboats, which are going to lure the big mother, copper and iron, yard by yard, finally letting her go off the rocky coast at a tangent, pulling her off away from the magnetism of the dock. All this is happening while Persio opens a black suitcase abstractedly, admires the closet into which everything fits so well, and the cut-crystal glasses, judiciously fastened to the wall, and the writing table with its light-colored leather furnishings. He feels as if he himself were the heart of the boat, the very center where the progressively accelerating beats pound with a final, lessening oscillation. He begins to see the ship as if he were installed on the bridge, in the tiny center window, from where, as captain, he would dominate the prow, the forward masts, the slicing curve which wakens the short-lived foam. Strangely, the vision of the prow appears to him with the same unreality as if one took a painting off the wall and, holding it flat on the palms of the hands, could see the lines and masses of the upper portion of the painting move out away from the foreground, so that all the relationships conceived vertically by the painter became organized into another order equally possible and acceptable. What Persio sees most clearly from the captain's bridge (though he is in his cabin, it looks as if he were dreaming or only watching the bridge on a radar screen) is a sort of greenish darkness with yellowish lights to port and starboard, and a white lantern, which hangs from what might be a phantom bowsprit (it would not do that the Malcolm, this modern freighter, pride of the Magenta Star Lines, should have a bowsprit). Through the tiny window with its thick violet-tinted glass, which protects it from the fluvial wind (all around them would be the clay banks of the Rio de la Plata, what a name, catfish and maybe giltheads, golden giltheads in the silver of the Rio de la Plata, an absurd mounting, the tawdriest jewelry shop), Persio starts to grasp and fathom the shape of the prow and the deck. He can see them better now. They remind him of something, a cubist painting for instance, that is, if the canvas were stretched out on the palms of his hands, the lower part becoming the front and the top part the back. In this way Persio can see irregular forms to port and starboard, and beyond, vague shadows, sort of bluish like Picasso's guitar player. There are two masts in the center which hold up cords, a filthy and humble occupation, two masts which are, in his memory of the painting, more like two circles, one black and another light green with black stripes, which is the mouth of the guitar, as if two masts could be planted in the painting lying across his hands, thereby creating a prow, the prow of the Malcolm, shipping out of Buenos Aires, a mass of a ship wavering in a kind of oily, fluvial frying pan, crackling occasionally.

Persio is going to start thinking again, but contrary to his usual disconcerted custom, he will not try to order everything about him, the yellow and white lanterns, the masts, the buoys, but rather he will think of an even greater disorder, he will open the arms of thought into a cross and throw deep into the river everything that sinks in given, established forms: cabin, passageway, hatchway, deck, ship's course, tomorrow, the cruise.

Persio doesn't believe that what is happening is rational: he doesn't even want it that way. He feels the perfect disposition of the pieces in a fluvial puzzle, from Claudia's face to Atilio Presutti's shoes, to the steward who marauds (it can very well be) through the corridor outside his cabin. Once more Persio feels that, in this hour of initiation, the thing every traveler calls tomorrow can be determined by principles decided this evening. His only anxiety is the wide range of possible choice. Should he let himself be guided by the stars, the compass, cybernetics, chance, principles of logic, occult sciences, the boards in the floor, the state of his gall bladder, sex, character, palpitations and presentiments, Christian theology, Zend Avesta, royal jelly, Portuguese railroad timetables, a sonnet, the Weekly Financier, the shape of Galo Porriño's chin, a papal bull, the cabala, necromancy, Bonjour Tristesse, or simply by adjusting shipboard discipline to the encouraging instructions found in all packages of Valda's Coughdrops?

Persio recoils in horror before the risk of forcing just any reality, and his continual hesitation is like that of a chromophile insect which runs across the surface of a painting in an attitude resolutely antichameleonic. The insect, lured by the blue, will advance, tracing the outlines of the central parts of the guitar, where the dirty yellows and olive green reign, and then will perch on the edge as if it might swim to the other side of the ship, and upon reaching the central orifice through the starboard bridge, will discover the blue zone interrupted by vast green surfaces. Its hesitation, its search for a bridge toward another blue region, are comparable to the vacillations of Persio, who is always afraid to transgress secret laws. Persio envies those who only pose the problem of liberty egocentrically. For him, the act of opening the door includes his action and that of the door indissolubly joined, insofar as his action of opening the door contains a finality that can be mistaken and can damage the link in an order that he does not sufficiently understand. To say it more clearly, Persio is at once a chromophile insect and blind, and the obligation or imperative to run only on the blue areas of the painting is blocked by a permanent and hateful incertitude. He takes pleasure in these doubts, which he calls art or poetry, and believes it his duty to consider every situation with the greatest possible latitude, not only as a situation but rather from all its imaginable derivatives, beginning with the verbal formula he trusts (probably ingenuously), and the ramifications extending as far as his projections, which he considers magic or dialectical, according to the palpitations of his heart or liver.

It is very likely that the smooth rocking motion of the Malcolm and the wearing anxieties of the day will end by conquering Persio, who will sleep enchanted in the perfect cedarwood bed. First, however, he will amuse himself by turning on and off the diverse mechanical and electrical gadgets which contribute to the passengers' comfort. But for the moment, a prior choice of a somewhat experimental nature has occurred to him, a choice hardly touched upon some seconds before when he decided to pose the problem. There is no doubt: Persio will take pencils and papers from his briefcase, as well as a railroad timetable, and spend a good while making calculations, forgetting the trip and the ship precisely because he would like to take one step more toward appearance and enter into the beginnings of a possible or available reality. He will be busy pondering all this at the same time in which the others on board will have already accepted this appearance and will have qualified and classified it as extraordinary and almost unreal—a measure of being quite sufficient to bump their nose against and yet be convinced that it was no more than a mere allergic sneeze.

XIV

"*Eksta vorbeden?* You two married? *Êtes vous ensemble?*"

"*Ensemble plutôt que mariés,*" Raul said. "*Tenez, voici nos passeports.*"

The officer was a short man with a glib manner. He scratched out Paula's and Raul's names and signaled a red-faced sailor.

"He will accompany you to your cabin," he recited textually, and he bowed before going on to the next passenger.

Walking behind the sailor, they heard the whole Trejo family talking at once. Paula immediately liked the smell of the ship and the way the sounds grew muffled in the passageways. It was difficult to imagine that a few yards from there stood the filthy dock, the Inspector, and the policemen.

"And further on Buenos Aires begins," she said. "Doesn't it seem incredible?"

"More incredible when you say 'begins.' You've adjusted quite rapidly to your new surroundings. As far as I'm concerned, the port was always where the city ended, and now more than ever. And this isn't the first time I've traveled by ship."

"Begins," Paula repeated. "Things don't end that easily. I like the lavender odor of the disinfectant, flykiller, and mothspray on this ship. When I was little I liked to stick my head in Aunt Carmela's wardrobe; everything was black and mysterious, and it smelled a little like this."

"This way, please," said the sailor.

He opened a cabin and, after switching on the lights, gave them the key. He disappeared before they could offer him a tip or even say "Thank you."

"How lovely, but how lovely," said Paula. "And how gay."

"Yes, now it does seem unbelievable that the port buildings are so close," Raul said, counting the suitcases piled up on the carpet.

Nothing was missing, and they began to hang up their clothes and arrange all their belongings, some of them rather unusual. Paula appropriated the far berth, under the porthole. Lying back with a sigh of contentment, she looked at Raul, who was lighting his pipe as he continued to take out toothbrushes, toothpaste, books, and tobacco cans. It would be curious to see Raul go to sleep in the other bed. For the first time they would sleep together in the same room, after having known each other in thousands of living rooms, parlors, streets, cafés, trains, cars, beaches, and woods. For the first time she would see him in pajamas (they were already visibly spread out on the bed). She asked him for a cigarette and he lit it and sat down at her side, gazing at her with a look both amused and skeptical.

"*Pas mal, hein?*" said Raul.

"*Pas mal du tout, mon choux,*" said Paula.

"You're very pretty, stretched out like that."

"Oh, come now," said Paula, and they burst into laughter.

"Should we take an exploratory turn around the deck?" asked Raul.

"Hm, I'd rather stay here. If we go up on deck, we'll see the lights of Buenos Aires."

"And what do you have against the lights of Buenos Aires?" Raul asked. "I'm going up."

"Go ahead. I'll continue arranging this flowery bordello, because what you call arranging . . . What a pretty cabin, I never thought they were going to give us such gorgeous quarters."

"Yes, thank God it doesn't look like the cabins they have on the queen of the Italian liners. The advantage of this freighter is that it tends toward austerity. The oak and ash always lend a Protestant note."

"We don't know for sure that it's a Protestant ship, though you're probably right. I like the smell of your pipe."

"Be careful," said Raul.

"Why careful?"

"I don't know, the smell of the pipe, I suppose."

"Is the young man talking in enigmas?"

"The young man is going to arrange his own things," said Raul.

"If I leave you alone with my suitcase, I'll find a brassiere in the middle of my handkerchiefs."

He went to the table and put the books and notebooks in order. He tried the lights, studying the various possibilities of illumination. He was delighted to find that the lights over the bed could be adjusted to all possible inclinations. Intelligent Swedes, if they were Swedes. Reading was one of the hopes of the trip, reading in bed without having anything else to do.

"Right now," Paula said, "my darling brother Rodolfo must be lamenting my dissipated conduct for the benefit of the family circle. A girl of good family leaves on a trip, destination unknown. She refuses to announce the hour of departure to avoid farewells."

"I'd like to know what he'd think if he knew you were sharing your cabin with an architect."

"Who wears blue pajamas and cultivates, the sweet angel, unattainable nostalgias and even madder hopes."

"Not always unattainable, not always nostalgias," said Raul. "Do you know, in general sea air brings me luck. Brief luck, to be sure, and ephemeral like one of the birds you'll soon see trailing after the ship for a while, sometimes even for a day, but birds which eventually lose their way. It has never mattered to me that happiness is short-lived, dear Paula; the evolution from happiness to habit is one of death's best weapons."

"My brother wouldn't believe you," Paula said. "My brother would consider me seriously taken in by your satyric intentions . . . My brother . . ."

"One never can be sure," said Raul. "Against the possibility of a mirage, of a mistake because of the darkness, a dream which lasts into one's waking moments, against the effects of the sea air, pay attention and don't uncover yourself too much. A woman with the sheet up to her neck has insurance against fires."

"I think," said Paula, "that if you suffered a mirage I'd greet you with the sharp edges of this volume of Shakespeare."

"Quite an unusual way to be using Shakespeare," said Raul, opening the door. And at that moment, framed in the doorway, was Carlos Lopez, in profile. He was just lifting his right leg to take a step forward. His sudden appearance gave Raul the impression of a snapshot of a horse in motion.

"Hello," said Lopez, stopping short. "Did you get a good cabin?"

"Very good. Take a look."

Lopez glanced in and blinked when he saw Paula stretched out on the far berth.

"Hello," said Paula. "Come in, if you can find a place to put your feet."

Lopez said that their cabin was very similar to his, except for the size. He added that he had just met Señora Presutti, as he left his cabin, and that she had allowed him to contemplate her face, in which a green color was mounting to clearly cadaverous proportions.

"She's seasick already?" asked Raul. "Be careful, Paula dear. What will happen to the ladies when we begin to catch sight of the behemoth and other prodigious sea creatures? I suppose elephantiasis will set in. Should we take a turn around the deck? You're Lopez, I believe. I'm Raul Costa, and that languid odalisque answers to the noble name of Paula Lavalle."

"Noble yourself," said Paula. "My name sounds like an incognito for a movie actress, the Lavalle included. Paula Lavalle starring in *The House on Seventh Street East*. Raul, before you go up to the lion-colored river, tell me where my green purse is."

"Probably under the red jacket, or hidden in the grey suitcase," said Raul. "The palette is so varied . . . Shall we go, Lopez?"

"Let's go," said Lopez. "See you later, señorita."

Paula listened to the "señorita" with her sharp Buenos Aires ear, quick to detect all the nuances of the word.

"Just call me Paula," she said in a tone of voice which showed Lopez that she had understood, and that now she was pulling his leg a bit.

Raul, standing at the door, sighed as he looked at them. He knew Paula's voice so well, the certain way that a certain Paula had of saying certain things.

"So soon," he said, as if to himself. "So, so soon."

Lopez looked at him. They went out together.

Paula sat at the edge of the bed. Suddenly the cabin seemed extremely small and confining. She looked for a fan and finally managed to locate the air conditioning system. She turned it on distractedly and then tried one of the armchairs, then another, and went on to arrange some brushes on a stand. She decided she was feeling well, even happy. They were things that she had to decide now to get them settled. The mirror verified her smile as she explored the pale green bathroom, and for a second she looked with sympathy at the redheaded girl, with the slightly almond-shaped eyes, and her good spirits fully returned. She went over the hygienic gadgets in detail and admired all the innovations which bespoke the ingenuity of the Magenta Star Lines. The odor of the pine soap, which she took out from her make-up case, together with a package of cotton and two combs, was the odor of her garden before it became, little by little, no more than the recollection of the odor of her garden. Why should the bathroom of the *Malcolm* have to smell like a garden? The pine-scented soap felt pleasant in her hand. All unused soap has something lovely about it, and its loveliness is enhanced by its being intact and delicate. Even the suds are different, as the soap wears away imperceptibly; and it lasts for days and days, during which pine forests invade the bath; there are pines in the mirrors and on the shelves, in one's hair and on one's legs, which she has now suddenly decided to strip bare so she can try out the splendid shower which the Magenta Star Lines so kindly offers her.

Without bothering to close the connecting door to the cabin, Paula slowly took off her brassiere. She liked her breasts, in fact, she liked her entire body which sprouted forth from the mirror. The water which poured from the faucet was so hot that it was necessary for her to examine the shiny tap, the hot and cold water mixer, before stepping into the almost ridiculous miniature pool. She pulled the plastic curtain around the pool and felt as if she were surrounded by a toy city wall. The pine scent blended with the warmth of the air, and Paula soaped herself with both hands and then with a red rubber sponge. She spread the soapsuds slowly over her body, between her thighs, under her arms, and against her mouth. At the same time, she tried to balance herself imperceptibly, and over and over, she had to take hold of the

spigots, out of pure play, and say an affable dirty word for her own
secret pleasure. Interregnum of the bath, the parenthesis of the dry
and dressed existence. Naked like this, she freed herself of time,
and was once again the eternal body (and why not, then, the
eternal soul?) offered up to pine-scented soap and the spray of the
shower, which was always the same, thus confirming its perma-
nence in the same interplay of differences in places, temperatures,
and perfumes. But the moment she wrapped herself in the yellow
towel, which hung within hand's reach, she went back once more
to the tedium of the dressed woman, as if every garment tied her
to history and returned every year of her life, every cycle of memory, and pressed the future against her face as if it were a clay mask.
Lopez (if that young man, so distinctly Argentinian, was Lopez)
seemed likable. To have so common a name as Lopez was a misfortune like any other; undoubtedly, that "see you later, señorita"
had been a joke, but it would have struck her as far worse if he had
said "señora." Who, on board the *Malcolm*, would believe she
didn't sleep with Raul? She didn't have to ask people what they
thought of things like that. She thought of her brother Rodolfo
again; he was so much of a lawyer, such a drag, such a necktie with
red dots on it. "The poor idiot will never know what it's like to
truly fall, to dive into the middle of life, as if from the twenty-foot
board. The poor mug with his court calendar and his decent-chap
look." She began to brush her hair furiously, standing naked in
front of the mirror, wrapped in the gaiety of the steam that a discreetly situated fan near the ceiling swallowed up little by little.

XV

The passageway was narrow. Lopez and Raul walked through it
without a very exact idea of where they were going, until they
reached a locked bulkhead. Somewhat taken aback, they stood
staring at the steel panels painted in grey and the mechanism of
the automatic lock.

"Strange," said Raul. "I could have sworn that I came through
here with Paula a little while ago."

"Some contraption!" said Lopez. "An emergency door in case

of fire, or something like that. What language do they speak on board?"

The sailor on guard next to the door looked at them with an expression that indicated he did not understand or did not want to understand. They made signs to show they wanted to go through the door. The reply was a completely clear gesture ordering them to retrace their steps. They obeyed, passed Raul's cabin again, and finally came to an outside stair which went down to the steerage deck at the prow of the boat. Talk and laughter sounded in the shadows, and Buenos Aires was already in the distance, like a city on fire. They approached the rail, step by step, to avoid the benches, coils of rope, and winches which they could sense on the darkened bridge.

"It's strange to see the city from the river," said Raul. "Now its oneness and its entire outline are visible. One is always so involved in it that one forgets its true shape."

"Yes, it is intelligible this way, but the heat's following us all the same," said Lopez. "The smell of mud that reaches as far as the arched street beyond the docks."

"The river has always frightened me a bit; I suppose its muddy bottom is to blame, the dirty water seems to mask what's further down. The stories of drownings perhaps, which seemed so terrifying to me as a boy. But it's not unpleasant to swim in the river, or to go fishing there."

"This ship is quite small," said Lopez, who was beginning to make out the shapes. "Odd that steel door should have been locked. Looks like we can't get through this way either."

They saw that a high bulkhead ran from one side of the bridge to the other. There were two doors behind the tiny staircases, which one climbed to reach the cabin corridors, but Lopez, worried without really knowing why, quickly found out that they were also locked. Above, on the captain's bridge, the full, round windows showed a violet-tinted light. The silhouette of an officer, standing quite still, was scarcely visible. Higher up, the radar arc revolved lazily.

Raul would have liked to go back to the cabin and talk to Paula. Lopez was smoking, his hands in his pockets. A figure walked by, followed by a massive silhouette: Don Galo was exploring the bridge. They heard coughing, as if someone were looking for a pretext to get into a conversation, and Felipe Trejo joined them, busily lighting a cigarette.

"Hello," he said. "Are your cabins good?"

"They aren't bad," said Lopez. "And all yours?"

It irritated Felipe that they included him immediately with his family.

"I'm with my father," he said. "My mother and sister share the cabin next door. There's a bathroom and everything. Look, there are lights over there, must be Berisso or Quilmes. Maybe it's La Plata."

"Do you like to travel?" Raul asked, tapping his pipe. "Or is this the first big adventure?"

Felipe was irritated again by these inevitable references to his youth. He almost decided not to answer, or to say that he had traveled a lot, but Lopez would be well aware of his pupil's background. Felipe answered vaguely that anyone liked taking a cruise.

"Yes, it's always better than going to school," Lopez said amiably. "Some people feel that traveling is quite instructive to the young. We'll see if that's true."

Felipe laughed, more uncomfortable every minute. He was convinced that if he were alone with Raul or any other passenger, he would have been able to chat easily. But sure as rain, between the presence of his father, sister, and two teachers, especially the Black Cat, life would be unbearable for him. He had a fantasy of a clandestine debarkation, a disappearance in the night, all by himself. "Yes," he thought, "just to cut out on my own, that's all that matters." And yet, he wasn't sorry that he'd approached the two men. Buenos Aires over there, with all those lights, depressed and exalted him simultaneously; he would have liked to sing, to climb up a mast, to run across the deck; he would have liked it to be the next morning, or the next port of call, filled with weird characters, broads, and a swimming pool. He was frightened and happy, and the sleepiness which always came over him at nine o'clock was beginning again, a sleepiness which was even difficult for him to disguise sitting in cafés or parks.

They heard Nora laugh as she came down the little stairway with Lucio. The light of their cigarettes indicated their passage. Nora and Lucio also had a splendid cabin. Nora was tired (she hoped it was not seasickness, please) and would have liked it if Lucio had talked less about the cabin they were sharing. She thought it would have been quite all right if they had been given two cabins, after all, they were only engaged. "But we're going to get married," she told herself anxiously. No one knew about the Hotel Belgrano (except for Juanita Eisen, her best friend and confidante) and besides that night . . . Probably they'd be taken for a married couple among the people on board; but the passenger list, the gossiping . . . How beautiful Buenos Aires was, all lit up, the lights from the Kavanagh and Comega buildings. It reminded her of a Pan-American calendar photograph which she had hung in her bedroom, only that was the bay at Rio, not Buenos Aires.

Raul caught a glimpse of Felipe's face each time someone inhaled on a cigarette. They had stayed a bit to one side, and Felipe enjoyed talking to a stranger, especially someone as young as Raul, who was probably not even twenty-five. He took a sudden liking to Raul's pipe, his sport jacket, his vaguely aristocratic appearance. "But he's no phony, that's for sure," he thought. "He's got dough, that I'm sure of. When I get money like that . . ."

"It's already beginning to smell like the open river," Raul said. "A bad enough odor, but full of promises. Little by little, we'll feel what it is to pass from city life to life on the high seas. It will be something of a purification."

"Oh, yes?" said Felipe, not understanding the last phrase.

"And gradually we'll learn new forms of boredom. But for you it'll be quite different, it's your first trip, and everything will seem so . . . well, supply the adjectives yourself."

"Oh, yes," Felipe said. "Of course, it's going to be terrific. Nothing to do all day . . ."

"That depends," said Raul. "Do you like to read?"

"Sure," said Felipe, who read occasional thrillers. "Do you think there's a swimming pool on board?"

"I wouldn't know. It's a little difficult on a freighter. They'll probably improvise some sort of pool with wood and canvas. They do that on third-class steamers."

"No kidding," said Felipe. "With canvas? That's great."

Raul lit his pipe again. "Once more," he thought. "Once more the elegant torture, the perfect statue spouting inane babble. And to have to listen to all this, making excuses for everything like an imbecile, even convincing oneself that it really isn't so terrible, that all adolescent boys are like this and that one can't expect miracles . . . One should be the anti-Pygmalion, the petrifier. But after-ward?

"Illusions as usual. To think that the wingèd words, the books loaned with such eagerness, with underlined paragraphs, with ex-planations . . ." He thought of Beto Lacierva, his presumptuous smile those last times, the ridiculous meetings in Lezama Park, the conversation on the bench, the abrupt ending, Beto keeping the money he had asked him for, as if it were coming to him, the in-nocently perverse, vulgar words.

"Did you see the old boy in the wheelchair?" asked Felipe. "Some case, eh? That's a nice pipe."

"Not bad," said Raul. "It draws well."

"Maybe I'll buy one myself," said Felipe, and he blushed. Just what he shouldn't have said; the guy would take him for a kid.

"You'll find what you're looking for at the ports we'll stop at," said Raul. "Anyway, you can try mine out in the meantime. I al-ways take two or three with me."

"Really?"

"Sure, sometimes it's nice to change. They probably sell good to-bacco on board, but I also have some, if you like."

"Thanks," said Felipe, slightly confused. He felt a kind of hap-piness mounting in him and a desire to tell Raul that he liked talk-ing with him. Maybe they'd be able to talk about women; after all, he did look older than his age, and lots of people took him for nineteen or twenty. He thought of the Negrita but without really wanting to this time; she'd be in bed by now, and if she felt lonely she'd be crying foolishly, as when she had to obey her Aunt Su-sana, who was as bossy as the devil. It was odd to think about the Negrita just when he was talking to a guy as sharp as Raul. He would have laughed at him, without a doubt. "He must have all kinds of dames," he thought.

Raul said good night to Lopez, who was leaving, then wished Felipe good night, and slowly went up the little staircase. Nora and Lucio were behind him, and Don Galo's chair wasn't around. The chauffeur must have had a time getting Don Galo down as far as the bridge. In the corridor he ran into Medrano, descending a red-carpeted interior stairway.

"Have you found the bar?" said Medrano. "It's up there, to one side of the dining room. Unfortunately, I saw a piano in a corner, but we could always cut the strings one of these days."

"Or tune it so whatever they play on it will sound like Krenek."

"God, yes," said Medrano. "But then you'd infuriate my composer friend, Juan Carlos Paz."

"We'd reconcile immediately," said Raul, "thanks to my twelve-tone record collection."

Medrano looked at him.

"Well," he said, "this trip is going to turn out better than I expected. You never begin a shipboard friendship with a conversation like this."

"I agree. Up till now my conversations have dealt mainly with the weather, except for a brief digression on the art of smoking. Well, I'm going to get acquainted with the upper lounges; there might be some coffee."

"There is, and it's excellent, too. See you tomorrow."

"Tomorrow," said Raul.

Medrano looked for his cabin, which was off the passageway on the port side. His suitcases were still unpacked, but he took off his jacket and lit a cigarette, pacing listlessly back and forth. Maybe this was happiness. There had been an envelope addressed to him on the tiny desk. In it he found a welcome note from the Magenta Star Lines, as well as the hours meals would be served, some practical suggestions for life on board the ship, and a list of passengers with their respective cabin numbers. He learned that on his corridor were Lopez, the Trejos, Don Galo, and Claudia Freire and her son Jorge. There was also a note in English and French informing the passengers that the doors leading to the deck at the stern would remain locked for technical reasons, and that passage beyond these limits was strictly forbidden.

"Sweet Jesus," murmured Medrano. "It's hardly believable."

But why not, after all? After the London, the Inspector, Don Galo, the black bus, the semiclandestine embarkation, why not a

regulation to keep the passengers from crossing over to the poop
deck? Stranger than that, there were two teachers and a pupil
among the winners, all from the same school. And the queerest
thing of all was to have heard Krenek mentioned casually in a
ship's gangway.

"This isn't going to be bad."

The *Malcolm* pitched back and forth a few times, gently. Medrano started to unpack his luggage. He thought approvingly of
Raul Costa, and then he made a mental review of the other passengers. All things considered, it wasn't too terrible a crowd; the
differences were clearly obvious, and very likely two cordial
groups would be formed at the outset: one group in which the redhead of the tangos would shine, while the other would include
amateurs of the Krenek style. Don Galo would be marginal, joining neither group, but attentive to everything as he rolled around
on his four wheels—a kind of crafty, sarcastic supervisor. Not
difficult to imagine Don Galo and Dr. Restelli striking up a respectable friendship. The adolescent with the black lock of hair in
his eyes would veer between the easy crew of youngsters like
Atilio and Lucio, and the more respectable group of mature older
men. The shy young couple would sunbathe a good deal, take a
lot of pictures, and stay out late on deck to count the stars. There'd
be some conversations about art and literature, maybe the trip
would even last long enough for a few love affairs, some sniffles,
and certainly for friendships which would end in the exchange of
calling cards and affectionate slaps on the back in the customs shed.

By this time Bettina would know that he had left town. The
farewell note he had put next to the telephone dully concluded
an amorous trip begun in Junín, culminating in a number of
jaunts around the Buenos Aires coastline, with side trips to the
mountains and the sea. Right now Bettina would be saying, "I'm
glad of it," and she really would be glad—that is, before she decided to cry. Tomorrow—really two different tomorrows, but the
same nevertheless—she would call up Maria Helena to tell her of
Gabriel's leaving; later the same afternoon she would have tea in
the Aguila with Chola or Denise and begin to settle on her story.
The angry version or the one that was pure imagination would be
dropped, and she would acquire a definitive text in which Gabriel

wouldn't come out too badly, because deep down, Bettina would
be happy that he had left for a little while or even for good. One
afternoon she would receive his first letter from the high seas, and
perhaps would answer, writing out whatever general-delivery address he had put on his envelope. "But where are we heading?" he
thought, hanging up his jackets and trousers. For the time being,
they were forbidden access to the stern. It was not so encouraging
to find oneself confined to such limited quarters, even if it were
only temporary. He remembered his first trip, traveling third class,
with sailors standing guard in the passageways to protect the sacro-
sanct peace of the first- and second-class passengers, the economic
caste system, and many other things that had both amused and exasperated him. Later, he had traveled first class and put up with
even worse nonsense . . . "But nothing like a locked door," he
thought, piling up the empty suitcases. It occurred to him: for
Bettina the first days of his absence were going to be like a locked
door, which she would scratch and claw at until her fingernails fell
out, fighting to break down the barrier of air and nothingness
("No, I don't know where he's going," "No, there's no letter," "A
week, two weeks, a month . . ."). He lit another cigarette, irritated. "Oh, fuck the ship," he thought. "I didn't make this trip for
that." He decided to try the shower, just to do something.

XVI

"Look," said Nora. "With this hook you can leave the door open
a little."

Lucio tried the gadget and duly admired it. At the other end of
the cabin Nora was opening a red plastic bag and taking out her
make-up case. Leaning against the door, he was watching her
work, diligent, methodical.

"Do you feel all right?"

"Oh, yes," said Nora, as if surprised. "Why don't you open your
suitcases and put your things away? I picked that closet for my
things."

Lucio listlessly opened a suitcase. *I picked that closet for my
things*, he thought. Apart, always apart, still choosing for herself as

if she were alone. He was watching Nora work, her capable hands arranging her blouses and stockings on the shelves. She went into the bathroom, set some bottles and brushes on the shelf, and tried the lights.

"Do you like the cabin?" Lucio asked.

"It's lovely," said Nora. "Much prettier than I had imagined, and yet I had imagined it, I don't know how to say it, more luxurious."

"Like the ones in the movies, maybe?"

"Yes, but on the other hand, this is more . . ."

"More intimate," said Lucio, coming up close to her.

"Yes," said Nora, standing quite still, gazing at him, eyes very wide. She was beginning to recognize this look of Lucio's, the way his mouth quivered, as if he were muttering something. She felt his warm hand on her back, but before he could embrace her, she swung completely around and avoided him.

"Come on," she said. "Don't you see how much there is to do? And we left the door . . ."

Lucio lowered his eyes.

He put his toothbrush in the rack and turned off the bathroom light. The ship was scarcely rocking; the noises on board began to gradually situate themselves in the shockproof zone of his memory. The cabin was purring discreetly. If he pressed his hand against a piece of furniture, he could feel it vibrate as though a smooth electric current were running through it. The open porthole let the moist river air in.

Lucio had taken his time in the bathroom, so that Nora would be able to get in bed first. It had taken more than half an hour to unpack and arrange; then she had locked herself up in the bathroom and reappeared in a robe under which a pink nightgown could be perceived. But instead of going to bed, she had opened a make-up case with the clear intention of filing her nails. Then Lucio had taken off his shirt, shoes, and socks and carried his pajamas to the bathroom. The water was delicious, and Nora had left a fragrance of cologne and Palmolive soap.

When he came back in, all the cabin lights were switched off except for the two little lamps over the beds. Nora was reading a woman's magazine. Lucio turned out the light over his bed and sat down next to Nora, who closed her magazine and rolled the sleeves of her nightgown down to her wrists, with a gesture which feigned distraction.

"Are you happy here?" Lucio asked.

"Yes," said Nora. "It's so different."

He took the magazine away from her gently, and held her face between his palms. He kissed her on the nose, hair, and lips. Nora closed her eyes. A strange, tense smile was frozen on her face, a smile which reminded Lucio of the night in the Hotel Belgrano, the useless, exhausting persecution. He kissed her violently and painfully on the mouth, but did not let go of her head, which she pulled back. Sitting up, he pulled back the sheet and ran his hands up under the pink nylon nightgown, seeking flesh. "No, no," she said in a stifled voice; her legs were already bare up to the thighs. "No, no, not like that, no." Begging. He threw himself over her, holding her tightly between his arms, and pressed a long kiss on her half-open mouth. Nora was looking up toward the little light over the bed, but he would not turn it off, just like the other time, but later, in the dark, she had defended herself better, and then the tears, the intolerable wailing, as if he had hurt her. Abruptly, he turned on his side and pulled up her nightgown, put his head to her tightened thighs, to her stomach, which Nora's hands wanted to hide from his lips. "Please," murmured Lucio. "Please, please." But at the same time he kept lifting her nightgown, forcing her to straighten her back, to let the cold pink nylon bunch and rise until it reached her throat, and then suddenly disappear into the shadows beside the bed. Nora had curled, pulling up her knees and turning over until she was almost on one side. Lucio sat up suddenly in a single movement, and returned naked, stretching out against her. He ran his hands along her waist, kissing her from behind and biting her on the neck with kisses, which his hands sustained and prolonged on her breasts and thighs, handling them thickly, as if only now he was really going to begin to undress her. Nora stretched out her arm and turned off the light. "Wait, wait, please, just a minute, please. No, no, not like that, not yet, please." But he was not going to wait; she felt him against her back. And to the pressure of his hands and arms which encircled and caressed her, was added the other presence, the hard, burning

touch of what she had shrunk from looking at or knowing that
night in the Hotel Belgrano; the thing that Juanita Eisen had described to her (but you couldn't call that a description) until she
was terrified; that which would be able to hurt her and make her
scream, helpless in the arms of the male, crucified against him by
his mouth, hands, knees; and that which was all blood and rend-
ing; the thing forever present and awful in the dialogues of the
confessional, in the lives of saints, that was as horrible as a corncob, poor Temple Drake (yes, Juanita Eisen had said so), the horror of a corncob brutally penetrating there, where fingers could
scarcely enter without hurting. And now there was this hot body
against her back, this anguished pressure, as Lucio panted in her
ear and held himself tight against her, harder and harder, his
hand forcing her to half-open her legs, and then suddenly something like a flash of liquid fire between her thighs, a convulsive
groan and a weak provisional feeling of relief because he had not
been able to do it this time either. She felt him vanquished,
crushed against her back, burning the nape of her neck with his
panting, interspersed with disjointed words, a mixture of reproach
and tenderness, a messy sadness of words.

Lucio lit the lamp. There had been a long silence.

"Turn over," he said. "Please turn over."

"Yes," said Nora. "Cover us up, if you don't mind."

Lucio sat up, looked for the sheet, and pulled it up over them.
Nora turned over in a single movement and pressed up against
him.

"Tell me why," Lucio wanted to know. "Tell me why,
again . . ."

"I was afraid," said Nora, closing her eyes.

"Of what? Do you think I'd hurt you? You think I'm such an
animal?"

"No, it's not that."

Lucio lowered the sheet little by little as he caressed Nora's face.
He waited until she opened her eyes to say: "Look at me, look at
me now." She stared fixedly against his chest and shoulders, but
Lucio knew that she could see further down, and suddenly he sat
up and kissed her, pressing himself against her lips so as not to let
her escape. He felt her mouth twitch as she shrank weakly from

the kiss; he released her for a brief instant, then continued again
to kiss her and run his tongue across her gums, and gradually he
felt her yield, as he penetrated the depths of her mouth and slowly
excited her toward him. His hand searched gently for the deep
passage, the certainty. He heard her groan, but then his own cry
prevented him from hearing any more, and her moans died out,
muffled by his cry, her hands stopped fighting and throwing him
off and everything retreated back into itself and descended slowly
into silence and sleep. One of them turned off the light, their
mouths found one another again, and Lucio could taste something
salty on Nora's cheeks; he kept searching for her tears with his lips,
swallowing them while he caressed her hair, and then he heard her
breathe more regularly, the sob growing smaller each time, already
at the edge of sleep. Seeking a more comfortable position, he
moved away a bit and looked at the porthole barely outlined in
the darkness. It was good this time . . . He was not thinking, for
this was a kind of complete tranquillity which scarcely needed reflection. Yes, this time made up for the others. He had the taste of
Nora's tears on his now-dry lips. Ready cash, when I get to the
counter I lay it down. And the words came pouring out one after
another, rejecting the tenderness of his hands, the salty taste of her
lips. "Cry, cutie," one word, another, exact ones: the return to
reason. "Cry all you like, cutie, it was time that you learned. You
weren't going to hang me up all night." Nora stirred, moved an
arm. Lucio caressed her hair and kissed her on the nose. Further
back the words flowed freely, revenge at the fore, yes, cry, cutie,
go ahead, but the words were already foreign to the hand which
kept on stroking Nora's hair, mechanically and carelessly.

XVII

Claudia was well aware that Jorge would not fall asleep without
some special news or some extraordinary discovery. The best seda-
tive was for him to learn that there was a centipede in the bathtub
or that Robinson Crusoe had *really* existed. For lack of a better
contrivance, she gave him a medical prospectus, which she had just
found in one of the suitcases.

"It's written in a mysterious language," she said. "Maybe there's news about the star in it."

Jorge sat up in bed and began to read the pamphlet diligently; it left him in a state of wonder.

"Listen to this part, Mama," he said. "Berolase 'Roche' is the pyrophosphoric ester of the aneuryn, a cofermenter which intervenes in the phosphorization of glucids and assures decarbonization of pyruvic acid in the body, a common metabolic factor in the decomposition of glucids, lipids, and protids."

"Amazing," said Claudia. "Are you comfortable with one pillow or do you want another?"

"I'm comfortable, Mama. What's the metabolic factor? We'll have to ask Persio. This certainly must come from the star. The lipids and protids must be enemies of the antmen."

"Very likely," said Claudia, turning off the light.

"Night, Mama. It's a lovely ship."

"Very lovely, indeed. Sleep well."

The cabin was the last one which opened on the portside corridor. Apart from the fact that she liked the number thirteen, Claudia also was happy to find she was facing the staircase which led to the bar and restaurant. She met Medrano at the bar. He had come back to have a brandy after a last, vain attempt to unpack his clothes. The bartender greeted Claudia in slightly stiff Spanish, and offered her the menu, decorated with the Magenta Star insignia.

"The sandwiches are good," said Medrano. "In place of a real dinner . . ."

"The *maître* wants you to feel free to eat and drink anything you would like," said the bartender, who had already said the same thing in the same words to Medrano. "Unfortunately, we could not serve you dinner, as you came on board so late."

"That's odd," said Claudia. "On the other hand they had time to prepare and assign us our cabins without any hurry."

The bartender made an evasive gesture and waited for their orders. They asked for beer, brandy, and sandwiches.

"Yes, everything's odd," said Medrano. "For example, the noisy crowd, which seem to be presided over by the young redheaded fellow, haven't shown their noses around here yet. Just offhand, one would think they'd have better appetites than we sluggish types, if you'll forgive my lumping us together."

"The poor things must all be seasick," said Claudia.

"Is your son already asleep?"

"Yes, after having eaten a pound of butter cookies. It seemed better that he go to bed right away."

"I like your boy," said Medrano. "He's a handsome kid—sensitive face."

"Too sensitive sometimes, but as he has a great sense of humor and an unusual interest in football and mechanical things, he manages. Tell me, do you really think all this is . . . ?"

Medrano just looked at her.

"Better you talk to me about your son," he said. "What can I tell you? An hour ago I found out that it's forbidden to cross over to the stern deck. They didn't give us supper, but on the other hand, the cabins are extravagant."

"Yes, as far as suspense goes, you can't ask for more," said Claudia.

Medrano offered her a cigarette, and she felt pleased with this thin-faced, grey-eyed man, who dressed with a studied negligence which suited him very well. The armchairs were comfortable and the purring of the motors helped one not to think, to just sit back and rest. Medrano was right: why ask? If everything suddenly ended, it would have been a pity not to have taken better advantage of these absurd, happy hours. Then she would have to go back to Juan Bautista Alberdi Street, Jorge's school, chain-reading novels while she listened to the roaring buses, the no-life of Buenos Aires with no future for her, the placid, humid weather, the news over the radio.

Medrano, smiling, was thinking of the events in the London. Claudia wanted to know more about him, but she had the feeling that he was not a man given to confidences. The waiter brought another brandy; in the distance, a siren sounded.

"Fear is the father of strange things," Medrano said. "Right now, several passengers must be starting to get worried. We'll enjoy ourselves, you'll see."

"You can laugh if you like," said Claudia, "but it's been a while since I've felt quite so happy or calm. I like the *Malcolm*, or whatever it's called."

"Perhaps the novelty of it all is a bit romantic?" Medrano said, looking at her out of the corner of his eye.

"Novelty alone is enough in a world where people, like children, almost always prefer repetition. Have you seen the latest ad for Argentine Airlines?"

"Maybe, I don't know."

"They advertise their airplanes by saying that we'll feel as if we're in our own homes when we're in them. 'Like being in your own home,' or something like that. I can't conceive of anything more awful than going in an airplane and feeling as if I were at home again."

"And I suppose they stuff you with maté, spareribs, and spaghetti, all to the tune of a moaning accordion."

"All of which is fine in Buenos Aires, but only on condition that one is able, at any given moment, to substitute something else for it. The exact word is availability. This trip could be a kind of test."

"I suspect that for some of these people it's a test that's going to turn out to be a bit difficult. But speaking of airline ads, I remember with a special aversion, one from I don't know what American company, which underlines the fact that the passenger will be treated in a very special way. 'You'll feel like an important personage,' something on that order. When I think of my colleagues, who pale at the thought of someone calling them 'Señor' instead of 'Doctor' . . . yes, that company must do a lot of business."

"The theory of the VIP," said Claudia. "Has anyone written on the subject yet?"

"Too many vested interests, I fear. But you were telling me why you liked the trip."

"Well, in the end, all of us or almost all of us will become good friends, and there's no sense in mystifying the *curriculum vitae*," said Claudia. "The truth is that I'm a perfect failure, but I haven't resigned myself to my lot."

"Which makes me question what you say about your being a failure."

"Oh, probably my lack of resignation is the only thing that gets me to do something like buying a lottery ticket and winning. It's worth being alive just for Jorge, for him and a few other things. For certain music which one goes back to, and certain books . . . All the rest is dead and buried."

Medrano stared fixedly at his cigarette.

"I don't know much about married life," he said, "but it doesn't seem as if it's been too satisfactory in your case."

"I was divorced two years ago," said Claudia. "For reasons as numerous as they are trivial: neither adultery, nor mental cruelty, nor alcoholism. My ex-husband is Leon Lewbaum; the name may mean something to you."

"Cancerologist or neurologist, I think."

"Neurologist. I divorced him before I became one of his patients. He's an extraordinary man, and I can say it with more sureness than ever now that I think of him in a way we would probably consider posthumous. I'm referring to myself, to that which remains of me, which isn't much."

"However, you divorced him."

"Yes, I divorced him, perhaps to save what remained of my own personality. You know, one day I discovered that I liked to go out at the hour he came in, to read Eliot when he decided to go to a concert, to play with Jorge instead of—"

"Ah," said Medrano, looking at her. "And you stayed with Jorge."

"Yes, everything worked out perfectly. Leon visits us every so often, and Jorge loves him in his own way. I live the way I want, and here I am."

"But you spoke of a failure."

"A failure? Actually, the failure was marrying Leon. And that's something that didn't work out by getting divorced, or even by having Jorge for a son. It began before all that; it's the absurdity that got me into this life to start with."

"Why, if it's not too much to ask?"

"Oh, the question isn't new; I've asked myself the same thing since I've begun to understand myself a little. I make use of a series of answers: for sunny days, for stormy nights . . . An assorted collection of masks, and behind everything, I think, a black hole."

"Should we have another brandy?" said Medrano, calling over the bartender. "It's strange, but I have the feeling that the institution of marriage doesn't have a single representative among us. Lopez and I are bachelors, I believe Costa is too, Dr. Restelli is a widower, there are a couple of girls of marriageable age . . . Ah, Don Galo! But who knows what Don Galo's matrimonial status is? Your name is Claudia, isn't it? I'm Gabriel Medrano, and my biography is lacking in interest altogether. To your health and Jorge's."

"To your health, Medrano, and let's talk about you."

"Through interest or courtesy? Forgive me, one says things that are mere conditioned reflexes. But I'm going to deceive you by first telling you I'm a dentist and then by telling you that I spend my life not doing anything useful, just cultivating a few friends, admiring a few women, and building a castle of playing cards. It tumbles down every few months. Paf, all fall down. But I begin again, you know, I start over again."

He looked at her and began to laugh.

"I like talking to you," he said. "Mother of Jorge, the little lion."

"We both talk a great deal of nonsense," Claudia said, laughing too. "Always masquerading, of course."

"Oh, masquerading. One usually gives too much importance to the face that's hidden. Actually it's the mask itself that counts, that it's this one, not another. Tell me what mask you wear, and I'll tell you what face you have."

"The most recent one," said Claudia, "is called *Malcolm*, and I believe a number of us share it. Listen, I'd like you to meet Persio. Could we have him called from his cabin? Persio is a marvelous person, a true magician; at times I'm almost afraid of him, but he's like a lamb, except that we already know how many symbols are concealed in the lamb."

"Is he the short, bald man who was with you at the London? He reminded me of a photograph of Max Jacob I have at home. Speak of the devil . . ."

"A lemonade is enough to re-establish the proper level of spirits," said Persio. "And maybe a cheese sandwich."

"What an awful combination," said Claudia.

Persio's hand had slid like a fish through Medrano's. He was dressed all in white, including his shoes. "All bought at the last minute in any shop at all," thought Medrano, looking at him sympathetically.

"The trip is beginning under disconcerting signs," said Persio, sniffing the air. "The river, which surrounds us, is like orange marmalade. And as far as my cabin is concerned, it's really sublime. Why try to describe it? It's sparkling and replete with mysterious things, with buttons and placards."

"Do you like to travel?" Medrano asked.

"Well, it's what I do all the time."

"He's referring to the subway," said Claudia.

"No, I'm not, I travel in infraspace and hyperspace," said Persio. "Two idiotic words which don't signify much, but I travel. At least my astral body fulfills vertiginous courses. Meanwhile, I work at Kraft Publishers, and my job is to correct galley proofs. You see, this cruise is going to be very useful to me in order to make stellar observations and decipher astral signs. Do you know what Paracelsus thought? That the firmament is a pharmacopoeia. Nice, isn't it? Now I'm going to have the constellations within hand's grasp. Jorge says that you can see the stars better from the sea than from land, especially from Chacarita where I live."

"You go from Paracelsus to Jorge without making a distinction," laughed Claudia.

"Jorge knows things, or maybe he's a spokesman for a knowledge he'll later forget. When we play magic games, the great Provocations, he always finds more than I. The only difference is that he becomes distracted quickly, like a monkey or a tulip. If I could hold his interest a little longer, especially on those things which he has insight into . . . But constant activity is the law of childhood, as Fechner probably would say. The problem is Argus, of course, always Argus."

"Argus?" asked Claudia.

"Yes, the polyfaceted, the ten-thousand-eyed, the simultaneity. Yes, the simultaneity!" Persio exclaimed enthusiastically. "When I pretend to add Jorge's vision to mine, am I not denouncing the most awful nostalgia of the race? To see through other eyes, to be both my eyes and yours too, Claudia, whose eyes are so beautiful, and those of this gentleman, which are so expressive. All eyes together, because that kills time, liquidates the whole thing. Goodbye, out it goes. Beat it!"

He made a gesture as if to scare off a fly.

"Do you know, if I simultaneously saw everything that the eyes of the race, the four billion eyes of the human race saw, reality would no longer be successive, it would petrify in an absolute vision in which the *I* would disappear, completely annihilated. But what an annihilation, what a triumphal blaze, what a Response! It's impossible to conceive of space as beginning at one special moment, and even more impossible to conceive of time, which is the same thing in a consecutive form."

"But if you should survive such a glimpse," said Medrano, "you would begin to feel time once more. It would be dizzily multiplied by the number of partial visions, but always time."

"Oh, they wouldn't be partial," said Persio, raising his eyebrows. "The idea is to encompass the whole cosmic system in a total synthesis, which is only possible by making an equally total analysis. You understand, human history is the sad result of each one looking out for himself. Time is born in the eyes, everybody knows that."

He took a pamphlet from his pocket and consulted it anxiously. Medrano, who was lighting a cigarette, saw Don Galo's chauffeur look in through the door, observe the scene for a moment, and approach the bartender.

"With a bit of imagination you can get a vague idea of Argus," said Persio, turning the pages of the pamphlet. "I, for one, exercise my imagination on things like this. It's not good for anything except to rouse my imagination, but it excites me to a cosmic feeling and gets me out of my sublunar torpor."

The cover of the pamphlet read *Official Railroad Guide for Portugal*. Persio shook the guide like a banner.

"If you like, I'll demonstrate for you," he proposed. "You could also use a photograph album, an atlas, a telephone book, but this little booklet is extremely useful for unfolding into simultaneity, for fleeing from this spot at any given moment . . . Maybe I'd better go on explaining. The official time is 22:30. Now you know that this isn't astronomical time, you know that we're four hours behind in relation to Portugal. But we're not interested in fixing a horoscope, we're simply going to imagine that it's about 18:30 in Portugal. A beautiful hour in Portugal, I suppose, an hour when all the Portuguese tiles are glowing."

He resolutely opened the guide and examined page thirty.

"The Great Northern line, are we there? Now look closely. At this very moment train 125 is passing between the stations of Mealhada and Aguim. Train 324 is pulling out of the Torres Novas station, just one more minute, actually much less. Train 326 is coming into Sonzelas, and on the Vendas Novas line, the 2721 has just left Quinta Grande. Can you see what I mean? Here is the Lousã branch, where the 629 has just stopped at the station of that name before going on to Prilhão-Casais . . . But thirty seconds have already elapsed; that means that we've hardly had time to imagine five or six trains, and yet there are many more. On the eastern line the 4111 is going from Monte Redondo to Guia; the 4373 has stopped at Leiria; the 4121 is coming into Paúl. And what about the western line? The 4026 left Martingança and is crossing Pataias; the 4028 has stopped at Coimbra, but the seconds are passing, and here on the Figueira line, the 4735 has arrived at Verride; the 1429 is about to leave Pampilhosa, and the whistle is already sounding, it's leaving . . . and the 1432 is pulling into Casal . . . Should I go on?"

"No, Persio," said Claudia, tenderly. "Drink your lemonade."

"But you grasped the idea, didn't you? The exercise . . ."

"Oh, yes," said Medrano. "I felt a little as if I could see all the trains in Portugal from far above, almost at the same time. Wasn't that the meaning of the exercise?"

"One's got to imagine that one sees," said Persio, closing his eyes. "It means erasing the words and only seeing how, at this very moment, on nothing more than an insignificant bit of the world, an insurmountable mountain of trains fulfill their schedules to the minute. And then, a while later, you can imagine all the trains of Spain, of Italy, and then on to all the trains that at this moment, 18:32, are at some place, or are arriving at or leaving some place."

"I'm getting dizzy," said Claudia. "Oh, no, Persio, not this first evening, with this magnificent cognac."

"All right, but the exercise is useful for other things," Persio conceded. "Especially for magical purposes. Have you thought about drawings? If, on this map of Portugal, we mark all the points where there's a train at 18:30, and then connect all the marks, the resulting drawing could be interesting. Then, we could modify the drawing every quarter of an hour, so as to appreciate the comparison or superposition as the drawing changes, improves, or worsens. I've had curious results, working with these drawings in my free moments at Kraft; I've about reached the conclusion that one day I'll see the birth of a drawing which will exactly correspond to some famous masterpiece, the Picasso guitar, for instance, or a Petorutti fruit bowl. If that happens, I'll have a code, a modulus. In that way, I'll begin to encompass creation from its true analogical base and I'll break with the time-space concept, which is an invention plagued with defects."

"The world is magical, then?" Medrano asked.

"Even magic is infected with Western prejudices," said Persio, bitterly. "Before reaching a formulation of cosmic reality, it would be necessary to retire, so as to have more time to study the astral pharmacopoeia and to palpate subtle material. What's the good of a forty-hour week?"

"Let's hope the trip gives you some time to study," said Claudia, standing up. "I'm beginning to feel a delicious touristic tiredness. See you tomorrow."

Medrano returned to his cabin a little later and this time found the energy to unpack his suitcases. "Coimbra," he thought, smoking his last cigarette. "Lewbaum the neurologist." It all blended so easily; perhaps it was also possible to extract a meaningful drawing of those meetings and memories of which Bettina was now forming a part, looking at him with an expression of shock and pique, as if the act of switching on the bathroom light was an unpardonable offense. "Oh, leave me alone," thought Medrano, turning on the shower.

XVIII

Raul switched on the bed lamp and blew out the match which had guided him that far. Paula was sleeping, turned toward him. In the weak light of the night lamp her reddish hair looked like blood on the pillow.

"How pretty she is," he thought, as he undressed without embarrassment. "When her face relaxes, the deep wrinkles between

her brows disappear, and they're there even when she laughs. And
her mouth . . . She looks like a Botticelli angel; something so
young, so virginal . . ." He laughed ironically. "*Thou still un-
ravish'd bride of quietness,*" he recited. "Ravish'd and archirav-
ish'd, the poor darling." Poor little Paula, punished too soon for
her own insufficient rebellion, in a Buenos Aires which had given
her only guys like Rubio, the first (if he was the first, but naturally
he was, Paula didn't lie), or Lucho Neira, the last, not counting
the x's, y's, and z's or the boys on the beach and the weekend adventures, or her flings in the back seat of some Mercury or DeSoto.
Putting on his blue pajamas, he walked barefoot to Paula's bed; it
touched him a bit to see her asleep, even if it was not the first
time, but now Paula and he were entering into a period of intim-
acy and secrecy, which would last weeks or months, if it was going
to last, and that first image of her sleeping trustfully at his side
filled him with tenderness. Paula's daily unhappiness had been intolerable to him during these last few months: her three o'clock in
the morning telephone calls, her backsliding to drugs, her desultory
walks, her dormant suicide wish, her sudden tyrannical moods
("Come immediately or I'll jump out of the window"), her rap-
tures of joy over a poem which had turned out well, her desperate
weeping which ruined ties and jackets. The evenings when Paula
arrived unexpectedly at his apartment, which irritated him endlessly, because he had continually asked her to call before coming;
her way of looking at everything, of asking: "Are you alone?" as if
she were afraid there was someone under the bed or sofa, and
then the burst of laughter or tears and the endless outpouring of
confidences between whisky and cigarettes. And in spite of everything, she did not deprive herself of injecting criticism, which was
even more irritating because of its aptness: "Who in the world
would think of hanging that piece of junk there?" or: "Don't you
see there's a vase too many on that stand?" Or her sudden fits of
raging morality, her ridiculous catechizing, her hatred of his friends,
her indubitable meddling in the Beto Lacierva affair, which perhaps explained the brusque rupture and Beto's flight. But at the
same time, there was Paula the splendid, the sweet loyal Paula, the
comrade of so many exciting evenings, of political discussions at
the university, of literary loves and hates. Poor little Paula, daugh-

ter of a local political boss and his pretentious, despotic family,
tied like a little dog to her first communion, to a convent school,
to "my parish priest" and "my uncle," to *La Nación* and the
Colón Opera House, and then suddenly, into the street like a
scream, the absurd and irrevocable act which had isolated her
from the Lavalles, forever and for nothing, the initial act of her
meticulous plunge. Poor little Paula, how could she be so stupid at
moments of decision. Besides (Raul was gazing at her, shaking
his head) her decisions had never really been radical. Paula was
still eating the bread provided by the Lavalle family, a bourgeois
family, capable of throwing dirt over the scandal and paying the
rent on an apartment for the black sheep of the family. And this
was a further reason for neurosis, for crises, for revolts, for plans to
sign up with the Red Cross or to go abroad. Meanwhile, everything
was debated in the luxury of a living room–bedroom flat, with central heating and automatic incinerators. Poor little Paula! It was
gratifying to see her sleeping deeply ("Is it Luminal or Nembutal?"
Raul wondered) and to know that she would be there all night,
breathing near him. And now he went back to his bed and turned
off the light. He lit a cigarette, concealing the flame between his
hands.

In cabin five, on the port side, Señor Trejo sleeps and snores exactly as if he were in the matrimonial bed on Acoyte Street. Felipe
is still up, though he couldn't be more exhausted; he has already
showered and is looking in the mirror at his chin, where an in-
cipient beard is beginning; he combs his hair meticulously, for the
pure pleasure of seeing himself, of feeling himself alive in mid-
adventure. He goes from the bathroom to the cabin and puts on
his linen pajamas and sits down in an armchair to smoke a
Camel, after adjusting the movable lamp, which shines on an issue
of *Sports International*, which he glances through unhurriedly. If
only the old man wouldn't snore . . . but that would be too much
to ask. Felipe is not resigned to the fact that he hasn't the cabin to
himself; if by any chance he lines up a girl, it's going to be a mess.
And how simple it all would have been if his old man slept somewhere else. Dreamily, he recalls movies and novels where the passengers have great love scenes in their cabins. "Why did I invite

them?" Felipe asks himself, and then thinks of the Negrita, who would be in the middle of undressing in the attic, surrounded by movie magazines and postcards of James Dean. He keeps turning the pages of the magazine, pausing at the fight photographs; he imagines himself the winner of an international boxing match, signing photos after having knocked out the former champion. "Tomorrow we'll be out to sea," he thinks suddenly, and yawns. The armchair is wonderful, but the Camel is beginning to burn his fingers; he is getting more and more tired. He turns off the overhead light, switches on the bed lamp, and then slides into bed, enjoying every square inch of the sheet and the soft but firm mattress. It occurs to him that Raul is going to bed too, after having smoked a final pipe, but instead of a snoring old man in his cabin, he'll have that gorgeous redhead. Raul is probably already warmly pressed up against her, and Felipe is sure that the two of them are naked and enjoying each other. For Felipe the verb "to enjoy" is replete with all that the solitary hand, the reading, and intimate bull sessions with school friends can evoke and suggest. Switching off the light, he gradually turns over on his side and stretches his arms into the shadows so as to wrap the Negrita's body in his arms, as well as the redhead's, a composite in which a friend's younger sister and his cousin Lolita also join. It is a kaleidoscope, which he caresses gently until his hands encircle the pillow; then he pulls the pillow out from under his head and pushes it up against his body, which fastens to it convulsively, while his mouth bites into the flat, lukewarm material. To enjoy, enjoy, not even knowing how he got out of his pajamas, and there he is naked against the pillow, stiffening and falling mouth down, pushing with the small of his back, hurting, never getting to the pleasure, shaken by a quiver which makes him burn and despair. He bites the pillow, presses it against his legs, coming close in to it and drawing back, and finally, he yields to habit, the easiest way. He falls onto his back and his hand starts the rhythmic race, the sheath whose pressure changes gradually, slowing down or accelerating knowledgeably, again it's the Negrita, now she's on top of him like some of the French photos Ordoñez has shown him, the Negrita, who keeps her breathing down, muffling her cries so she won't wake Señor Trejo.

. . .

"At last," said Carlos Lopez, turning off the light. "In spite of my fears, this aquatic monstrosity has set sail."

The light from his cigarette made patterns in the shadows, and then a milky clarity outlined the porthole. He was feeling fine in bed; the gentle rocking was inviting him to sleep without more ado. But Lopez thought first of how lucky it was that he had found Medrano among his traveling companions, and of how he had enjoyed the story of Don Galo, and he recalled Costa's redheaded girlfriend, and the disconcerting behavior of the Inspector. Then his thoughts returned to the brief visit to Raul's cabin, the exchange of barbs with the green-eyed girl. That was some girl Raul had. If he had not seen it . . . But he had seen it, and there was nothing odd about it, simply a man and a woman sharing cabin number ten. Curious, if he had met her with Medrano, for example, it would have seemed perfectly natural. But with Costa, he didn't know exactly why . . . It was ridiculous, but that's how it was. He remembered that Costals from the Montherlant novels had called himself Costa at first; he remembered another Costa, a former schoolmate. Why did he keep going back to the same idea? There was something that didn't fit here. Paula's voice, when she had spoken to him, had seemed like a voice on the margin of the presumed situation. Of course there are women who can't do anything about their high spirits. And Costa at the door, smiling. Both so pleasant. And so different. There lay the mystery; such a dissimilar couple. He did not feel the connection, the continual change in coloration of love play or friendship play in which the most blatant antagonisms revolve within something that connects and places them.

"I'm kidding myself," Lopez said out loud. "In any case, they'll be great traveling companions. And one never knows . . ."

The cigarette flew like a firefly and was lost in the river.

D

Exactly at midnight, Persio, furtive and slightly frightened, but nevertheless excited and irrepressible, takes his place at the darkened prow to stand watch. The southern sky fascinates him, and he raises his bald head to look at the resplendent clusters of stars, but

Persio also wants to establish and hasten a contact with the ship
which carries him, and because of that he has waited for the hour
of sleep when all men become equal, and has imposed a jealous
vigil on himself which must put him in communication with the
fluid substance of night. He is standing next to what is like a coil
of cables (on principle there are no serpents aboard ships), and he
feels the humid air of the estuary on his forehead, and then he col-
lates, in a low voice, the various elements of judgment gathered
upon leaving the London, and he establishes meticulous nomencla-
tures in which the incongruity of including three accordions and a
refreshing Cinzano and water, together with the shape of the prow
bulkhead and the oily revolving of the radar, resolves itself for him
in a slow geometry, a gradual approximation of the causes of the
situation which he shares with the rest of the passengers. There is
nothing in Persio which tends to a normative formula, yet a per-
petual anxiety possesses him regarding the vulgar problem of his
environment. He is sure that an order scarcely perceivable by analogy governs the chaos which includes a singer taking leave of his
brother and a wheelchair embellished by a chrome crank; like the
dark certainty that there exists a central point in which every discordant element can finally become visible as a spoke in the wheel.
Persio's ingenuousness is not so overpowering that he could possibly
fail to ignore the necessity of breaking down the phenomena before
going on to any architectonic attempt, but at the same time, he
cannot prevent his love for the incalculable kaleidoscope of life;
he savors the feeling of his feet encased in brand-new tennis shoes;
he listens with tenderness to the creaking of the boat's framework
and to the gentle lapping of the river against the keel. Incapable of
renouncing the concrete in favor of installing himself on a plane in
which things pass from being mere things to cases and where the
sensual repertory gives way to a vertiginous balance of vibrations
and energy tensions, he chooses, by means of a humble astrological
labor, a traditional approach by way of the concealed image, the
tarot pack, and the favor of some enlightening chance event. Persio
puts his faith in a kind of winged genie which orients him in the
tangled yarn of facts, and like the prow of the Malcolm which cuts
the river, night, and time in half, he quietly goes forward in his
meditation which casts aside the trivial—the Inspector, for in-

stance, or the odd prohibitions which reign on board—so as to concentrate on elements conducive to a greater coherency. A while ago his eyes were exploring the captain's bridge, pausing at the wide, empty window from which a violet light shines. Whoever is steering the ship must be in the back of the translucent cabin, far from the windows, which flow phosphorescently in the light river haze. Persio feels a gradual horror mounting in him. Visions of fatal ships without helmsmen run through his memory; recent reading has furnished him with visions of the sinister region of the northeast (and Tuculca, the god, menaces threateningly with a green staff in his hand), and the visions combine with Arthur Gordon Pym and Erik's boat drifting in the subterranean lake of the Opera. What a combination! But at the same time Persio fears, and he does not know why, the foreseeable moment in which the silhouette of the pilot will be outlined in the little window. Up until now everything has happened in a kind of amiable delirium, decipherable and intelligible, with little material to pad out the isolated elements; but something tells him (and that something could be precisely the unconscious explanation of all that has happened) that in the course of the night an order is going to be established, a disturbing causality chained and unchained simultaneously by the angular stone, which will present itself at the top of the arch in the window at any moment. And that is why Persio trembles and recoils when at this very moment a silhouette is outlined on the captain's bridge, an upright black torso appears, motionless, framed in the glass. High above, the stars turn slightly. The arrival of the captain has been enough for the ship to vary its course; now the large mast no longer caresses Sirius, but wavers toward the Little Bear, jabs it and lashes it, and then moves away. "We have a captain," Persio thinks, shaken, "we have a captain." And it is as if in the disorder of rapid thought and in the fluctuation of his blood, a law is slowly coagulating, the law which is the mother of the future and the beginning of an inexorable route.

FIRST DAY

> . . . *le ciel et la mer*
> *s'ajustent ensemble pour*
> *former une espèce de guitare* . . .
> —AUDIBERTI, *Quoat-Quoat*

XIX

Atilio Presutti's nocturnal activities ended with a room change. With the help of a sullen, almost mute steward he pulled one of the beds out of his cabin and carried it to the cabin next door, which his mother, Nelly's mother, and Nelly herself would share. The installation was complicated by the shape and size of the cabin, and Doña Rosita talked several times about leaving things as they were and going to sleep in her son's cabin, but Pelusa rocked his head between his hands and said that three women together was different from a mother with her son, and besides, there were no screens or any other kind of separation in the cabin. At last they managed to set up the bed between the bathroom door and entranceway, and Pelusa reappeared with a little box of peaches which Rusito had given him. Even though they were all hungry, none of them dared ring the bell to ask about dinner. Instead, they ate peaches, and Nelly's mother took out a bottle of cherry brandy and a Hershey bar. Completely at peace, Pelusa went back to his cabin, threw himself down on his bed, and slept like a log.

It was seven when he woke up, and a misty sun was filtering into the cabin. Seated on his bed, he scratched himself through his undershirt and admired the cabin's luxury and size in the clear light of day. "What luck the old lady's a woman and has to sleep with the other dames," he thought, satisfied, calculating the independence and importance a private cabin gave him. Cabin number four: Señor Atilio Presutti. Should we go up and see what's

happening? The ship seems to be standing still, maybe we reached
Montevideo already. Good God, what a bathroom, what a toilet
seat, *mamma mia!* And pink paper, this is great! Maybe this afternoon or tomorrow I'll try out the shower. It should be terrific. But
take a look at this washbowl, it's like the swimming pool at the
Sports Club, and you could wash your neck here without splashing
a drop, and good hot water . . .

Pelusa soaped up his face and ears energetically, careful not to
wet his undershirt. Afterward, he put on his new striped pajamas,
his tennis shoes, and touched up his hair before going on deck. In
his hurry he forgot to brush his teeth, even though Doña Rosita
had bought him a new toothbrush.

He walked past the cabins on the starboard side. The rest of
those guys would still be snoring, he thought, sure that he'd be the
first one out on deck. But there he bumped into the kid traveling
with his mother, who looked at him in a friendly way.

"Morning," said Jorge. "I see I beat everyone up."

"How are you, kid," Pelusa condescended. He approached the
rail and grasped it with both hands.

"My God," he said. "But we're anchored in front of Quilmes!"

"Is that Quilmes, with all those tanks and cranes?" Jorge asked.
"Is that where they manufacture beer?"

"But don't you see what's happened?" Pelusa cried. "And I
thought we were in Montevideo already and maybe we could get
off the ship and all that, I don't know . . ."

"Quilmes must be pretty close to Buenos Aires, isn't it?"

"Sure, you take the streetcar and you're there in two shakes! The
Jap gang could be catching me from the seawall; they're all of them
from there . . . But what kind of a trip is this, would you tell me?"

Jorge examined him with wise eyes.

"We've been anchored for a half hour," he said. "I came up at
six, I wasn't tired any more. Do you know that you never see anyone here? Two sailors came by in a hurry to do something about
the tackle, but I don't think they understood me when I talked to
them. They were probably lipids."

"What?"

"Lipids. They're very strange fellows, never talk. Unless they
were protids. It must be pretty easy to mix them up."

Pelusa looked at Jorge out of the corner of his eye. He was going to ask him something when Nelly and her mother appeared on the little staircase. They were both in slacks and fancy sandals, wearing sunglasses and handkerchiefs around their heads.

"Oh, Atilio, what a divine ship!" Nelly said. "It's a pleasure to see everything so sparkling. And the air, what air!"

"What air!" echoed Doña Pepa. "And what an earlybird you are, Atilio."

Atilio went over to them, Nelly lifted her cheek to him, and he deposited a kiss on it. He immediately stretched out his arm and showed them the coast.

"But I know that," said Nelly's mother.

"Berisso!" said Nelly.

"Quilmes," said Pelusa, lugubriously. "Would you tell me what kind of a cruise is this?"

"I was thinking we were out to sea already and that the ship wasn't rocking any more," said Nelly's mother. "Maybe there's something broken and they have to fix it."

"Maybe they came to tank up on gasoline at Quilmes," Nelly said.

"These ships use fuel oil," Jorge said.

"Yes, that's what I mean," said Nelly. "And this little boy is here all alone? Is your mama downstairs, darling?"

"Yes," said Jorge, looking at her out of the corner of his eye. "She's counting the spiders."

"The what, little boy?"

"The spider collection. Whenever we make trips we always take our collection with us. Last night five escaped, but I think Mama has already found three."

Nelly and her mother opened their mouths. Jorge ducked down to dodge Pelusa's friendly but awkward slap.

"Don't you see the kid is pulling your leg?" said Pelusa. "Let's go up and see if they'll give us a cup of coffee. I'm dying of hunger."

"I heard that breakfasts on these ships are very complete," said Nelly's mother peevishly. "I read that they even serve orange juice. Do you remember that movie, honey? The one where the young girl was working . . . and the father was something in a newspaper and didn't want her to go out with Gary Cooper?"

"But no, Mama, it wasn't in that movie."

"Yes, don't you remember it was in technicolor and she sang that bolero in English at night . . . But you're right, it wasn't with Gary Cooper. It was the one with the train accident, do you remember?"

"No, Mama," Nelly said. "It's really something how she always mixes them up."

"But they were serving orange juice, all the same," Doña Pepa insisted.

Nelly hung on her sweetheart's arm to go up to the bar, and on the way she asked him in a low voice if he liked her in slacks. Atilio answered by letting out a kind of stifled howl and squeezing her arm until it hurt.

"You know," said Pelusa, whispering in her ear, "you'd be my wife already if it wasn't for your old man."

"Oh, Atilio," said Nelly.

"We'd have the cabin all to ourselves and everything."

"You think I don't think of it at night? I mean, that we could be married already?"

"And now we'll have to wait till your old man puts out with an apartment for us."

"Oh yes. You know what Papa's like."

"A stubborn mule," said Pelusa respectfully. "Well, at least we can be together the whole trip, we can play cards, and at night we can go out on deck. You know those coils of rope on the deck? Great to hide behind. I'm starving . . ."

"The river air is very bracing," said Nelly. "What do you think of Mama in trousers?"

"They're okay on her," said Pelusa, who had never seen anything more like a mailbox. "My old lady doesn't like to wear those things. She's old-fashioned, and anyway the old man would go wild if he caught her in a pair of pants. You know how it is."

"They're very impulsive at your house," said Nelly. "Go call your mother and we'll go up. Just look at those doors. Aren't they clean?"

"Listen to all that yakyak at the bar," said Pelusa. "It sounds like they all show up for breakfast call. Let's go get the old lady together. I don't like you going to the bar alone."

"But Atilio, I'm not a baby."

"They're all kinds of sharks on this ship," said Pelusa. "You come with me and that's that."

XX

Breakfast was ready in the bar. There were six tables laid, and the waiter was placing the last flowered napkin when Lopez and Dr. Restelli walked in almost simultaneously. They chose a table and were joined immediately by Don Galo, who, after dismissing his chauffeur with a snap of his fingers, appeared to take it for granted they had all been introduced. Lopez, incredulous that the chauffeur could have carried Don Galo and the wheelchair up the stairs (suspended in the air like a laundry basket; what a trick!), asked:

"How are you this morning?"

"Fair enough," Don Galo replied with a Galician accent undiminished by fifty years of Argentine commerce. "Too damp, though. And no dinner last night."

Dr. Restelli, in white suit and golfing cap, allowed that, although the organizational details might be somewhat deficient, the responsible authorities could plead the existence of attenuating circumstances.

"Not at all, not at all," said Don Galo. "Positively intolerable! Always is when bureaucracy tries to supplant private enterprise. If Thomas Cook and Sons had organized this trip you can be sure we wouldn't have had all these headaches."

Lopez was amused. With his gift for provoking arguments, he insinuated that private agencies were not above selling a pig in a poke now and then, and that in any event the Tourist Lottery was invented by officialdom.

"Of course, of course," Dr. Restelli seconded him. "Señor Porriño—that is your name, I believe—you must remember that the initial inspiration must be attributed to the intelligent vision of our authorities, and that—"

"Contradicting yourself!" Don Galo cut him off. "Never yet seen authorities with any vision. Look, there's not a single government decree covering retail commerce that's not a complete calamity. The regulation for importation of textiles, for example. What do you say about that? A disaster, naturally! In the Retail Association —I've been honorary president for three terms now—I've given my opinion in two open letters and a protest to the Ministry of Commerce. The results, gentlemen? None! That's government for you!"

"Just a moment." Dr. Restelli struck the fighting-cock pose which always delighted Lopez. "Far be it from me to defend government actions in their entirety, but a professor of history has, so to speak, a feeling for comparisons, and I can assure you that this government—that most governments, generally speaking—represents moderation and balance as compared with private interests, which may be very respectable, if you like, but which usually try to seize that which cannot be granted them without seriously undermining the national interest. And not only the majority interest, good sir, but we must also consider the interests of political parties, public morale, and community councils. What must be avoided at all costs is anarchy, albeit in its most rudimentary forms."

The waiter, who was serving coffee and cream, listened to the dialogue with intense interest, moving his lips as if repeating the more overwhelming words.

"Tea with lots of lemon for me," Don Galo ordered without looking up. "Oh yes, of course. Everyone starts talking about anarchy when it's perfectly clear that the real anarchy is officially sponsored, disguised behind laws and ordinances. You'll see! This trip is going to be a mess! A perfect mess!"

"In that case," Lopez asked offhandedly, "why did you come?"

Don Galo started visibly.

"But man, that's two different things. Why shouldn't I come as long as I won the lottery? I'll wait for the defects to crop up as we go along."

"Given your ideas, though, defects are to be foreseen, aren't they?"

"Of course! But what if things should accidentally turn out well?"

"In other words, you recognize that official initiative can be sound in certain cases," Dr. Restelli interposed. "Personally, I always try to be understanding and to imagine myself in the position of the governor." (That's what you'd like, you poor, frustrated politician, thought Lopez with more sympathy than malice.) "Guiding the ship of state is a serious affair, my esteemed friend, but fortunately the helm is in excellent hands. Not sufficiently energetic, perhaps, but eminently well-intentioned."

"There you are!" said Don Galo, buttering his toast furiously. "There you are with your dictatorial government. No sir! What we need is intensive commerce, freer flow of capital, opportunity for everybody—within certain limits, naturally."

"Those things are not incompatible," said Dr. Restelli, "but we certainly must have a vigilant authority armed with ample powers. I admit that, and there is no more staunch defender of Argentine democracy than myself. When it comes to confusing liberty with license, however, you'll find in me a determined adversary."

"Who's speaking of license?" Don Galo bristled. "When it comes to moral questions I'm as strait-laced as anybody, goddamn it!"

"I did not use the word in that sense, but since you employ its common meaning, I am delighted that we find ourselves on common ground there."

"And we agree about the strawberry jam, which is very good," interjected Lopez, who was seriously bored. "I don't know whether you've noticed, but we've been anchored for some time now."

"A breakdown!" Don Galo exclaimed with satisfaction. "You! A glass of water!"

They greeted politely the gradual arrival of Doña Pepa and the rest of the Presutti family, who installed themselves with running commentaries at a table loaded with butter and jam. Pelusa came over to their table, apparently to allow them a close and detailed view of his pajamas.

"Morning, how goes it?" he said. "Did you see what's up? We're opposite Quilmes, Quilmes, understand?"

"Quilmes!" Dr. Restelli exclaimed. "Impossible, young man, we ought to be at Montevideo!"

"I know the gas tanks," Pelusa assured him. "My fiancée over there wouldn't let me lie. You can see the houses and factories, I'm telling you it's Quilmes."

"Why not?" said Lopez. "We've the preconceived idea that our first stop should be Montevideo, but if we're on another course, south, for instance—"

"The south?" said Don Galo. "And what will we do in the south?"

"Well, I suppose we'll find out about that right now. What's the itinerary?" Lopez asked the waiter.

The waiter had to confess that he did not know. That is, he had known it until the day before: they were supposed to have been sailing for Liverpool, with stops at eight or nine regular ports en route. But after negotiations had begun with the home office, he had been left in the dark as to the plans. He cut his explanation short to attend to Pelusa's urgent demand for more coffee. Lopez turned back to the others with a puzzled expression.

"We'll have to find an officer," he said. "They must have established an itinerary by now."

Jorge, who had taken a liking to Lopez, came running over to their table.

"The others are on their way," he announced. "But the ship's crew is invisible. Can I sit down with you? I'd like some coffee with milk and bread and jam, please. There they come, the ones I said were on their way."

Medrano and Felipe came in, looking surprised and sleepy, Paula and Raul behind them. While they were all shaking hands and greeting one another, Claudia and the Trejo family arrived. Only Lucio and Nora were missing, not counting Persio, because Persio never gave the impression of being missing from anywhere. The bar was filled with the scraping of chairs, conversation, and cigarette smoke. The majority of the passengers began to see one another really for the first time. Medrano, who had invited Claudia to share his table, found her younger than he had thought the night before. Paula *was* younger, but her eyelids looked heavy, and a tiny nerve caused one side of her face to contract occasionally. Just then, she seemed as old as Claudia. The news that they were anchored off Quilmes had spread to every table, provoking laughter and ironic remarks. Medrano, who suddenly had the feeling of a particularly ridiculous anticlimax, saw Raul Costa go up to a porthole and talk to Felipe. They ended up by joining Paula at a table where she was already seated, while Lopez maliciously savored the Trejo family's obvious displeasure at their son's secession. The chauffeur reappeared to take Don Galo away, and Pelusa immediately ran over to help him. "What a nice fellow," Lopez thought. "How can you tell him he ought to leave his pajamas in the cabin?" He mentioned it to Medrano in a low voice, leaning across to the other table.

"It's the same old story," Medrano said. "You can't be offended by these people's ignorance or coarseness when neither of us has done anything to help change matters. We'd rather organize our lives so as to have the least possible contact with them, but when circumstances oblige us to live together—"

"We're lost," said Lopez. "At least I am. I feel overwhelmed, overcomplicated in the face of so much pajama, so much *Woman's Day*, so much innocence."

"An excellent opportunity which they unconsciously exploit to throw us off balance, given that we also bother them. Every time one of them spits on the deck, it's as though they were putting a bullet between our eyes."

"Or when they turn the radio up, then scream at one another over it; but then they can't hear the radio very well and turn it up still more, etcetera, *ad infinitum*."

"And above all," Medrano said, "the worst is when they decide to show off the traditional sterling qualities of the commonplace and the stereotype. In their way, they're extraordinary, like a boxer in the ring or a trapeze artist, but one can scarcely imagine traveling for any length of time with athletes or acrobats."

"Don't get melancholy," Claudia said, offering them cigarettes, "and don't show your bourgeois prejudices so fast. What do you think of the intermediary link, the student's family? There you have some nice people who are even more unhappy than we are; they don't get along with the group around the pajamaed redhead or with our cozy table. They aspire toward the latter, of course, but we back off terrified."

The party referred to were quietly arguing, except for a few sudden hisses and interjections, about Felipe's rudeness. Señora Trejo was not going to let that whippersnapper of a son take advantage of the situation to emancipate himself at sixteen and a half years old, and if his *father* was not going to reprimand him . . . But Señor Trejo would certainly do it, she could be sure of that. As for Beba, she was the very image of disdain and disapproval.

"Well," Felipe was saying, "we sailed so much last night that when I looked through the porthole this morning and saw chimneys I almost went back to bed."

"That will teach you not to be such an earlybird," said Paula, yawning. "And you, my dear, that will be the last time you wake me. I come from an honorable line of sleepyheads, on both sides, the Lavalles as well as the Ojedas, and I have to keep our coats of arms well polished."

"That's all right with me," said Raul. "I did it only for your health, but it's clear my efforts have not been well received."

Felipe listened, completely bewildered. It was a little late now to come to any agreement about matters of sleep. He set himself diligently to the task of eating a hard-boiled egg, looking out of the corner of his eye at his family's table. Paula was observing him between two clouds of smoke. Neither better nor worse than the others; it seemed as if age was the great leveler, making them all vaguely stubborn, cruel, and delicious. "He's going to suffer," she said to herself, but she wasn't thinking about Felipe.

"Yes, that will be best," said Lopez. "Look, Jorge, if you're already through with your breakfast, go see if you can find someone from the ship, and ask him to come up here for a minute."

"An officer or an ordinary lipid?"

"An officer is better. Who are the lipids?"

"Don't know," said Jorge. "But I'm sure they're enemies. See you later."

Medrano signaled the waiter, who was leaning over the bar. He approached listlessly.

"Who's the captain?"

To everyone's surprise the waiter did not know.

"That's how it is," he explained, a bit sadly. "Until yesterday it was Captain Lovatt; but last night they said . . . Because you people came on there were some changes, and . . ."

"What do you mean, changes?"

"Yes, some new arrangements. I don't think now we're going

to Liverpool. Last night I heard—" He interrupted himself and
looked around. "I think it would be better if you talked to the
maître, maybe he knows something. He'll be here any minute."

Medrano and Lopez exchanged looks, and let the waiter off
the hook. It seemed as if the only thing left was to admire the
coast around Quilmes and talk. Jorge returned with the news that
there were no officers in sight, and that two sailors painting a cap-
stan didn't understand Spanish.

XXI

"Hang it here," said Lucio. "It'll only take a minute to dry in
front of the fan and then we'll put it on again."

Nora had just finished wringing out the part of the sheet she
had been washing.

"You know what time it is? Nine-thirty, and we're anchored
somewhere."

"I always get up about now," said Nora. "I'm hungry."

"I am, too. But they've probably served breakfast already. Meals
on board ship are at different times than we're used to."

They looked at each other. Lucio approached Nora and gently
embraced her. She put her head on his shoulder and closed her
eyes.

"Do you feel all right?" he asked.

"Yes, Lucio."

"You love me a little, don't you?"

"A little bit."

"And are you happy?"

"Hm."

"Aren't you happy?"

"Hm."

"Hm," said Lucio, and kissed her on the hair.

The waiter looked at them disapprovingly, but hurried to clear
the table which the Trejo family had just left. Lucio waited
until Nora sat down, and then he went over to Medrano, who
brought him up to date on what had happened. When he went

back and repeated it to Nora, she refused to believe him. In general, the women on the trip were quite scandalized, as if each had personally planned her itinerary in advance and it was being thwarted from the very outset. On deck, Paula and Claudia were looking disconcertedly at the manufacturing spectacle along the coast.

"To think that we could get home on a bus from there," Paula said.

"I'm beginning to think it wouldn't be a bad idea," laughed Claudia. "But all this has a comic side which amuses me. All we have to do now is run aground on Maciel Island, and we'll have a great view of Buenos Aires."

"And Raul was visualizing us in the Marquesas in under a month."

"And Jorge was getting ready to walk the lands of his beloved Captain Hatteras."

"What a lovely boy you have," said Paula. "We're great friends already."

"I'm glad, because Jorge isn't easy. If someone doesn't strike him just right . . . He gets it from me, I'm afraid. Are you glad you're taking this trip?"

"Well, glad isn't exactly the word," said Paula, blinking, as if sand had blown in her eye. "I'd rather say hopeful. I think I need to change my life a little, the same goes for Raul, and that's why we decided to make the trip. I suppose the same is true for everyone."

"But you're not traveling for the first time."

"No, I was in Europe six years ago, and the truth is my trip was pretty awful."

"It can happen," said Claudia. "Europe isn't only the Uffizi or the Place de la Concorde. It is for me, at the moment, but that's because I live in a world of literature. And perhaps, seen from this part of the world, there's a higher percentage of deception than one imagines."

"It's not that, at least not in my case," said Paula. "To be perfectly frank, I'm completely incapable of truly playing the part I'm supposed to play. I was raised in an atmosphere of constant illusion as far as personal fulfillment is concerned and I've never been able to live up to it. Here, facing Quilmes, right on this

river the color of baby shit, I could invent a solid chapter of justi-
fications. But the day comes when you compare yourself on the
scale of older models, measure yourself against the Greek columns,
for instance—and you sink still lower. I'm surprised," she added,
taking out her cigarettes, "that certain trips don't end with a bullet through the head."

Claudia accepted a cigarette and looked at the approaching
Trejo family, as well as Persio, who was waving wildly to her
from the prow. The sun was beginning to burn.

"I know why Jorge likes you," Claudia said, "aside from the fact
that he's fascinated by green eyes. It's not fashionable any more
to quote, but do you remember the phrase by a Malraux character:
'Life is worth nothing, but nothing is worth a life.' "

"I'd like to know how that character ends up," said Paula, and
Claudia felt that her voice had changed. She put her hand on
Paula's arm.

"I don't remember," she said. "Maybe with a bullet through
the head. But probably someone else pulled the trigger."

Medrano looked at his watch.

"To tell the truth, this is beginning to be a bore," he said. "Since
we're the only ones here, what do you say we delegate someone to
penetrate the wall of silence?"

Lopez and Felipe agreed, but Raul suggested that they go together to look for an officer. There were only two blond sailors on
the prow who shook their heads and exchanged some words in a
language which might have been Norwegian or Finnish. They
crossed the starboard passageway without finding anyone. The
door of Medrano's cabin was open, and a steward greeted them
in labored Spanish. It was better if they went to see the *maître*,
who would be in the dining room preparing for lunch. No, it was
not possible to cross over to the poop deck, but he could not tell
them why. Captain Lovatt, yes. Captain Lovatt was no longer captain? Up until yesterday it was Captain Lovatt. One more thing:
he requested that the gentlemen lock their cabins, if they had val-
uable items . . .

"Let's go look for the famous *maître*," said Lopez, bored.

They returned to the bar, unwillingly, and found Lucio and

Atilio Presutti discussing the reason for the *Malcolm*'s anchoring. From the bar they all went into the reading room, where a Scandinavian piano glowed ominously, and then into the dining room, whose dimensions brought a whistle of admiration from Raul. The *maître* (it had to be the *maître* because he had the smile of a *maître* and was issuing orders to a waiter who looked at him with a taciturn expression) was setting out flowers and napkins on the tables. Lucio and Lopez walked up ahead, and the *maître* raised his greying eyebrows and greeted them with a certain indifference, which did not exclude a touch of amiability.

"You see," said Lopez, "these gentlemen and I are somewhat surprised. It is ten in the morning and we still do not have the slightest notion of the trip we are going to make."

"Oh, a notion of the trip," said the *maître*. "I believe they're going to send you some sort of bulletin or dispatch. I'm not really up to date on things myself."

"No one here is very up to date on what's going on," said Lucio, his voice pitched just a little too high. "Does it seem proper to have us . . . in Never-Never Land?" he finished, blushing, vainly looking for a way to continue.

"Sir, I beg your pardon. I didn't think that in the course of the morning . . . We're quite busy," he added. "Lunch will be served at eleven sharp, and dinner at eight. Tea will be served at five in the bar. Those who wish to eat in their cabins—"

"Speaking of wishes," said Raul, "I'd like to know why we can't cross over to the poop deck."

"Technical reasons," the *maître* said quickly.

"Is the *Malcolm* damaged in some way?"

"Oh, no."

"Why have we been anchored out here in the river all morning?"

"We'll weigh anchor immediately, sir."

"To where?"

"I don't know, sir. I suppose it will be announced in the bulletin."

"Can we talk to an officer?"

"I've been informed that an officer will come to welcome you at lunch."

"Is it possible to send a cable?" asked Lucio, just to say something practical.

"To where, sir?" the *maître* asked.

"What do you mean where? Home," said Pelusa. "To find out how the family is. I have a cousin stuck in bed with appendix."

"Poor kid," Raul said with sympathy. "Well, we'll wait to see if the oracle will show up with the *hors d'oeuvres*. I'm going out to admire the Quilmes coast, homeland of Victorio Cámpolo, our celebrated boxer, and other great founding fathers."

"It's curious," said Medrano to Raul as they left, slightly hangdog. "I keep having the feeling that we've gotten into a big fix. Amusing, in a way, but I don't know up to what point. How does it strike you?"

"*Not with a bang but a whimper,*" said Raul.

"Do you know English?" Felipe asked him as they went down the steps to the bridge.

"Yes, of course." Raul looked at him and smiled. "I said 'of course' because almost everyone I know does. You study English at school, I suppose."

"A little," said Felipe, who failed his examinations regularly. He wanted to remind Raul of the pipe he had offered him, but was embarrassed. Not exactly embarrassed, but it was a question of waiting for the right moment. Raul spoke, but not too insistently, of the advantages of knowing English, listening to himself the whole time with a kind of pitiable mockery. "The inevitable histrionic phase," he thought, "the sinuous and wise search, the first round of study . . ."

"It's beginning to get hot," he said mechanically. "The traditional humidity of the Rio de la Plata."

"Oh, yes. But that shirt you have on must be terrific," Felipe said, as he enthusiastically touched the material between two fingers. "It's nylon, isn't it?"

"No, it's only a silk poplin."

"It looks like nylon. We have a prof who wears nylon shirts. Someone brings them to him from New York. We call him 'The Old Smoothie.' "

"Why do you like nylon so much?"

"Because . . . well, it's in style, and all the magazines advertise it a lot. It's a shame it costs so much in Buenos Aires."

"But why do *you* like it?"

"Because you don't have to iron it," said Felipe. "Just wash the shirt, hang it out, and there it is. Old Smoothie told us."

Raul looked him squarely in the face, while he took out his cigarettes.

"I see you're a practical man, Felipe. But who would have guessed you had to do your own washing and ironing."

Felipe blushed red and hurriedly accepted a cigarette.

"Don't kid me," he said, turning his eyes away. "But nylon, for trips . . ."

Raul agreed, helping him get over his momentary embarrassment. Nylon, of course.

XXII

A boat with a man and boy in it came along the starboard side of the *Malcolm*. Paula and Claudia waved to them and the boat came up even closer.

"Why are you anchored out here?" the man asked. "Is something wrong?"

"Mystery," said Paula. "Or a strike."

"How can there be a strike, miss, something must be broken."

Claudia opened her wallet and showed him two ten-peso bills.

"Do us a favor," she said. "Paddle around to the poop deck and see what's happening on that side. Yes, the poop deck. Look and see if there are some officers there, or if they're repairing something."

They rowed off, and the man, obviously disconcerted, did not even risk another word. The boy, who had thrown out a line, began to pull it in hurriedly.

"What a good idea," said Paula. "But how absurd this all seems, doesn't it? To send a kind of spy is ridiculous."

"Perhaps it's no more ridiculous than guessing a number with five digits within all the possible combinations. There's a certain proportion in all this ridiculousness, even though I'm probably catching some of Persio's madness."

While she was explaining who Persio was, the little boat and its occupants pulled away without so much as a glance back toward the *Malcolm*. Claudia was not surprised.

"A failure of the *astuzie femminile*," Claudia said. "I hope the men manage better than we have. Are you both comfortable in your cabin?"

"Fine, just fine," said Paula. "For such a small ship the cabins are perfect. Poor Raul will soon begin to be sorry he ever brought me along; he's order itself, while I'm . . . Don't you get a certain sense of satisfaction out of throwing things about?"

"No, but I have a house to run and a child. Sometimes . . . But no, I think that I really do prefer to find petticoats in the petticoat drawer, etcetera."

"Raul would kiss your hand if he could hear you," laughed Paula. "The first thing I did this morning was to brush my teeth with his brush. And poor Raul, he really does need rest."

"Count on the ship for peace and quiet. In fact, it's almost too quiet."

"I don't know, he's upset already, and this story about an off-limits rear deck infuriates him. But really, Claudia, Raul is going to have a terrible time with me."

Claudia had the feeling that behind that insistence there was a desire to add something else. It did not interest her very much, but she liked Paula, the way she blinked, her sudden changes of position.

"I suppose he must be used to your using his toothbrush."

"No, not exactly the toothbrush. The books of his I lose, the cups of coffee I knock over onto the rug . . . but the toothbrush no, not until this morning."

Claudia smiled, without saying anything. Paula wavered and made a gesture as if to scare away a fly.

"Perhaps it's better if I just tell you: Raul and I are simply good friends."

"He's a very nice young man," said Claudia.

"As no one or almost no one on board will believe it, I'd at least like you to know about it."

"Thanks, Paula."

"I'm the one who has to do the thanking for having met someone like you."

"Yes, sometimes it happens that . . . sometimes I've felt the necessity to be thankful for a mere presence too, a gesture, or even a silence. Or to know that one can begin to speak, to say something one wouldn't ever say to anyone, and suddenly it's so easy."

"Like offering a flower," said Paula, and she pressed her hand lightly on Claudia's arm. "But I can't be trusted," she added, withdrawing her hand. "I'm capable of an infinite number of bad deeds, and I'm incurably perverse with myself and with others. Poor Raul bears with me up to a point . . . You can't imagine how good and understanding he is, perhaps because I really don't exist for him; I mean that I only exist on an intellectual level, to put it one way. If, by some unlikely chance, we should ever go to bed together, I think he'd begin to detest me the next morning. And he wouldn't be the first."

Claudia turned her back to the rail to avoid the sun, which was already too strong.

"Aren't you going to say anything?" Paula asked sullenly.

"No, nothing."

"Well, maybe it's better if you don't. Why should I be boring you with my problems?"

Claudia noticed the excitement in her voice, her irritation.

"It occurs to me," she said, "that if I had asked a question or made a comment you would have distrusted me. With the perfect and ferocious distrust of one woman toward another. Doesn't it frighten you to confide in someone?"

"Oh, confidences . . . This wasn't any confidence." Paula crushed out her scarcely smoked cigarette. "I didn't do anything but show you my passport. I'm horrified at the idea of being judged for something I'm not, that a person like you should care for me on the basis of a dirty misunderstanding."

"And so you told me about Raul, and your perversity, and your unhappy love affairs . . ." Claudia began to laugh and suddenly bent over and kissed Paula on the cheek. "What an idiot. You're a big dope."

Paula lowered her head.

"I'm much worse than that," she said. "But don't trust me, don't trust me."

Nelly thought the orange blouse was too daring, but Doña Rosita, on the other hand, was more indulgent with the youth of today. Nelly's mother was of an intermediary opinion: the blouse was fine, but the color was loud. When Atilio was asked his opinion he remarked judiciously that you wouldn't notice the blouse except on a redhead, but anyway he'd never let his fiancée show her shoulders like that.

The sun was burning the tops of their heads, and they took refuge in the area which two sailors had just topped over with canvas. Once they were comfortably seated in deck chairs of various colors, they felt quite happy. Actually, the only thing missing was a cup of maté, and that was Doña Rosita's fault, for she had not wanted to bring the thermos and maté pot with the silver straw—a gift of Nelly's father to Don Enzo Presutti. At bottom, Doña Rosita regretted her decision, but she remarked that it wasn't refined to drink maté on the first-class deck, to which Doña Pepa answered that they could have gathered in the cabin to drink it. Pelusa suggested they go up to the bar and have a beer, but the ladies were too pleased with their comfortable chairs and the view of the river.

Don Galo, whose every descent of the staircase was followed with terrified eyes by the women, reappeared at this moment to interrupt the conversation and to thank Pelusa for the help he gave the chauffeur in these delicate operations. The women and Pelusa answered in unison that it was the least they could do, and Doña Pepa asked Don Galo if he had traveled a good deal. Well, yes, he knew a bit of the world, especially the entire Lugo region and the province of Buenos Aires. He had also traveled as far as Paraguay in a boat of Mihanovich's, a terrible trip in '28, and what heat, what heat . . .

"And always . . . ?" Nelly insinuated, vaguely motioning toward the chair and chauffeur.

"Come, come, girl. In those days I was as strong as an ox. Once there was a fire in the Pehuajó store . . ."

Pelusa signaled Nelly to bend toward him so that he could whisper in her ear.

"The old lady's going to pee her pants," Pelusa whispered. "When she wasn't looking I packed the maté pot in the suitcase and four pounds of tea. We'll drag it up here this afternoon and you're going to see their mouths fall open . . ."

"But Atilio!" said Nelly, who was still admiring Paula's blouse at a distance. "You're a . . . you're . . ."

"Well, what can you do," Pelusa said, satisfied with life.

The orange blouse got to Lopez too, as he was coming on deck after having arranged his things. Paula was reading, facing the sun, and he leaned up against the railing and waited until she looked up.

"Hello," said Paula. "How are you, professor?"

"*Horresco referens,*" Lopez murmured. "Don't call me professor or I'll throw you overboard, book and all."

"Françoise Sagan, and she doesn't merit that kind of treatment. I see the river air awakes piratelike instincts in you. Walk the plank or something like that, no?"

"You've read novels about pirates? Good sign, very good sign. I know by experience that the most interesting women are those who have ventured into masculine reading as children. Stevenson, for example?"

"Yes, but my buccaneer erudition comes from my father who kept a complete file of *Tit-Bits* where the great novel titled *The Treasure of the Island of the Black Moon* was published."

"Ah-hah, but I've read that too! The pirates had some great names—Sennacherib Eden, Maracaibo Smith."

"I bet you don't remember the name of the nimble swordsman who dies doing battle for the good cause?"

"Sure I remember: Christopher Dawn."

"We're twin souls," said Paula, extending her hand. "Long live the black flag! The word professor is forever banished."

Lopez went to look for a chair, after assuring himself that Paula had rather go on talking than reading *Un Certain Sourire.* Quick and agile (he was not small, but he sometimes gave the impression of being so, partly because he wore unpadded jackets and narrow trousers, and because he moved with great speed), he returned with a deck chair which spouted green and white stripes, sat down next to Paula with obvious voluptuousness, and watched her for a while, silently.

"*Soleil, soleil, faute éclatante*," she said, staring back at him. "What protective divinity, Max Factor or Helena Rubinstein, will save me from this cruelest of scrutinies?"

"The scrutiny," Lopez observed "offers the following analysis: extraordinary beauty, slightly counteracted by excessive exposure to dry Martinis and the air conditioning in north-side *boîtes*."

"Right you are."

"Treatment: sun in moderate doses and piracy *ad libitum*. The latter is dictated by my experience as a thaumaturge, because I know well enough that I would not be able to rid you of your vices all at once. When you've savored the salt of taking over a ship, when you've put a hundred crew members to the sword . . ."

"Of course, the scars remain, as in the tango."

"In your case they simply diminish to an excessive photophobia, caused by the batlike life you lead, as well as your constant reading, undoubtedly. Besides, I've heard the awful rumor that you write poems and stories."

"Raul," Paula murmured. "The damn squealer. I'm going to make him walk the plank naked, rub his body with tar."

"Poor Raul," said Lopez. "Poor, lucky Raul."

"Raul's fortune is always precarious," Paula said. "Risky speculations: sells mercury, buys petroleum, liquidates at any price, panic at midday and caviar at midnight. And it isn't bad that way."

"Yes, it's better than a salary from the Board of Education. As for me, I not only don't have any stocks, I don't take any stock in them. I live without taking stock in anything . . ."

"The fauna of Buenos Aires is all the same, my dear Jamaica John. And that's why we've come aboard the *Malcolm* with so much enthusiasm and that's why we've already begun to infect it with immobility and don't-get-involved kind of thinking."

"The difference is that I was joking, while you seem launched upon a species of self-criticism worthy of a Muscovite."

"No, not that. I've already told enough about myself to Claudia. Quite enough for one day."

"Claudia seems nice."

"Very nice. Really, there's a group of interesting people on board."

"And another quite picturesque. Let's see what alliances, schisms, and desertions take place during the course of the trip. I see Don Galo talking with the Presutti family over there. Don Galo will act as a neutral observer, he'll go from table to table in his strange vehicle. Isn't it curious to see a wheelchair on a ship, one medium of transport on top of another?"

"There are even stranger things," said Paula. "Once when I was coming back from Europe, the captain of the *Charles Tellier* made an intimate confession to me: the venerable old gentleman admired motor bikes and had his on board. He scooted around Buenos Aires with great enthusiasm on his Vespa. But your strategic and tactical vision of all of us interests me. Go on."

"The Trejos are the only problem," said Lopez. "The boy will hang around us, for sure." (*Tu parles*, Paula thought.) "The others will be received politely but it won't go any further than that. At least in your case and in mine. I've already heard them talking, and that's enough. For example: 'Do you want a whipped-cream pastry? It's homemade.' I wonder if Dr. Restelli won't gear himself toward the most conservative side of his personality. Yes, he's the likely candidate for a card game with them at seven-thirty. The poor girl, she'll have to submit to the hideous humiliation of playing with Jorge. Undoubtedly, she was hoping to meet someone her own age, but if the rear deck doesn't hold some surprise in store for us . . . As far as you and I are concerned, I anticipate an offensive and defensive alliance, a meeting, absolutely coincidental, in the pool, if there is a pool somewhere, and even supercoincidental meetings at lunches, teas, and dinners. Unless Raul—"

"Don't worry about Raul, you talk like the incarnation of von Clausewitz."

"Well, if I were Raul," Lopez said, "I wouldn't be overjoyed to hear you say that. In my role as Carlos Lopez, I consider our alliance more indissoluble as time goes on."

"I'm beginning to think," Paula said offhandedly, "that Raul would have done better asking for two cabins."

Lopez looked at her a moment and felt troubled in spite of himself.

"I'm already aware of the fact that these things don't happen in Argentina, and perhaps nowhere else," said Paula. "And it's precisely why Raul and I do them. I don't expect you to believe me."

"But I do believe you," said Lopez, who actually did not believe her at all. "What does it have to do with anything?"

A muffled dinner gong sounded in the hallway, and then more clearly from the top of the staircase.

"That's how it is," Lopez said lightly. "Will you have me at your table?"

"As one pirate to another, with great pleasure."

They stopped at the foot of the portside staircase. Atilio was energetically helping the chauffeur carry up Don Galo, who was shaking his head affably. The others followed him in silence. They were already upstairs when Lopez suddenly remembered something.

"Tell me: have you seen someone on the captain's bridge?"

Paula stared at him.

"Now that I think of it, no. Of course, as we're anchored at Quilmes I hardly think the eagle eye of an argonaut is necessary."

"I agree," Lopez said, "but it's strange all the same. What would Sennacherib Eden have thought?"

XXIII

Hors d'oeuvres variés

Potage Impératrice

Poulet à l'estragon

Salade tricolore

Fromages

Coupe Melba

Gâteaux, petits fours

Fruits

Café, infusions

Liqueurs

At table one, Beba Trejo arranges herself to sit facing the other diners. That way everyone will be able to admire her new blouse and the bracelet of synthetic topazes.

Señora Trejo is of the opinion that glasses of cut crystal are the most elegant by far,

Señor Trejo checks his vest pockets to make sure he has brought his liver pills and Alka Seltzer,

Felipe looks gloomily at the neighboring tables, knowing how much happier he would be at one of them.

At table two, Raul tells Paula that the fish forks and knives remind him of some new Italian designs he has seen in a magazine,

Paula listens to him absent-mindedly and selects tuna fish in oil and olives,

Carlos Lopez feels mysteriously exhilarated, and his middling appetite grows as he eats shrimps in vinegar sauce and celery with mayonnaise.

At table three, Jorge outlines a circle with his finger over the *hors d'oeuvres* tray, and his ecumenical order brings a smile of approval from Claudia,

Persio reads the wine label attentively, observes the color of the wine, and sniffs it for a long minute before filling his glass to the brim,

Medrano watches the *maître*, who watches the waiter, who watches his tray,

Claudia butters some bread for her son and decides to take a nap after lunch, preceded by a Bioy Casares novel.

At table four, Nelly's mother announces that vegetable soup makes her belch, for which reason she prefers a soup with fine noodles,

Doña Pepa has the feeling that she's a little seasick, even though no one can say it's because the boat is moving,

Nelly is looking at Beba Trejo, Claudia, and Paula, and is thinking that people with social standing always dress very unusually,

Pelusa is marveling at the fact that the rolls are so tiny, so individual, but when he breaks one open, what a drag, they're all crust.

At table five, Dr. Restelli is filling the glasses of his fellow diners and vigorously discussing the relative merits of Burgundy and the Côte du Rhône wines,

Don Galo smacks his lips and reminds the waiter that the chauffeur will eat in his cabin and that he's a man with a good, solid appetite,

Nora is suffering because she has to sit with two older men, and she wonders if Lucio won't be able to arrange something with the *maître* to change their table,

Lucio lets his plate be filled with sardines and tuna fish, and is the first to notice a slight vibration of the table, followed by the gradual disappearance of the red chimney pipe which was bisecting the circumference of the porthole.

A burst of happiness jumped through the dining room: Jorge leaped from his chair to go see the maneuver, and Dr. Restelli's optimism was drawn like a halo around his smiling physiognomy, which, however, did not in the slightest relax Don Galo's grimace of reserved skepticism. Only Medrano and Lopez, who had exchanged glances, continued to wait for the arrival of an officer. To a question asked by Lopez in a low voice, the *maître* raised his hands dispiritedly and said he would try to send a waiter to insist. What did he mean he was going to *try?* Yes, because until new orders were received communications with the rear deck were going to be slow. Why? It seems that there were some technical difficulties. Was it the first time that this had happened on the *Malcolm?* In a certain sense, yes. What did "in a certain sense" mean, exactly? It was just a way of putting it.

Lopez resisted the temptation to tell him in the best Buenos Aires fashion: "Look, buddy, go jump," and accepted, instead, a slice of smelly, delicious Limburger cheese.

"Nothing to be done with him," he said to Medrano. "We're going to have to straighten this thing out ourselves."

"Not without coffee and brandy," said Medrano. "We'll get together in my cabin, and let Costa know, too." He turned to Persio who was talking volubly to Claudia. "How do things look to you, my friend?"

"To tell the truth, I don't see them," Persio said. "I've had so much sun I feel luminous inside. I'm more to be contemplated than to contemplate. All morning I thought of the publishing house, my office, and no matter what I did I couldn't bring them into focus. How is it possible that sixteen years of daily work should suddenly be transformed into a kind of mirage, with nothing more than the river around me and the sun burning into my skull? The metaphysical side of this experience must be carefully analyzed."

"That," said Claudia, "is simply called a paid vacation."

Atilio Presutti's voice rang out above the others, enthusiastically celebrating the arrival of the peach Melba. Beba Trejo rejected hers with a look of elegant disdain; only she could have calculated the sacrifice involved. Looking at Paula, Nelly, and Claudia, all of whom were savoring the ice cream, she felt superior in her martyrdom; but her supreme triumph was to crush Jorge, that worm in short pants who had used the familiar form to her when he came in, and who was swallowing his ice cream with one eye fixed on the waiter's tray, where two filled dishes remained.

Señora Trejo was stunned:

"How is it possible! Don't you like ice cream?"

"No, thanks," said Beba, avoiding the omniscient and amused glance of her brother.

"What a silly girl you are," said Señora Trejo. "But since you don't want . . ."

She was setting the dish in front of her none-too-small bust, when the skillful hand of the *maître* whisked it away.

"It's a bit melted already, señora. Take this one instead."

The señora blushed violently, to the delight of both her children and husband.

Seated on the edge of his bed, Medrano swung his foot to the rhythm of the ship's almost imperceptible roll. The aroma of Raul's pipe brought back the memory of evenings in the Foreign Residents' Club and conversations with Scott, his English teacher. He was thinking about it now, about having left Buenos Aires without telling any of his friends at the Club. Perhaps Scott would let them know, perhaps not, depending on how he felt at the moment. By now Bettina would have already telephoned the Club, talking in a carefully detached voice. "She'll call again tomorrow and ask for Willie or Marquez Cey," he thought. "Poor fellows, they won't know what to tell her. Really, I've gone too far. Why, after all, did I have to come and go all that secretly, keeping the news of the prize to myself?" It had occurred to him the previous night, before going to sleep, that in his cat-and-mouse game there was cruelty underlying the whole thing. "It's almost more a vengeance than an abandonment," he told himself. "But why, when she's such a good girl? Unless it was just because of that." He had also thought that during these last months he could see nothing but faults in Bettina: it was too common a symptom, too ordinary. His club, for example—Bettina refused to understand that. "But you're not a foreign resident" (in an almost patriotic tone of voice). "With all the clubs in Buenos Aires, you decide to join one full of gringos . . ." It was sad to think that because of remarks like that he would never see her again. But that was that.

"It's not a matter of offended dignity," said Lopez suddenly. "It would be a pity to spoil something enjoyable right from the start. On the other hand, we can't stand around with our arms folded. It's getting to be an uncomfortable position for me, and God knows I'm not surprised."

"I agree," said Raul. "The iron fist in the velvet glove. I suggest we cordially open a way to the *sanctum sanctorum*, utilizing, as much as possible, the falsely unctuous manner which the Yankees attribute to the Japanese."

"Let's go," said Lopez. "Thanks for the drink, old man, it's excellent."

Medrano offered another drink which they accepted, drank quickly, and went out.

The cabin was just two steps away from the lowered bulkhead door which cut across the portside corridor. Raul began examining the door with a professional glance, and jiggled a lever painted green.

"Nothing to do. This only opens by steam pressure, and it's operated from some other spot. They've put the emergency lever out of action."

The door on the starboard passageway withstood all their efforts, too. A shrill whistle swung them about, somewhat startled. Pelusa greeted them with something between confusion and enthusiastic relief.

"You too? I had a go at it a while back, but these doors are really the end. What are those birds cooking up over there? They shouldn't be doing that, do you think?"

"That's for sure," said Lopez. "And you didn't find another door?"

"Everything's condemned," said Jorge solemnly; he had appeared like a hobgoblin.

"You talking about the doors?" asked Pelusa. "There are two locked ones on the deck. If we don't find a basement or something like that . . ."

"Are you preparing an expedition against the lipids?" Jorge asked.

"That's right," said Lopez. "Have you seen some?"

"Only the two Finns, but the ones on this side are not lipids, they must be glucids or protids."

"Listen to the things this kid says," marveled Pelusa. "Beginning today he's got it in for the lipads."

"Lipids," Jorge corrected.

Without knowing exactly why, Medrano was disturbed about Jorge's going along on the exploration.

"Look, we're going to entrust a delicate mission to you," he said. "Get up to the deck and carefully guard the two doors. Maybe the lipids will appear through there. If you notice anything at all, whistle three times. Do you know how to whistle loudly?"

"A little," Jorge admitted, shamefully. "My teeth have spaces between them."

"You don't know how?" asked Pelusa, anxious to demonstrate. "Look, do like this."

He put his thumb and index finger together in his mouth, and let out an earsplitting whistle. Jorge put his fingers together, but thought better of it, nodded his head, and raced off.

"Well, should we go on looking around?" asked Lopez. "Perhaps it would be better to separate, and the first one to find a passage can let the rest of us know immediately."

"Terrific," said Pelusa. "Like cops and robbers."

Medrano returned to his cabin for cigarettes. Raul saw Felipe at the end of the passageway. He was wearing his new bluejeans for the first time and a checked shirt, which outlined him like a movie against the door at the farthest end of the hallway. He explained what they were doing, and together they went to the central passage which joined both corridors.

"But what are we looking for?" Felipe asked, disconcerted.

"How should I know?" Raul said. "How to get to the rear deck, for instance."

"It's probably the same as this, more or less."

"Maybe. But since we can't get there, that changes everything."

"You think so?" said Felipe. "Probably it's because of something they're fixing. Later this afternoon they'll open the doors."

"Then, of course, it will be the same as the prow."

"Oh, of course," said Felipe, who was understanding less every minute. "Well, if it's just for fun, okay; maybe we'll find the way through before the others."

Raul wondered why only Lopez and Medrano felt the same as he. The rest could only see it as a game. "It's a game for me too, after all," he thought. "What's the difference? Well, there is a difference, that's for sure."

They were just getting to the port passageway when Raul discovered the door. It was very narrow, painted the same white as the walls in the corridor, and the door knob, set into the door itself, was almost invisible in the darkness of the hallway. Without much hope of success, Raul turned the knob and felt it give. The half-opened door revealed a tiny staircase which descended until it was lost in shadows. Felipe gulped excitedly. They could hear Lopez and Atilio talking in the starboard passageway.

"Should we let them know?" Raul asked, looking sideways at Felipe.

"Better not. Let's go alone."

Raul began the descent, and Felipe closed the door behind them. The staircase led to a passageway, which was faintly lit by a violet light. There were no doors to either side and the sound of the motors was very near.

They walked silently as far as a locked bulkhead door. To either side there were doors like the one they had just discovered in the passageway.

"Right or left?" Raul said. "You choose."

It struck Felipe strangely to hear himself suddenly addressed in the familiar form. He motioned to the left, not daring to answer

Raul with the same familiarity. He slowly probed for the knob, and
the door opened onto a darkened compartment. It smelled musty.
There were metal cabinets and shelves painted white on both sides.
There were tools, boxes, and an ancient compass, cans of nails and
screws, pieces of carpenter's glue, and metal cuttings. While Felipe
approached the porthole and wiped it with a rag, Raul raised the
lid of a tin box and then shut it immediately. More light was seep-
ing through now and they were getting used to the diffuse aquarium
clarity.

"The tool locker," Raul said mockingly. "We're still not doing
too brilliantly."

"We can try the other door," Felipe said. He had taken cigarettes out and offered one to Raul. "Doesn't this ship feel mysterious? We don't even know where it's taking us. It reminds me of
a movie I saw a long time ago. John Garfield was in it. They got on
a ship that didn't even have sailors, and it finally turned out to
be the ship of the dead. Some kind of fake thing or other, but it
gave you the creeps just the same . . ."

"Yes, that's from a Sutton Vane play," Raul said. He sat down
on a carpenter's bench, and exhaled smoke through his nose. "You
really like the movies, eh?"

"Sure."

"Do you go often?"

"Pretty often. I have a friend who lives near one and we always
go to the Roca or to one downtown. It's pretty good Saturday
nights."

"Do you think so? Oh, of course, downtown is more lively, and
you can pick up a girl."

"Sure," said Felipe. "You must have enough fun at night."

"A little, yes. Now, not so much."

"Oh, of course, when you get married . . ."

Raul was watching him, smiling and smoking.

"You're wrong, I'm not married."

He enjoyed the blush, which Felipe attempted to hide by
coughing.

"Well, I meant . . ."

"I already know what you meant. Actually, it must annoy you

a little to have to come on this trip with your parents and sister, doesn't it?"

Felipe avoided his glance, uncomfortably.

"What're you going to do?" he said. "They think I'm still a kid, but I had the chance to take them with me, then . . ."

"I think you're a kid, too," said Raul. "But I would have liked it better if you'd come alone. Or as I've come," he added. "That would have been the best because on this ship . . . But then, I don't know what you think."

Felipe didn't know either, and he stared at his hands and then at his shoes. "He feels naked," Raul thought, "not completely grown up, not a baby either, but somewhere between the two. Just like his sister." He stretched out his arm and clapped Felipe on the head. Felipe, surprised and humiliated, backed away.

"But you at least have a friend now," said Raul. "That's something, no?"

He relished, as if it were wine, the slow, shy, and earnest smile which was growing on Felipe's puckered, petulant mouth. Sighing, he got up from the bench and vainly tried to open the cabinets.

"Well, I think we should get on with it. Do you hear voices?"

They half-opened the door. The voices came from the cabin on the right, where people were talking in some unfamiliar language.

"The lipids," Raul said, and Felipe looked at him in amazement. "It's a term Jorge uses to designate the sailors from this side of the ship. Well?"

"Let's go if you want to."

Raul pushed the door wide open.

The wind, which at first had blown from the stern, shifted until it came head on to the *Malcolm*, which was now sailing into the open sea. The women decided to leave the deck; but Lucio, Persio, and Jorge settled at the tip of the prow, and there, anchored to the bowsprit—as Jorge fancifully expressed it—they watched the slow replacement of river water by a growing green surge of rough sea. This was no novelty for Lucio, for he was well acquainted with the Delta and water was the same everywhere. He liked it, of course, but only half-followed Persio's commentaries and explanations, and kept running back inevitably to Nora, who had preferred (but why?) to stay with Beba Trejo in the reading room leafing through magazines and travel folders. He kept going over, in his memory, Nora's confused words when she awoke, and he thought of the shower they had taken together despite her protests, and of Nora, naked under the water. He had wanted to soap her back and kiss it warm and shrinking away from him. But Nora had gone on stubbornly refusing him the sight of her naked from the front, concealing her face and turning around in search of the soap or the comb, until he had found it necessary to wrap a towel around himself hurriedly and stick his face under a shot of cold water.

"The scuppers look like wooden troughs," Persio said.

Jorge absorbed the explanations, and kept asking questions and taking in the answers, and admiring (in his own unceremonious way) Persio the magician, Persio the knowitall. He liked Lucio, too, because like Medrano and Lopez, Lucio did not call him "kid" or "pipsqueak," nor did he speak of the "child" like Beba's fat mother, that other idiot who thought she was a great lady. But at the moment the only important thing was The Ocean, because this was The Ocean, this was salt water, and down below them were acanthopteriges and other marine denizens, and they'd see jellyfish, too, and algae, like in Jules Verne novels, and maybe St. Elmo's fire.

"You used to live in the St. Elmo district, didn't you, Persio?"

"Yes, but I moved because there were rats in the kitchen."

"How many knots do you think we're making?"

Persio calculated some fifteen knots. Little by little, precious words were turned adrift, words Jorge had learned from books and that were enchantments to him: latitudes, ship's course, rudder, reflection circle, navigation on the high seas. Jorge regretted the disappearance of sail, for his reading had furnished him with hours and hours of discussion of rigging, mainsail, fore-topmast. He was recalling entire phrases, without remembering where they came from: "It was an enormous binnacle, with a glass covering and two copper lamps at either side to illuminate the compass."

They passed some ships: the *Haghios Nicolaus*, the *Pan*, the

Falcon. A hydroplane flew over them for a moment as if observing them. Later the horizon spread open, already tinted the yellow and sky-blue of dusk, and then they were alone, and they felt themselves alone for the first time. There was no coast, nor were there buoys, nor ships, nor even gulls or a great sea spreading its arms. At the center of the immense green wheel, the *Malcolm* advanced southward.

"Hello," said Raul. "Can you get to the rear deck through here? The poop?"

One of the two sailors watched him indifferently, as if he had not understood. The other, a broad-shouldered fellow with a prominent abdomen, made a step backward and opened his mouth.

"*Hasdala,*" he said. "No poop."

"Why no poop deck?"

"No poop deck through here."

"Through where then?"

"No poop."

"This guy doesn't waste any words," murmured Felipe. "What a bear, *madre mía.* Look at the snake he has tattooed on his arm."

"What did you expect?" asked Raul. "They're lipids, they're just lipids."

The smaller sailor had backed away to the rear of the cabin, where there was another door. He leaned against the wall, smiling good-naturedly.

"Officer," said Raul. "I want to talk to an officer."

The talkative sailor raised his hands, palms forward. He was watching Felipe, who stood casually, his fists sunk in the pockets of his bluejeans.

"Call an officer," the lipid said. "Orf call one."

Orf agreed from the rear of the cabin, but Raul was not satisfied. He studied the cabin in detail. It was bigger than the one on the port side: two tables, some chairs and benches, a berth spread with a rumpled sheet, and two maps of submarine depths fastened to the wall with gilded tacks. There was a phonograph on a bench in the corner. A black cat was sleeping on a piece of torn carpet. It was a mixture of storeroom and cabin where the two sailors (in

striped undershirts and filthy white trousers) only half fit. But neither could this be an officer's cabin unless the mechanic . . . "But
how should I know how mechanics live?" Raul said to himself.
"Conrad and Stevenson novels, but hardly any kind of bibliogra-
phy for a ship of this day and age . . ."

"Well, go ahead and call an officer."

"*Hasdala,*" the loquacious sailor said. "Back to prow."

"No. Officer."

"Orf inform officer."

"Now."

Felipe asked Raul in a low voice if it wouldn't be better to go
back and find the others. This talking in circles was beginning to
worry him a little, as if none of the people there really wanted to
commit themselves one way or another. The enormous, tattooed
sailor went on looking at him blankly, and Felipe had the disagreeable feeling of being stared at and, at the same time, of not being
able to face these attentive eyes, rather friendly and curious, but so
intense he could scarcely return the glance. Raul stubbornly kept
pressing his point to Orf, who was listening in silence, still leaning up against the door, making an occasional gesture of complete
ignorance.

"Well," said Raul, shrugging his shoulders, "I think you're right,
it'll be better if we go back."

Felipe left first. At the door, Raul stared hard at the tattooed
sailor.

"Officer!" he screamed and shut the door. Felipe had already
started back but Raul remained a moment, pressed close to the
door. In the cabin he could hear Orf's voice rise, a screechy voice
which seemed to parody itself. The other sailor burst into guffaws,
which made the air vibrate. Tightening his lips, Raul dodged
through the door to the left and came out again carrying the tin
box, whose lid he had raised a while before, under his arm. He ran
through the corridor as far as the foot of the staircase, where Felipe
stood waiting for him.

"Hurry," he said, taking the steps by twos.

Felipe turned around, surprised, thinking they were being followed. He saw the box and raised his eyebrows. But Raul put his

hand against his back and forced him to continue up. Felipe vaguely remembered that Raul had begun to use the familiar address with him precisely on this staircase.

XXIV

An hour later the bartender went from cabin to cabin and scoured the deck to inform the passengers that an officer was waiting for them in the reading room. Some of the ladies were already suffering from seasickness; Don Galo, Persio, and Dr. Restelli were resting in their cabins, and only Claudia and Paula accompanied the men, who were already informed about Raul's and Felipe's expedition. The officer was lean and looked preoccupied, and kept running his hand through his grey crew-cut. He spoke Spanish with difficulty, but with few mistakes. Medrano, without knowing why, thought he was either Danish or Dutch.

The officer welcomed them in the name of the Magenta Star Lines and in the name of the captain of the *Malcolm*, who was unable to do so in person at the moment. He regretted that an unexpected increase in work had prevented an earlier meeting, and he expressed his understanding of the slight concern which the passengers must have felt. All measures had now been taken to assure them a cruise that would be completely enjoyable; the passengers would find a swimming pool, a solarium, a gymnasium, a game room, two ping-pong tables, and recorded music at their disposal. The *maître* would take charge of collecting any suggestions the passengers might for-mul-ate, and of course, the officers would remain at the disposition of all the guests.

"Some of the women are already quite seasick," Claudia said, breaking the uncomfortable silence which followed the speech. "Is there a doctor on board?"

The officer had the understanding that the doctor would not be long in paying his respects to sick and well alike. Medrano, who had been waiting for this moment, came forward.

"Very well, many thanks," he said. "There are still a couple of things we should like to have cleared up. The first is this: have

you come of your own free will or only because one of these gentlemen insisted on having an officer here? The second is very simple: why is the deck at the stern forbidden to us?"

"Yeah, why?" yelled Pelusa, whose face was slightly green, but
who was standing up to seasickness like a man.

"Gentlemen," said the officer, "this visit should have been made
before, but it was not possible for the same reasons which force us
to . . . to momentarily suspend communication with the rear
deck. There is little to see there," he added quickly. "The crew, the
cargo . . . You're much more comfortable here."

"And what kind of reasons are those?" asked Medrano.

"I regret that my orders—"

"Orders? We're not at war," said Lopez. "We're not being trailed
by submarines, and you're not transporting atomic weapons, or
anything like that. Or are you?"

"Goodness no, what an idea!" said the officer.

"Does the Argentine government know we've embarked under
these conditions?" Lopez continued, laughing inwardly over the
question.

"Well, the negotiations were made at the last minute, and we
had to resolve certain technical aspects by ourselves. The Magenta
Star," he added with discreet pride, "has always had a reputation
for treating its passengers well."

Medrano knew they were simply going around in circles.

"What's the captain's name?" he asked.

"Smith," the officer said. "Captain Smith."

"Like me," said Lopez, and Raul and Medrano laughed. But the
officer felt the sting of the mockery and he wrinkled his brow.

"He used to be named Lovatt," said Raul. "Ah, one other thing:
can I send a cable to Buenos Aires?"

The officer thought a minute before answering. Unfortunately,
the radio installation on the *Malcolm* did not take ordinary mes-
sages. When they reached Punta Arenas, the post office . . . The
way he ended the phrase gave the impression that for the moment
Raul would not need to telegraph anybody.

"These are temporary circumstances," added the officer, inviting
them with a gesture to sympathize with such circumstances.

"Look," said Lopez, more irritated by the minute. "You have a group of people before you who haven't the slightest interest in spoiling a fine cruise. But personally the methods employed by the captain or whoever he is are insufferable. Why doesn't he tell us the cause of our imprisonment on the prow? And don't give us that insulted look."

"And another thing," Lucio spoke up. "Where are we going after Punta Arenas? Punta Arenas is a very unusual stopover."

"Oh, to Japan. It's quite a nice cruise across the Pacific."

"*Mamma mia*, Japan!" said Pelusa, open-mouthed. "Then we're not going to Copacabana?"

"Forget the itinerary until later," said Raul. "I want to know why the poop deck is forbidden to us. Why do I have to sneak around like a rat looking for a hole, and then bump into two sailors, who won't let me through?"

"Gentlemen, gentlemen . . ." Looking around him, the officer seemed to be searching for someone who would not yield to the growing rebellion. "Please try to understand our point of view . . ."

"Once and for all, what is the reason for all this?" Medrano asked dryly.

After a silence in which only the clear clink of a spoon dropped on the bar was heard, the officer shrugged his narrow shoulders, obviously discouraged.

"In short, gentlemen, I would have preferred to have kept silent, since you are beginning a well-earned vacation. We are on schedule . . . Yes, I see now . . . Oh well, it's very simple: there are two cases of typhus among our men."

The first to react was Medrano and he did so with a cold violence that shocked them all. No sooner had he begun to tell the officer that we were no longer in the age of bloodlettings and leeches than the officer raised his arms with a gesture of fatigue and irritation.

"Excuse me, but I must have expressed myself badly. I should have said that we are dealing with typhus 224. Undoubtedly, you're not up on the disease, and this is exactly our problem. Very little is known about 224. The doctor is using the most modern treatment, but he's of the opinion that what is needed right now is a kind of . . . sanitary barrier."

"But just tell me something," Paula burst out. "How were we able to sail from Buenos Aires last night? Weren't you already aware of your two hundred and something?"

"Yes, of course," said Lopez. "They closed the rear deck off from us from the very beginning."

"And how was it that the health officers at the port let you leave? And how is it you were allowed to come into port in the first place, when typhus was declared?"

The officer lifted his eyes to the ceiling. He was looking more fatigued every minute.

"Don't force me to say more than what my orders allow, gentlemen. This situation is only temporary, and I have no doubt that within a few days the patients will have passed out of the contagious phase. For the moment—"

"For the moment," said Lopez, "we would be completely correct in assuming that we've fallen into the hands of a gang of profiteers . . . Yes, you heard right. They take on a good contract at the last minute, keeping their mouths shut about anything happening on board. Your Captain Smith must be the world's perfect slaver, and you can tell him so for me."

The officer took a step back, and swallowed hard.

"Captain Smith," he said, "is one of the two patients. The sicker."

He left before anyone had time to answer.

Holding onto the railings with both hands, Atilio returned to the deck and threw himself down in a chair next to the ones in which Nelly, her mother, and Doña Rosita, who were taking turns groaning, were sitting. Seasickness was attacking them all with varying degrees of seriousness, as Doña Rosita had already explained to Señora Trejo, who was just as sick as the others. She, for instance, had the dry type of seasickness, while Nelly and her mother vomited all the time.

"I told them not to drink so much soda; now they have a kind of dysentery. You don't feel well, do you? You can tell right away, you poor dear. Fortunately, as I have dry seasickness, I hardly throw up; it's more an upset stomach than anything else. Poor Nelly, look how she suffers. I've only eaten dry things today, so I've kept everything down. I remember when we went to the river restaurant La Dorita in the launch, and I was practically the only one who didn't vomit on the way back. All the others, poor things . . . Oh, look how sick Doña Pepa is."

Armed with buckets and sawdust, one of the Finnish sailors was trying to maintain the cleanliness of the deck which was being so poorly treated. Pelusa, with a moan both furious and disgusted, held his head between his two hands.

"It's not that I'm seasick," he told Nelly, who looked at him with a trace of consciousness. "It's probably the ice cream didn't go down right, and worse because I sent two in a row straight down to my belly . . . How do you feel?"

"Awful, Atilio, really awful . . . Look at poor Mama. Couldn't the doctor look at her?"

"But what doctor, *mamma mia*," Pelusa sighed. "If I told you the latest . . . Better I don't, it would turn you inside out all over again."

"But what's the matter, Atilio? You can tell me. Why does this ship move so much?"

"The tides," said Pelusa. "The baldheaded guy was telling us all about the sea. Ugh, how it leans. Look, look, it's just like that block of water is going to come right over us . . . Do you want me to get you your perfume for the handkerchief?"

"No, no, but tell me what's happening."

"You mean what's going to happen," said Pelusa, fighting against an odd kind of tennis ball rising in his throat. "We have the bubonic plague on board, that's what."

XXV

A burst of laughter from Paula broke the silence and was followed by a series of furious phrases, not directed toward anyone in particular. Then Raul decided to ask Medrano, Lopez, and Lucio to go with him to his cabin for a minute. Felipe, who was anticipating brandy and men's conversation, was aware that Raul had not made the slightest indication that he join them. He lingered a moment, unbelieving, but Raul was the first to leave the salon. Unable to say a word, and feeling as if his pants had dropped down in front of everybody, he remained alone with Paula, Claudia, and Jorge, who were talking of going to the deck. Before they were able to say a word, he rushed out and ran to lock himself in his cabin, where, luckily, he did not find his father. So great was his confusion and despair that for a brief moment he stayed leaning against the inside of the cabin door, vaguely rubbing his eyes. "But what can he be thinking?" he managed to wonder. "What the hell is he thinking about?" There was no doubt that the meeting had been called to discuss a plan of action, and they had left him out. He lit a cigarette and threw it away immediately. He lit another; it sickened him and he crushed it out under his shoe. So much talk, so much friendship, and now . . . But when they had started to go below and Raul had asked if they should tell the others, he immediately had accepted his negative answer, as if he liked sharing the adventure with him alone. And after the conversation in the empty cabin . . . and goddamn it, why had he come on like a friend and used the familiar form, if he meant to drop him like a hot potato in the end and lock himself up with the others? Why had he told him now he could count on a friend, why had he promised him a pipe . . . He felt himself choking, the section of the bed he was staring at was no longer visible, and in its place a blur of revolving rays and sticky lines popped from his eyes and fell across his face. Furious, he ran his hands across his cheeks, went into the bathroom and plunged his head into a basin full of cold water. Then he went and sat at the foot of the bed, where Señora Trejo had set out some handkerchiefs and clean pajamas. He took a handkerchief and gazed at it fixedly, muttering insults. Along with his rancor, a story of sacrifice was gradually building up, a fantasy in which he would save all of them, although he did not know what he would save them from; and then, with a knife through his heart, he would fall at the feet of Paula and Raul; he would listen to their words of sorrow and remorse, Raul would take his hand and desperately squeeze it, Paula would kiss him on the forehead . . . The damned bastards would kiss him on the forehead, begging his forgiveness, but he would fall silent like a god and would die as real men die (a phrase he had read somewhere, which had impressed him a good deal at the time). But before dying as real men die, he was going to show that bunch of wiseguys. To start with, there would be absolute disdain, an icy indifference. Good morning, good night, and that was it. They'd be coming to look for him, to confide their worries, and then there would be the hour of revenge. Ah, so that's what you think? Well, I don't agree with you. I have my own opinion, but that's my affair. No, why should I tell it? You hardly trusted me up until now, although I was the first one to discover the passage below. One does what one can to help and this is the outcome. And if something had happened to us below? Go on, laugh all you want, I don't intend to lift a finger for anybody. Of course then they would go on investigating on their own; that was practically the only amusement on board this lousy ship. Oh well, so could he, after all, investigate on his own. He thought about the two sailors in the ship's cabin to the right, about the tattooing. The one named Orf seemed more approachable, and if he found him alone . . . He could see himself stepping onto the poop, discovering first the deck, then the hatchways. Ah, but that plague, supercontagious, and no one on board vaccinated. But after all, a knife in the heart or the two hundred and something plague, in the end . . . He half-closed his eyes so he could feel the grazing of Paula's hand across his forehead. "Poor darling," Paula murmured, caressing him. Felipe slid down until he was stretched out in bed, turned toward the wall. The poor darling, so brave. It's me, Felipe, it's Raul. Why did you do that? All that blood, poor kid. No, no, I'm not suffering at all. It's not the wounds that hurt, Raul. And Paula would say: "Don't talk, darling, wait till we take off your shirt," and he would have his eyes profoundly closed, just like now, yet he still would be able to see Paula and Raul crying over him, he would be able to feel their hands, just as he could now feel his own hand, deliciously opening a way through his clothes.

"Be an angel," said Raul, "and act like Florence Nightingale with the poor seasick ladies, not to mention that your face is passably green, too."

"A lie," said Paula. "I don't see why you have to throw me out of my cabin."

"Because," Raul explained, "we have to hold a council of war. Go like a good little ant and pass out Dramamine to the needy.

Come in, friends, and sit down where you can, beginning with the beds."

Lopez came in last, after watching Paula leave, looking bored and carrying a bottle of pills which Raul had handed her as an all-powerful argument. An odor of Paula still lingered in the cabin; he smelled it as soon as the door was closed. Over and above the smell of pipe tobacco and the soft fragrance of wood, was the odor of cologne, wet hair, perhaps make-up. He remembered Paula stretched out on the bed at the rear of the cabin and instead of sitting there, next to Lucio, who was already seated, he remained standing next to the door, his arms folded.

Medrano and Raul were praising the electrical installations in the cabins, the latest gadgets provided by the Magenta Star. But as soon as they were alone, everyone looked curiously at Raul. Raul dropped his nonchalant attitude and opened the wardrobe to take out the strongbox. He put it on the table and then sat down on one of the armchairs, tapping his fingers on the lid of the box.

"I think," he said, "that we've discussed our situation more than enough for today. In any case, I don't know your points of view in detail, and I should think we ought to be able to profit from getting together off by ourselves. Well, I'll begin by giving my opinion. All of you are aware of the fact that the Trejo boy and I had a very instructive conversation with two inhabitants of the depths of this vessel. As a result of this conversation, or rather, as a result of the atmosphere and air we breathed during the course of this conversation, much the same as during the instructive lecture we just received from the ship's officer, I get the impression that not only are they making fools of us but that there is something more serious involved. In a word, I don't think there's really any joke being played, but that we're simply victims of a swindle. Not just an ordinary swindle, of course; but something more . . . metaphysical, if you don't mind the awful word."

"Why is it such an awful word?" asked Medrano. "Oh, these Argentine intellectuals, scared of big words."

"Let's understand one another," said Lopez. "Why do you say metaphysical?"

"Because, if I've followed Costa's thinking correctly, I would

say that the immediate reasons for this quarantine, true or false,
conceal something else, which eludes us, precisely because it is
more . . . well, the word in question."

Lucio watched them, astonished, and for a moment he asked
himself if they hadn't conspired to make fun of him. It irritated
him not to have the vaguest idea of what they meant, and he
ended up by coughing and assuming an air of intelligent attention.
Lopez, who had noticed his gesture, raised his hand amiably.

"Let's invent a small class plan, as Dr. Restelli and I would say
in our illustrious faculty room. I suggest we put any extreme imaginings under lock and key and face up to the matter in the
most positive way. In this sense, I subscribe to the idea of a joke
and possible swindle, because I doubt very much if the ship's officer's speech convinced anyone. I think the mystery, to call it that,
is still as great as ever."

"Well, it's the question of this typhus," said Lucio.

"Do you believe the typhus story?"

"Why not?"

"Well, it sounds phony to me from beginning to end," said Lopez, "even if I can't tell you why. No matter how strange our embarkation was, the *Malcolm* WAS anchored at the north dock in
Buenos Aires, and it's hard to believe that two cases of such a serious illness on a ship known to be in harbor could have been concealed from the port authorities like this."

"Well, that's material for discussion," said Medrano. "I think our
mental health will benefit if we leave that out. I'm sorry to be such
a skeptic, but I think the authorities, such as they are, were put on
the spot yesterday at six P.M., and that they got out of it as well as
possible, that is, without burdening themselves with scruples or responsibilities. I know this doesn't explain the previous stage, the arrival of the *Malcolm* in port with a plague aboard. But I suppose
the arrival, as well as the departure, was also arranged with the port
authorities in some underhanded way."

"The illness could have broken out on board after the ship was
already at the dock," said Lucio. "These things can be latent, can't
they?"

"Yes, it's possible. And Magenta Star didn't want to lose a good thing, which came up at the last minute. Why not? But that doesn't get us anywhere. Let's take it for granted that we're aboard ship and far from the coast. What are we going to do?"

"Well, first we have to reverse the question," said Lopez. "Should we do something? We should be in agreement on this point."

"The ship's officer explained the typhus situation to us," said Lucio, still confused. "Maybe we should just calm down, at least for a few days. The trip is going to be so long . . . Isn't it terrific that they're taking us to Japan?"

"The ship's officer," said Raul, "could have lied."

"Lied! Then . . . there isn't any typhus?"

"My dear boy, this typhus business feels to me like a trick. Like Lopez, I can't tell you why, but I feel it in my bones, as they say."

"I agree with you," said Medrano. "Perhaps there is someone sick on the other side, but that doesn't explain the captain's conduct (unless he really is one of the patients) or the officers'. It's as if they've been asking themselves how they should manage us ever since we've come onto the ship, and that all this time has been spent in discussion. If they'd started by acting a little more civilized, we probably wouldn't have suspected a thing."

"Yes, this is where our self-esteem comes in," said Lopez. "We resent this lack of courtesy, and maybe we're even blowing that up. In any case, I won't conceal the fact that aside from any personal joke or insult involved here, there's something in this whole thing about locked doors that annoys me. It's as if this really weren't a trip at all."

Lucio, who was more and more surprised by these reactions, which he only feebly shared, lowered his head in agreement. If they were going to take it all so seriously, everything would certainly be spoiled. Some pleasure trip . . . Why were they so touchy? One door more or less . . . When they dived into the pool and started some games going, what would the rear deck matter to them then? There were ships on which the poop (or the prow for that matter) was forbidden territory, and people didn't get nervous about it.

"If we were only sure it really is a mystery," said Lopez, sitting down on the edge of Raul's bed, "but maybe it's just stubbornness, discourtesy, or the fact that the captain considers us a cargo to be carefully stashed away in one part of the ship. And that's exactly where the idea begins to hurt."

"And if we come to the conclusion that it has to do with that," said Raul, "what should we do?"

"Force our way through," Medrano said curtly.

"Ah, well, we now have one opinion, and I'm with you . . . I see Lopez is too, and that you—"

"Me too, of course," Lucio said hurriedly. "But before we do anything we have to be sure we're not being shut up on this side just because of some whim."

"The best thing would be to insist on cabling Buenos Aires. The officer's explanation seemed ludicrous to me, because any kind of radio equipment on ship can be used for that. We'll insist, and from their answer we'll be able to see just what the intentions of the . . . of the lipids are."

Lopez and Medrano burst into laughter.

"Let's adjust our vocabulary," said Medrano. "Jorge calls the sailors from the poop deck lipids. The officers, judging from what I heard at the table, are glucids. And, gentlemen, it is with the glucids we must do battle."

"Death to the glucids," said Lopez. "And I spent my morning talking about pirate novels . . . Well, suppose they refuse to send our message to Buenos Aires, which is more than likely if they're playing dirty and are afraid that this will ruin their business. In that case, I don't see what the next move is."

"I do," said Medrano. "I see it clearly enough. It will be a question of breaking down a door and taking a look around the other side of the ship."

"But if things start going wrong . . ." said Lucio. "You know that laws at sea are different, there's another . . . discipline. I don't understand anything about this, but it seems to me we shouldn't go beyond the limits without thinking it through."

"As far as going beyond the limits, the example the glucids are setting seems to me sufficiently eloquent," said Raul. "Tomorrow, if it strikes Captain Smith's fancy to lock us in our cabins for the remainder of the trip, it would almost be within his rights."

"That's talking like Spartacus," said Lopez. "If we give him a finger, he'll take an arm, as our friend Presutti would say, a friend whose noticeable absence I deplore under the circumstances."

"I was for having him come, too," said Raul, "but the truth is
he's so unpolished I thought better of it. Later, we'll be able to
present him with a résumé of the situation and enlist him in our
redeeming cause. He's an excellent fellow, and he likes the glucids
and lipids as much as he likes someone stepping on his bunion."

"In short," said Medrano, "I believe we decided, *primo*, that
we're all sufficiently in agreement concerning the unconvincing
typhus story, and that, *secundo*, we should insist that the walls of
the oppressors be brought down and we be allowed to look at the
ship from any spot we feel like."

"Exactly. Method: a cable to Buenos Aires. Probable result: a
refusal. Subsequent action: break down a door."

"Everything seems easy enough," said Lopez, "except for the
door. Ripping down a door is not going to please them at all, not
by a long shot."

"Of course they're not going to like it," said Lucio. "They'll
feel justified in taking us back to Buenos Aires, and that would be
a nuisance, I think."

"I realize that," said Medrano, who was watching Lucio with a
certain irritable sympathy. "To return and find ourselves on Peru
and Avenida the morning of the day after tomorrow would be
rather ridiculous. But, my friend, at least on Peru and Avenida
there are no locked bulkhead doors."

Raul ran his hand across his forehead as if to push away a
troublesome thought, but since the others had fallen silent, he
decided to speak.

"Well, you see, this more and more confirms my feeling of a little
while back. Except for Lucio, who wants to see the geisha girls and
listen to the sound of the koto, all of which seems perfectly
justifiable to me, the rest of us would happily sacrifice the Land of
the Rising Sun for a Buenos Aires café, where the doors are wide
open to the street. Is there a common measure between the two
things? In point of fact, there isn't. Not even the most remote of
measures. Lucio is quite right when he talks about calming down,
since this passivity will be highly rewarded with kimonos and Fu-
jiyama. And yet, and yet . . ."

"Yes, and that brings back the word of a little while ago," said Medrano.

"Exactly, the little word. It doesn't have anything to do with doors, dear Lucio, nor glucids. Probably, the rear deck will turn out to be a filthy place, stinking of tar and bales of wool. What we'll see from there will be the same as what we see from the prow: the sea, and more sea, forever beginning again. And yet . . ."

"In short," said Medrano, "it would appear as if there was an agreement of the majority on this point. You too? Good, then there's unanimity. It remains to be decided if this is to be discussed with the others. For the moment, apart from Restelli and Presutti, it seems better to do what we have to do on our own. As they say, there's no reason to alarm the women and children."

"There probably won't be any cause for alarm," said Lopez. "But I'd like to know how we're going to manage to force our way if it comes to that."

"Ah, that's very simple," said Raul. "Since you like playing pirate, take this."

He lifted the lid of the box. Inside were two .38 revolvers and a .32 automatic, also five boxes of ammunition made in Rotterdam.

XXVI

"*Hasdala*," said one of the sailors, lifting an enormous board with no apparent effort. The other sailor agreed with a dry "*Sa!*" and hammered a nail into the end of the board. The wooden frame for the pool was almost finished, and the construction, as simple as it was solid, was mounted in the middle of the deck. While one of the sailors was nailing the last supporting board, the other unfolded a canvas tarpaulin and began to fasten it to the sides with straps and buckles.

"And they call that a pool," complained Pelusa. "Just look at that piece of junk. It looks more like a place to wash pigs. What do you think, Don Persio?"

"I detest bathing in open air," said Persio, "especially when there's the possibility of swallowing someone else's dandruff."

"Yeah, but it's nice, even so. D'ja ever go to the pool at the Sport Barracks? They add disinfectant and it has the Olympic measurements."

"Olympic measurements? And what're those?"

"Well . . . the measurements for the Olympic games, what else would they be? The Olympic measurements, they're in all the newspapers. But take a look at this getup a second, nothing but boards and a canvas bag inside. My buddy Emilio went to Europe two years ago, and he told me in third class on his boat there was a pool all green marble. If I knew about this fake I swear I wouldn't of come."

Persio was looking at the Atlantic. They had lost sight of the coast, and the *Malcolm* was sailing in waters suddenly calm, of a metallic blue, almost black along the crest of the waves. Only two gulls were following the ship, stubbornly perched on the mast.

"Gulls are big eaters," said Pelusa. "They could swallow nails. I like it when they see a fish and zoom down to take it. Poor fish, what a stab those gulls must deliver . . . Do you think we'll see some schools of delphin on this trip?"

"Dolphin? Yes, probably."

"Emilio told me on his ship he saw schools of delphin and flying fish all the time. But we . . ."

"Don't get discouraged," Persio told him affectionately. "The trip has hardly begun, and the first day, what with seasickness and the novelty of it all . . . But later you'll like it."

"Well, I like it. You learn things. Don't you think? Like the army . . . They lead you a dog's life, with all those exercises and that food . . . I remember once they gave us a stew that the best thing in it was a fly . . . But pretty soon you learn how to sew on a button and get down any crap they set in front of you, at least it doesn't turn your stomach. This'll probably be the same, don't you think?"

"I suppose so," agreed Persio, attentively following the activities of the Finns, who were now connecting a hose to the pool. Beautifully green water began to rise in the bottom of the canvas, or at least Jorge proclaimed it to be so. He was perched on top of the boards waiting to jump in. A bit recovered from seasickness, the ladies approached to inspect the work and take strategic positions for the moment when the bathers would begin to appear. They did not have to wait long for Paula, who came down the staircase slowly so that everybody could absorb, definitively and in detail, her red bikini. Behind her came Felipe in green trunks and a sponge towel over his shoulders. They were preceded by Jorge, who extolled the excellence of the water temperature at the top of his lungs, and then they jumped into the pool and splashed around awhile in the modest space it afforded them. Paula showed Jorge how to sit at the bottom of the pool holding his nose, and Felipe, still put out and scowling, but incapable of resisting the joy of the water and the shouts around him, climbed onto the frame to dive, among displays of fright and admonishment from the ladies. Nelly and Pelusa joined them; Pelusa kept up his barrage of disparaging remarks. Meticulously sheathed in a one-piece suit, which featured alternating blue and purple diamonds, Nelly asked Felipe if Beba wasn't going to swim, to which Felipe answered that his sister was still under from one of her attacks, and it would be very strange if she did come down.

"She has attacks?" Nelly asked, horrified.

"Attacks of romanticism," said Felipe, wrinkling his nose. "Poor stupid nut."

"Oh, you scared me! Your little sister is so nice, poor girl."

"You don't know her yet, you'll see. What do you think of the trip?" Felipe asked Pelusa. "Who could have been the brain who thought this one up? If I meet him I'll take care of him, believe me."

"You're telling me," said Pelusa, trying to conceal the act of blowing his nose with his two fingers. "What a pool, *mamma mia!* There are only three or four of us in here, and we're already packed like sardines in a can. Come on, Nelly, I'll show you how to swim under water. Don't be afraid, dope, let me show you, you'll look like Esther Williams."

The Finns had installed a horizontal board on one side of the frame, and Paula sat down to sun herself. Felipe dived again, snorted as he had seen them do in swimming tournaments, and clambered up next to her.

"Your . . . isn't Raul going to go swimming?"

"My . . . how do I know?" Paula said, mockingly. "He must still be busy conspiring with his bloody friends, and thanks to them the cabin stinks of black tobacco. You weren't there, were you?"

Felipe looked at her out of the corner of his eye. No, he hadn't been there; after eating he liked to stretch out in bed to read. Oh, and what did he read? Well, right now he was reading an issue of the *Reader's Digest.* Sure, excellent reading for a young student. Yes, it wasn't bad; it carried condensed versions of the world's masterpieces.

"Condensed," said Paula, staring out to sea. "Of course. Obviously, it's more practical."

"Of course," said Felipe, who was feeling more and more ill at ease. "There's no time to read long novels in this day and age."

"But novels don't really interest you too much," said Paula, who had stopped joking and was looking at him kindly. There was something touching about Felipe; he was too much of an adolescent, too much of everything: too handsome, too stupid, too ridiculous. Only when he was silent did he attain a certain balance; then his face accepted his age, and his hands, with their chewed nails, hung to either side with perfect indifference and grace. But if he spoke, if he wanted to tell a lie (and at sixteen to open your mouth was to lie), the gracefulness came crashing to the ground and nothing more than an awkward pretense of self-sufficiency remained, just as touching but irritating, a muddy mirror in which Paula could once again see herself in her own schooldays, the first attempts at freedom, the humiliating conclusion of so many things that should have been lovely. She felt sorry for Felipe, she would have liked to stroke his hair and tell him something which would bring back his poise and self-possession. Now he was explaining that he liked to read, but that his studies . . . What? Don't you have to read when you study? Yes, of course he had to read, but only textbooks or notes. Not anything that could be called a book, like a Somerset Maugham or A. J. Cronin novel. He wasn't, of course, like some of his schoolmates at the National who went around with glasses because they read too much. First and foremost, life. Life? What life? Well, you know, life: going out, seeing things, traveling, as they were doing now, meeting people . . . Their teacher Peralta always told them that the only important thing was experience.

"Ah, experience," said Paula. "Of course, that is important. And your teacher Lopez, does he talk to you about experience, too?"

"No, he doesn't. Of course if he wanted to . . . You can see he gets along with the women, but he doesn't go around bragging about it. We have a good time with Lopez. You have to work for him, that's for sure, but when he's satisfied with your work he can spend half an hour talking about last Sunday's football game."

"Don't tell me," said Paula.

"Sure, Lopez is okay. He doesn't take things as seriously as Peralta."

"Who ever would've known it," said Paula.

"It's absolutely true. Maybe you were thinking about the Black Cat?"

"The Black Cat?"

"Mr. Starched Collar, I mean."

"Ah, the other teacher."

"Yes, Restelli."

"No, I wasn't thinking of him," Paula said.

"Oh well," said Felipe. "There's no comparison. Lopez is okay, everyone thinks so. I even study for him sometimes, no kidding. I'd like to be a friend of his, but, you know . . ."

"You'll have the opportunity here," said Paula. "There are a number of people worth getting to know. Medrano, for instance."

"Probably, but it's different with Lopez. And also your . . . Raul, I mean." He lowered his head and a drop of water ran down his nose. "They're all nice," he said, flustered, "even though they're much older. Except for Raul, who's very young."

"He's not as young as all that," said Paula. "Sometimes he turns terribly old, because he knows so much and is worn out with what your teacher Peralta would call experience. Then at other times he's almost too young, and he acts perfectly idiotic."

She saw the baffled look in Felipe's eyes and stopped talking. "Go a little further and I'll be pimping for them," she thought, amused. "Let them dance their dance alone. Poor Nelly, she looks like an actress out of the silent films, and her boyfriend is absolutely swimming with his bathing trunks creeping up on him . . . Why doesn't she shave under her arms?"

As if it were the most natural thing on earth. Medrano bent over the box, chose a revolver, and put it in his back pocket after checking to see if it was loaded and if the cylinder spun easily. Lopez was about to do the same, but he thought of Lucio and stopped himself halfway. Lucio stretched out his hand and then withdrew it, shaking his head.

"I understand less every minute," he said. "Why these weapons?"

"You don't have to take one," said Lopez, free of scruples. He took the second revolver and offered the pistol to Raul, who was watching him with an amused smile.

"I'm old-fashioned," said Lopez. "I've never liked automatics. There's something base about them. My affection for revolvers can probably be explained by all the cowboy films I've seen. You can tell I'm pre-George Raft. Do you remember William S. Hart? . . . It's strange, but today is a day of recollections. First the pirates and now the cowboys. I'll take this box of bullets, if you don't mind."

Paula knocked twice and came in, asking them to kindly be on their way because she wanted to put on her bathing suit. She looked with amazement at the strongbox, which Raul was just closing, but said nothing. They all went out to the corridor, and Medrano and Lopez went back to their cabins to put away the guns. They both felt vaguely ridiculous with their pockets bulging with weapons, as well as bullets. Raul suggested they meet a quarter of an hour later in the bar, and he returned to his cabin. Paula, who was singing in the bathroom, heard him open a drawer in the wardrobe.

"What does this arsenal mean?"

"Ah, so you knew they weren't *marrons glacés*," Raul said.

"You didn't bring that box on board, that much I know."

"No, it's war booty. From a more or less cold war, at the moment."

"And you intend to play bad men?"

"Not without first exhausting all diplomatic channels, dear heart.

Although I know there's no need to tell you, I'd appreciate it if you didn't mention these warlike preparations in front of the women and children. All this will probably end in a most laughable manner, and we'll keep the weapons as souvenirs of the *Malcolm*. But right now we are quite resolved to take a snoop around the poop deck, peaceably or otherwise."

"*Mon triste coeur bave à la poupe, mon coeur couvert de caporal*," Paula said in a singsong, as she reappeared in her bikini. Raul whistled in admiration.

"Anybody would think this is the first time you've see me dressed down to the skin," said Paula, looking at herself in the wardrobe mirror. "Aren't you going to change?"

"Later. Now we have to launch our hostilities against the glucids. What svelte legs you've brought on this trip."

"So I'm told. If you can use me as a model, you're authorized to make all the drawings you like. But I suppose you've already picked out others for that."

"For God's sake, pull in your fangs," said Raul. "Hasn't the good salt air begun to have an effect on you? At least leave me alone, Paula."

"Okay, sweet prince. See you later." She opened the door and turned around. "But don't do anything foolish," she added. "I don't really give a damn, but you three are the only tolerable creatures on board. If something happens to all of you . . . Will you let me be your godmother of war?"

"Of course, as long as you keep on sending me packages of magazines and chocolates. Did I tell you that you're stunning in that bathing suit? Yes, I told you. You're going to raise the blood pressure of those two Finns, not to mention the blood pressure of one of my friends."

"Speaking of fangs . . ." said Paula. She came back into the cabin. "Tell me something first. Did you believe the story about the typhus? No, I didn't think you did. But if we don't believe that, it's even worse, because then nothing is clear."

"That's similar to what I thought as a kid when I was starting to become an atheist," said Raul. "That's when the troubles began. I suppose the typhus story is being used to cover some other sordid business. Maybe they're carrying hogs to Punta Arenas or accordions to Tokyo, all very unpleasant, as everyone knows. And I have a series of similar hypotheses, each more sinister than the next."

"And if it turned out there was nothing on the rear deck? If this whole act was just a caprice of Captain Smith's?"

"We've all thought of that, darling. I thought of it myself when I boosted this box. I repeat, it's much worse if nothing is happening on the poop. I hope with all my heart that we find a band of Lilliputians there, or a cargo of Limburger cheese, or just a rat-infested deck."

"Must be the salt air," said Paula, closing the door.

Mercilessly sacrificing the hopes of both Señor Trejo and Dr. Restelli, who were counting on him to reanimate a languishing conversation, Medrano approached Claudia, who preferred the bar and her coffee to deck games. He ordered a beer and told her the results of their meeting, what they had just decided, without mentioning the strongbox. It was an effort to talk seriously because he constantly had the feeling that what he was saying was pure invention, something that grazed reality without involving either the narrator or listener. As he was listing the reasons for the decision to force a way to the rear deck, he almost felt a solidarity with the other side, as if, climbing to the top of the mast, he could judge the game in its entirety and get an impartial view.

"It's so foolish, if you think about it a little. We should name Jorge captain and let him run things; I'm sure his idea of it has more to do with reality than ours."

"Who knows," said Claudia. "Jorge is aware that something strange is going on. He told me a minute ago: 'We're in a zoo, but we're not the spectators,' or something like that. I understood him completely because I have the same impression. But are we right in rebelling? I'm not talking through fear; it's more like being afraid to tear down some partition which might turn out to be indispensable to the proportions of the room."

"A room . . . yes, perhaps. I see it more as a special kind of game we're playing with the people on the other side. At noon they made the first move and now they're waiting, their watches

set and ticking, for us to answer. They're playing the white pieces
and . . ."

"We're going back to the idea of play. I suppose that it's part
of the true concept of life, no illusions and no transcendency.
One adjusts to being a good bishop or a good castle, to moving
diagonally or castling to save the king. After all, the *Malcolm* isn't
too different from Buenos Aires, at least not from my life in Buenos Aires. It's become more functional and plasticked up every day,
with more electrical gadgets in the kitchen and more books in the
library."

"To be like the *Malcolm* you should have a touch of mystery in
your house."

"There is, his name is Jorge. What greater mystery is there than
a present without anything of the present, absolute future. Something lost beforehand which I lead, help, and encourage as if he
were going to be mine forever. To think that any little girl at all
will take him away from me in a few years, a little girl, who right
this minute is reading a storybook or learning a cross-stitch."

"You don't say it with grief, it seems to me."

"No, grief is too tangible, too present, and too real to apply to
this. I see Jorge from two levels, today's level, which makes me
quite happy, and the other level, situated far in the distance, where
I see an old lady on a sofa, surrounded by an empty house."

Medrano nodded silently. The delicate wrinkles which were beginning to rim Claudia's eyes were visible during the day, but the
tiredness in her face wasn't artificial, as it was in Raul Costa's
girl. She reminded him of a *résumé*, a price well paid, a slight
ash. He liked Claudia's serious voice, her way of saying "I" without emphasis, but at the same time with a resonance which made
him want her to repeat the word and wait for it with anticipated
pleasure.

"Too lucid," he told her. "And that's a high price to pay. How
many women live in the present without thinking about the day
they'll lose their children? Their children and so many other
things. Like me, like all of us. The sides around the chessboard pile
up with pawns and queens taken in the game, but to live is to
have your eyes fixed on the pieces you need to go on playing."

"Yes, and to prepare for yourself a precarious calm, generally with prefabricated materials. Art, for instance, or trips . . . The best part is that, even with these, one can achieve an extraordinary happiness, a sort of false, and definite, settling into an existence. And a good number of really extraordinary people will settle for this. But I . . . don't know, it's something to do with these last years. I feel less happy when I'm happy; a little bit of joy begins to hurt me, and God knows I'm capable of being joyous."

"Frankly, this has never happened to me," Medrano said pensively, "but I think I can understand it. It's a little like the drop of aloes in the honey. In my case, up till now, if I've suspected the drop of aloes was there, it's heightened the sweetness."

"Persio would claim that, on another level, honey itself could be considered one of the most bitter forms of aloes. But without leaping off into outer space, as he says with so much delight, I think that my uneasiness these days . . . Oh, it isn't an interesting uneasiness, not metaphysical, more like a scarcely perceptible sigh . . . I've felt unjustifiably anxious, a little like a stranger to myself, for no apparent reasons. And it's exactly this lack of reasons that worries me instead of reassuring me, because you know, I have a kind of faith in my instincts."

"And so this trip is a defense against the uneasiness?"

"Well, defense is a very solemn word. I'm not as threatened as all that, and luckily I think I'm pretty far from accepting the usual fate of Argentine women once they have children. I haven't resigned myself to establishing what they call a home, and probably I'm responsible in good measure for having destroyed my own. My husband could never understand my lack of enthusiasm for the latest model refrigerator or a vacation in Mar del Plata. I shouldn't have gotten married, that's all, but there were other reasons, one being my parents, their naïve faith in me . . . They're dead now; I'm free to show my real self."

"But you don't give the impression of being what they call an emancipated woman," said Medrano. "Not even a rebel, in the bourgeois sense of the word. Neither, thank God, are you a superstitious bourgeois or a member of the Woman's Club. Curious, but I can't pigeonhole you and I'm not sorry about it. The classical wife and mother . . ."

"I know that men recoil in terror before women who are too classical," said Claudia. "But that's always before they marry them."

"If by classical you mean lunch at noon, ashes in the ashtray, and Saturday night at the movies, then I think my reticence would be as marked after as before matrimony, all of which, by the way, makes the latter impossible for me. Don't think I go around cultivating bohemians, or anything like that. I, too, have a special little hook in my closet where I hang my ties. It's something deeper, the suspicion that a . . . a 'classical' woman is just as lost as any other woman. The mother of the Gracchi is famous for her children, not for herself. History would be sadder than it already is if all her heroines were recruited from that class of woman. No, you baffle me because you have a serenity and balance that don't fit in with what you've told me. All to the good, you can believe me; these beautifully well-balanced types usually develop into perfect monotony, especially on a cruise to Japan."

"Oh, Japan. You say it so skeptically."

"I don't think you're very sure of getting there either. Tell the truth, if it's the thing to do at this hour: Why did you come on the *Malcolm*?"

Claudia stared at her hands and thought a moment.

"Not long ago someone was talking to me," she said. "Someone very desperate, for whom life is no more than a series of precarious postponements, which can be canceled out at any moment. This person thinks of me as strong, well balanced, so much so that she confides in me and confesses all her weaknesses. I wouldn't want this person to find out what I'm going to say, because the sum of two weaknesses can become a terrible force and unchain catastrophes. But you know, I'm very much like this person. I think I've come to a point where the most tangible things have begun to lose all sense, to become blurred, to give way. I think . . . I think I'm still in love with Leon."

"Ah."

"And at the same time I know that I can't stand him, that the mere sound of his voice repels me every time he come to see Jorge, to play with him. Can anyone make any sense out of that? Can anyone love a man whose presence alone is enough to change each minute into a half hour?"

"How should I know?" Medrano said abruptly. "Personally, my complications are far simpler. How should I know if anyone can love someone like that?"

Claudia looked at him and then averted her eyes. The sullen note in Medrano's voice was familiar to her: it was the tone of voice used by men who were irritated by subtleties that they were incapable of understanding, and especially, of accepting. "He'll limit himself to classifying me as a hysteric," she thought pitilessly. "And he's probably right, not to mention that it's ridiculous even to be discussing these things." She asked him for a cigarette, and waited until he offered her a light.

"All this talk is absolutely useless," she said. "When I began to read novels, and I began very young, I always had the feeling that the dialogue was usually ridiculous. For the simple reason that the slightest incident would have put an end to these conversations or cut them short. For instance, what if I had been in my cabin, or you had decided to go on deck instead of coming here to have a beer? Why place any importance on an exchange of words provoked by the most absurd coincidence?"

"The worst of it," said Medrano, "is that it can be applied to every act in life, including love, which, until now, has seemed the most serious and fatal of our activities. To accept your point of view means that all of our existence becomes trivial, to toss it to the dogs of pure absurdity."

"Why not?" said Claudia. "Persio would say that what we call absurd is only our ignorance."

Medrano stood up when he saw Lopez and Raul come into the bar. They had just met on the staircase. Claudia started to turn the pages of a magazine.

The three friends avoided the Trejo-Restelli table, and instead went over to the far corner of the bar to talk to the bartender. Lopez took charge of directing operations, and the bartender turned out to be more accessible than they had thought. The poop deck? The telephone was disconnected for the moment and the *maître* was personally establishing a connection with the officers. Yes, the *maître* had been vaccinated, and they were probably subjecting him to a special disinfecting before returning from that area, unless he didn't actually get to the danger zone and all communication was being made orally, from a distance. Yes, he was only guessing at all this.

"Besides," the bartender added unexpectedly, "starting tomorrow there will be a beauty parlor and barber shop open from nine until twelve."

"Fine, but now we want to send a cable to Buenos Aires."

"But the officer said . . . the officer said, gentlemen. How do you expect me to . . . ? I've only been aboard this ship a short time," the bartender added, complaining. "I came on in Santos two weeks ago."

"Let's leave the autobiography for later," said Raul. "Just show us the way to the rear deck, or at least take us to some officer."

"I'm very sorry, gentlemen, but my orders . . . I'm new here." He saw Medrano's and Lopez' faces and he swallowed quickly. "The most I can do is show you the way there, but the doors are locked, and . . ."

"I know one way that doesn't take you anywhere," said Raul. "Let's see if it's the same one."

Rubbing his hands (though they were perfectly dry) on a towel bearing the Magenta Star insignia, the bartender reluctantly left the bar and led them down the staircase. He stopped in front of a door opposite Dr. Restelli's cabin, and opened it with a small Yale key. What they saw was a very simple but elegant cabin. There was an enormous photograph of Victor Emmanuel III on the wall and a party hat hung from a hook. With the look of a Newfoundland dog on his face the bartender asked them to come in, and immediately shut the door. At one side of the bunk was a tiny door, hardly visible between the cedar paneling.

"My cabin," said the bartender, drawing a semicircle with his spongy hand. "The maître has one on the larboard side. Do you really . . . ? Yes, this is the key, but I insist you shouldn't . . . The officer said . . ."

"Open up and no more talk," Lopez ordered. "Go back and serve the thirsty old bucks beer. And it's not necessary to talk to them about all this."

"Oh, no, I won't say anything."

The key turned twice and the little door opened onto a stairway. "There are many roads which lead to hell," thought Raul. "As long as this doesn't also lead to a tattoed giant, Charon with snakes on his arms . . ." He followed the others down a dark passage. "Poor Felipe, he must be tearing his hair. But he's too much of a kid for all this . . ." He knew he was lying, that it was only a pleasurable perversity which had made him deprive Felipe of this adventure. "We'll let him have another mission to compensate for this," he thought, a bit repentant.

They stopped when they came to a turn in the passageway. There were three doors, one of them half open. Medrano pushed it wide open. It was a storeroom for empty boxes, boards, and rolls of wire. It led nowhere. Raul suddenly realized that Lucio hadn't joined them at the bar.

The second door was closed and the third led to another, brighter passageway. Three axes with red-painted handles hung on the walls, and the passage ended at a door with a printed sign reading: GED OTTAMA, and in smaller letters: *P. Pickford.* They entered a large cabin, full of metal lockers and three-legged stools. A man stood up, surprised, and then took a step back. Lopez spoke to him in Spanish, with no success. He tried French. Raul, sighing, asked a question in English.

"Ah, passengers," said the man, who was dressed in light blue trousers and a short-sleeved red shirt. "But you can't go through here."

"Excuse the intrusion," said Raul. "We were looking for the radio room. It's an urgent matter."

"You can't go through here. You have to . . ." He glanced quickly at the door to his left. Medrano reached it a second before him. With both hands in his pockets, he smiled amiably.

"Sorry," he said. "You see we have to go through. Pretend you haven't seen us."

Breathing nervously, the man backed away until he almost bumped into Lopez. They went through the door and closed it quickly. Things were starting to get interesting.

The *Malcolm* seemed to be made up principally of passageways, which made Lopez feel slightly claustrophobic. They were approaching the first turn, without having found a door, when they

heard a bell ring. It might have been an alarm. It lasted five seconds and left them half deaf.

"There's going to be hell to pay," said Lopez, more and more
excited. "Let's see if these damn Finns come pouring out."

A little beyond the turn they found a half-opened door, and
Raul couldn't help thinking that the ship's discipline was worse
than arbitrary. Lopez pushed the door open and they were greeted
by an angry meowing. A white cat leaped back, offended, and began to lick its paw. The cabin was empty, but it was luxuriously
furnished with doors: three of them. Two were locked and the
third opened with difficulty. Raul, who had stayed behind to pet
the cat, a female, inhaled the odor of mustiness and bilge. "But
we're not very deep," he thought. "We must be at the same level
as the prow deck, or a little lower." The blue eyes of the white cat
followed him with a vacuous intensity, and Raul leaned over to
pet it again before joining the others. The bell was still audible
in the distance. Medrano and Lopez were waiting for him in a
storeroom stacked with cooky boxes. The labels were in English
and German.

"I'd like to be wrong," said Raul, "but I have the feeling that
we're practically back to where we started from. Behind that
door . . ." He saw that it had a safety latch on it and he pulled it
back. "I'm right, unfortunately."

It was one of the two locked doors they had seen at the end of
the entrance passageway. The stale smell and the darkness overwhelmed them. None of them felt like going back to find the
man in the red shirt.

"Actually, the only thing missing is a meeting with the Mino-
taur," said Raul.

He tried the other locked door, and looked at the third which
would bring them back to the storeroom of empty boxes. In the
distance, they heard the white cat meowing. Shrugging their
shoulders, they went back to find the door marked GED OTTAMA.

The man was still there, but he looked as if he had had more
than enough time to prepare for another meeting.

"Sorry, but this is not the way to the captain's bridge. The radio room is up above."

"Remarkable information," said Raul, whose fluent English gave

him the captaincy at this stage of operations. "And how do you get
to the radio room?"

"Up above, following the passageway until . . . Ah, of course,
the doors are locked."

"Can you take us around the other way? We'd like to speak
with an officer, since the captain is sick."

The man looked at Raul, astonished. "Now he's going to say he
didn't know the captain was sick," thought Medrano, who felt
like going back to the bar for a brandy. But the man only puckered
his lips in disapproval.

"My orders are to take care of this section," he said. "If you
need me, let me know. I can't go above with you, I'm very sorry."

"Don't you want to open the doors, even though you can't
come with us?"

"But sir, I don't have the keys. I've already told you that this is
my section."

Raul consulted his friends. They all felt as if the ceiling were
lower than ever, the stale odor more oppressive. They nodded to
the man in the red shirt and retraced their steps in silence. They
did not speak until they reached the bar, where they ordered
drinks. Bright sunlight poured in through the portholes and
flashed back from the brilliant blue of the ocean. Sipping his
first drink, Medrano regretted having lost so much time in the bow-
els of the ship. "Playing Jonah like an imbecile, and in the end
they'll make a fool of me," he thought. He felt like talking to
Claudia, or going up on deck, or stretching out on his bed to
smoke and read. "Actually, why are we taking this so seriously?"
Lopez and Raul were gazing out toward the open sea, and they
both looked as if they had just come up to the surface after a
long immersion in a well, in a movie, or in a book which could
not be put down before the end.

XXVII

The sun turned red at dusk and a fresh breeze started up,
forcing the bathers from the pool. The ladies, fairly recovered
from seasickness, were provoked into a disorderly rout. Señor Trejo

and Dr. Restelli had discussed the situation on board at great length, and had come to the conclusion that everything was fine as long as the typhus got no further than the rear deck. Don Galo shared their opinion, but perhaps his optimism was influenced by the fact that the three friends—they already were quite friendly—had moved their chairs to the most forward part of the prow, where the air they breathed could not be contaminated. Señor Trejo went to his cabin for a moment to look for his sunglasses and found Felipe, who was showering before putting on his bluejeans again. Suspecting that he knew something about the strange conduct of the men around Medrano (their conspiratorial air and sudden exit from the bar had not escaped him), Señor Trejo began to question his son in a friendly fashion and quickly learned of the expedition to the depths of the ship. Too clever for punishments and other paternal reproaches, he left his son, who was gazing at himself in the mirror, and returned to the prow to inform his friends of the latest news. And when Lopez approached them a half hour later with a bored expression on his face, he was received in the most circumspect manner and was informed that on a ship, or anywhere else, the principles of democratic referendum should be respected at all times, although the fieriness of youth might excuse . . . Staring out at the perfect line of the horizon, Lopez listened without blinking to the tart homily mouthed by Dr. Restelli, whom he regarded too highly to send *ipso facto* to the devil. He answered that they had limited themselves to a few reconnoitering patrols, since the visit and explanations of the officer had not seemed satisfactory to them. And that their investigations had been most unrewarding, but that their abortive attempt to obtain more precise details had only encouraged them to continue thinking the typhus story a complete hoax.

At this point Don Galo became as agitated as a fighting cock, insisting that only the most warped imagination could doubt the perfectly lucid and proper explanations given by the officer. As far as he was concerned, he wanted to make it clear that if Lopez and his friends continued to disturb the work of the ship's captain and to spread obvious insubordination on board, the consequences would be most troublesome for everyone involved. And he considered this reason enough for him to step forward to express his dissent. Señor Trejo felt the same way, more or less, but as he was not at all acquainted with Lopez (and he couldn't conceal the annoying sensation of being, in a certain way, a parvenu on board), he limited himself to saying that they all should show themselves united as good friends, and consult one another before adopting any decision that would affect the lives of the others.

"Look," said Lopez, "if it's any consolation to you, we haven't been able to make head or tail out of anything, and besides, we've been bored to hell—missing a swim in the pool, among other things," he added laughingly.

It seemed ridiculous to start an argument with these old gaffers; besides, the dusk and setting sun invited silence. He went to the rail and leaned over the cutwater, watching the play of foam turning red and violet. The early evening was unusually serene, and the breeze seemed to float around the *Malcolm*, scarcely grazing it. Far off, on the larboard side, he could see a plume of smoke. Lopez indifferently recalled his home—the house of his sister and brother-in-law in which he had a separate apartment; right now Ruth would be bringing back onto the covered patio the straw chairs which had been taken out to the garden during the afternoon. Gómara, his brother-in-law, would be talking politics with his colleague Carpio, who defended a vague kind of communism, overlarded with poems by Chinese authors translated into English and then to Spanish for the publishing house in which he worked, and Ruth's children would be listening respectfully and sadly for the order to go up and take baths. All that was yesterday, all that was happening over there, a little beyond the silvery, reddish-purple horizon. "It already seems like another world," he thought, but probably a week later the recollections would gather some force, when the novelty of the present faded. He had been living in Ruth's house for fifteen years and for ten of those fifteen years he had been a teacher. Fifteen years, ten years, now one day at sea, a redhead (but actually the redhead didn't have anything to do with it) had been enough to scramble and pulverize that previous part of his life, that long third of his lifetime, into a dream image. Maybe Paula was at the bar, but she could be in her cabin with Raul, at the loveliest time, the time when night was falling, making

love. Making love on a gently rolling ship, in a cabin where every
object, every scent, and every light were symbols of distance, of
perfect liberty. Of course they were making love; he didn't believe
a word of that ambiguous story, that declaration of independence
she had made. One didn't get on a ship with a woman like that to
talk about the immortality of the crab. She could tease him amiably; he'd let her play around a while, and then . . . "Jamaica
John," he thought, a little angry. "I won't play Christopher Dawn
for you, tootsie." What would it be like to run his hands through
that red hair, to feel it run through his fingers like blood? "I think
of blood too much," he told himself, looking at the horizon,
which was turning redder by the moment. "It's Sennacherib
Eden's fault. No doubt." But what if she were at the bar? And he
here, wasting time . . . He turned and set off rapidly toward the
staircase. Beba Trejo, seated on the third step, scooted to the
other side to let him pass.

"Lovely evening," said Lopez, who still did not know what to
make of her. "You haven't been seasick?"

"Me, seasick?" protested Beba. "I haven't even taken any pills.
I never get seasick."

"That's what I like to hear," said Lopez, who had nothing more
to say on the subject. Beba was waiting for something more. If
only Lopez would stay and talk a little. She watched him walk
off, waving to her, and she stuck out her tongue when she saw he
couldn't see her. He was a fool, but nicer than Medrano. She
preferred Raul to all of them, but so far Felipe and the other
men had monopolized him, it was revolting. He looked a little like
William Holden—no, more like Gérard Philippe. No, not like
Gérard Philippe either. So thin in those fancy shirts, with that
pipe. That woman doesn't deserve a boyfriend like that.

That woman was at the bar drinking a gin fizz.

"How did the expedition go? Are you getting the black flag
and the boarding sabers ready?"

"For what?" asked Lopez. "Actually, an acetylene torch to cut
through the bulkhead doors and a dictionary in six languages to
get along with the glucids would be more useful. Hasn't Raul
told you?"

"No, I haven't seen him yet. Tell me."

Lopez told her, and used the incident to gently mock himself, as well as the other two men. He also told her about the old men's prudent reaction, which made them both laugh. The bartender made very excellent gin fizzes, and only Atilio Presutti was in sight, drinking a beer and reading a sports magazine. What had Paula done all afternoon? Well, she had swum in the pool, stared at the horizon, and read Françoise Sagan. Lopez noticed that she had a green-covered notebook with her. Yes, sometimes she took notes or wrote something. What kind of thing? Oh, well, a poem.

"Don't act like you're going to confession," Lopez said impatiently. "What is it with Argentine poets? They walk around as if they're hiding. I have two poet friends, one of them very good. And they both act like you: a notebook in the pocket and the expression of a Graham Greene character being tracked down by Scotland Yard."

"But this couldn't interest anyone," said Paula. "We write for ourselves and for a group so insignificant that it doesn't have the vaguest statistical importance. You know that now the importance of things has to be measured statistically. Tabulations and that sort of thing."

"Not true," Lopez said. "And if a poet has that attitude the first thing to suffer is his poetry."

"But if no one reads it, Jamaica John. Friends fulfill their debt; of course, and sometimes a poem falls into the hands of a reader as though it were his fate or at some special bidding. That's already a lot, and more than enough to keep the poet going. As for you, you don't have to feel obliged to ask me for my things. Maybe I'll lend them to you one day, just out of the blue. Isn't it better that way?"

"Yes," said Lopez, "as long as that day comes."

"That depends a little on both of us. At the moment I'm feeling rather optimistic, but do we know what's in store for us tomorrow, as Señora Trejo would say? Have you ever seen the likes of Señora Trejo?"

"The woman is touching," said Lopez, who had no desire at all to talk about Señora Trejo. "She looks a lot like one of Medrano's drawings—no, not our friend, but the inventor of graphodramas. I just exchanged a few words with her adolescent daughter, who is attending the arrival of night on the front staircase. That girl is going to get bored."

"On board and everywhere else. Don't make me think back to the age of fifteen, the hours before the mirror, and . . . and so many curiosities, false reports, and equally false monstrosities and delights. You like Rosamond Lehmann novels?"

"Yes, sometimes," said Lopez. "I like you better, to hear you, to talk to you, and to look at your eyes. Don't laugh, the eyes are there and there's nothing to do about it. All afternoon I thought of the color of your hair, even when we were skulking about the damn passageways. What's it like when it's wet?"

"Well, like a soapbark tree or a bowl of borsht. The most repulsive thing you can think of. Do you really like it, Jamaica John? I wouldn't put that much faith in first impressions. Ask Raul, he knows me better. I have a bad reputation among the people who know me because I'm a little like *la belle dame sans merci*. I exaggerate, of course, but basically what's really wrong with me is that I feel too sorry for myself and for others. Every time anyone stretches out a hand I put a coin in it, and it seems like this is a bad idea in the long run. Don't look so pained, I don't intend to tell you my life story. I already poured my heart out to that lovely, lovely, and very good Claudia. I like Claudia, Jamaica John. Tell me you like Claudia."

"I like Claudia," said Jamaica John. "She uses a marvelous cologne, has an enchanting son, and everything's great, including this gin fizz . . . Let's have another," he added, putting his hand on hers. She let it stay there.

"You could've asked to get by," said Beba. "You already stepped on my skirt with that dirty sneaker."

Felipe whistled two bars of a mambo and leaped up to the deck. He had been in the sun too long, sitting beside the pool, and his shoulders, back, and face were burning. But all this too was part of the trip, and the fresh air at dusk filled him with pleasure. Except for the old ginks on the prow, the deck was empty. Taking shelter behind a ventilator, he lit a cigarette and looked scornfully at Beba, who was sitting languidly and quietly on the

little staircase. He took a few steps, and then leaned up against
the rail. The sea looked like . . . *The sea was like a vast and
trembling sheet of crystal,* and Freilich, that queer, who was reciting it, as the literature prof looked on with a smile of approval.
That imbecile, Freilich. Head of the class, the goddamned faggot.
"Yes ma'am, I'm going there, ma'am, yes ma'am. Would you like
the colored chalk, ma'am?" And the lady teachers, of course, bam-
boozled by the ass licker, gave him a hundred on everything.
Well, he didn't fool the men so easily, more than a couple were
on to him, but just the same he always came out with a hundred,
studying all night, dark circles under his eyes . . . But those dark
circles weren't from studying; Durruty said that Freilich walked
around downtown at night with a big guy, who must have a lot
of dough. He had met them one afternoon in a pastry shop on
Santa Fe, and Freilich blushed and pretended not to see him
. . . He was sure that the other guy was the bull, that's for sure.
He was well aware of how these things happened, ever since the
night of the festival in third year, when they had put on a play
and he had played the role of the husband. Alfieri had come up
to him during intermission saying: "Look how pretty Viana is!"
Viana was a fellow from third C, more of a queer than Freilich
ever was, one of those guys that let himself be beaten up and
kicked around during recess, wiggling around the whole time, delighted, making faces. But at the same time, you had to admit
that he was a good guy, generous. He always went around with
things in his pockets: American cigarettes, tiepins. This time
Viana was playing the role of a young girl dressed in green, and had
made himself up something terrific. How he must have enjoyed
himself when they put his make-up on; once or twice, he was
talked into going to school with the remains of mascara on his
lashes. What a sensation! He had been greeted by falsetto voices,
embraces, pinches, and kicks. But that night Viana was happy
and Alfieri was looking at him, repeating: "Look how pretty she is,
she looks like Sofia Loren." Another funny guy, Alfieri, so stern, always the perfect school monitor, but suddenly, if you didn't watch
out, he'd have a hand on your back, with a fake smile, and a way
of saying: "Do you like girls, kid?" and he'd wait for the answer
with his eyes half-closed. And when Viana had looked out over

the audience, anxiously searching for someone, Alfieri had said to him: "Watch, now you're going to see why she's so worried," and suddenly a little guy showed up, dressed in a grey suit and a snazzy raincoat, a silk scarf around his neck, and gold rings on his fingers. Viana was waiting for him, smiling, a hand at his waist (just like Sofia Loren), while Alfieri, pressed close to Felipe, murmured: "Now he's a piano manufacturer. You dig, baby, the kind of life Viana has with him? Wouldn't you like to have loot all the time and be driven around to the Tigre and Mar del Plata?" Felipe, absorbed by the scene before him, didn't answer. Viana and the piano manufacturer spoke excitedly, and he looked as if he were reproaching him for something, and then Viana lifted the skirt he was wearing, staring at his white shoes, as though admiring them. "If you want to, one night we'll go out together," Alfieri had said. "We'll go on the town and I'll introduce you to some women which you must be hot for at this point . . . unless you like men, I don't know," and his voice was lost between the noise of the hammering of the mechanics and the murmur of the audience. Felipe freed himself of Alfieri's arm, pretending he hadn't realized it was there, lightly slung around his shoulders, and said he had to get ready for the next act. He still remembered the smell of Virginia tobacco on Alfieri's breath, his face with the half-closed eyes, which he didn't change even in front of teachers or the principal. He had never known what to think of Alfieri; sometimes he seemed like such a ladies' man, talking to the fifth-year crowd in the patio. Once Felipe had sidled up behind them to listen and he heard Alfieri telling about laying a married woman he knew, and he was describing it in detail, the furnished room they'd gone to, because at first she was frightened of her husband who was a lawyer, but afterwards they had screwed for three hours, and the word was repeated again and again. Alfieri bragged of interminable prowess, of not having let her sleep for even a minute, of not wanting to get her pregnant, how they'd taken precautions but what a drag that always was, of rapid changes of position in the dark and of something flying around that banged up against the door or wall with a whizzing sound, how the room looked after the night was over and the fuss the maid would kick up . . . The meaning of some of the things was lost on Felipe, but they were things you didn't ask about; someday he'd know what they meant and that would be the end of that. Luckily, Ordoñez wasn't one of those guys who kept his mouth shut, and he was always giving detailed illustrations, lending him books that he didn't dare buy or even hide in his house, with Beba around; she was like a flea when it came to getting into places she didn't belong, especially drawers. What really upset him was that Alfieri hadn't been the first to go after him. Did he look like a fairy to them? There were too many vague things about the whole business. Alfieri, for instance, didn't look like one either . . . Couldn't compare him with Freilich or Viana who were out-and-out faggots. He'd occasionally seen Alfieri go up to some second- or third-year kid at recess, making gestures to them as he did with him, and there was nothing sissyish about them, they were regular kids too. What he meant was that Alfieri liked this kind of fellow, not whores like Viana or Freilich. And surprised, he also remembered the day they had gone on the bus together; Alfieri paid for both of them, even though he had pretended that he hadn't seen him in line, and when they were sitting down on the back seat, on the way to the Retiro, he began to talk about his fiancée, very naturally, that he had to see her this afternoon, that she was a teacher, that they would get married when they found an apartment. All this in a low voice, almost in Felipe's ear, and Felipe was listening somewhere between interest and suspicion because Alfieri was a monitor, an authority at any rate, and after a pause, when the subject of his fiancée seemed to be exhausted, Alfieri added with a sigh: "Yes, I'm going to get married soon, but you know, I like boys so much . . ." and again he wanted to get away, not to have anything to do with Alfieri, even though right now Alfieri was confiding in him as an equal, and when he talked about boys that didn't mean full-fledged men like Felipe. He scarcely dared look out of the corner of his eye, smiling with difficulty, as if this were extremely natural and he were used to talking about such things. It would have been easy with Viana or Freilich, he would have jabbed them in the ribs or something like that, but Alfieri was a school monitor, a man past thirty, and a smooth character besides who took lawyers' wives to furnished rooms with him.

"They gotta have something wrong with their glands," he thought, throwing away his cigarette. Looking in at the door of the bar for a second, he had seen Paula chatting with Lopez. And he had looked at them with envy. Just fine. Daddy Lopez wasn't losing a second working over the redhead; it remained to be seen how Raul would react. If only Lopez would drag her out and haul her off to his cabin and bring her back all done in like the lawyer's wife. Everything would be settled in very simple terms: have a go at it, come on to the chick, feel her up, throw it into high gear, and finish it off on the bed. And the other guy would have the choice of acting like a man or settling down as a cuckold. Felipe walked about deck, satisfied with his outline, where everything was well lit and in its place. Not like with Alfieri, who used words with double meanings, and that business of not ever knowing whether he was talking seriously or looking for something else . . . He saw Raul and Dr. Restelli standing on the deck, and he turned his back on them. He could just stand around with his English goddamned pipe. Raul had tried his patience long enough. Felipe had wasted enough time on him this afternoon. Ha, and they hadn't managed to accomplish a thing; he was already informed by his father of the expedition's failure. Three grown men, and they hadn't even gotten through to the rear deck to see what was going on.

It suddenly occurred to him, and he made up his mind without even giving it a second thought. In a matter of two leaps he ducked out of sight and hid himself behind a roll of rope. Besides avoiding a meeting with Raul, he saved himself from a possible conversation with the Black Cat, who must be more than put out by his lack of . . . how did he say it in class? . . . of civility (or was it urbanity? Eccchh, some junk or other). When he saw them at the railing, he started running toward the staircase. Beba watched him go by with a look of immense pity on her face. "You act as if you weren't three years old yet," she murmured. "Running like a baby, you're going to make us look like fools in front of everyone." Felipe swung around at the top of the staircase and insulted her sharply. He ran into his cabin, which was almost next to the side of the joining passage between the corridors, and spied out through a crack in the door. When he was sure it was clear, he left quickly and groped for the door of the passageway. It was open as before, the staircase just below. It was there that Raul had first used the familiar form in addressing him. It all seemed unbelievable now, completely unbelievable. When he closed the door he was enveloped in darkness, much darker than it was in the afternoon when he'd gone down with Raul; it was strange that the place seemed dimmer now, the light was lit, just as it was earlier. He hesitated a second, halfway down the staircase, and listened to the noises from below; the motors were beating heavily, an odor of grease and bitumen was rising from the depths. They had walked around down there talking about the movie with the ship of death in it, and Raul had said that the movie was from a certain . . . And later he had agreed that it was a great pity that Felipe had to have his family along with him. He remembered the wording perfectly: "I would have liked it better if you had come alone." What did it matter to *him* if he had come alone or with others? The door to the left was open; the other one was closed, as it had been before, but hammering could be heard inside. Motionless in front of the door, Felipe felt something sliding down his face; he dried the sweat with the sleeve of his shirt. Whipping out another cigarette, he lit it quickly. He'd show those three wiseguys.

XXVIII

"Last month she finished her fifth year at the conservatory," said Señora Trejo. "And with school honors. Now she's going on to become a concert performer."

Doña Rosita and Doña Pepa were really impressed. Doña Pepa had wanted Nelly to go on to be a concert performer too, but it was a constant battle. And what talent! Ever since she was a little girl she had sung all the tangos by heart, as well as other things, and spent hours listening to the programs of classical music on the radio. But when she had to practice, there was nothing doing.

"Believe me, señora, I begged her . . . a battle, believe me. If I tell you . . . But what can you do, she didn't like to practice."

"Of course, señora. On the other hand, Beba practices the piano four hours every day and I assure you it's a sacrifice for my husband and me; after all, so much practicing is tiring and the house is tiny. But then, when she finishes her exams with honors, there's some compensation. You should hear her . . . Maybe they'll invite her to play; they often have concerts on these trips, and they ask some artist to play. Of course, Beba didn't bring her music, but as she knows the 'Polonaise' and 'Clair de lune' by heart . . . She's always playing them . . . It isn't just that I'm her mother, but she does play them with such feeling."

"You have to know how to play classical music," said Doña Rosita. "It isn't like the music you hear today; it's just noise, these modern things on the radio. I immediately say to my husband, I tell him: 'Oh, Enzo, turn off that junk, it gives me a headache.' They should forbid it, I think."

"Nelly says that the music you hear today isn't like the music of the old days, Beethoven and all that."

"Beba says the same thing, and she's in a position to know," said Señora Trejo. "There's too much modern music right now. My husband has written twice to the National Radio to have them improve the programs, but you know how that is, and there's so much favoritism . . . How are you, darling? You don't look so well."

Nora was feeling well enough but Señora Trejo's observation upset her. Entering the reading room she had suddenly run into the ladies, and somehow she didn't know how to turn around and go back to the bar. She had to sit down with them, smiling as if she were feeling happy. She wondered if there wasn't something in her face that . . . But that couldn't be. Impossible.

"This afternoon I felt a little seasick," she said. "Nothing much. It went away as soon as I took a Dramamine. And are you all well?"

Sighing, the ladies told her that the present calmness of the sea allowed them to keep down a little tea with milk, but if it began to get rough, as it had at midday . . . Ah, happy were the young, and Nora was one of them, who only thought of having a good time, for they still didn't know what life was like. Of course, traveling with a fellow as nice as Lucio, she could scarcely help but see

only the rosy side of life. So much the better for her, sweet girl.
And just as well. One never knew what tomorrow would bring,
and as long as there was health . . .

"You must have gotten married very recently?" asked Señora
Trejo, watching Nora attentively.

"Yes, ma'am," said Nora. She felt as if she were going to blush
and she didn't know what to do to conceal it from them; the three
of them were looking at her with tapioca smiles, their spongy
hands resting on their bulging stomachs. "Yes, ma'am." She
decided to put on a violent coughing fit and she covered her face
with her hands, and the women asked if she had a cold, and Doña
Pepa advised her to rub herself down with Vicks Vaporub. Nora
felt her lie in the pit of her stomach, and her cowardice even more:
she hadn't the courage to face the question. "What do I care what
they think, as long as we're going to get married later anyway?"
Lucio had said so many times. "It's the best proof you can give me
that you trust me, and besides you have to fight bourgeois prejudices . . ." But she couldn't, and now less than ever. "Yes, ma'am,
very recently."

Doña Rosita was explaining that dampness did her no good at
all, and if it weren't for her husband's work, she would never have
stayed on Maciel Island. "I have a kind of rheumatism which attacks me all over," she was informing Señora Trejo, who continued to look at Nora, "and no one can get rid of it. I've seen all the
big doctors, and I even had Pantaleon come, the famous healer,
but nothing could be done. It's the humidity, you know. It's bad
for the bones. It's like the mildew inside the body and no matter
how much you take physics or hepatic fungus waters, nothing
helps . . ." Nora saw an opening in the conversation and she
stood up, glancing at her watch, as if she had an appointment.
Doña Pepa and Señora Trejo exchanged a knowing look and a
smile. They understood; of course, how could they not understand
. . . Go on, darling, somebody's waiting for you. Señora Trejo
was a bit sorry that Nora was leaving, for at least Nora was of her
class, not like these ladies, who were so good, sweet dears, but so
below her station . . . Señora Trejo vaguely began to suspect that
she wasn't going to have anyone else to talk to on the trip, and she
was worried and upset. The little boy's mother only spoke to men;

it was obvious that she must be some kind of artist or writer because the really feminine things were of no interest to her, and she was forever smoking and discussing incomprehensible things with Medrano and Lopez. The redheaded girl was not at all pleasant, and besides, she was too young to understand life and talk of serious matters, apart from the fact that she wasn't thinking of anything more than showing herself off in that disgusting bikini, and even flirting with Felipe, no less. She'd have to speak to her husband about it. It wasn't the thing for Felipe to fall into the hands of this vamp. And just then she remembered Señor Trejo's eyes when Paula had stretched out on the deck to take the sun. No, it wasn't the trip she had imagined it would be.

Nora opened the door of the cabin. She didn't expect to see Lucio; she had a vague idea that he was on the deck. He was sitting on the edge of the bed, staring off into space.

"What are you thinking about?"

Lucio was not thinking about anything, but he knit his brows as if he had just been torn from serious thoughts. Then he smiled and motioned her to sit down next to him. Nora sighed sadly. No, nothing had happened. Yes, she had been at the bar talking to the ladies. Of course, a little of everything. Her lips did not open when Lucio took her face between his two hands and kissed her.

"Don't you feel well, sweetie? You must be tired—" He stopped short, fearing that she might interpret it as an allusion. But why not, what the devil. Of course it's tiring, like any other hard exercise. He felt a bit worn out too, but he was certain it didn't come from . . . Before he had lost himself in total distraction to sit without a thought in his head, he had been remembering the scene in Raul's cabin; it had left a bad taste in his mouth. He hoped something would happen to let him make up for everything, to get involved again in the situation from which he suddenly found himself excluded. But he hadn't acted stupidly; it was ridiculous to dream up murder mysteries and go around passing out firearms. Why ruin the trip right from the start? All afternoon he had gone around wanting to talk with one of them alone, especially with Medrano, whom he had known slightly before and who seemed the most sensible. To tell him they could count on him

completely if things began to look bad (which was inconceivable),
but that it didn't seem to him very smart to be looking for useless
trouble. What a bunch of nuts, instead of getting a good poker
game started.

Sighing, Nora stood up and took a brush from her make-up bag.
"No, I'm not tired, I feel fine," she said. "I don't know, I suppose it's because it's the first day of the trip . . . How should I
know? It's always a change."

"Yes, you have to get a good night's sleep tonight."

"Of course."

She began to brush her hair slowly. Lucio was watching her. He
thought: "Now I'll always see her like that, brushing her hair."

"When will we be able to send a letter to Buenos Aires?"

"I don't know. I guess from Punta Arenas. I think we're stopping there. Are you going to write home?"

"Well, of course. Just imagine how awful they must feel . . . I
better let them know I went on a trip . . . I don't know . . .
mothers imagine all sorts of things. The best thing to do would be
to write to Mocha, and have her explain everything to Mama."

"I suppose you'll tell her you're with me."

"Yes," said Nora. "In any case, they know it. I never would have
gone alone."

"That's going to please your mother no end."

"Well, she has to know it some time. But I'm mainly worried
about Dad—he's so sensitive, and I wouldn't want him to suffer
too much."

"Here we go with the suffering," said Lucio. "What the devil,
why should he suffer? You came with me, I'm going to marry
you, and that's that. Why do you have to talk about suffering right
away, as if it were a tragedy?"

"I was just talking, that's all. Dad is so good . . ."

"It's always my fault," Lucio said bitterly. "I destroyed your
peaceful household, I'm the one who keeps your famous parents
awake at night."

"Please, Lucio," said Nora. "It has nothing to do with you. I'm
the one who decided to do what we're doing."

"Yes, but that part of the story doesn't interest them. I'll always be the Don Juan who ruined the after-dinner conversation and the lotto games, well, fuck that."

Nora didn't answer. The lights flickered for a second. Lucio went to open the porthole and paced across the cabin, his hands behind him. At last he came back to Nora and kissed her on the neck.

"You always make me say something stupid. I know everything is going to be all right, but I don't know what's the matter today, I see things in a way . . . Actually, we couldn't have done anything else, if we wanted to get married. Either we went away together or your mother created a scene. This is better."

"We could have gotten married before, in any case," Nora said in a thread of a voice.

"And for what? Why should we have gotten married before? Yesterday, for instance? Just tell me why."

"I'm not going to say any more."

Lucio sighed and went to sit down on the bed again.

"It's true. I keep forgetting the lady is Catholic," he said. "Of course we could have gotten married yesterday, but it would have been idiotic. We would have had the marriage certificate in my jacket pocket and that would be all. You know that I don't even entertain the thought of getting married in the church, either now or later. As much civil ceremony as you want, but I'll have nothing to do with those black crows, thanks. I'm thinking of my father, too, even though he's dead. When someone's a socialist, he's a socialist. And that's forever."

"All right, Lucio. I never asked for us to be married in the church. I was only saying . . ."

"You were only saying what they all say. They all have a terrible fear of being left in the lurch after going to bed with a man. Bah, don't look at me like that. We've slept together, haven't we? It wasn't a stand-up in a hallway, was it?" He closed his eyes, feeling wretched and dirty. "Don't make me say such hideous things, sweetie. Please believe that I have confidence in you too, and I don't want to suddenly find myself on the floor and discover you're like the others . . . I already told you about Maria Esther once, didn't I? I don't want you to be like her, because then . . ."

Nora gathered that then he would have dropped her like he had dropped Maria Esther. Nora understood him extremely well but said nothing. She continued to see Señora Trejo's face in the bar before her, like a smiling ectoplasm. And Lucio went on talking, talking, getting more nervous every minute, but she was beginning to realize that his nervousness did not come from what he had just finished saying, but rather from something deeper, something else. She put her brush back in the case and went to sit down next to him. She rested her head on his shoulder and rubbed herself gently against his arm. Lucio grunted something, but it was a satisfied grunt. Little by little their faces drew together, and they kissed. Lucio caressed Nora's flanks with long strokes; she was smiling, her hands in her lap. He pulled her toward him violently, slid his arm around her waist, and pushed her gently down. She resisted, laughing. She saw Lucio's face on top of her, so close she hardly could distinguish an eye or his nose.

"Idiot, little idiot. Baby bird."

"Big idiot."

She felt his hand running along her body, awakening her. She thought, slightly amazed, that she almost wasn't afraid of Lucio. It still wasn't easy, but she wasn't afraid any more. A church marriage . . . She protested, ashamed, hid her face, but the deep caress carried its own cure and filled her with an anxiety, a desire in which she lost her caution. It wasn't right, no it wasn't. No, Lucio, no, not like that. She closed her eyes, protesting.

At this moment Jorge was playing P_4K and Persio, after much reflection, answered with K_2K. Implacable, Jorge fired back Q_1R, and Persio could only answer with K_4K. The white pieces descended then with Q_5K, the blacks trembled, hesitated ("Neptune is letting me down," said Persio) until hitting the mark with P_6K, and then there was a brief pause, interrupted by a series of guttural sounds which Jorge produced, and it ended by his giving up Q_4K, and directing a look of cunning toward Persio. When he produced K_4K as his answer, Jorge didn't have to do anything but give a tiny push with Q_5B and kill off all the men.

"Poor Persio," said Jorge magnanimously. "You know, you put your foot in it right off the bat and then couldn't pull yourself out of the mess."

"Remarkable," said Dr. Restelli, who had stood watching the game. "A very remarkable Nimzowich defense."

Jorge looked at him out of the corner of his eye, and Persio quickly began to put away the pieces. Outside, the muffled sound of the dinner gong could be heard.

"The boy is an unusual player," said Dr. Restelli. "As for me, with my modest limitations, I would like very much to play with you, Señor Persio."

"Be careful of Persio," Jorge warned. "He always loses, but one can never be sure."

With the cigarette stuck in his mouth, he opened the door suddenly. At first he thought the two sailors were there, but the mass at the back of the cabin was only an oilskin hanging from a hook. The big-bellied sailor was hammering a strap with a wooden club. The blue serpent tattooed on his upper arm moved rhythmically up and down.

Without stopping hammering (why the devil was this bear hammering a leather strap?), he watched Felipe, who had closed the door and was looking at him, his cigarette still in his mouth and both hands in the pockets of his bluejeans. They remained this way for a moment, studying one another. The serpent took one more leap, the last dull blow of the wood on the strap (the big fellow was softening the leather; it was probably going to be a wide belt to hold in his belly, yeah, sure it was for that), then the serpent came to rest at the edge of the table.

"Hi," said Felipe. The smoke from the Camel drifted into his eyes, and he hardly had time to snatch it out of his mouth before he sneezed. For a second everything blurred through his tears. Shitty cigarette! When was he going to learn how to smoke without taking it out of his mouth?

The sailor kept looking at him, a half-smile on his thick lips. He seemed to find it very amusing that Felipe was in tears on account of the smoke. Slowly, he started to roll up the leather strap; his enormous hands were moving like hairy spiders. He continued rolling it with an almost feminine delicacy.

"*Hasdala*," said the sailor.

"Hi," Felipe repeated, as he felt his initial bravery slip away into thin air. He advanced a step and looked at the tools on the work table. "Are you always working . . . doing these things?"

"*Sa*," said the sailor, tying the strap together with another thinner one. "Sit down there, if you want to."

"Thanks," said Felipe, realizing that the man had just spoken to him in a Castilian Spanish much more intelligible than that of the afternoon. "Are you Finnish?" he asked, trying to get his bearings.

"Finns? No, why should we be Finns? There's a bit of everything here, but there aren't any Finns."

The light from the two bulbs set in the ceiling fell hard on their faces. Sitting on the edge of a bench, Felipe felt uncomfortable and could find nothing to say, but the sailor continued securing the strap with extreme care. Then he began to put away two pair of pliers and an awl. He lifted his eyes repeatedly to look at Felipe, who could feel the cigarette growing smaller and smaller between his fingers.

"You know it's not permitted to come this side of the ship," said the sailor. "You shouldn't have come."

"Hell, what's the difference?" said Felipe. "If I feel like coming down to talk a little . . . It's dull over there, you know."

"Maybe so, but you're not supposed to come here. Now that you're here, you may as well stay awhile. Orf won't get back until later and no one will find out."

"Just as well," said Felipe, not really understanding exactly what risk it was that the others might find out about. More sure of himself, he pushed the bench against the wall until his back had some support; he crossed his legs and took a long drag on the Camel. He was beginning to enjoy himself, and it was time to get on with it.

"Actually, I came to talk to you," he said. (Why in hell did that other guy use the familiar form, while he . . . ?) "I don't like all these mysterious goings-on here."

"Oh, there's no mystery," said the sailor.

"Why don't they let us go to the deck at the stern, then?"

"They give me an order and I carry it out. Why do you want to go back there? There's nothing much there, you know."

"I want to see it," said Felipe.

"There's nothing to see, kid. Sit quiet now you're here already. You can't go through."

"Can't I get through this way? That door?"

"If you want to go through that door," the sailor said laughing, "I'll have to break your head open like a coconut. And you have such a good-looking head, I just don't want to split it like a coconut."

He was speaking slowly, choosing his words. Felipe knew right away that the sailor wasn't just talking, and that he'd better stay put. At the same time he liked the man's attitude, the way he smiled as he threatened to break his head. He took out the pack of cigarettes and offered him one. The sailor shook his head.

"That's tobacco for women," he said. "Smoke mine, sailor's tobacco, you'll see."

Part of the serpent disappeared into his pocket and came out with a black cloth sack and a book of cigarette papers. Felipe shook his head, but the man pulled off a cigarette paper and handed it to him as he tore another one off for himself.

"I'll show you, see. Do the same thing I do, just watch and do what I do. See, you tap the tobacco in like that . . ." The hairy spiders were dancing gracefully around the cigarette paper, and suddenly the sailor ran his hand along his mouth, as if he were playing a harmonica, and a perfect cigarette lay poised on his fingers.

"Look how easy it is. No, it's going to fall like that. Well, you smoke this, I'll make another one for myself."

When he put it in his mouth, Felipe tasted the dampness of the still-wet saliva on the paper and was on the verge of spitting the cigarette out. The sailor was looking at him, gazing at him steadily, and smiling. He began to roll his cigarette, and then took out an enormous, blackened lighter. A thick, penetrating smoke choked Felipe, and he made a gesture showing his appreciation.

"Better not inhale too much," said the sailor. "It's a little stronger than you're used to. Now you'll see how good it is with a shot of rum."

He took out a bottle and three tumblers from a tin box under the table. The blue serpent filled two tumblers and passed one to Felipe. The sailor sat next to him, on the same bench, and raised the tumbler.

"Here's to you, kid. Don't drink it all at once."

"Hm, it's very good," said Felipe. "It must be rum from the Antilles."

"Sure is. So now you like my rum and tobacco, eh? And what's your name, kid?"

"Trejo."

"Trejo, eh. But that's not your first name, that's your last name."

"Naturally, it's my last name. My first name is Felipe."

"Felipe. That's good. How old are you, kid?"

"Eighteen," Felipe lied, hiding his mouth in the tumbler. "And what's your name?"

"Bob," said the sailor. "You can call me Bob even though I actually have another one, but I don't like it."

"Tell me anyway. I told you my real name."

"Oh, it'll sound ugly to you, too. Imagine something like Radcliffe, you wouldn't like it, would you? Bob's better, kid. Here's to you."

"*Prosit*," said Felipe, and they drank again. "Hm, it's nice here."

"Of course it is."

"A lot of work on board?"

"So-so. It'd be better if you didn't drink any more, kid."

"Why?" asked Felipe, bristling. "Great, just when I'm beginning to like it. This rum and tobacco are terrific . . . Why shouldn't I drink any more?"

The sailor took the tumbler away and left it on the table.

"You're very nice, kid, but then you'll have to go back up alone, and if you drink all that, they're going to guess something."

"But I can drink anything I want at the bar."

"Hm . . . with the bartender they have up there, anything you drink won't be too strong," mocked Bob. "And your mama must have her eye peeled besides . . ." he said. He seemed to enjoy watching Felipe's eyes and the sudden blush on his face. "Go on, kid, we're friends, Bob and Felipe are buddies."

"O.K.," Felipe said sullenly. "And that door."

"Forget that door," said the sailor, gently, "and don't get sore, Felipe. When can you come back?"

"Why should I come back?"

"Kid, to drink rum and smoke with me and talk," Bob said. "In my cabin, where no one will bother us. Orf can walk in here any minute."

"Where's your cabin?" asked Felipe, half-closing his eyes.

"There," said Bob, pointing to the forbidden door. "There's a passageway that goes to my cabin, just before the hatchway to the poop."

XXIX

The sound of the dinner gong reverberated while Medrano was in the middle of Miguel Angel Asturias. He shut the book and stretched out on the bed, wondering if he really felt like eating supper. The soft light from the headboard was inviting, and he thought of staying in to read; besides, he liked *Hombres de maíz*. In a certain sense reading was a way of temporarily putting aside all the novelty of his surroundings and getting back to the order of his Buenos Aires apartment, where he had begun the book. Yes, like a house that he carried with him, but he did not like the idea of taking refuge in a story to forget the absurdity of having a Smith and Wesson .38 in a dresser drawer, within arm's reach. The revolver was a symbol of everything: the *Malcolm* and its passengers, and all the hazy frustrations of the day. The pleasure of being gently rocked, the masculine and minute convenience of the cabin, were more allied to the virtues of the book. It would have taken something completely unexpected, like hearing a horse galloping through the corridor or smelling incense, to make him jump out of bed and face the events around him. "I'm too comfortable here to budge," he thought, remembering the faces of Lopez and Raul after they had returned from the ineffectual evening expedition. Perhaps Lucio was right, maybe it was ridiculous to start playing detective. But Lucio's reasons were suspect; at the moment the only thing that mattered to him was his woman. And this cheap mystery and scaffolding of lies that surrounded them was just as irritating to Lopez and Raul as it was to him. More irritating yet was to think, whenever he pulled himself away from the open page, that if they hadn't been so comfortable on board they would have put more into it, pressuring the situation until their doubts were cleared up. The delights of Capua, etcetera. More austere delights, of course, in Nordic tonality, modulating in scale from cedar to ash. Lopez and Raul would probably propose a new plan, or even he would, if it was boring at the bar, but everything they did would be more of a game than any real act of recovery. Perhaps the only wise move would be to imitate Persio and Jorge, to play chess and pass the time as well as possible. The poop deck, bah! First and foremost, the poop. Even the word sounded like a mush for infants. The poop, what idiocy!

He chose a dark suit and a tie that Bettina had given him. He had thought of Bettina a couple of times while reading *Hombres de maíz*, because she didn't care for Asturias' poetic style, the alliteration and the resulting magical quality. But until this moment he hadn't been even slightly preoccupied with what had happened with Bettina. He was enjoying himself too much with the events of the embarkation and the small-scale setback to think of the immediate past. Nothing better than the *Malcolm* and the people on it, hurrah for the poop-mush soup (a poor man's Asturias, he burst into laughter thinking of rhymes): bloop and croup. Buenos Aires would have to wait, there would be time enough to think of Bettina—if it came on its own, if he decided to think of it as a problem. But yes, it was a problem; he would have to analyze it, and in the way he liked to analyze problems, in bed at night, his hands behind his head. At any rate, this uneasiness (Asturias or eating; eating, tie, Bettina's gift, ergo Bettina, ergo annoyance) was growing like an anticipated conclusion of the analysis. Unless it was only the ship's roll or the tobacco-filled air of the cabin. It wasn't the first time he had left a woman in the lurch, and a woman had left him once, too (to marry a Brazilian). Ridiculous that Bettina and the poop deck were a bit of the same thing at the moment. He would ask Claudia what she thought of his attitude. But no, why did he have to think of Claudia's arbitration in terms of obligation? Of course, he didn't have any reason at all to talk to Claudia about Bettina. Trip talk comes and goes, but nothing more. The poop and Bettina; it was really stupid that all this was just a painful point in the pit of his stomach now. Stupid, especially for Bettina, who was probably getting herself invited to the Embassy Club already, God forbid that she should miss a night. Yes, but she must have cried, too.

Medrano tightened his tie with one stroke. The knot didn't come out right; this tie had always been rebellious. The psychology of ties. He remembered a novel in which a crazed valet madly cut up his master's entire tie collection with a pair of scissors. The room was littered with pieces of ties, a butcher shop of ties on the floor. He picked out another, a modest grey, which agreed to a perfect knot. Of course she must have cried, all women cry, and for much less than that. He imagined her opening the dresser drawers, taking out photographs, complaining to her friends on the telephone. This was all fated; it had to happen. Claudia must have done the same thing after separating from Lewbaum, Claudia and all other women. He kept repeating: "All of them, all of them," as if he wanted to lump the diversity of experiences into one miserable episode in Buenos Aires, a mere drop of water in the ocean. "But after all is said and done, it's cowardice," he heard himself think, and he did not know if the cowardice was the drop of water in the ocean or the bare fact of having left Bettina in the lurch. A little more or a little less weeping in this world . . . Yes, but to be the cause, even though none of this was important, and Bettina would be window-shopping on Santa Fe or having her hair done at Chez Marcelle. What did Bettina matter to him, it wasn't Bettina, it wasn't Bettina herself and it wasn't not being able to go to the poop, and it wasn't typhus 224. In spite of everything, he had this pain in the pit of his stomach, though when he opened the door he was smiling, and once in the corridor he ran his hand through his hair, still smiling, as if he were making an agreeable discovery: as if he were on the brink of discovery, almost seeing what he was searching for, and feeling the pleasure of having accomplished all his goals. He promised himself to retrace his steps, to dedicate the beginning of the evening to thinking things through more slowly, more calmly. Perhaps it wasn't Bettina but rather that Claudia had talked so much about herself, she had spoken about herself in her serious voice, of how she was still in love with Leon Lewbaum. But he'd be damned if that mattered to him, even if Claudia also cried in the night thinking of Leon.

Raul left Pelusa explaining to Dr. Restelli why the Boca Juniors team had to take the championship and went to his cabin to dress for dinner. He thought cheerfully of the various getups they'd see in the dining room that evening; probably poor Atilio would show up in shirtsleeves and the *maître* would look both satisfied and scandalized, typical of servants when they watch their masters disgrace themselves. He was seized with a desire to return and get back into the conversation. Hardly able to cut short the sporting enthusiasm of Pelusa (who had found Dr. Restelli a prudent fellow, but a hot defender of the merits of the Western Railway team), Raul casually mentioned that it was time to dress for dinner.

"Actually, it's too hot to have to dress," he said, "but we'll respect the tradition of the sea."

"What do you mean get dressed?" said Pelusa, disconcerted.

"I mean to put on an uncomfortable tie and jacket," said Raul. "We do it for the ladies, of course."

He left Pelusa delivered over to his thoughts and climbed the little staircase. He was not quite sure he had done the right thing, since he had a tendency to doubt the justification of almost all his acts lately. If Atilio preferred to appear in the dining room with a striped shirt on, that was his affair; in any case, the *maître* or some passenger would end up by letting him know that it was incorrect, and the poor fellow would have a worse time of it, unless he told them off. "I act only out of aesthetic reasons," thought Raul, amused again, "and I try to justify them from the social point of view. The only thing certain is that I'm exasperated by anything out of step, out of kilter. That poor man's shirt would ruin my *potage Hublet aux asperges*. The lighting in the dining room is bad enough already . . ." With his hand on the knob, he looked toward the entrance of the corridor which connected the two passageways. Felipe stopped suddenly, losing his balance a bit. He seemed very confused, as if he didn't recognize Raul.

"Hello," said Raul. "I haven't seen you all afternoon."

"It's that . . . How dumb of me, I took the wrong turn. My

cabin is on the other side," said Felipe, as he started to turn around. The light fell full on his face.

"You look like you've had too much sun," said Raul.

"Naw, it's nothing," said Felipe, adopting a sullen tone of voice that was only half effective. "I spend all my afternoons in the pool at the club."

"But the air in your club isn't as strong as it is here. Do you feel all right?"

Raul came up to Felipe and looked at him in a friendly fashion. "Why don't you stop fucking around with me?" thought Felipe, but at the same time he was flattered that Raul was talking to him again in that tone, after the dirty trick he had played. He answered with a nod and finally turned toward the corridor, but Raul didn't want to let it go at that.

"You probably didn't bring anything for a burn, unless your mother . . . Come with me a minute, I'll give you something to put on before you go to bed."

"Don't bother," said Felipe, leaning his shoulder on the partition. "I think Beba has some kind of junk with her."

"Take it anyway," Raul insisted, stepping back to open the door of his cabin. Paula wasn't there but she had left the lights on. "Besides, I have something else for you. Come on in a second."

Felipe seemed determined to stay in the doorway. Raul, who was going through his overnight case, motioned him to come in. Suddenly, he realized he didn't know how to get him over the puppy-dog hostility. "I'm the one who sought him out, like an imbecile," he thought, shuffling through the drawer full of socks and handkerchiefs. "But how badly he's taken it, my God." Straightening up, he repeated the motion to come in. Felipe took two steps, and only then did Raul realize that he was staggering a little.

"I didn't think you were feeling well," he said, pulling up a chair for him. He pushed the door closed with his foot, and then he took two or three deep breaths and burst into laughter.

"Bottled sun, then. And I thought you had sunstroke . . . But what kind of tobacco is that? You smell frightfully of tobacco and alcohol."

"So what?" Felipe murmured, fighting a rising nausea. "If I take a drink and smoke . . . I don't see that . . ."

"Of course," said Raul. "I didn't have the slightest intention of bawling you out. But the combination of sun and the other stuff is a little explosive, you know. I could tell you . . ."

But he didn't feel like telling him; he preferred looking at Felipe, who was turning a little pale and staring intently in the direction of the porthole. They remained silent for a moment which, to Raul, seemed long and perfect, and to Felipe, a whirlwind of red and blue points dancing before his eyes.

"Take this salve," Raul finally said, putting a tube in his hand. "Your shoulders must be burning."

Felipe instinctively opened his shirt and looked at himself. His nausea was subsiding, and a malicious pleasure was rising in its place, the pleasure of keeping quiet, of not talking about Bob, of the meeting with Bob and the glass of rum. Only he would get the credit for . . . It seemed that Raul's mouth was trembling a little; he looked at him, surprised. Raul straightened up and smiled.

"You'll sleep without any irritation if you use this. And take that too; a thing promised is a thing due."

Felipe took the pipe with an uncertain hand. He had never seen such a beautiful pipe. Raul, his back to him, was taking something out of a jacket pocket hanging in the wardrobe.

"English tobacco," he said, giving him a bright-colored box. "I don't know if I have any extra pipe cleaners, but in the meantime you can use mine when the pipe's dirty. Do you like it?"

"Yes, of course," said Felipe, looking respectfully at the pipe. "You didn't have to give me this. It's too good a pipe."

"That's exactly why I'm giving it to you," said Raul. "And so you'll forgive me."

"You . . ."

"Look, I don't know why I did that. You suddenly seemed too much of a kid to get involved in a possible row. After I thought about it, I was sorry. Forgive me, and let's be friends, do you want to?"

The nausea was returning little by little, a cold sweat was breaking out on Felipe's forehead. He managed to put the pipe and tobacco away in his pocket and then stood up with difficulty, swaying back and forth. Raul stood next to him and stretched out his arm to hold him up.

"I . . . I'd like to go to the bathroom for a minute," Felipe murmured.

"Of course, why not," said Raul, opening the door hurriedly. He closed it again and paced around the cabin. He heard the water running in the sink. Raul went to the bathroom door and rested his hand on the knob. "Poor kid, maybe he'll fall and hit himself," he thought, but he was lying and he bit his lips. If he opened the door, he would see him . . . Perhaps Felipe might never forgive him that humiliation, unless . . . "Not yet, not yet." And Felipe would be vomiting in the sink—no, actually it was better to leave him alone. And if he lost consciousness and fell? But he wasn't going to fall, it was practically monotonous lying to himself like this, looking for pretexts. "He liked the pipe so much," he told himself, pacing again in a circle. "But now he's going to be ashamed for having locked himself in my bathroom . . . And as usual, the shame will be ferocious, he'll rip me up from top to bottom, unless the pipe, perhaps, yes, maybe the pipe . . ."

Buenos Aires was indicated by a red dot, and from there a blue line descended almost parallel to the curve of the province, some distance from the coast. As the passengers came into the dining room they could follow the tedious exactitude of the map decorated with the insignia of Magenta Star, and the route covered that day by the *Malcolm*. The bartender admitted, smiling discreetly, that the author of the progressive itinerary was none other than himself.

"And who gives you the data?" Don Galo asked.

"The pilot sends it down to me," the bartender explained. "I was a draftsman when I was young. I like to fool around with a drawing triangle and compass in my spare time."

Don Galo signaled the chauffeur to leave and take the wheelchair with him, and watched the bartender out of the corner of his eye.

"How's the typhus coming?" he asked.

The bartender blinked, but just then the impeccable silhouette of the *maître* appeared at his side. His *aperitif* smile fell on all the diners, one after the other.

"It seems that everything is going along fine, Señor Porriño,"

said the *maître*. "At least I haven't received any alarming news. Go
back to the bar," he said to his subordinate, who was displaying a
tendency to linger in the dining room. "Let's see now, Señor Porriño, would you like a *potage champenois* to begin? It's excellent."

Señor Trejo and his wife made their appearance at this moment,
followed by Beba, wearing a dress she wished were cut lower. Raul
came in behind them and went to sit down with Paula and Lopez, who lifted their heads at the same time and smiled abstractedly. The Trejos scarcely glanced at the menu, but instead discussed Felipe's sudden and unexpected illness. Señora Trejo was
very thankful that Señor Costa had bothered to look after Felipe
and to accompany him as far as his cabin, calling Beba on the way
so that she might let Papa and Mama know about it. Felipe was
sleeping deeply now, but Señora Trejo was still concerned about
the cause of this sudden malaise.

"Too much sun, my dear," Señor Trejo assured her. "He spent
the afternoon on deck and now he looks like a lobster. You didn't
see him, but when he took off his shirt . . . Just as well that
young fellow brought some salve along; it seems to do wonders."

"What you forget is that he smelled of whisky a mile away," said
Beba, reading the menu. "He does anything he feels like on this
ship."

"Whisky? Impossible," said Señor Trejo. "He could have had a
beer, that's possible."

"You'll have to speak to the man who serves the drinks," said
his wife. "He shouldn't be given anything but lemonade or things
like that. He's still too much of a child to handle himself alone."

"If you think you're going to straighten him out, you've got
another think coming," said Beba. "It's already too late. Strict rules
for me, but for him—"

"Don't you start."

"You see? What did I tell you? If I accepted an expensive gift
from some passenger, what would you say? I can hear you now
screaming to high heaven. But *he* can do whatever he feels like, of
course. Always the same thing. Why wasn't I born a boy . . ."

"Gifts?" said Señor Trejo. "What's this about gifts?"

"Nothing," said Beba.

"Speak up, speak up. Now that you've begun, finish. Actually,

Osvaldo, I wanted you to talk to Felipe. That girl there—the one in the bikini, you know."

"Bikini?" said Señor Trejo. "Ah, the redhead. Yes, that girl."

"The girl that spent the afternoon making eyes at our boy, and if you didn't see it, I did, I'm his mother and I have a sure instinct about these things. Don't you get involved, Beba, you're too young to know what we're talking about. Oh, these children, what sacrifice."

"Making eyes at Felipe?" asked Beba. "Don't make me laugh, Mama. Do you really think that woman is going to waste her time with a baby?" ("If he could only hear me now," thought Beba. "He'd blow his stack.")

"What's this about a present, then?" said Señor Trejo, suddenly interested.

"A pipe, a can of tobacco, and I don't know what else," said Beba indifferently. "I'm sure they're worth a lot of money."

The Trejos exchanged glances, and then Señor Trejo looked over in the direction of table number two. Beba was watching them slyly.

"That man is really quite nice," said Señora Trejo. "You ought to thank him, Osvaldo, and in passing tell him that our boy shouldn't be spoiled. It's obvious that seeing Felipe sick like that worried him, poor fellow."

Señor Trejo said nothing but thought about mothers' instincts. Beba, still peevish, figured that now Felipe would have to return the gifts. *Langue jardinière*, which was then served, took them by surprise in the middle of their deliberations.

The Presutti group made their resolute and timorous appearance, waving to various tables, checking the mirror out of the corners of their eyes, with Doña Pepa and Doña Rosita whispering together excitedly. Paula felt like laughing and she looked at Raul with an expression which reminded him of evenings in the lobbies of Buenos Aires theaters, or in suburban living rooms, where they went to amuse themselves maliciously at the expense of poetesses and pompous businessmen. He was expecting one of those remarks at which Paula excelled, a remark which synthesized the situation, pinning it down like a butterfly. But Paula said nothing because she had just felt Lopez' eyes on her, and suddenly the desire to make the wisecrack already on the tip of her tongue evaporated. There was neither sadness nor anxiety in Lopez' look, but rather a placid contemplation, in the face of which Paula felt slowly drawn back into herself, back to what was less spectacular, less superficial in herself. After all, she told herself ironically, the Paula of the epigrams was also she, and the perverse or simply malicious Paula could also be thrown into the bargain; but Lopez' eyes settled on her in their least complicated manner, under which sophism and frivolity turned into something forced. Going from Lopez to Raul, to Raul's sensitive and intelligent face, was jumping from today to yesterday, from the temptation to be frank to that of indulging one more time in the flashy lie of appearances. But if she did not conquer the kind of friendly censureship that Lopez' look was beginning to mean to her (and the poor guy didn't have the vaguest idea that he was playing this role), the trip would turn into a meaningless nightmare. She liked Lopez, she was glad that his name was Carlos, that the contact of his hand on hers did not displease her. He did not interest her too much, was probably a typical Argentine like so many of her other male friends, more cultivated than cultured, more enthusiastic than passionate. There was something clean about him which bored her a little. A cleanliness which immediately destroyed any verbal treachery, any desire of hers to describe in detail Atilio's fiancée's toilette, or the brick-red jacket Atilio wore. Not that Lopez' presence prevented frivolous remarks on the rest of the passengers; he too was smiling and looking over at Doña Pepa's plastic necklace and at Atilio's efforts to make his spoon coincide with his mouth. But behind his smile was a purity of intention, which turned his enjoyment into something quite different. Jokes were only worth something for themselves, and were not to be used as double-edged weapons. Yes, it was going to be terribly boring unless Raul hurled himself into a counterattack, which would re-establish the balance. Paula was well aware that Raul would immediately sense what was in the atmosphere, and probably fly into a rage. He had already rescued her once from a most ominous influence (a theosophist who could be a very good lover at the same time). Armed with an immodest insolence, he had managed to undo in a matter of a few months the fragile and esoteric scaffolding by which Paula thought she would climb to heaven like a shaman. Poor Raul, he would begin by feeling pangs of jealousy, which would have nothing to do with jealousy, but merely ordinary spite at not being master of her intelligence and her time, at not being able to share each moment of the trip in the same exigent spirit of communion, the same coincidence of taste that they shared. Although Raul let himself be dragged into any kind of adventure, he would, just the same, be at Paula's side demanding his cut of attention. His jealousy would be more disillusion than anything else, and in the end it would disappear because he knew that Paula would once again return (but would she return this time?), a nostalgic story on her lips, and with the face of return, deposit the weight of her current boredom and disappointment in his lap, so that again he could take care of his capricious and spoiled cat. That's how it had happened after she had made love with Rubio, after she had broken with Lucho Neira, and with all the others. A perfect symmetry ruled her relations with Raul because he, also, passed through confessional phases; he brought back his black cat after his sad adventures in the suburbs and on the terraces, and together they healed their wounds with the resurgence of comradeship from college days. How much they needed one another, and what a bitter fabric was this friendship woven of, a friendship exposed to a double wind, an alternating fugue. What did Carlos Lopez have to do with this table, with this ship, with this placid habit of walking everywhere together? Paula began to detest him violently, while he, happy just looking at her, so very happy, was like an innocent walking smilingly into a cage of tigers. But he was not innocent, Paula knew it only too well, and if he was (but he wasn't), he'd just have to stand for it, tiger Raul, tiger Paula. "Poor Jamaica John," she thought, "if you could only escape in time . . ."

"What happened to Jorge?"

"He's running a little fever," Claudia said. "I suppose he sat in the sun too long this afternoon, unless it's his tonsils. I've persuaded him to stay in bed and I've given him an aspirin. We'll see what kind of night he has."

"Aspirin is terrible," said Persio. "I've taken it two or three times and it had a deadly effect on me. It completely upsets the intellectual order and then the sweating starts. All in all, it's very disagreeable."

Medrano, who had eaten without much enthusiasm, suggested a second cup of coffee at the bar, and Persio went off to the deck, where he had to make stellar observations, promising to first stop in the cabin to see if Jorge had fallen asleep. The lighting in the bar was pleasanter than in the dining room, and the coffee was hotter. Once or twice Medrano asked himself if Claudia was concealing the anxiety she must be feeling over Jorge's fever. He would have liked to know, to help her later in any way he could, but Claudia did not go back to the subject of her son and they talked of other things. Persio returned.

"He's awake and he'd like you to go see him," he said. "It's probably the aspirin."

"Don't be silly. Go study the Pleiades and Ursa Minor. Would you like to come with me, Medrano? Jorge would like to see you."

"Yes, of course," said Medrano, feeling happy for the first time in hours.

Jorge received them sitting up in bed, a notebook of drawings on his lap, which Medrano had to examine and comment on, one by one. His eyes were shining, but his hot skin was largely the result of the sun he had had on the deck. He wanted to know if Medrano was married and if he had children, where he lived, if he was also a teacher like Lopez or an architect like Raul. He said he had slept for a moment but had a nightmare about the glucids. Yes, he was a little sleepy, and thirsty. Claudia gave him something to drink and arranged a paper shade over the light at the headboard.

"We'll sit here in the armchairs until you fall asleep. We're not going to leave you alone."

"Oh, I'm not scared," said Jorge. "But when I sleep, I can't defend myself, you know."

"Hit the glucids hard," Medrano suggested, bending over and kissing him on the forehead. "Tomorrow we'll talk about a whole pile of things. Now sleep."

Three minutes later Jorge stretched, sighed, and turned toward the wall. Claudia switched off the light at the head of the bed and only the one next to the door remained on.

"He'll sleep like a dormouse all night. In a while he'll start to talk, he says all kinds of strange things . . . Persio loves to hear him talk in his sleep and immediately draws all sorts of extraordinary conclusions."

"Of course, Persio, priest and seer," Medrano said. "You've noticed the change in people's voices when they talk in their sleep? It's hard to imagine that they're the same ones talking . . ."

"They are and they aren't."

"Mmm . . . Years ago I slept in the same room as my older brother, one of the dullest people you could imagine. He hardly closed his eyes before he began to talk; sometimes, not always, he'd say such incredible things that I'd write them down and show them to him the next morning. He never believed me, poor guy. It was too much for him."

"Why frighten him with a mirror he didn't expect?"

"You're right. You'd have to be as simple and direct as a dowser or situated firmly on the opposite pole to accept that. We're so afraid of breakthroughs or invasions of the unconscious, of losing the precious day-after-day identity . . ."

Claudia was listening to Jorge's breathing, which was growing calmer and more steady. Medrano's voice restored her peace of mind. She felt a little weak, and half-closed her eyes with relief and fatigue. She hadn't wanted to admit that Jorge's fever was worrying her, that through habit she had concealed her worry, maybe through pride, too. No, what Jorge had was nothing, it had nothing to do with the poop deck. It seemed ridiculous to imagine any relationship; it was all fine; the smell of Medrano's tobacco was the essence of order, of normality; and his voice, his quiet and somewhat sad way of saying things, was peace itself.

"Let's be charitable when we talk about the I," said Claudia, breathing deeply, as if escaping her latest imaginings. "It's too precarious, too fragile—if one thinks about it objectively—not to wrap it in cotton. Doesn't it amaze you that your heart goes on beating during every passing minute? It never fails to astonish me. I know that the heart isn't I, but if it should stop . . . In short, it would be better if we didn't get onto transcendent subjects; I've never had the luck to have a worthwhile conversation on such matters.

Better to stay on the side of the simple life, it's amazing enough in itself."

"Yes, let's be methodical," said Medrano, smiling. "Besides, we couldn't set up the final questions without first knowing a little more about ourselves. Honestly, Claudia, right now my only interest is biographical, the first stage of a solid friendship. I'd like to be clear, I'm not asking you to tell me the details of your life, but I'd like to listen to you talk about your tastes, Jorge, Buenos Aires, I don't know what else."

"No, not tonight," said Claudia. "I've already bored you enough this afternoon with sentimental details which are probably irrelevant. I'm the one who knows nothing about you, apart from the fact that you're a dentist and that one of these days I intend to ask you to look at one of Jorge's molars that hurts him sometimes. I like your laughing at that, another person would be indignant over such a worldly parenthesis, secretly, at least. Is it true that your name is Gabriel?"

"Yes."

"Did you always like it? Your name. As a boy, I mean?"

"I don't remember. I probably thought of the name Gabriel as something fated, like a cowlick, something I did have on the back of my head. Where did you spend your childhood?"

"In Buenos Aires, in a house in Palermo where frogs sang at night and where my uncle set off marvelous fireworks at Christmas."

"And I in Lomas de Zamora, a chalet in an enormous garden. I must be some kind of imbecile, because childhood still seems to be the most profound part of my life. I was too happy as a child, I'm afraid. It's a bad beginning for life; as soon as you put on long pants, the evil eye is on you. Would you like to hear my *curriculum vitae*? We'll stop at adolescence, as all adolescences seem too much alike to be terribly interesting. I became a dentist without knowing why, too frequent a case in our country, I'm afraid. Jorge's saying something. No, he's only sighing. Perhaps my talking is bothering him. My voice must be strange to him."

"He likes your voice," said Claudia. "Jorge doesn't take long to tell me these kinds of things. He doesn't like Raul Costa's voice and he makes fun of Persio's, which actually does sound something like

a parrot's. But he likes Lopez' voice and yours, and he says Paula
has pretty hands. He looks at hands, too, a good deal; his description of Presutti's hands made me laugh until I cried. Then you
studied dentistry, poor thing."

"Yes, and besides, a while ago I lost the house of my childhood,
which still exists, but which I didn't want to ever see again. I have
that kind of sentimentality; I'd walk ten blocks out of my way not
to pass under the balconies of an apartment where I was happy
once. I don't run away from memory, but I don't cultivate it either; besides, my misfortunes, like my good luck, have always been
low pressure."

"Yes, occasionally you have the look of . . . I'm not gifted
with a sixth sense, but sometimes my intuitions are sharp."

"And what's your intuition?"

"Nothing too important, Gabriel. That you go around in circles
a bit, looking for something that doesn't appear. I hope it's not
only a shirt button."

"Neither is it the Tao, dear Claudia. Something very modest and
very selfish: a kind of happiness that will give the least possible
hurt to others, a difficult enough requirement, which doesn't make
me feel either bought or sold, and which allows me to keep my
freedom. You see, it's not too easy."

"Yes, people like us almost always represent happiness in those
terms. Marriage without slavery, for instance, or living with someone openly without debasement, or a job which doesn't prevent us
from reading Chestov, or children who don't turn us into maids.
Very likely the simple posing of this problem is mean and false
from the beginning. Just read the Bible . . . But we've agreed not
to overstep our boundaries. Fair play above all."

"Perhaps," said Medrano, "the mistake is in not wanting to overstep our boundaries. Maybe it's the surest way of falling flat even
from the everyday, social point of view. Well, I chose to live alone
very early. I went out to the provinces. Life wasn't easy, but in
that way I didn't succumb to the scattering from which the man
from Buenos Aires usually suffers, and one fine day I returned to
the city, from which I haven't budged. Apart from the standard
trip to Europe, and the vacations in Viña del Mar when the Chil-
ean peso was still cheap . . . My father left me a bigger inherit-

ance than either my brother or I had thought possible; I was able
to reduce my practice to the minimum and I became an *aficionado,*
a fan. Don't ask me of what, that would be too hard to answer.
Let's say football, for instance, Italian literature, kaleidoscopes,
women of easy virtue."

"You put them at the end of the list, but maybe you keep them
in alphabetical order. Explain what you mean by women of easy
virtue now Jorge's sleeping."

"I mean that I've never had a fiancée," said Medrano. "I think
I'd be lousy as a husband, and I've got enough decency not to
want to test it out. And I'm not what women refer to as a seducer.
I like women who don't present any problem other than themselves, which is quite enough."

"You don't like to take responsibility?"

"I don't think so. Perhaps I have too high-flown an idea of responsibility. So fancy I have to run away from it. A fiancée, a se-
duced girl . . . Everything becomes pure future, suddenly it's necessary to live for and through the future. Do you think the future
can enrich the present? In marriage perhaps, or when one feels a
sense of paternity . . . It's strange, considering how much I like
children," Medrano murmured, looking at Jorge's head buried in
the pillows.

"Don't think you're an exception," said Claudia. "In any case,
you're heading rapidly toward that human product classified as a
bachelor. That also has its merits. A certain actress used to say that
bachelors were the best box-office material, real benefactors of art.
No, I'm not joking. But you think you're more cowardly than you
really are."

"Who said anything about being a coward?"

"Well, your rejection of all possibility of engagement or seduction, of all responsibility, of all future . . . That question you
asked me a minute ago . . . I think the only future that can enrich
the present is one that rises from a present that one can face up to.
Naturally, I don't think anyone should work thirty years like a
mule in order to retire and live in peace afterwards, but on the
other hand, it seems to me, any momentary cowardice will not
only *not* deliver you from an unpleasant future, but will only help

create it, in spite of yourself. Coming from me this might seem a
little cynical, but if you don't seduce the girl only because you fear
the consequences, your refusal only helps create another void in
the future, a future phantasm, efficient enough to bring any adventure to an untimely end."

"You're thinking of me, but not of the girl."

"I guess so, but I'm not trying to talk you into becoming a Casa-
nova. I suppose a certain firmness is necessary to resist the temptation of seduction; and moral cowardice in that case would become
a source of positive values . . . Now that's a laugh."

"The problem's not valid; there's neither cowardice nor courage,
but just the preliminary decision which eliminates most opportunities. A seducer looks to seduce, and then he seduces. If you
eliminate the search . . . To put it bluntly, it's easy enough to
avoid the virgins; and there're very few of them in the social milieu
I frequent . . ."

"If those poor girls were aware of the metaphysical conflicts
they're capable of creating with their innocence alone," said Claudia. "Well, tell me about the others, then."

"No, not like that," said Medrano. "I don't like the way you ask
me or your tone of voice. Nor do I like what I've been saying, and
even less, what you've said. Be better if I go back to the bar and
have a brandy."

"No, wait a minute. I know that I speak foolishly sometimes.
But we can always discuss something else."

"Excuse me," said Medrano. "It wasn't foolish, quite the contrary. My bad temper derives precisely from the fact that it wasn't
foolish talk. You treated me like a coward, on a moral level, and
you're perfectly right. I'm beginning to wonder if love and responsibility don't come to the same thing at some point in our lives, at
some very special point on the road . . . I still don't see it very
clearly, but for a long time . . . Yes, I'm in a bad mood, especially
because of all that. I never would've believed that one event, and a
frequent enough one in my life, would begin to bother me . . .
Like canker sores on your gums, and each time your tongue runs
over them there's a very unpleasant sensation . . . And this is
like a mental canker sore, it comes back again and again . . ." He

shrugged his shoulders and took out his cigarettes. "I'll tell you what it is, Claudia, because . . . I think I'll feel better if I do."

He told her about Bettina.

XXX

Her anger subsided during the course of dinner and was replaced by irony and an urge to make fun of him. Not that she had any particular reason to make fun of him, but that he could disarm her this way, even in the way he looked at her, continued to bother her. For a minute she had been tempted to believe that Lopez was an innocent, that his strength derived precisely from his innocence. Then she mocked her own ingenuousness; it wasn't hard to see that Lopez was equipped with all the prerequisites for hunting big game, even though he didn't make a great point of his equipment. Paula was not flattered by the immediate effect she had produced on Lopez; quite the contrary (what the hell, they hadn't even known one another the day before, two strangers in an enormous Buenos Aires), she was annoyed to see herself reduced so quickly to the traditional state of royal prey. "And all because I'm really the only available, interesting woman on board," she thought. "He probably wouldn't even have noticed me if we'd been introduced at a party or at the theater." It was exasperating to feel automatically incorporated into a series of voyage amusements. They were nailing her to the wall like a cardboard target game, so that Mr. Hunter might have some target practice. But Jamaica John was so appealing, she really couldn't feel irritated with him. She wondered if he were thinking something like this. She knew very well that he could take her for a flirt, first, because she was one, and secondly, because she had a way of being, of acting, which was easily misunderstood. As a good Argentine, poor Lopez might be thinking that he would make a bad show if he didn't do everything possible to make her. An idiotic situation, but with something fated about it, a situation set up with Guignol marionettes, who were forced to give and take the ritual blows of the cudgels. She felt a little sorry for Lopez, as well as for herself, and at the same time she was glad that she wasn't kidding herself. Both of them could play that game to perfection, and God hope that Punch was as skillful as Judy.

At the bar, where Raul had invited them for a gin, they managed to get past the Presuttis who were squeezed into one corner, but found themselves directly in front of Nora and Lucio, who had not eaten supper and seemed worried. The inevitable arrangement of chairs and tables brought them all together, and they spoke a little about everything, each gladly abandoning his personality to the comfortable monstrosity of collective conversation, always somewhat beneath the total of those who compose it, and for that reason restful and welcome. Lucio was relieved by the appearance of the others, because Nora had become depressed after writing a letter to her sister. Although she said it was nothing, she immediately fell into an abstracted state that exasperated him somewhat, since he could find no way of avoiding it. He had never spoken so much with Nora, it was she who usually made the conversation; actually, their tastes were quite different, but that, between a man and a woman . . . In any case, it was a mess and Nora was becoming despondent over nonsense. Maybe it was a good idea for her to enjoy herself with the others for a while.

Paula had scarcely spoken with Nora until now, and both of them smilingly crossed their weapons while the men ordered drinks and passed cigarettes around. Sheltered in a silence broken only by an occasional friendly comment, Raul studied them, and at the same time he exchanged impressions with Lucio about the map and itinerary of the *Malcolm*. He saw joy and confidence born again in Nora; the social monster caressed her with its many tongues, pulled her out of the mere dialogue, this disguised monologue, brought her into a small world, both polite and trivial, sparkling with clever phrases and meaningless laughter, and filled with the aroma of chartreuse and Philip Morris. "A real beauty treatment," thought Raul, as he watched Nora's features take on a glow that made them lovely. Lucio was more difficult; he continued to look a bit recalcitrant, absorbed in himself. And as for Lopez, poor Lopez! He was dreaming out loud, poor fellow. Raul began to feel sorry for him. "So soon," he thought, "so soon . . ."

But perhaps he didn't know that Lopez was happy and that he was dreaming of pink elephants, of enormous glass globes filled with colored water.

"And thus it happened that the three musketeers, who weren't four this time, went to the rear deck and returned shorn of their fleece," said Paula. "Whenever you want, Nora, we two can take a walk around, and we can even take along Presutti's fiancée in order to make our party a sacred number. I'm sure we'll get as far as the propellers."

"We'll catch typhus," said Nora, who tended to take Paula seriously.

"Oh, I have some Vicks Vaporub," Paula said. "Who would have thought that these gallant hoplites would bite the dust like ordinary cowards?"

"Don't exaggerate," said Raul. "The ship is very clean and there's nothing to bite at the moment."

He wondered if Paula would keep her word or if she was going to mention the revolvers and pistol now. No, she wouldn't say anything. Good girl. Completely mad but absolutely straight. Nora, a bit surprised, was asking for some details of the expedition. Lopez watched Lucio out of the corner of his eye.

"Bah, I didn't tell you because it wasn't worth the bother," Lucio said. "You heard what Miss Lavalle said. Just a waste of time."

"I'm not sure we wasted our time," said Lopez. "Any reconnaisance has some value, as a famous strategist must have already said. And as far as I'm concerned, the expedition has been useful even if it only convinced me that there's something rotten about the Magenta Star Lines. Nothing fierce, of course, it's not that they have a cargo of gorillas on the poop deck; more like a too-visible kind of contraband or something along those lines."

"That's possible, but actually it's not a matter that concerns us," said Lucio. "Everything's all right on this side."

"Apparently, yes."

"Why apparently? It's perfectly clear."

"Lopez, very wisely, doubts any excessive clarity," said Raul. "As the Bengal poet of Santiniketan said, there's nothing like excessive clarity to render one blind."

"Well, those are just poetic phrases."

"That's why I quote it, and I even have the modesty to attribute it to a poet who has never said any such thing. But getting back to Lopez, I share his uneasiness, and so does Medrano. If something's not right on the rear deck, the prow will become contaminated sooner or later. Call it typhus 224 or a ton of marijuana; from here to Japan there's a long salty route, dear friends, and many voracious fish under the keel."

"Brr . . . don't make me shiver!" said Paula. "Look at Nora, poor dear, you've really frightened her."

"I don't know if you're joking," said Nora, flashing a look of surprise at Lucio, "but you told me . . ."

"And what did you want me to tell you, that Dracula was prowling loose on the ship?" Lucio protested. "Everyone's exaggerating here, and it might be fun as a pastime, but it's hardly necessary to make people think that all this talk is serious."

"As far as I'm concerned," said Lopez, "I'm absolutely serious, and I don't intend to sit back and fold my arms."

Paula applauded mockingly.

"Jamaica John, no less! I didn't expect less of you, but really this heroism . . ."

"Don't be a fool," Lopez said bluntly. "And give me a cigarette; I'm out of mine."

Raul feigned a gesture of admiration. Oh, brother. No, this was going to be good. He began to watch Lucio, who was trying to regain lost territory, and Nora, the sweet innocent lamb, who was depriving him of the pleasure of having his explanations accepted. For Lucio it was all very simple: typhus, the sick captain, the contaminated area, therefore, an elemental precaution. "It's inevitable," thought Raul, "the pacifists have to spend their lives at war, poor souls. Lucio is going to buy himself a machine gun at the first port of call."

Paula seemed more merciful, and was listening to Lucio's explanations with an extremely attentive air, which Raul knew all too well.

"I've finally found someone with a little common sense. I've spent the day surrounded by conspirators, from the Last of the Mo-

hicans to dynamiters from St. Petersburg. It feels good to meet a
person with solid convictions, who isn't carried away by dema-
gogues."

Lucio, not sure that she was paying him a compliment, intensi-
fied his explanations. If something was to be done, it was to send a
note signed by everyone (by anyone who wanted to, of course) so
that the first pilot might know that the passengers of the *Malcolm*
understood and respected the unusual situation on board. And at
worst, it could be suggested that the contact between officers and
passengers had not been completely open . . .

"Come on, now," Raul murmured, bored. "If those fellows had
typhus on board in Buenos Aires, they were sons of bitches to start
out on this trip."

Nora, who was not used to such strong talk, blinked. Paula had
difficulty repressing a guffaw, but she took Lucio's side again and
conjectured that the epidemic must have broken out suddenly
when the ship was scarcely out of the bay. The unfortunate officers, confused and uncertain, had stopped for one evening in front
of Quilmes, where the fumes must certainly not have helped the
atmosphere on the poop deck.

"Yes, yes," said Raul. "And the whole thing in radiant technicolor."

Lopez was listening to Paula, an amused and ironic smile on his
face. She amused him, but it was only a bittersweet kind of amusement. Nora was trying to understand, but was so disconcerted that
she ended up staring into her coffee cup, and it was a good while
before she stopped.

"Well, in short," said Lopez. "The free play and expression of
opinions is one of the benefits of democracy. I, in any case, subscribe to the healthy epithet which Raul employed a minute ago.
And we'll see what happens."

"Nothing will happen, unfortunately for you," said Paula.
"You'll be deprived of your toy, and the trip will turn out to be
hideously boring just as soon as they let you cross to the rear deck.
Apropos of decks, I'm going out to look at the stars, which must be
very phosphorescent."

She stood up without looking at anyone in particular. She was
beginning to be bored with this facile game, and it was annoying

her that Lopez had not helped her by taking a stand, either for or against. She realized that he didn't see any way of following her, and he wouldn't leave the table until later. And she knew that something else was going to happen and she began to enjoy herself again, especially since Raul would be aware of it, and everything was always more enjoyable when shared with Raul.

"Aren't you coming?" said Paula, looking at Raul.

"No thanks. The stars, all that costume jewelry . . ."

She thought: "Now he's going to get up and say . . ."

"I'm going to the deck, too," said Lucio, standing up. "Are you coming, Nora?"

"No, I'd rather read a bit in the cabin. See you later."

Raul stayed with Lopez. Lopez crossed his arms like one of the executioners from the illustrations in the *Arabian Nights*. The bartender began to clear off the coffee cups while Raul sat expecting the shrill whistle of a scimitar and the fall of a head onto the floor.

Persio, standing motionless at the extreme end of the prow, heard them approach, preceded by bits and pieces of sentences, broken in the warm wind. He lifted his arm and showed them the sky.

"Look how splendid this is," he said enthusiastically. "This is not the same sky that's over Chacarita, believe me. There's always a kind of noxious vapor in Chacarita, a greasy repellent curtain between my eyes and this splendor. Do you see it, do you? This is the supreme god, spread over the world, the god of the infinite eyes . . ."

"Yes, very lovely," said Paula. "Slightly repetitive in the long run, like anything majestic and solemn. Only in the smallest things is there true variety, don't you think?"

"Ah, demons are speaking for you," Persio said courteously. "Variety is the authentic promise of hell."

"It's incredible how crazy this guy is," Lucio murmured, when they continued on their way and became lost in the shadows.

Paula sat down on a roll of cord and asked for a cigarette; it took a long time to light it.

"It's hot," said Lucio. "Funny, but it's hotter here than in the bar."

He took off his jacket, and his white shirt clearly silhouetted his body in the dark. There was no one on this part of the deck, and the breeze would occasionally hum along the length of the stretched cables. Paula was smoking silently, looking toward the invisible horizon. When she inhaled, the light of the cigarette made the red stain of her hair grow even redder in the night. Lucio was thinking of Nora's face. But what an ass she was! And she just might as well begin to learn what the score was. A man is free, and there's nothing wrong in taking a walk around the deck with another woman. Damn bourgeois conventions, and convent educations, oh Mary, mother of God, and other nonsense, complete with white flowers and holy cards in three colors. Affection was one thing, freedom was something else, and if she thought she was going to keep him all to herself for the rest of her life, as she had recently, simply by not giving in to him, she was quite mistaken . . . He felt Paula's eyes on him, even though he couldn't see them. It seemed all the same to good old Raul if his girl was out alone with someone else; he had even looked at her with an amused air, as if he were already well aware of her tricks. He hadn't often met people as strange as the ones on this ship. And Nora, what a way she had of sitting with her mouth open when she was listening to the things Paula said. And being shocked at strong language! And then Paula's sudden way of picking up a theme and making sense of it.

"I'm happy that you, at least, understood my point of view," he said. "It's all very well to act interesting, but it's hardly necessary to jeopardize the success of the trip."

"Do you think this trip is going to be a success?" asked Paula, indifferently.

"Why not? It depends on us a bit, it seems to me. If we declare ourselves enemies to the ships' officers right off, they can make life impossible for us. I have my pride like anyone else," he added, stressing the word pride, "but it's hardly worth ruining the whole cruise simply because of a stupid whim."

"Is this really called a cruise?"

"Come on, don't joke."

"I mean it, these elegant words always take me by surprise. Look, look, a falling star."

"Make a wish, quickly."

Paula wished. For a fraction of a second the sky had opened toward the north; a delicate rent of light broke through which must have fascinated the vigilant Persio. "Well, my boy," thought Paula, "now we're going to make short work of this stupidity."

"Don't take me too seriously," she said. "I really wasn't too sincere when I took your side a while ago. It was a question . . . of sport, let's say. I don't like to see anyone acting inferior; I'm one of those people who run to the defense of the smallest or dumbest."

"Ah," said Lucio.

"I joked about Raul and the others because it amused me to see them transformed into Buffalo Bill and company; but it could very well be that they're right."

"Go on then," said Lucio, annoyed. "I was glad when you took my side, but if you only did it because you thought I was an idiot . . ."

"Oh, don't take things so literally. Besides, you defend the principles of order and established hierarchies, a thing that in some cases requires more courage than the iconoclasts suspect. It's easy for Dr. Restelli, for instance, but you're very young, and your attitude, on first glance, is disagreeable. I don't know why it's necessary to represent young people with a stone in each hand. It's probably an invention of old people, a good reason for not letting loose the *polis*, not for love or money."

"The *polis?*"

"Yes, that's right. Your wife is charming, her innocence is very appealing. Don't tell her, for women don't forgive that kind of compliment."

"She's not all that innocent, don't you believe it. She's a little . . . there's a word for it . . . It isn't timorous, but something like it."

"Quiet, inhibited."

"Yes, exactly. It comes from her bringing-up, not to mention the sweet nuns. I suppose you're not Catholic."

"Oh, yes," said Paula. "Fervent, besides. Baptism, first communion, confirmation. I still haven't managed to become an adulterous wife, nor a Samaritan, but if God grants me health and time . . ."

"It seemed so to me," said Lucio, who had not understood too well. "Of course, I have very liberal ideas on these matters. It's not that I'm an atheist, but I'm not what you'd call religious, either. I've read a good deal on the subject and I think the Church is bad for humanity. Does it seem conceivable to you that in a century of artificial satellites there should still be a Pope in Rome?"

"Well, in any case, he isn't artificial," said Paula, "and that's something in itself."

"I mean . . . I'm always arguing with Nora on the same theme, and I'll finally end up convincing her. She's already accepted some things—"

He interrupted himself, for he had the unpleasant feeling that she was reading his mind. But after all, it was a good idea to tell everything, for one never knew with such a liberal girl.

"If you promise not to spread this around, I'm going to confess something very personal to you."

"I know what you're going to say," said Paula, surprised by her own assurance. "There's no marriage license."

"Who told you? But no one—"

"You did yourself. The young socialists always begin by convincing the young Catholic girls, but the young girls end up having the last word. Don't worry, I'll be discreet. And one thing: marry that girl."

"Yes, of course. But I'm too big for advice."

"Too big?" Paula said in a provoking voice. "You're a nice little boy and nothing more."

Pleased and annoyed at the same time, Lucio came up to her. Since she gave him an opening and since she was challenging him like that, and being very familiar besides, he was going to teach her a lesson about acting like an intellectual.

"As it's so dark here," Paula observed, "one sometimes doesn't know where to put one's hands. I advise you to put yours in your pockets."

"Don't act dumb," he said, tightening his arms around her waist. "Warm me up, I'm cold."

"Ah, Dashiell Hammett style. Is that how you won your woman?"

"No, not like that," said Lucio, trying to kiss her. "Like that, and like that. Come on, don't be like that, baby, you don't understand . . ."

Paula pushed his arms away and jumped to her feet.

"Poor Nora," she said, starting toward the staircase. "Poor kid, I'm really beginning to feel sorry for her."

Lucio followed her, furious because he realized that Don Galo was up and about that part of the deck. Don Galo was a strange hippogriff under the light of the stars, a multiple and unique shape —chauffeur, chair, and the cripple himself—who assumed disturbing proportions. Paula sighed.

"I know what," she said. "I'll be the witness at your wedding, and I'll even give you a silver centerpiece for a wedding present. I saw one just recently in town."

"Are you mad?" asked Lucio, quickly dropping the familiar address. "Paula . . . let's be friends, okay?"

"In other words, you want me to keep quiet, right?"

"It's all the same to me. What do I care what you say? But it will matter more to Raul, it seems to me."

"Raul? See for yourself, if you like. If I don't say anything to Nora it will be because I don't feel like it, and not because I'm afraid. Go drink your Ovaltine," she added, suddenly furious. "And give my regards to the Socialist party."

E

Just as it's marvelous that the contents of an inkwell may be converted into The World as Will and Representation, or that the grazing of a cutaneous papilla against a dried and taut cylinder of gut might weave the first polygon of a fugue development in space, it is not less marvelous that meditation, secret ink, and subtle fingernail tapping against the tense parchment of night ends up by invading and penetrating the opaque material which surrounds the thirsty rims of the hollow. At this advanced hour of the evening on the prow of the ship, unconnected intuitions slide along the precarious surface of conscience; they search for incarnation, and for this reason they bribe the word which will concretize them in that disorderly conscience; they surge like remnants of phrases, like declensions and contradictory cases occurring amid an expanding whirlwind, fed by hope, terror, and happiness. Rendered a service or disservice by the sentimental radiations, which emanate more from the skin and viscera than from the delicate antennae crushed by so much meanness, the intuitions of a spatial loftiness, of that which begins where the fingernail ends (fingernail the word and fingernail the thing), battle mercilessly against the ordinary canals and plastic or vinylite molds of the stupefied and furious conscience; they search for the direct route, the detonation, the cry of alarm, or the suicide by gas, they pursue those who pursue them, they even pursue Persio, who presses his two hands up against the rail, lost in the stars, a migraine headache, and red wine. Sated with light, the day, and faces like his own, with prechewed conversations, similar to a little Sumerian facing the terrifying mystery of night and stars, his bald head fastened to the celestial vault, Persio battles with a head-on wind, which isn't even recorded by the ostentatious anemometer installed on the captain's bridge. He half-opens his mouth to receive the wind and savor it, and who can say that it is not the intermittent puff of air from his own lungs which has engendered the gust of wind that goes through his body like a stampede of corralled deer. In the absolute solitude of the prow, which the inaudible snores of the sleepers in the cabins transform into a Cimmerian world, in the unsurvivable world of the northwest, Persio lifts his precarious stature with the gesture of personal sacrifice, the figurehead carved from the same wood as Erik's dragons, the libation of lemur blood splashed on the spume. He has heard the guitar of the ship's cables resound weakly, the gigantic fingernail of space scratches out its first sound, almost immediately drowned out by the vulgarity of the waves and wind. A damnable sea, because of its monotony and poverty, an immense, gelatinous green cow girding the ship which violates it persistently, in an endless battle between the iron penis and the viscous vulva, which shudders at every towering of spume. Momentarily, above the inane and common copulation, the guitar of space flings down its exasperating call to Persio. Uncertain of what he has heard, his eyes closed, Persio knows that only the stammered vocabulary, the hesitant luxury of the largest words, loaded down like eagles with their royal prisoners, will, in the end, answer to his inmost self, his deepest feelings of his inner being and comprehension, the intolerable resonance of the strings. Fearful and small, moving like a fly over immeasurable surfaces, the mind and lips feel hesitantly the mouth of the night, the fingernail of space, and the pale hands of the mosaic maker piece in the fragments of blue, gold, and beetle-back green in the too tenuous outlines of this musical drawing which is taking form. Suddenly a word, a well-rounded and heavy noun (but the brick doesn't always stick in the mortar) halfway constructed, collapses with a snail's scream lost in the flames. Persio lowers his head and stops understanding, he no longer even understands that he has stopped understanding. But his fervor is like the music that floats effortlessly in the air of memory, and he again half-opens his lips, closes his eyes, and dares proffer another word, then another, and still another, exuding them with a breath which lungs alone could not explain. Instantaneous refulgent flares blind Persio and survive such fragmentary prowess, rough supports of the kind his anxiety would naturally back away from, just as if someone had tried to put his face in a pumpkin filled with centipedes; tied to the gunwale, as if his body itself was on the edge of a horrendous joy or joyous horror, since nothing of what was subjected to the conditioned reflexes survives at this moment, he persists and excites and shelters the half-visions which tumble down, disfigured and distraught, upon him. He moves his shoulders awkwardly amid the cloud of bats, shreds of opera, galley proofs composed in eight-point type, fragments of trolleys with advertisements of wholesalers, and disjointed verbs lacking a context in which to gel. The trivial, the rotten and pointless past, the conjectured and illusory future, coagulate in one single fatty, smelly pudding, which flattens out the tongue and covers the gums with a bitter coating. He would have liked his arms to open in a harrowing gesture, to undo with one blow and only one scream this pitiful pullulation which destroys itself in a writhing and hostile finale to a wrestling match Greco-Roman style. He knows that at any given moment a sigh will escape from his everyday self, pulverizing everything with a slobbering admission of the impossible, and then the employee on vacation will say: "It's already late, in the cabin there's light, the sheets are made of linen, the bar is open," and perhaps he'll add the most abominable of renunciations: "Tomorrow is another day," and his fingers sink into the iron of the gunwale, grasping it in such a way that the quality of survival of the dermis and epidermis pass over to the providential. On the verge—and this word returns and returns, everything is on the verge and will stop being so at some time or another—Persio is on the verge, the ship is on the verge, the present is on the verge, the verge is on the verge: resist, stand still, offer himself for the taking, destroy himself as conscience in order to be the prey and hunter simultaneously, the meeting which annihilates all opposition, the light which illumines itself, the guitar which is the ear that listens to itself. And he has lowered his head because he feels his energy ebbing, and he also feels misfortune like lukewarm soup or a big oily spot creeping along the lapels of his new jacket, the obstreperous battle of yes and no seems to subside, the uproar which split his temples dies down, the contest goes on, but now it takes place in icy air, in a block of glass, Uccello horsemen freeze in their homicidal undertaking, a snowfall from a Russian novel trembles in a paperweight of suspended flakes. Up above, the music also has its own hierarchy, and a tense and sustained note gradually begins to become heavy with meaning, it accepts a second note, it gets away from the melody in order to become part of and lose itself in an ever richer chord, and from this dying sound surges a new music, the guitar falls to pieces, falls like a hair on a pillow, and all the fingernails of the stars fall on Persio's head and claw him in an exquisite torture of consummation. Closed to the ship, the night, and even himself, desperate availability which is pure waiting, pure admission, Persio feels he is descending, while the night is growing and stretching itself over him, and then there is a movement which shakes him open like a ripe pomegranate, offering him at last its own fruit, its last blood which is one with the forms of the sea and sky, with the barricades of time and place. And so it is he who sings, thinking he hears the song of the immense guitar, it is he who begins to see beyond his eyes, to the other side of the screen, the anemometer, the standing figure in the somber violet of the captain's bridge. And at the same time it is hopeful attention in its most extreme degree and also (without its surprising him) the clock at the bar which signals 23:45, and also (without its hurting him) freight train 8730 which enters the station at Villa Azedo, and the 4121, which goes from Fontela to Figueira da Foz. But a minimum reflection of his memory has sufficed, expressing itself in the involuntary desire to clear up the diurnal mystery, the excentration finally

achieved and lived smashes like a mirror under an elephant's step,
the paperweight filled with snowflakes drops suddenly, the sea
waves creak curling agitatedly, and only the stern remains, the
diurnal desire, Persio's vision of the stern, as it looks at him, while
he remains at the farthest reach of the prow, drying a hideously hot
tear which has slid down his face. He sees the stern, only the stern:
no more trains, nor Rio Branco Avenue, nor the shadow of the
horse of a Hungarian farmer, now, no more—and everything is
crowded into this tear that burns his cheek and falls on his left
hand, sliding imperceptibly to the sea. In his memory, shaken by
terrifying blows, three or four images scarcely remain of the totality
that has come to be: two trains, the shadow of a horse. He sees the
deck at the stern and weeps for everything at one time, he falls into
an unimaginable contemplation, finally concerted, and cries as we
cry, without tears, upon waking from a dream of which only a few
threads remain between our fingers, threads of gold or of silver or
of blood or of haze, the threads saved from a thundering forgetfulness that is not forgetfulness at all but rather the return to the
diurnal, to the here and now in which we hang on, just to keep on
going. The stern, then. That which is over there, the stern. A play
of shadows and red lanterns? The stern, over there. Nothing remi-
niscent of nothing: neither capstans, nor quarterdecks, nor topsails,
nor crew, nor a pratique flag, nor gulls flying over the stays. But the
stern, over there, this thing which is Persio in the process of looking at the stern, the monkey cages on the port side, cages of wild
monkeys to port, a zoo full of wild beasts on the scuttle of the
stowage, the lions and the lioness turning slowly in the enclosure
surrounded by wire and the reflection of the full moon on the
phosphorescent skin of their flanks; they bellow cautiously, never
sick, never seasick, indifferent to the gabble of hysterical baboons,
to the orangoutang that scratches its behind and examines its nails.
And among them, free to wander on the bridge, are the herons, the
flamingos, the hedgehogs and moles, the porcupine, the marmots,
the parakeets and penguins. Little by little he determines the order
of the cages and fenced-off enclosures; the confusion and disorder
changes from second to second into forms at once elastic and rigid,
like those which give solidity and elegance to Picasso's musician
which belonged to Apollinaire; in the black and purple and noc-

turnal, blue and green glowing flashes filter through, and so do
yellow circles, perfect black zones (the trunk, perhaps the head of
the musician), but all persistence in this analogy is already mere
remembrance and therefore incorrect, because from one of the
edges a fugitive figure appears, perhaps Vanth, the one with immense wings, countersign of fate, or perhaps Tuculca, the god with
the vulture face and she-ass ears, just as another contemplation
was able to paint his shape in the tomb of Orcus, unless a masquer-
ade of boatswains and pilot's mates, given over to the artifice of
papier-mâché, is taking place this evening in the stern castle, or the
fever of typhus 224 is taking hold of the air with the delirium of
Captain Smith, stretched out on a cot soaked with phenic acid, as
he declaims psalms in English with a Newcastle accent. Opening
a track through his passivity the idea of a possible circus penetrates
Persio's thought, a circus where anteaters, clowns, and ducks dance
on deck under a tent of stars, and only because of his imperfect
vision of the stern can this momentary irruption of scatological
figures, of shades of Volterra or Cerveteri, merge themselves with
a zoo monotonously consigned to Hamburg. When he opens his
eyes still more, his eyes fixed intently on the sea which the prow
divides and outlines, the colors of the spectacle mount sharply and
burn his eyelids. With a cry he covers his face; what he has just
seen piles up in a disorderly heap about his knees and forces him
to double over, groaning, disconsolately happy, almost as if a soapy
hand had just finished tying a dead albatross around his neck.

XXXI

At first he thought of going up to the bar for a whisky, for he
was sure he needed it, but once in the corridor he felt a touch of
the night outside, under the sky, and he was filled suddenly with
the desire to look at the sea and to put his thoughts in order. It
was past midnight when he leaned up against the port rail, glad to
be alone on the deck (he could not see Persio, who was hidden by
one of the ventilators). Far off a bell sounded, probably at the
stern or on the captain's bridge. Medrano looked up to that

height: the same as always; the violet light, which seemed to emanate from the very substance of the glass, gave him an unpleasant sensation. He wondered vaguely if those who had spent the afternoon on the prow, swimming in the pool or sunbathing, had noticed the captain's bridge. At the moment, he was interested only in his long conversation with Claudia, which had ended on a strangely calm, collected note, almost as if he and Claudia had gradually fallen asleep next to Jorge. They hadn't slept, but perhaps what they had said to one another had done them some good. And perhaps not; personal confidences didn't resolve anything, at least not for him. The past was not at all clear yet. On the other hand, the present was suddenly more pleasant, fuller, like an island of time surprised by night, by the imminence of dawn, and at the same time by the waves of a stale sea, the bad taste of the day before yesterday, and yesterday, and this morning and afternoon, but an island where Claudia and Jorge were at his side. Accustomed to never gelding his thought, he asked himself if this smooth, insular vocabulary were not a product of some feeling and if, like so many other times, his ideas were not merely reflecting the colors of attraction or protection. Claudia was still a lovely woman; speaking to her presupposed a primary and subtle approximation to an act of love. It occurred to him that it no longer was irritating that Claudia should still be in love with Leon Lewbaum, as if he could now accede to another of Claudia's realities. It was strange, almost beautiful.

They already knew one another so much better than they had a few hours before. Medrano could not remember another incident in his life in which a personal relationship between two people might have been established so easily, almost like a necessity. He smiled when he thought of the exact moment—he was absolutely sure of his feeling—in which they had both abandoned the ordinary level of relationship and descended hand in hand to a different rung where words became objects heavy with affection or blame, with deliberation or reproach. It had occurred at the exact moment in which he—so shortly before, actually such a short time before—had said to her: "Mother of Jorge, the little lion," and she had understood that it was not a heavy-handed word-

play on her husband's name, but rather that Medrano was putting
something into her open hands, something like a warm loaf of
bread or a flower or a key. Their friendship was beginning on the
soundest footing—differences and disagreements. Claudia had just
said some very hard words to him, almost denying him the right to
make his life what he had already decided to make it. And at the
same time she had added, vaguely embarrassed: "Who am I to reproach you for a trivial life, when my own . . ." And both had
fallen silent, looking at Jorge, who was now sleeping with his face
toward them, exquisite under the soft light, sighing occasionally
or babbling a bit out of his dreams.

Persio's slight silhouette took him by surprise, but it did not annoy him to find Persio here at this hour and place.

"An interesting voyage, for the most part," Persio said, leaning
up against the rail, at Medrano's side. "I've examined the passenger
list, and I've drawn some astonishing conclusions."

"I'd like to know them, Persio."

"They are not too clear yet, but the principal buttress (lovely
word, incidentally, so solid and reassuring) is the fact that practically all of us are under the influence of Mercury. Yes, the list
is grey. The instructive uniformity of this color in which the violence of white and the annihilation of black are fused to make
pearl grey, just to mention one of its precious nuances."

"If I understand you correctly, you think that there are none of
us out of the ordinary, no unusual types?"

"More or less that."

"But this ship is just an ordinary slice of life, Persio. The unusual is only found in a very small percentage, except in literary
creations, and that is exactly what makes literature. I've crossed
the ocean twice, apart from other travels. Do you think I ever met
extraordinary people on any of these trips? Ah, yes, once on a train
which went to Junín I lunched across from Luis Angel Firpo, who
was already fat and old, but always pleasant."

"Luis Angel Firpo, a typical example of the Ram with Mars as
his most important influence. His color is red, as is natural, and his
metal iron. Probably Atilio Presutti is on that side too, or Señorita
Lavalle, who has a particularly demoniac nature. But the dominant
tones are monochords . . . It's not that I'm complaining, it would

be much worse if the ship were loaded with saturnine or plutonian types."

"I'm afraid novels are influencing your concept of life," said Medrano. "All of us who come on a ship for the first time think we're going to meet humanity of a different kind, that aboard ship a sort of transfiguration is going to take place. I'm less optimistic and I agree with you that there is no hero here, no grand-scale tortured soul, no interesting case."

"Oh, scales. Of course, that's very important. Up till now I was looking at the list in a more ordinary, prosaic way, but I'll have to study it on different levels; perhaps you're right."

"Perhaps. Look, today several small things have happened that can have enormous repercussions. Don't trust tragic gestures, grand pronunciamentos; that's all literature, believe me."

He thought of the mere fact that Claudia had rested her hand on the arm of the chair, moving her fingers now and again, and of what it meant to him. The big problems: weren't they just inventions for the public? The leaps into the absolute, in the style of Karamazov or Stavrogin . . . There were also the Julien Sorels, with their banality, their meanness, and in the end their leap was as fabulous as that of any other mythical hero. Perhaps he was missing the point of what Persio wanted to say. He took him by the arm and they walked slowly along the deck.

"You're thinking about the stern too, aren't you?" he asked, unemphatically.

"I see it," said Persio, with even less emphasis. "It's an unimaginable mess."

"Ah, you see it."

"Yes, sometimes. A little while ago, to be exact. I see it and I don't see it, and it's all confused . . . Like thinking, it's on my mind constantly."

"It must strike you as odd that we don't do anything about it. You don't have to answer, I think it's like that. Well, it seems odd to me, too, but basically it has something to do with the smallness and meanness of things that we were talking about before. We made a couple of attempts, which left us looking ridiculous, and here we are, and this is just where the small-scale comes into play. Minutiae: a match lit for someone, a hand resting on the arm of a

chair, a fast joke, like a glove slapped across someone's face . . .
All that is happening, Persio, but you live face to face with the
stars and you only see it cosmically."

"One can be looking at the stars and at the same time see the
tips of one's eyelashes," said Persio, slightly piqued. "Why do you
think I told you that the list was interesting a while ago? Exactly
because of Mercury, because of the grey, because of the will-less-
ness of practically everyone. If these things didn't interest me, I'd
be at Kraft correcting proofs on a Hemingway novel, where things
always happen on a very grand scale."

"Anyway," said Medrano, "I'm far from justifying our inactivity.
But I don't think anything will be straightened out if we insist, unless we get involved in the grand gesture, though perhaps that
would only lead to nothing and things would end up even more
ridiculous than they are already: in the fashion of the mountain
which labored and brought forth a mouse. There it is, Persio: the
ludicrous. And that's what we're afraid of, and this is buttressed
(I go back to your lovely word) by the difference between the
hero and a man like me. The ridiculous or ludicrous is always on a
small scale. The idea that we can be made fun of is simply intolerable, and for that reason the poop deck is there and we're
here."

"Yes, I think that Señor Porriño and I are the only people on
board who wouldn't be afraid of the ridiculous," said Persio. "And
not because we're heroes. But the rest . . . Ah, the grey, that
most difficult of colors, so unwashable . . ."

It was an absurd conversation and Medrano wondered if someone would still be in the bar; he needed a drink. Persio was obviously ready to follow him, but the door of the bar was closed and
they left one another with a certain melancholy. While he took out
his key, Medrano thought about the color grey and how he had
purposely cut short his conversation with Persio, as if he had
needed to be alone again. Claudia's hand on the arm of the chair
. . . But again this slight nuisance in the pit of his stomach, this
malaise which hours before he had called Bettina, but which was no
longer Bettina, nor Claudia, nor the fiasco of the expedition, although it was a little of everything together and something else,

something that was impossible to grasp, yet was there, too close, too far inside him to be recognized or trapped.

Following hard on the footsteps of the talkative ladies, who were there for no reason in particular before going to bed, was the most ponderous presence of Dr. Restelli, who prattled on, for the benefit of Raul and Lopez, about a plan which he and Don Galo had engineered during the evening. The social relations on board left something to be desired, since several people had scarcely had any opportunity to meet, not to mention the fact that others tended to isolate themselves, for which reason he and Don Galo had come to the conclusion that an amusing soirée would be the best way to break the ice. If Lopez and Raul would collaborate, as undoubtedly all the passengers of a certain age and health would, and be kind enough to exhibit their special talents, the soirée would be enormously successful, and the trip could be carried on in a more tightly knit and cordial atmosphere, one definitely more in keeping with Argentine nature: a little withdrawn at the beginning, but of limitless expansiveness once the first step was taken.

"Well, let's see," said Lopez, a little taken aback. "I know how to do some card tricks."

"Excellent, my dear colleague," said Dr. Restelli. "These things, so insignificant at first glance, are of maximum importance from the social point of view. I've presided over numerous literary circles, co-operatives, and social groups for many years, and I can assure you that magic games are always received with the greatest of pleasure. And I'd like you to take note, moreover, that this soirée, whose purpose is to achieve a spiritual and artistic *rapprochement*, will dissipate the worries—most justified, of course—that the wretched news of the epidemic has provoked among the feminine element on board. And you, Señor Costa, what will you be able to offer us?"

"I haven't the slightest idea," said Raul, "but if you give me some time to talk to Paula, we'll think of something."

"Fine, fine," said Dr. Restelli. "I'm positive that all will turn out well."

Lopez wasn't so positive. When he was alone again with Raul (the bartender was beginning to turn off the lights, for it was time to go to sleep), he decided to say something about it.

"Even if Paula decides to make fun of us again, what do you say we take another little trip into the nether regions?"

"At this hour?" Raul asked, surprised.

"Well, down there time does not seem to be of the essence. We'll avoid witnesses and maybe we'll find the right passage. It will be a question of trying the way that you and the Trejo kid followed this afternoon. I don't really know where you go down, but at least show me the entrance and I'll go alone."

Raul looked at him. This Lopez, how badly he took Paula's beating. How delighted Paula would be if she could hear him.

"I'll accompany you with great pleasure," he said. "I'm not tired and maybe we'll enjoy ourselves."

It struck Lopez that it would have been a good idea to let Medrano know, but then they decided that he'd probably be in bed already. The door in the passageway was still inexplicably open, and they went down without meeting anyone.

"I found the guns there," Raul pointed out. "And here there were two lipids, one of them of good-sized proportions. You see, the light's still on; it's probably some kind of guardroom, though it looks more like the back part of a dry-cleaning establishment or something equally wild. Let's go."

At first they didn't see him, because the fellow named Orf was squatting behind a heap of empty bags. He stood up slowly, a black cat in his arms, and looked at them without surprise, but with a certain annoyance, as if it were hardly the hour to come around bothering him. Again Raul was put off by the appearance of the storeroom, which looked something like a cross between a cabin and a guardroom. Lopez stared at the hypsometric maps, which reminded him of his childhood atlases, his passion for the colors and lines, where the diversity of the universe was reflected, everything that was not Buenos Aires.

"His name's Orf," said Raul, pointing out the sailor. "He doesn't talk much. *Hasdala,*" he added, amiably, with a wave of the hand.

"*Hasdala,*" said Orf. "I warn you, it is forbidden to come here."

"He's not so untalkative as all that," said Lopez, trying to guess Orf's nationality by his accent and name. He came to the conclusion that it was easier to think of him simply as a lipid.

"They already told us that this afternoon," Raul observed, sitting down on a bench and taking out his pipe. "How's Captain Smith doing?"

"I don't know," said Orf, letting the cat climb down his pants leg. "It'd be better if you left."

He did not say it too convincingly, and ended up by sitting down on a stool. Lopez had settled himself on the edge of a table, and was studying the maps in detail. He had seen the door at the rear and he wondered if by leaping forward he might be able to open it before Orf could block his way. Raul offered his tobacco pouch and Orf accepted. He was smoking an old pipe made of carved wood, which vaguely resembled a mermaid, without making the mistake of representing her in detail.

"Have you been a sailor long?" Raul asked. "I mean on the *Malcolm*."

"Two years. I'm one of the newer ones."

He stood up to light his pipe with the match that Raul held out to him. At the same moment that Lopez jumped down off the table to get to the door, Orf lifted the stool and took a step forward. Raul stood up too, because Orf had seized the stool by one of its legs, which was not the way to hold a stool under normal circumstances, but before Lopez fathomed the sailor's threatening gesture, Orf brought the stool down and planted it in front of the door, sitting down on it in a way that made the whole thing seem like a single movement, like a ballet step. Lopez looked at the door, put his hands in his pockets, and turned toward Raul.

"Orders are orders," said Raul, shrugging his shoulders. "I think our friend Orf is an excellent chap, but friendship ends at the point where doors begin, eh Orf?"

"You insist, you insist," he said complainingly. "It's forbidden, you can't cross over there. You'd do a lot better by . . ."

He exhaled the smoke appreciatively.

"Excellent tobacco, señor. Did you buy it in Argentina?"

"I buy this tobacco in Buenos Aires," said Raul. "At Florida Street and Lavalle. It costs me my right eye, but I believe that smoke has to please Zeus's nostrils. What were you going to advise us to do, Orf?"

"Nothing," Orf said, his eyebrows knit.

"In the name of our friendship," said Raul. "You may as well make up your mind, we plan to come visit you very often, you as well as your colleague with the blue snake on his arm."

"Speaking of Bob . . . why don't you go and see him? I'm glad that you came, but . . ." he added, slightly disconsolately, "it's not because of me, but if something happens . . ."

"Nothing's going to happen, Orf, that's what's terrible. Visits and more visits, and you with your three-legged stool in front of the door. But at least we'll smoke and you'll talk to us of the kraken and the Flying Dutchman."

Irritated by their failure, Lopez was following the conversation listlessly. He glanced again at the maps, inspected the portable gramophone (there was an Ivor Novello record on it), and looked at Raul, who seemed to be enjoying himself well enough and showed no sign of impatience. He returned to the edge of the table with an effort; perhaps there might be another chance to reach the door. Orf seemed ready to talk, even though he contin- ued playing watchdog.

"You're passengers and you don't understand," Orf said. "As for me, there would be no inconvenience in showing you . . . But Bob and I have already taken enough chances. Because of Bob it might happen that . . ."

"Yes?" said Raul, encouragingly.

"This is a nightmare," Lopez thought. "He's not going to finish any of his sentences; he talks like a rag torn into shreds."

"You're adults and you should be careful of him, because . . ."

"Be careful of whom?"

"The young boy," said Orf. "The one who came with you be- fore."

Raul stopped tapping the edge of the stool.

"I don't understand," he said. "What's going on with the boy?"

Orf again assumed a pained expression and looked toward the rear door, as if he thought someone were spying on him.

"Actually, nothing's happened," he said. "I tell you only so you'll tell him . . . None of you should come here," he finished, almost furious. "And now I have to go to sleep; it's late."

"Why can't we go through this door?" Lopez asked. "Can you get to the stern through here?"

"No, it goes to . . . well, further on it begins. There's a cabin behind here. You can't get through."

"Let's go," said Raul, putting his pipe in his pocket. "I've had enough for one night. So long, Orf, see you later."

"Better you don't come back," said Orf. "Not because of me, but . . ."

In the corridor Lopez wondered out loud what sense these bits and pieces of sentences made. Raul, behind him, whistling softly, snorted impatiently.

"Certain things are beginning to set clearer for me," he said. "The business about getting drunk, for instance. It did seem odd that the bartender should have given him so much alcohol. I thought he got drunk on one drink, but he surely had more than one. And the smell of tobacco . . . It was lipid tobacco . . . I'll be damned."

"The kid must've wanted to do the same as we did," Lopez said, bitterly. "After all, we're all looking for a way to look good by uncovering the mystery."

"Yes, but he runs a greater risk."

"Do you think so? He's a kid, but not that much of one."

Raul kept quiet. Lopez, who was at the top of the staircase, turned around suddenly and was struck by the look on Raul's face.

"Tell me one thing: why don't we do the only thing left for us to do with those birds?"

"Mm?" Raul said, distracted.

"Beat 'em up. A minute ago we could have gotten to that door."

"Perhaps, but I doubt the efficiency of the system, at least at this stage of the game. Orf seems okay and I can't see myself pinning him to the floor while you get the door open. I don't know, basically we don't have any real reason to act that way."

"Yes and that's bad. See you tomorrow."

"See you," said Raul, as if he didn't even know he was speaking.

Lopez saw him go into his cabin, and he turned to walk to the opposite end of the hall. He stopped to look at the steel beams and gears, thinking that Raul, at this moment, must be in the process of telling Paula about their latest pointless expedition. He could imagine Paula's mocking expression. "Ah, so Lopez was with you, of course . . ." and then some biting commentary would follow, as well as a reflection on their collective stupidity. At the same time, he could still see Raul's face on the staircase, a face full of fear, of preoccupation which had nothing to do with the stern or the lipids. "Truthfully, it wouldn't surprise me at all," he thought. "Then . . ." But it wasn't a good idea to build up his hopes, though what he was beginning to suspect would match what Paula had said. "I wish I could believe it," he thought, suddenly very happy, anxious and happy, idiotically full of hope. "I'll always be an imbecile," he mumbled, looking at himself in the mirror with satisfaction.

Paula did not make fun of them. Comfortably settled in bed, she was in the middle of a new novel when Raul came in, and she received him with such good humor that Raul, after pouring himself a whisky, sat down on the edge of the bed and told her that the sea air and sun were beginning to tan her beautifully.

"In three days, I'll be turned into a Scandinavian goddess," Paula said. "I'm delighted you've come, because I was feeling the need to talk literature. Since we left, I haven't talked with you about books, and that's not like us."

"Okay," Raul said, slightly distracted. "New theories?"

"No, a new impatience. Something rather evil is happening to me, Raulito, in that the better the book I'm reading is, the more it repels me. I mean that its literary excellence repels me, or it may be that literature itself repels me."

"You should just stop reading, and you'll have no problems."

"No, because once in a while I find a book which couldn't possibly be classified as great literature, but which doesn't sicken me. I'm beginning to suspect the reason why: because the author has renounced effects, formal beauty, without falling into journalism or a cut-and-dried monographic style. It's difficult to explain; I don't understand it very well myself. I think it's necessary to go ahead toward a new style, which we'll be able to continue calling

literature, if you wish, even if it would be more correct to change
the name to something else. This new style could only come from
a new vision of the world. But if one day it's accomplished, how
stupid these novels we admire today are going to seem, these novels full of infamous tricks, chapters and subchapters, with well-calculated entrances and exits . . ."

"You're a poet," said Raul, "and all poets, by definition, are
enemies of literature. But we, the sublunar creatures, still find a
chapter from Henry James or Juan Carlos Onetti beautiful, and
luckily for us, these authors have nothing of the poet about them.
Basically, what you have against novels is that they lead you around
by the nose, or rather that their effect on the reader is accomplished from the outside in, and not the other way around, as in
poetry. But why does the element of fabrication or gimmickry
annoy you? You think the same thing in Picasso or Alban Berg is
perfectly fine."

"It's not perfectly fine; I'm simply not aware of it. If I were a
painter or a musician, I'd react against it with the same violence.
But it's not only that; what really grieves me is the poor quality of
literary methods, their repetition to infinity. You'll say there's no
progress in the arts, and how sorry I am about that. When you
compare the treatment of a certain theme by an old writer and a
modern one, you realize immediately that at least as far as rhetoric
is concerned, there's hardly any difference between them. The
most we can say is that today we're more perverse, more informed, and that we have a more ample repertory; but the tricks
are the same, the women pale or blush, something that never
really happens (I sometimes turn a little green, I'll admit that, and
you bright red), and the men act, think, and answer in a kind of
universal code, which applies in exactly the same way to a novel
about India as to a Yankee best-seller. Do you understand me better now? I'm talking about exterior forms, but if I denounce them
it's because this repetition proves the basic sterility, the mere varia-
tions around a thin theme, like that Hindemith hodgepodge on
a Weber theme we heard one miserable night, poor us."

Relieved, she stretched out in bed and rested her hand on
Raul's knee.

"You don't look well, sweetie. Tell Mama Paula all about it."

"Oh, I'm all right," said Raul. "Our friend Lopez looks even worse after the way you mistreated him."

"He, you, and Medrano, all three of you deserved it," said Paula. "You all acted as if you didn't have a brain among you, and the only sensible person is Lucio. I suppose I don't have to explain to you that—"

"I suppose, but Lopez must think that you really were siding with the cause of order and *laissez faire*. It's hit him hard. You're his archetype, his Valkyrie, his Freya, and look what you've done. I'm sure Lucio will end up as a petty official in a municipal government or as chairman of a society of blood donors, that's in the books. What an idiot, *madre mía*."

"And so Jamaica John is going around with a hangdog expression? My poor pirate, his cape is drooping . . . You know I like Jamaica John very much. It shouldn't seem strange to you that I treat him badly. I need—"

"Oh, don't start in with your catalogue of needs," Raul said, finishing his whisky. "I've seen you ruin too many mayonnaises by throwing in the salt or lemon at the wrong moment. And besides, I don't give a damn about how Lopez strikes you and what you have to discover in him."

"*Monsieur est fâché?*"

"No, but you're more sensible when you talk about literature than when you talk about feelings, which is pretty usual with women. I know already, you're going to tell me that this only proves I know nothing about women. Save your words."

"*Je ne te le fais pas dire, mon petit.* But maybe you're right. Give me a swallow of that crap."

"Your tongue will be coated tomorrow. Whisky has a horrible effect on you this late; besides it's very expensive and I only have four bottles."

"Give me a little, you dirty pig."

"Go and get it yourself."

"I'm naked."

"So?"

Paula looked at him and smiled.

"So," she said, pulling up her legs and shoving her feet out from under the sheet. She felt around for her slippers, while Raul watched her, annoyed. She stood straight up in one leap, tossed the sheet at his face, and walked toward the shelf where the bottles were. Her back was silhouetted in the darkness of the cabin.

"You have pretty buttocks," said Raul, getting the sheet off. "Let's see the front."

"The front is going to be less interesting to you," Paula said in the voice which infuriated him. She poured whisky into a tall glass and went to the bathroom to add some water. She came back, walking slowly. Raul looked her in the eyes, and then lowered his glance to her breasts and stomach. He knew what was going to happen and was ready: the slap shook him from head to toe, and almost at the same moment, he heard Paula's first sob and the muffled sound of the glass falling on the carpet without breaking.

"The air in here is going to be unbreathable," said Raul. "It would have been better if you had drunk it. After all, I do have Alka Seltzer."

He leaned over Paula, who was crying, face down on the bed. He caressed her shoulder and the scarcely visible shoulder blade, his fingers traced the delicate spine and stopped at the edge of her rump. He closed his eyes to better see the image he wished to have.

". . . who loves and thinks of you always, Nora." She stood looking at her own signature, then rapidly folded the sheet of paper, addressed the envelope, and sealed the letter. Seated in bed, Lucio was trying to work up interest in an issue of the *Reader's Digest*.

"It's very late," Lucio said. "Aren't you going to sleep?"

Nora didn't answer. Leaving the letter on the table, she took some clothes and went into the bathroom. The sound of the shower seemed endless to Lucio as he tried to grasp the problems of conscience of a bomber pilot from Milwaukee, who was converted to Anabaptism in the middle of a raid. He decided to forget it and go to sleep, but before he could do that, he had to wait his turn to wash up, unless . . . Gritting his teeth, he went to the door and turned the knob: no luck.

"Can't you open up?" he asked in the most natural tone of voice possible to him.

"No, I can't," Nora's voice answered.

"Why?"

"Just because. I'll be right out."

"Open up, I'm telling you."

Nora didn't answer. Lucio put on his pajamas, hung up his clothes, arranged his slippers and shoes. Nora finally returned with a towel wrapped around her head like a turban, her face slightly flushed.

Lucio noticed that she had put her nightgown on in the bathroom. Sitting down in front of the mirror, she began to dry her hair, to brush it with long, endless gestures.

"You know, I'd like to know what's the matter with you," Lucio said, in an assertive tone of voice. "Did you get sore because I took a turn around the deck with that girl? You could have come too, if you'd wanted."

Up, down, up, down. Nora's hair began to shine, little by little.

"Don't you trust me? Or did you think I wanted to come on with her? You're mad because of that, aren't you? You don't have any other reason that I know of. Talk, say something. You didn't like my going out with that girl?"

Nora put her brush on the dresser. She gave the impression of being very tired, or not having the energy to talk.

"Maybe you're just not feeling well," he said, changing his tone, looking for an opening. "You're not angry with me, are you? You saw I came back right away. What's wrong with it, after all?"

"It would seem there *was* something wrong with it," said Nora softly, "since you're carrying on in such a way . . ."

"Because I want you to understand that with that girl . . ."

"Forget that girl, and furthermore, she looks like a little tramp to me."

"Then why are you sore at me?"

"Because you lie to me," Nora said sharply. "And because you said things tonight that made me sick."

Lucio tossed away his cigarette and went over to her. His face was almost comic in the mirror, a real actor playing the role of the virtuous man, indignant and offended.

"But what did I say? You mean to tell me you're catching the goofiness of the others? Do you want the trip to come to an end too?"

"I don't want anything. It just pains me that you kept quiet about what happened during the afternoon."

"I forgot about it, that's all. It seemed idiotic that they should be playing conspirator over something that's perfectly clear. They're going to ruin the whole goddamned trip with their fucking child's play."

"You can leave out the swear words."

"Oh, of course, I forgot the lady can't hear certain things."

"What I can't tolerate is vulgarity, and lies."

"I lied?"

"You kept quiet about what happened this afternoon, and that comes to the same thing. Unless you don't think I'm grown up enough to know about what you're doing on the ship."

"But sweetie, it wasn't important. It was just so much nonsense with Lopez and the others. They got me mixed up in something that didn't interest me and I told them so very clearly."

"It doesn't seem to me it was all that clear. They're the ones who are speaking clearly, not you. And I'm as scared as you are, but I don't go around pretending."

"Me, scared? If you're referring to the typhus two hundred and something . . . exactly, just what I've been saying all along, we have to stay put on this side of the ship and not get mixed up in that mess."

"They don't think it's typhus," said Nora, "but all the same, they're worried, and they don't pretend they're not, like you. At least they put their cards on the table, and they're trying to do something."

Lucio sighed, relieved. At this level, everything turned to dust, lost its weight and seriousness. He put his hand on Nora's shoulder, and bent over to kiss her on the hair.

"What a little idiot you are, pretty and foolish," he said. "I do everything so as to not hurt you . . ."

"That wasn't the reason you kept quiet this afternoon."

"Yes, it was. What other reason was there?"

"Because you were ashamed," said Nora, getting up and going to bed. "And you're ashamed now, and in the bar too, you didn't know where to hide yourself. Shame and nothing more."

It wasn't going to be so easy, after all. Lucio regretted the caress and kiss. Nora turned her back on him resolutely; her body under the sheet was a small hostile wall, full of irregularities, declivities, and crests, terminating in a forest of damp hair on the pillow. A wall between them. Her body, a silent, motionless wall.

When he came back from the bathroom smelling of toothpaste, Nora had turned off her light but had not changed her position. Lucio approached, rested a knee on the edge of the bed, and pulled the sheet to one side. Nora sat up brusquely.

"I don't want to. Go to your own bed. Let me sleep."

"Oh, come on," he said, holding her by the shoulder.

"Leave me alone, I'm telling you. I want to sleep."

"Okay, I'll let you sleep, but next to you."

"No, it's hot. I want to be alone, alone."

"Then you're that sore?" he said in a voice which one reserves for children. "The silly little baby girl is so mad?"

"Yes," said Nora, closing her eyes as if to wipe out his image. "Let me sleep."

Lucio stood up.

"You're jealous, that's what's the matter with you," he said, walking away. "It makes you mad that I went out on deck with Paula. You're the one who's been lying to me the whole time."

But she did not even answer, perhaps she didn't even hear him.

F

"No, I don't think my plan of attack could be clearer than a number containing fifty-eight ciphers, or one of those portolano charts which carry ships down to aquatic catastrophes. It's complicated by an irresistible kaleidoscopic vocabulary, words like masts adorned with capital letters like furious sails. Samsara, for example. I say Samsara and suddenly all my toes begin to shake, and it's not that my toes suddenly shake, nor that the poor ship that carries me, like a figurehead, more gratuitous than well carved, oscillates and vibrates under the blows of the Trident. Samsara, solidity sinks below me, Samsara, the smoke and vapor replace the elements, Samsara, work of the great illusion, son and grandson of Mahamaya . . .

"Thus they go out, famished bitches in heat, with their tall capital letters like columns, swollen with the more than splendid pregnancy of excessively adorned capitals. How direct myself to the

little one, to his mother, to all those Argentinian men of silence,
and to tell them, to speak to them, of the plan of attack which
breaks and scatters me into facets, like a diamond melted in the
middle of an icy battle of snowflakes? They'd like to turn their
backs on me, walk off, and if I chose to write to them—because
sometimes I think of the virtues of a prolix and distilled manu-
script, a résumé of long equinoxes of meditation—they would
throw my pronouncements away with the same negligence and
perplexity that induces them to prose, to self-interest, to intrigue,
to the explicit, to journalism with its many disguises. Monologue,
a lonely task for a soul immersed in the multiple! What a dog's
life!

(Persio pirouettes petulantly under the stars.)

"Finally, it's impossible to interrupt them while they digest a
plate of fish with dialectics, with anthropology, with the inconceivable narration of Cosmas Indicopleustes, with the sacred
Etruscan texts, with the desperate mantic which offers me its hot
ideograms from on high. And I myself, like a half-crushed cockroach, scurry around with what remains of my cockroach legs from
one plank to the next, and crash into the vertiginous height of a
small sliver, resulting from one of the nails in Presutti's shoe, like
a knot in the wood . . . And yet, I begin to understand it's something too close to trembling, I begin to see, it's less than a breath
of dust, I begin to begin, I run backwards, I turn back! To turn
back, yes, there the answers are sleeping their larval life, their first
night. How many times in Lewbaum's auto, frittering away a weekend on the plains around Buenos Aires, did I feel that I should sew
myself into a sack and throw myself onto the roadside, passing
Bolivar or Pergamino, near Casbas or Mercedes, in some spot or
other with owls on the telephone poles, with deplorable horses
searching for a bit of pasture land eaten away by the autumn. Instead of accepting the toffee Jorge insisted on slipping in my pocket,
instead of feeling happy next to the majestic and protective sim-
plicity of Claudia, I should have abandoned myself to a night on
the pampas, just like on this night here on a doubtful and unknown
sea, I should have stretched out on my back, so that the burning
sheet of sky might cover me up to my mouth, and let the juices
from below and above infest me rhythmically, the rice-powdered

clown which is the truth of the big tent set up above its bells, the carcass of a cow making the air reek for three hundred yards around, and making authenticity reek, as well as the truth, reeking only for those who reek, who hold their noses with a gesture of virtue and who run to hide in their Plymouth or in the memory of Sir Thomas Beecham recordings. Oh, such intelligent imbeciles, oh poor friends!

(The night opens for a second as a falling star speeds downward, and for an instant the *Malcolm* sprouts sails and topsails, is hung with the archaic rigging and tackle, and Persio trembles too, as if an unknown wind might be blasting him from one side; then, turned toward the horizon, he forgets the radar and telecommunications, and falls into a half-vision of brigantines and frigates, of Turkish caravels, Greek-Roman saiques, Dutch hookers, Tunisian sindales, and Tuscan galliots—more a result of Pio Baroja's maritime novels and long hours of loathing at Kraft's until four in the afternoon, than a true knowledge of the sense of those names spreading like trees.)

"Why such a confused agglomeration in which I can't tell the truth from recollection, names from presences? The horror of echolalia, of the inane quibble. But with everyday talk alone, one achieves only a table loaded down with victuals, a meeting with shampoo or the razor, rumination over a judicious editorial, a plan of challenge and response, figuring that this sandpaper on fire over my head reduces to less than ash. Covered by the grass of the pampas, I ought to have stayed long hours listening to the armadillo's running, or the laborious germination of cinacina grass. Sweet, stupid words of folklore, inconsistent preface of all sacred mystery, how their gummy paws caress my tongue, how they grow like deep honeysuckle and gradually offer me access to the true Night, far from here and contiguous, abolishing the distance from the pampas to the South Atlantic. My Argentina, out beyond, behind this phosphorescent curtain, darkened if not downright sinister streets of Chacarita, buses rolling poisoned with colors and advertisements! Everything joins in me because everything hurts me, I, the cosmic Tupac Amaru, ridiculous, babbling words that even to my stubborn ear seem inspired by the Sunday edition of La Prensa or by one of Dr. Restelli's dissertations, Dr. Restelli, a professor in secondary school. But crucified on the pampas, lying face up to the silence of a million shining cats, which look at me, impassively drinking from the milky trickle, I should have yielded, perhaps, to what my reading concealed from me, understood suddenly the second and third layers of meaning of all those railroad schedules and telephone books which I fended off yesterday for the enlightenment of the affable Medrano, and why the umbrella always breaks on me when I hold it pointing left, and that delirious search for exclusively pearl-grey nylons or Bordeaux-red ones. From knowledge to understanding or from understanding to knowledge, road uncertain, I discern it hesitantly with the aid of anachronistic vocabularies, Periclean meditations, obsolete vocations, the amazement of my bosses and the laughter of the elevator operators. No matter, Persio goes on, Persio, the dejected atom at the edge of the road, dissatisfied with the traffic laws, this atom of rebellion which is a prelude to the H-bomb, preface to the mushroom which delights the habitués of Calle Florida and the silver screen. I have seen the American land during the hours when it was closest to its final secret, I've traipsed on foot across the hills of Uspallata, I've slept with a wet towel over my face, crossing the Chaco, I've jumped off the train on the Pampa of Hell to feel the coolness of earth at midnight. I know the odors of Calle Paraguay, and also those of Godoy Cruz de Mendoza, where the wine's compass flows between dead cats and frames of reinforced concrete. I should have chewed coca on each trip, to exacerbate the solitary hopes that habit relegates to the depths of one's dreams, to feel the third hand growing in my body, the hand which knows how to seize time and bandy it about, because this third hand has to be somewhere, and sometimes suggests itself, explosively so, in a line of poetry, in a stroke of a brush, in a suicide, in a saintly figure, but which prestige and renown immediately mutilate and replace with flashy reasons, this work of a leprous stonecutter which one calls explaining and rationalizing. Ah, I feel the third hand opening and closing in some invisible pocket: if I could caress you with it, lovely night, to sweetly flay the names and dates which are gradually covering over the sun, the sun that once fell ill in Egypt and turned blind, and needed a god to cure it . . . But how can I explain all this to my fellow passengers,

to myself, if at every turn I look at myself in a mirror of scorn and
invite myself to go back to the cabin where a glass of cold water
awaits me, as well as a pillow, that immense white field where
dreams will gallop? How can one perceive the third hand without
already being one with poetry, that treason of words in ambush,
that pimp of loveliness, of euphony, of happy rhymes, of so much
prostitution framed in cloth and explained in handwriting insti-
tutes? I don't want intelligible poetry on board, or voodoo, or
initiates' rites. Something more immediate, something that words
cannot fuck, something free of tradition, so that finally, what all
tradition masks surges like a plutonium cutlass through a screen
decorated with painted stories. Stretched out in the alfalfa, I should
have been able to enter this order, to learn its forms, because these
are not words but rather pure rhythms, drawings on the most sensitive palm of the third hand, radiant archetypes, bodies without
weight where gravity sustains itself and softly bubbles up the germ
of grace. I feel something approaching, but I recoil, I don't know
how to reconcile myself with my shadow. If I could find the way to
say something about all this to Claudia, to the happy youths who
run toward unaccountable games, the words would then become
torches in dark passages, and perhaps right here, and not on the
plains where I reneged on my duty when I refused my embrace to
the arable earth, right here the third hand would fall like a leaf
at the gravest hour the first of eternity's clock, an encounter comparable to the setting of Saint Elmo's fire on a sheet stretched out
to dry. But I'm like them, we're all trivial, metaphysicians long before being physicists, we run away from questions so as not to get
our pants ripped off by a set of sharp eyeteeth, and so football has
been invented, and so one becomes a radical or a second lieutenant
or a proofreader at Kraft, incalculable felony! Perhaps Medrano is
the only person who knows it: we're trivial and we pay for it with
happiness and misfortune, the happiness of the marmot wrapped
in its fat, the silent unhappiness of Raul Costa who presses a swan
of ash against his black pajamas. And even if from our birth we are
destined to ask questions and pry into the answers, even then there's
something endlessly disconcerting in the yeast of Argentine bread,
in the color of railroad tickets and the amount of calcium in our
water, that throws us like desperados into the total drama; we leap

onto the table to dance the dance of Shiva with an enormous linga in our hand, or we run amuck to meet the shot that will lodge in our head or the escaping gas, poisoned by pointless metaphysics, nonexistent problems, invisible suppositions which comfortably screen the central void with smoke, the statue without head, without arms, without linga, without yoni, the appearance, the comfortable appurtenance, the dirty appetite, the pure rhythm carried to the infinite, where science and conscience also find a place. Why don't we first throw the venomous weight of history out the window, refuse commemorations, and weigh the heart on a scale of tears and fasting? Oh, Argentina, why this fear of fear, this emptiness to conceal emptiness? Instead of the judgment of the dead, why not the judgment of the living, the head which smashes against the monument in the Plaza de Mayo, so that the third hand may finally be born with an ax of diamonds and of bread, its newest flower, its tomorrow which would be purification and coalescence? Who is this whoreson who talks like the national anthem about 'the laurels we won'? We, have we won the laurels? But is it possible we're such scoundrels?

"No, I don't think my plan of attack could be clearer than a number containing fifty-eight ciphers, or one of those portolano charts which carry ships down to aquatic catastrophes. It's complicated by an irresistible kaleidoscopic vocabulary, words like masts adorned with capital letters . . ."

SECOND DAY

XXXII

Lucky she'd brought along four or five magazines of her own, because the books in the library were written in weird languages, and the few in Spanish were about war and Jewish problems and other philosophical things. While she was waiting for Doña Pepa to finish doing her hair, Nelly relished with intense gratification photos of various cocktail parties that had taken place in the largest homes in Buenos Aires. She was fascinated by Jacobita Echaniz' elegant style, as she chatted with her readers, really as if she were one of them, without acting at all snobbish about the best society, but at the same time letting them know (why did *her* mother wear her hair like a washerwoman, for heaven's sake?) that she belonged to a different world, where everything was rosy, perfumed, and gloved—I do nothing but go to fashion shows, Jacobita confessed to her faithful readers—Lucia Schleiffer, who is darling, and intelligent besides, gave a talk on the evolution of feminine fashion (on the occasion of the textile exhibition at Gath and Chaves), and the man in the street (the women too) are bowled over by the pleated, washable skirts, until just recently a part of North American magic . . . The wife of the French ambassador invited a select group of guests to the Alvear for a presentation of French fashions (as one designer remarked: Christian Dior takes the lead, and we all try to follow him). Each guest received a tiny flask of French perfume as a token gift, and everyone left madly delighted, clutching a small package . . .

"Well, here I am," said Doña Pepa. "You're here too, Doña Rosita? It looks like a lovely morning."

"It does, but the boat is beginning to rock again," said Doña Rosita morosely. "Are you coming, darling?"

Nelly closed the magazine, but not before learning that Jacobita had just visited a horticultural exhibit in Centenary Park, where she had run into Julia Bullrich de Saint, surrounded by baskets of flowers, as well as friends, and that she had also met Stella Morros de Careano and the indefatigable Señora de Udaondo. Nelly wondered why Señora Udaondo was indefatigable. And all that had taken place in Centenary Park, just around the corner from where her friend Coca Chimente lived, the girl who worked with her at the store. It would have been simple for the two of them to have gone one Saturday afternoon, to have asked Atilio to take them to see what the horticultural exhibit was like. But the ship really was rocking, her mother and Doña Rosita would get sick for sure as soon as they had breakfast, and even she, well . . . It was a shame to have to get up so early. On a pleasure trip breakfast shouldn't be served before nine-thirty, like the society people do it. When Atilio came in, all spruced up and in a good mood, she asked him if you couldn't stay in bed until nine-thirty and ring the bell and have breakfast served in the cabin.

"Of course," said Pelusa, who wasn't quite sure. "You do whatever you want here. I get up early because I like to look at the ocean when the sun comes up. Right now I'm starving. What do you think of the weather? Those are some waves, I'm telling you . . . ! We still didn't see those delphins, but I bet we will this afternoon. Good morning, señora, how's everything? How's the kid, señora?"

"He's still sleeping," said Señora Trejo, who wasn't sure "kid" was the proper word for Felipe. "The poor darling had a restless night, according to my husband."

"He was out too long in the sun," said Pelusa knowledgeably. "I told him a cuppla times: 'Look, kid,' I said, 'I know about this, I know what I'm saying, don't go crazy the first day . . .' But what can you do? Anyway, this way he'll learn. Look, when I did my—"

Doña Rosita cut the imminent evocation of his army life short, announcing the necessity of going up to the bar because she felt

the ship's rocking more in the corridor. That was enough to remind Señora Trejo of her stomach. She wouldn't have anything
but a cup of black coffee. Dr. Viñas had told her it was the best
thing when seasickness struck. On the other hand, Doña Pepa
thought that a good slice of bread and butter would keep a cup of
coffee down, but of course, without any jam on it, because jam
was full of sugar and that thickened the blood, the very worst
thing for seasickness. Señor Trejo, who had just joined the group,
thought there was some scientific basis for the theory, but Don
Galo, who had emerged from the staircase like a Cartesian devil
vividly raised on the chauffeur's iron hands, thought it sensible to
down a good plate of bacon and eggs. Other passengers were beginning to arrive at the bar. Lopez stopped to read an announcement which confirmed the opening of the barber shop; the hours
were given. Beba made one of her grand entrances, halting on
the last step and glancing languidly around her, and Persio came
in behind her, wearing a blue shirt and cream-colored trousers
which were too large for him. The bar was soon filled with talk
and good smells. Medrano, already smoking his second cigarette,
was watching for Claudia. Nervous, he went back to check at her
cabin.

"I'm the height of indiscretion, but it occurred to me that perhaps Jorge wasn't getting on too well and maybe you needed
something."

Claudia, wrapped in a red bathrobe, seemed younger. She
gave him her hand, although neither of them really understood the
need for such a formal greeting.

"Thanks for coming. Jorge's much better, and he slept very well
all night. This morning he asked if you had stayed a long time
. . . But better he ask his own questions."

"At last you're here," said Jorge, who used the familiar address
completely naturally. "Last night you promised to tell me a Davy
Crockett story. Don't forget."

Medrano promised to tell him some wild stories of the heroes
of the plains.

"But now I'm going to breakfast. Your mother has to get
dressed and you do too. I'll see you on deck. The weather's wonderful."

"All right," said Jorge. "Boy, did you talk last night!"

"Did you hear us?"

"Sure, but I dreamt about our star, too. Did you know Persio and I have a star?"

"A little like Saint-Exupéry's," Claudia confided. "Delightful, all the same, and they do make remarkable discoveries on it."

On the way back to the bar, Medrano was thinking that the interval (the night) had mysteriously transformed Claudia's face. She had said goodbye to him looking tired and discouraged, as if everything he had confessed had been painful to her. And the words she had used concerning his confidences—not many, perhaps reluctant, almost all hard and cutting—had only accentuated the bitter expression on her face; it seemed worn out with a sudden fatigue that was not entirely physical. She hadn't treated him rudely, but neither had she shown him any pity, returning sincerity with sincerity. And this morning he met the everyday Claudia again, mother of the little lion. "She's not the type to drag sadness around after her," he thought gratefully. "And neither am I. But Lopez, on the other hand . . ." Lopez said he felt fine, but that actually he hadn't slept much.

"Are you going to the barber's?" he asked. "In that case, let's go together and we can talk while we wait. I think barber shops are an institution worth cultivating."

"Pity there's no place to have our shoes polished," said Medrano, amused.

"A pity, yes. Look at Restelli, how dashing he is this morning."

Dr. Restelli had tied a red handkerchief with white polka dots under the open collar of his sport shirt. His rapid and decisive friendship with Don Galo was becoming more and more solid, aided, as it was, by frequent consultations over a list, which they were perfecting with the help of a pencil the bartender had lent them.

Lopez began to tell him about the events of the previous evening, warning him beforehand that there really wasn't much to tell.

"The net result is that I'm in a foul mood, ready to smash all those lipids or whatever you want to call them in the mugs."

"I wonder if we're not wasting our time," Medrano said. "I think of it as a kind of two-way staircase: it irritates me to waste time in pointless investigations, but it seems we're wasting our time if we go on like this. You have to admit that the partisans of the *status quo* look better than we do."

"But you don't think they're right."

"No, I'm simply analyzing the situation, that's all. Personally, I'd like to go on looking for a way to the afterdeck, but I don't see any way to do it except by force, and I don't want to ruin the trip for the others, especially when they seem to be having such a good time."

"While we go on making everything a problem . . ." said Lopez, slightly discouraged. "Actually, I got up in a bad mood and I'm looking for a way to blow off steam. Now why did I get up in a bad mood? A mystery—liver trouble, probably."

But it wasn't his liver, unless his liver had red hair. And yet, he had gone to sleep happy, certain that things were going to be better defined and that they would not turn out unfavorably. "But one is sad all the same," he said to himself, staring grimly into his empty cup.

"That fellow Lucio, has he been married long?" he asked before thinking much about it.

Medrano sat looking at him. Lopez saw he was hesitating.

"Well, I wouldn't want to lie to you, but I wouldn't want this to get around, either. I suppose they pass themselves off as newly-weds, but they haven't undergone that short ceremony conducted in an office fragrant with ink and old leather. At least that's what Lucio told me in Buenos Aires; sometimes we run into one another at the University Club. Calisthenics."

"It doesn't really interest me too much," said Lopez. "Of course, I'll keep it a secret for the unconscionable pleasure of making martyrs of the ladies, but I wouldn't be at all surprised that with their highly developed sense of smell . . . Look, there's one of them beginning to get seasick."

With a gesture which included both awkwardness and considerable power, Pelusa had taken his mother's arm and was beginning to haul her toward the door.

"A little fresh air will fix you up, Mama. Hey, Nelly, set a deck chair up someplace that's not too windy. Why'd you eat so much bread and jam? I told you, remember?"

Don Galo and Dr. Restelli motioned to Medrano and Lopez in a somewhat conspiratorial manner. Their list was growing longer.

"Let's have a little talk about the soirée," Don Galo proposed, as he lit a cigar of dubious quality. "It's about time we enjoyed ourselves, goddamn it."

"Good," said Lopez. "And then we're going to the barber shop. What a great schedule."

XXXIII

Things work out in a way you least expect, Raul thought as he woke up. Paula's slap had helped him fall asleep. But once awake, after a perfect rest, he thought again of Felipe going down into that Nibelung land of adventure and violet lights, just to prove his independence and courage. The devilish little snot, no wonder he'd tied on a bag complicated by a sunstroke. He imagined him (as he watched Paula stirring in bed) going into the cabin Orf shared with the big tattooed gorilla, being friendly, getting himself invited to a drink, passing himself off as the ship's cock of the walk, and probably slandering the other passengers. "A beating, a good beating," he thought, but he smiled, because beating Felipe would have been like . . .

Paula opened one eye and looked at him.

"Hello," said Raul. "*Look, love, what envious streaks Do lace the severing clouds in yonder east . . .*"

"The sun's shining, isn't it?"

"*Night's candles are burnt out, and jocund day . . .*"

"Come give me a kiss," said Paula.

"Perish the thought."

"Come on, don't be so rancorous."

"Rancorous is too big a word, dear heart. Rancor must be earned. Last night you seemed to me just plain crazy, but that's nothing new."

Paula jumped out of bed, and to Raul's surprise, she was wearing pajamas. She came over to him, tousled his hair, patted his cheek, kissed him on the ear, and tickled him. They were laughing like children, and he ended up hugging and tickling her until they both fell on the carpeted floor, rolling over into the middle of the cabin. Suddenly, Paula leaped up and pivoted on one foot.

"You're not angry, you're not angry," she said. Then she burst into laughter, still dancing. "But you're the one who acted like a beast, you let me get up like that . . ."

"I let you? You tramp, you got up naked because you're an exhibitionist and you knew I wouldn't go to Jamaica John and tell on you."

Paula sat on the floor, and put her two hands on her knees.

"Why Jamaica John, Raul? Why him and not someone else?"

"Because you like him," said Raul seriously. "And because he's mad for you. *Est-ce que je t'apprend des nouvelles?*"

"No, truthfully not. We have to talk about that, Raul."

"Nothing doing. You go find another confessor. But I'll absolve you, that, yes."

"Oh, you have to listen. If you don't listen, what will I do?"

"Lopez," Raul said, "is in cabin number one, on the opposite side. He'll listen to you, go see."

Paula looked at him thoughtfully, sighed, and then they both jumped up at the same time and raced for the bath. Paula won and Raul went back to bed and took out a cigarette. A good beating . . . There were several people who could use a good beating. A beating with flowers, with wet towels, with a slow perfumed scratch . . . A beating that would last for hours, interrupted by reconciliations and caresses, the perfect vocabulary of hands, capable of abolishing and justifying the blows only so they could begin again between moans and final forgetfulness, like a leopard skin or a dialogue between statues.

At ten-thirty, people began to crowd onto the deck. A perfectly meaningless horizon surrounded the *Malcolm*, and Pelusa was tired of looking out on all sides for signs of the marvels Persio and Jorge had prophesied.

But who was watching all this, taking it in? Not Persio, by any means, for he was busy shaving in his cabin. The spectacle, naturally, was available to anyone who cared to look, and all that was needed was to go out on deck and nonchalantly amble over to the prow, which was becoming more and more of a fixed image (people in deck chairs, people quietly leaning up against the rail, people stretched out on the deck or seated at the edge of the pool). And so, starting at the first floorboard, at foot level, the onlooker (whoever it was, for Persio was still rubbing his chin with after-shave) could progress, either slowly or quickly, or could stop a second to gaze at a brown or black tar-filled groove, or could lift up his eyes to glance at a ventilator, or even higher, to look at the lower part of the topmast, thickly covered with white paint, unless he preferred to take everything in at once, to suddenly settle on partial positions and instantaneous gestures before turning his back on the scene, as he dug down in his pocket where a pack of Chesterfields nestled warmly.

From high up—a valid point of view, even if not practical— the masts are abolished and reduced to two insignificant discs, in much the same way as Giotto's tower, seen by a swallow suspended over its exact center, is reduced to a ludicrous square, losing all its prestige, as height and volume recede. And a man on the street, observed from a fourth floor is, for an instant, a kind of hairy egg floating in the air above a pearl-grey or blue crossbar, sustained by a mysterious levitation which soon explains two active legs and sharp back, destroying all notion of pure geometries. The view from above, the most inefficient possible view: the angels see a Cezanne-like world: spheres, cones, cylinders. Then the onlooker is suddenly tempted to approach the spot where Paula Lavalle watches the waves. The approach, food for thought, mirror for larks (but is Persio thinking all this, or is it Carlos Lopez? Who is inventing all these similes? Who's looking for the best angle and focus in this conscientious photography?), and already at Paula's side, against Paula, almost in the middle of Paula, the discovery of an iridescent universe, fluctuating and altering constantly: her hair, brilliant in the sun, like a cat playing with a red ball of yarn, every strand of hair a burning bramble, an electric wire carrying the fluid which keeps moving the *Malcolm*, the machines of the world, the action of men, and the course of the galaxies. The absolutely inutterable cosmic swing is contained in this head of hair. The observer can't tear his eyes away from it, everything else is a cloudy background as in a close-up of Simone Signoret's left eye, where everything around it is like lukewarm soup, which eventually takes on the form and name of lover or mother or the bistro in District 7. And at the same time everything is like a guitar (if Persio were here he would proclaim the guitar, while denying the term of comparison—there is no *like*, each thing is petrified in its thingness, and the rest is trick and artifice—not allowing the guitar to be used as a metaphoric game, from which we can conclude that perhaps Carlos Lopez, or Gabriel Medrano, no, I guess Lopez, is both originator and victim of these visions, brought about and undergone beneath the blue sky). But going back to the idea that from above everything is a guitar, the mouth of the instrument becomes the circumference of the biggest mast, the strings are the innocent cables which vibrate and tremble as the guitarist's fingers rest on the frets, and the hand is Señora Trejo's (without her knowing it), who is stretched out on a green rocker, and the other hand is the burning sea off the port side, scratching the guitar's flank as gypsies do when they mark time between songs, the sea as Picasso felt it when he painted the man with the guitar, which belonged to Apollinaire. And it cannot any longer be Carlos Lopez thinking this, but it is Carlos Lopez next to Paula, his eyes lost in a single strand of her hair, who feels an instrument vibrate in the confused pleading of forces which is all a mass of red hair, the potential interlacing of thousands and thousands of hairs, each one the string of a secret instrument which would extend over miles and miles of a sea, a harp like the harp woman of Hieronymus Bosch, ancestor to Picasso's guitar, and the player of the same music which fills Carlos Lopez' mouth with a deep taste of berries and fatigue and words.

"Oh, fuck, what a hangover, Christ," Felipe mumbled, sitting up in bed.

He sighed, relieved to see that his father had already gone out on deck. Cautiously turning his head, he checked his condition and found out it wasn't all that bad. As soon as he had a shower (and a good dip in the pool) he'd feel fine. He pulled off his pajamas and examined his red shoulders, but they hardly hurt at all now; just an occasional prickling sensation ran along his skin, which required a delicate scratching. A splendid sun poured in through the porthole. "I'll spend the day in the pool," he thought, stretching. His tongue felt like a piece of rag in his mouth. "What a hunk that Bob is. That's some rum he's got," he added, with the completely masculine satisfaction of having committed some enormity, broken some principle or other. He suddenly thought of Raul and he looked for the pipe and tobacco. Who had brought him to the cabin and put him to bed? He remembered Raul's cabin, the mess in the bathroom, and Raul waiting outside, hearing everything. He shut his eyes, ashamed. Maybe Raul had brought him back to the cabin, but what did his parents and Beba say when they saw him like that? Now he remembered a hand rubbing salve on his arms, and some distant words, and the old man blowing his top. Raul's salve, Raul had talked about a salve or had given him some, oh, but what the hell did it matter, he was suddenly hungry, positive that everyone had eaten breakfast and that it must be very late. No, nine-thirty. But where was the pipe?

He took a few steps, testing himself. He felt fine. He found the pipe in a drawer in the dresser, between the handkerchiefs, and the can of tobacco mixed in with some socks. Beautiful pipe, and so English-looking. He put it in his mouth and went to look at himself in the mirror: but he looked strange standing there, half naked with that elegant pipe between his lips. He didn't feel like smoking; the taste of Bob's rum and tobacco was still with him. What a terrific talk he had had with Bob, what an incredible guy.

He stepped under the shower, turning the faucet from boiling hot to ice cold. The *Malcolm* was dancing a bit and it felt good to keep his balance without hanging onto the chrome faucets. He soaped up slowly, looking at his body the whole time in the big mirror which practically covered one of the bathroom walls. The whore in the call house had said to him: "You have a nice body, kid," and it had given him courage that time. Of course he had a terrific body, his back was a triangle like the guys in the movies or like boxers, and his legs were slim but he could kick a goal from halfway down the field any time. He turned off the shower and again looked at his body, sparkling with water, his hair falling onto his forehead; he pushed it back, changed the expression on his face to one of indifference, looked at himself from a three-quarter view, and then in profile. His stomach muscles were clearly defined; Ordoñez said they were the sure signs of an athlete. He contracted his muscles, so as to make his body ripple with as many muscular knots and protuberances as possible; he lifted his arms like Charles Atlas and thought that it would be nice to have a photograph taken like that. But who would take a picture of him like that? Even though he had seen some unusual photos, he wondered who could possibly have taken them? For instance those photos that some character had snapped of himself while he was with a chick in various positions, you could even see the rubber trigger the guy held between his toes to take the pictures, and everything else too, absolutely everything. Actually a woman with her legs open was disgusting enough, more so than a man, especially in a photo . . . It was different that time in the whorehouse because she was moving the whole time, and besides, he was interested in another way, but like that, looking at photographs in cold blood . . . He put his hands on his stomach, what a piece of brutality, he couldn't even think about it. He wrapped a bath towel around his waist and began to comb his hair, whistling. As he had washed his hair, it was very wet and soft, and he couldn't manage to comb down the slick fringe around his forehead. He stayed a while longer until he was satisfied with the results. Then he took off the towel and began to flex his muscles, looking at himself occasionally in the mirror to see if his fringe of hair was in place. His back was to the door, which had been left open, and he suddenly heard Beba scream. He saw her face in the mirror.

"Indecent," Beba said, quickly backing out of the field of vision. "You think it's all right to go around naked with the door wide open?"

"Eccchh, you're not going to fall over dead just because you see a bit of ass," said Felipe. "Between brother and sister . . ."

"I'm going to tell Papa. Do you think you're eight years old?"

Felipe put on his bathrobe and came out of the bathroom into the cabin. He began to fill the pipe, looking at Beba, who had sat down on the edge of the bed.

"Well, it looks like you're better," said Beba peevishly.

"It wasn't anything. I was in the sun too long."

"The sun doesn't smell."

"That's enough out of you. Don't get me sore. You can get out anytime you want to."

He coughed, choking on the first puff. Beba was watching him, amused.

"It thinks it can smoke like a big man," she said. "Who gave you the pipe?"

"You know who gave it to me, stupid."

"The redhead's husband, right? You're lucky, I'd say. First you flirt with the wife and then her husband gives you a present."

"You can shove your opinions up your ass."

Beba didn't take her eyes off him. Apparently, she was enjoying Felipe's progressive domination over the pipe, which was beginning to draw nicely.

"It's very funny," she said. "Mama was furious last night at Paula. Yes, don't look at me like that: furious. Do you know what she said? Swear you won't get mad."

"I won't swear to anything."

"Then I won't tell you. She said . . . 'That *woman* is the one getting mixed up with my little boy.' I defended you, believe me, but they ignored me as usual. You'll see, she's going to blow her top."

Felipe turned red with rage, choked again, and ended up by putting the pipe down. His sister modestly stroked the edge of the bedspread.

"The old lady's the end," Felipe said at last. "But what does she think I am? I'm fed up with this 'little boy' shit, one of these days I'm going to tell them all to—" (Beba had stuck her fingers in her ears.) "And you'll be the first, you rat. I'd bet my last nickel you were the one who went and egged her on about my . . . So now talking to women isn't permitted? And who do you think got you all here, would you mind telling me? Who paid for the trip? Look, get out of here, move, I feel like giving you a couple of . . ."

"If I were you," Beba said, "I'd watch my step flirting with Paula. Mama said . . ."

At the door she turned back. Felipe was still in the same place,

his hands in his bathrobe pockets, looking like a scared but
cocky boxer.

"Just imagine if Paula found out we call you Buddy," said
Beba, closing the door.

"A haircut is a metaphysical operation," Medrano remarked.
"Have they thought up a psychoanalysis and a sociology of the relationship between the barber and his customers yet? Especially
the ritual, which we countenance and conform to all of our lives."

"When I was little the barber shop impressed me as much as
church," Lopez said. "There was something mysterious when the
barber would bring out a special chair, and then that sensation of
a hand tightening around my head like a coconut and making it
turn from one side to another . . . Yes, a ritual, you're right."

They were leaning up against the rail, looking for anything in
the distance.

"The whole thing turns the barber shop into a kind of temple," said Medrano. "First, the fact that the sexes are separated
gives it a special importance. The barber shop is like a poolroom
or a urinal, a kind of strictly male society which gives us a certain
inexplicable freedom. We cross over into a territory very different
from that of the street, our homes, or streetcars. After-dinner talk
for men only and bars with ladies' entrances are part of the past already, but we've managed to salvage a few remnants."

"And the smell, you could recognize it any place on earth."

"Aside from which, this male ambience may perhaps have been
created so that a man, in the full pride of his virility, might be able
to yield to a kind of eroticism that he himself considers feminine,
maybe unreasonably so, but a fact nonetheless, which he would
deny indignantly under ordinary circumstances. The rubdowns, the
lotions, the perfumes, the meticulously described haircuts, the mirrors, the talcum powder . . . If you were to list these items out of
context, isn't it women's stuff?"

"Of course," said Lopez, "which proves that we're not even
free of them when we're alone. Thank God. Let's go look at the
tritons and nereids, who seem to be gradually invading the pool.
We could use a swim ourselves."

"Go ahead, old boy, I'll stay in the sun and walk around a while."

Atilio and his fiancée had just hurled themselves theatrically into the water, screaming that it was very cold. Jorge, looking decidedly miserable, came up to Medrano and told him that Claudia wasn't allowing him to go in.

"Well, you'll go in this afternoon. You weren't too well last night, and you heard them say the water's like ice."

"Cold," said Jorge, who loved precision in certain cases. "Mama spends her life making me take a bath when I don't want to, and . . . and . . ."

"And vice versa."

"That's it. And you, Persio-moon-man, aren't you going to swim?"

"Oh, no," said Persio, who warmly offered his hand to Medrano. "I'm too sedentary, and besides, I once swallowed so much water I was unable to speak for over forty-eight hours."

"You're talking through your hat," Jorge decided, not at all convinced. "Medrano, did you see the glucid up there?"

"No. On the bridge? But no one's ever there."

"I saw him, I'm telling you. When I came out on deck a while ago, he was there. There, right between those two windows; he must have been at the wheel."

"Curious," said Claudia. "When Jorge told me, it was already too late and I saw no one. One wonders how they do navigate this ship."

"It's not absolutely necessary for them to stay glued to the windows," said Medrano. "The bridge has some depth, I suppose, and they probably install themselves in the back or in front of the map table . . ." He had the feeling no one was paying much attention. "In any case, you were lucky, luckier than I . . ."

"The first night the captain stood vigil up there until very late," Persio said.

"How do you know it was the captain, Persio-moon-man?"

"You can tell. It's a kind of aura about him. Tell me: what was the glucid you saw like?"

"Small, and dressed in white like all the others, with a cap on like all the others, and hands with black hairs like all the others."

"You're not going to try and tell me you saw the hair on his hands from here."

"No," Jorge admitted. "But because of his smallness you could tell he had hair on his hands."

Persio held his chin between two fingers, and supported his elbow with two others.

"Curious, very curious," he said, looking at Claudia. "One wonders if he really saw an officer, or if an interior eye . . . as when he talks in his sleep, or deals cards. A catalyst, that's the word, a real lightning rod. Yes, one wonders," he added, lost in thought.

"I saw him, I'm telling you," Jorge murmured, slightly offended. "What's so funny about that, hey?"

"You don't say hey."

"Huh, then?"

"You don't say huh, either," said Claudia, laughing. But Medrano didn't feel like laughing.

"This is getting to be a nuisance," he said to Claudia, when Persio took Jorge off to explain the mystery of the waves. "Isn't it silly to be stuck in a zone we call the deck? My God, it's completely undecked. Don't tell me that these lousy canvas tarps the Finns have installed would be any kind of protection in a storm. I mean if it begins to rain, or when we hit cold weather in the Strait of Magellan, we'll have to spend the day at the bar or in our cabins . . . Hell, this is more like a troop transport or a slaver than anything else. You have to be like Lucio not to notice it."

"That's true," said Claudia, moving toward the rail. "But since the sun is shining so beautifully, even though Persio says it's basically black, we shan't worry about it."

"Yes, and that's how we are about so many other things in our lives," said Medrano in a soft voice. "Since last night I've had the feeling that what happens to me from outside in, to put it like that, isn't essentially different from what I am inside out. I'm not making myself very clear, I'm afraid I'm falling into pure analogy, those analogies Persio so enjoys. It's a little . . ."

"It's a little you and a little me, isn't it?"

"Yes, and a little bit of all the rest, too. The problem has to be set up with greater clarity, but I feel as if just thinking of it turns out to be the best way to lose sight of it . . . All this is so vague and insignificant. You see, a moment ago I was perfectly all right. All Jorge had to tell me was that he had seen a glucid on the bridge to make everything go to hell. What connection can there be between that and . . . ? But this is a rhetorical question, Claudia; I suspect the connection, and the connection is that there isn't any connection because everything is one and the same thing."

"My poor Gabriel," said Claudia, taking him by the arm and imperceptibly drawing him closer to her. "You've been having a bad time since yesterday. But that isn't why we came on the *Malcolm.*"

"No," said Medrano, half-closing his eyes to better feel the soft pressure of Claudia's hand. "Of course it wasn't because of that."

"Jantzen?" Raul asked.

"No, Robert Hall," Lopez said, and they broke into peals of laughter.

It seemed comical to Raul to run into Lopez in the starboard corridor when Lopez' cabin was on the opposite side. He's making the rounds, poor fellow, taking a turn around each time in the hope of producing a casual encounter. O enamored sentinel, *pervigilium veneris!* He really deserves a better bathing suit . . .

"Wait up a second," he said, not knowing if he should congratulate himself for his compassion. "The atomic whirlwind is getting ready to come along too, but naturally she's lost her lipstick or slippers someplace."

"Oh, all right," said Lopez, elaborately indifferent.

They began to talk, leaning against the corridor wall. Lucio went by in a bathing suit, greeted them, and kept going.

"Are you still in the mood for launching new sorties using commando tactics?" asked Raul.

"Not so much after last night's fiasco . . . But I guess we'll have to go ahead with it. Unless the Trejo kid does it first."

"I doubt it," said Raul, looking at him out of the corner of his eye. "If he comes back stoned every time like he did yesterday . . . Can't descend into Hades without a well-tempered soul; at least that's what all good mythology teaches us."

"Poor kid, all he wanted to do was retaliate," said Lopez.

"Retaliate?"

"Well, yesterday we left him out of our plans and I'd guess he didn't like it. I know him slightly, remember? I teach at his school. I don't think he has what they call an easy character. At that age they all want to be men and they're right, except that the means they use and the opportunities that come their way keep playing dirty tricks on them."

Why the devil is he talking to me about him? Raul wondered, nodding his head appreciatively the whole time. *You have a sharp sense of smell, you do, you see everything that's under water, and you're an okay guy besides.* He bowed solemnly before Paula who was opening the cabin door, and then turned to look at Lopez who wasn't feeling too comfortable in his bathing suit. Paula had put on a severe black one-piece suit, just the opposite of yesterday's bikini.

"Hello, Lopez," she said lightly. "Are you going to have a swim too, Raul? We're not all going to fit in there."

"We'll die like heroes," said Raul, leading the march. "*Madre mía*, the La Boca gang is already here; the only thing missing now is for Don Galo to throw himself in, chair and all."

Felipe appeared on the portside staircase, followed by Beba, who installed herself in an elegant pose against the railing, so she could survey the pool and deck. They waved to Felipe, and he waved back timidly, wondering what their remarks about his odd indisposition must have been. But when Paula and Raul met him, laughing and talking, and then dived into the water with Lopez and Lucio close behind, his self-confidence came back and he started to joke and play with them. The water in the pool lapped away the last remnants of hangover.

"Seems you're better," Raul said to him.

"Sure, it's all blown over."

"Careful of the sun. It's going to be strong again today. Your shoulders are very burned."

"Ecch, it's nothing."

"Did the salve help?"

"Yeah, I think so," said Felipe. "What a mess last night. Pardon me for getting sick in your cabin. I felt like a damn fool, but—"

"Forget it, it was nothing," said Raul. "It could have happened to anyone. I once vomited on my Aunt Magda's carpet, may she not rest in peace, and a lot of people said it looked better than ever, but I assure you Aunt Magda wasn't popular in our family."

Felipe smiled, not understanding too well. He was happy that they were friends again. Raul was the only one he could talk to on the ship. Too bad Paula was with him and not with Medrano or Lopez. He felt like talking more with Raul, but he could see Paula's legs hanging over the edge of the pool and he was dying to go and sit down next to her to find out what she'd thought of his getting sick.

"I tried the pipe today," he said awkwardly. "It's terrific, and the tobacco . . ."

"Better than what you smoked last night, I imagine," said Raul.

"Last night? Oh, you mean . . ."

No one could hear them; the Presuttis were bellowing at the other end of the pool. Raul came closer to Felipe, who was standing against the corner of the tarpaulin.

"Why did you go alone? You know, you can go wherever you want to, but I have a feeling it's not too safe down below."

"And what could happen to me?"

"Probably nothing. Who were you down there with?"

"With . . ." He was going to say "Bob" but he swallowed the word. "With one of those guys."

"Which one, the younger one?" asked Raul, who knew very well which one.

"Yeah, him."

Lucio came splashing over to them. Raul made a gesture Felipe didn't understand, slipped back into the water, and swam toward the other end of the pool, where Atilio and Nelly were ducking one another enthusiastically. He said something to Nelly, who was furtively admiring him, and then he and Pelusa began to teach her how to dive. Felipe watched him for a minute, listlessly replied to Lucio, and then pulled himself up next to Paula whose eyes were closed.

"Guess who."

"Judging from the voice, a very handsome boy," said Paula. "I hope his name isn't Alexander, because the sun is marvelous."

"Alexander?" asked Felipe, the pupil, who had managed to fail several semesters of ancient history.

"Yes, Alexander, Iskander, Aleixandre, as you like. Hello, Felipe. But of course, you're Alexander's father. Raul, come listen to this, it's tremendous! The only thing missing now is a *macédoine* of fruit brought in by a waiter."

Felipe let the incomprehensible garble pass and touched up the bangs on his forehead with a nylon comb he pulled out of his tight bathing suit. Stretching out, he delivered himself over to the first easy caress of sun.

"Well, are you over your hangover?" Paula asked, closing her eyes again.

"What hangover? I got sick from too much sun," said Felipe, startled. "Everyone here thinks I drank a quart of whisky. Look, once at a school dinner at the end of the term . . ." Paula had to endure a description which included several boys rolling under the table at the Electra restaurant, and a picture of Felipe arriving home, invincible and undaunted, at three in the morning, even though he had drunk two Cinzano bitters, switched to red wine, and then to a sweet liqueur the name of which he couldn't remember.

"Cast-iron stomach!" said Paula. "How come it had such a bad effect on you this time?"

"But it wasn't the booze, I told you—I think I was out too long in the afternoon. You're pretty burnt yourself," he added, looking for a way out. "It looks good on you, your shoulders are nice."

"Really?"

"Yes, really nice. I imagine you've been told that a thousand times."

"Poor baby," thought Paula, without opening her eyes. "Poor baby." But she wasn't thinking of Felipe. She was thinking of the price someone would have to pay for a dream, once more someone would die in Venice and would go on living after death, *a sadder but not a wiser man* . . . By this time even a child like Jorge would have found a heap of amusing, even subtle things to say.

But no, the bangs, the petulance, and that's it . . . "That's why they look like statues, and the truth is they really are, inside and out." She guessed what Lopez must be imagining, sitting alone, sulking. It was time to sign an armistice with Jamaica John, the poor honey was probably convinced that Felipe was coming on, and that she was listening, more and more flattered by his gallantries ("more of a galantine than gallantry"). "What would happen if I dragged him off to bed? He'd get as red as a lobster and not know what to do with himself . . . Yes, well, he'd know what to do, but before and after, the really important . . . Poor kid, I'd have to teach him everything . . . But isn't it extraordinary, the boy in *Le Blé en herbe* was named Felipe . . . Oh, no, this is too much. I'll have to tell Jamaica John, once he gets over the urge to wring my neck . . ."

Jamaica John was staring at the hairs on his legs. Without raising his voice much he could have spoken with Paula, now that the Presuttis were out of the water and all was quiet except for Jorge's far-off laughter. But instead, he asked Medrano for a cigarette and began to smoke, his eyes fixed on the water, where a cloud was struggling desperately not to lose its Williams-pear shape. He was just remembering a fragment of dream that he'd had toward dawn, and which must have influenced his mood. He occasionally had dreams like that; this time, a friend of his was being made a minister in the dream, both of them were attending the swearing-in ceremony. Everything was fine, his friend a marvelous person, but all the same, Lopez had felt vaguely unhappy—as if anyone could have been appointed minister except for him. And then, at other times, he dreamed that his friend would marry well: a marriage of yachts, the Orient Express, Superconstellations; in any case, waking up was painful until a shower put some order back into reality. "I don't even have an inferiority complex," he said to himself. "But asleep I'm a mass of misery." He tried to get at the truth about himself. Wasn't he satisfied with his life? Wasn't his work, his house (not his house, actually, but to live as a boarder at his sister's house was a more than satisfactory solution), his girl-friends of the moment or the semester enough for him? "The worst of it is that dreams are supposed to reflect the truth, but maybe it's just the opposite, and I'm worrying myself sick over nothing. With this kind of sun and a trip like this I must be a real idiot to get as worked up as this."

Alone in the water, Raul watched Paula and Felipe. And so the pipe was terrific, and the tobacco . . . But he'd lied to him about his trip to Hades. The lying didn't bother him, it was almost a kind of homage that Felipe paid him. It wouldn't have been difficult to tell the truth to someone else; after all, what was the difference? But he lied to *him*, because even though he wasn't aware of it, he sensed the force which brought them together (all the more powerful the more it was stretched, like a good bow); he lied to him and unconsciously he was offering him a flower with his lie.

Standing up, Felipe breathed deeply, joyously; his body and head were outlined against the deep blue background of sky. Raul leaned up against the tarp and took the full force of the wound; he stopped watching Paula and Lopez, and instead he heard a loud voice, way inside, reverberating as in a cavern, the screaming sound of a thought, a thought born of the words of Krishnadasa, a strange thought to be having beside a pool, at such a different time, in a body so foreign, but as if the words rightfully belonged to him, and they did belong to him, all the words of love belonged to him, Krishnadasa's, the pastoral lover's, the man tied to a bed of flowers, subjected to the sweetest and slowest torture. "Dearly beloved, I have but one desire," he heard the singing. "To be the bells that encircle your legs, to go wherever you go, to be wherever you are . . . If I don't tie myself to your feet, what good does it do to sing of love? You are the image of my eyes, I see you everywhere. If only I contemplate your beauty, I am capable of loving the whole world. Krishnadasa says: Look, look." And the sky looked black around the statue.

XXXIV

"Poor man," said Doña Rosita. "Just look at him there, like a saint, without anyone to talk to. I think it's a shame, I always say to my husband the government ought to do something about it. It isn't fair just because someone's a chauffeur he has to spend the day by himself in a corner."

"And he seems nice, poor fellow," said Nelly. "And how big he is! Have you noticed, Atilio? What a bear!"

"Oh, he's not all that big," said Atilio. "When I help him lift the old man's chair, don't think he beats me for strength. He's big, that's for sure, but it's all fat. He looks like a wrestler, but if Lausse got a hold of him he'd knock him flat in two seconds. Hey, how do you think Rusito's going to do when he goes against Estefano?"

"Rusito's very good," said Nelly. "I hope to God he wins."

"The last time he took it by the skin of his teeth. I don't think he's got enough punch, but he's got great legs . . . He looks like Errol Flynn in that thing about the boxer, you saw it."

"Yes, we saw it at the Rialto. Oh, Atilio, I don't like movies about boxers. Their faces get all bloody and you don't see anything but fighting all the time. There's no feeling, you know?"

"Bah, feeling," said Pelusa. "If women don't see some slicked-up character smooching everybody, they can't stand it. Life's something else, I'm telling you. Reality, get it?"

"You say that because you like Westerns better, but boy, when Esther Williams comes on you've got your mouth wide open, don't think I don't see you."

Pelusa smiled modestly and said that Esther Williams was something else, really gorgeous, after all. But Doña Rosita, reacting to the lethargy brought on by breakfast and the rolling of the ship, intervened to inform them that the actresses nowadays simply couldn't compare with those of her day.

"Absolutely right," said Doña Pepa. "When you think of Norma Talmadge and Lillian Gish, you think of real women. Remember Marlene Dietrich? She isn't what you'd call decent, but what emotion! And the technicolor one with a priest who escaped among the Moors, you remember, and she came out at night to the terrace wearing white veils . . . I think it had a sad ending, it was destiny . . ."

"Oh, I know," said Doña Rosita. "*Gone with the Wind*, what emotion, now I remember."

"No, it wasn't *Gone with the Wind*," said Doña Pepa. "It was with a priest called Pepe something-or-other. Everything happened in the desert, I remember, and what color!"

"No, Mama," said Nelly. "The one with a Pepe was another one with Charles Boyer. Atilio saw it too, we went with Nela. Remember, Atilio?"

Atilio, who didn't have much of a memory, began to shift the deck chairs around, occupants and all, so that they'd be in the shade. The women screamed a little, but they were delighted because now they had a good view of the pool.

"She's talking to the boy already," said Doña Rosita. "When I think of how bold she is . . ."

"Mama, don't exaggerate," said Nelly, who had been talking to Paula and was still dazzled by Raul's good nature, as well as his jokes. "You don't want to understand modern youth, remember when we went to see the one with James Dean? I swear, Atilio, she wanted to leave all through the whole thing and she kept saying they were just a bunch of bums, imagine."

"Oh, those hoods aren't exactly straight," said Pelusa, who'd had a long discussion of the problem with the boys at the café. "It's the kind of education they get, what can you do."

"If I were that boy's mother, he'd hear from me," said Doña Pepa. "I'm positive she's saying things to him he shouldn't hear at his age. And if it were only that . . ."

The three of them agreed, looking significantly at one another.

"Last night's business was the last straw," Doña Pepa went on. "Just imagine going out in the dark with a married fellow, and the wife there watching it all . . . The expression on her face, and I saw it, poor angel. What it amounts to is they have no religion. You see what it's like on the streetcar? You could drop dead before they'd get up and give you a seat, and they just go on reading magazines full of crime and Sofia Loren."

"Ah, señora, I could tell you . . ." said Doña Rosita. "Look, in our neighborhood, without going any further . . . Look at her, just look at that hussy, and if it were only with that fellow last night, but on top of that she runs after the teacher, and he looks like a serious decent person."

"What does that have to do with it?" said Atilio, lining up, as

the only man, with the faction under attack. "Lopez is a great guy,
I swear, you can talk to him about anything, he's no snob. Nothing
wrong with making a pass, in the long run it's the woman who has
the say-so."

"And how about her husband, then?" said Nelly, who admired
Raul and didn't understand his conduct. "I think he must know
what's going on. First one fellow, then another, and another."

"There you have it, exactly," said Doña Rosita. "One goes off
and she immediately starts talking to the teacher. What does she
say to them? I can't understand how her husband puts up with it."

"It's modern youth," said Nelly, at a loss for another explanation. "It's in all the novels."

Wrapped in a wave of moral authority and a blue and red sun-
dress, Señora Trejo greeted the present company and sat down in
a deck chair next to Doña Rosita. Lucky her son had already left
the Lavalle woman's side, because now . . . Doña Rosita took her
time before leading the conversation back to the subject of interest, and between one thing and another she vigorously discussed
the rolling of the ship, the breakfast, the typhus scare—if it weren't
caught in time and if the rooms weren't disinfected—and the
indisposition (fortunately nothing serious) of the nice Trejo boy,
so much like his father, especially the way he moved his head.
Bored, Atilio suggested that he and Nelly take a walk around the
ship to warm up after their swim, and the women closed ranks,
compared their skeins of wool and the beginnings of respective
knitted bedjackets. Later (Jorge was singing at a scream, accompanied by Persio, whose voice sounded remarkably like a cat's) the
women unanimously agreed that Paula was a disturbing element
on board and that something like that shouldn't be permitted, especially when it took so long to get to Tokyo.

The discreet appearance of Nora was received with lively curiosity disguised as Christian friendliness. The women were immediately disposed to cheer Nora up, for those circles under her eyes
eloquently confirmed what she must have suffered. It was under-
standable, poor girl, only just married and to a hummingbird of a
man who was already going out in the dark with someone else to
do only God knows. A great pity Nora wasn't more given to be-

ing confidential; all the dialectic ability the ladies possessed was necessary to draw her into the conversation, which opened with a reference to the good quality of the butter on the ship, and immediately progressed to an analysis of the furnishings in the cabins, the ingeniousness displayed by the sailors in constructing the pool on open deck, that excellent fellow Costa, the slightly sad air which Lopez the teacher had worn this morning, and the youthfulness of Nora's husband, although it was strange that she hadn't gone swimming with him. Perhaps she was a little seasick; the ladies didn't feel like getting into the pool either, besides, at their age . . .

"Yes, I didn't feel like going in today," Nora said. "It's not that I'm feeling badly, just the opposite, but I didn't sleep much and . . ." And then she blushed violently because Doña Rosita had looked at Señora Trejo, who had looked at Doña Pepa, who had looked at Doña Rosita. Everyone understood perfectly, they had been young once, but in any case Lucio ought to be more gallant and come to fetch his young wife, so that he could walk with her in the sun or swim with her. Ah, men were all the same, very demanding for some things, especially when they had just married, but then later they liked to go out alone or with other men, to tell off-color stories while the wife sat home knitting. However, to Doña Pepa it seemed that a newly married woman shouldn't permit her husband to leave her alone, because it was just like giving him wings, and in the end the man would go off to play cards in the café, after having gone alone to the movies, after having come home late from work, after God knows what else.

"Lucio and I are very independent," Nora offered weakly. "Each of us has a right to live our own lives, because . . ."

"This is what modern youth is like," said Doña Pepa, firm in her opinion. "Each to his own and one fine day they find out that . . . I don't mean it about you, my dear, you know, you're both so nice, but I've had experience, I've brought up Nelly, and what a battle . . . Right now, not to go any further, if you and Señor Costa don't pay more attention, it wouldn't surprise me at all if . . . But I didn't mean . . ."

"There's nothing, Doña Pepa," Señora Trejo said quickly. "I un-

derstand perfectly what you meant to say and I'm in complete
agreement with you. I've also had to watch out for my children,
believe me."

Nora was beginning to realize they were talking about Paula.
"I don't like the lady's behavior either," she said. "Not that it
has anything to do with me personally, but she has a way of
flirting . . ."

"Exactly what we were saying when you came," Doña Rosita
said. "The exact words. A shameless hussy, that one."

"Well, I didn't say . . . I think you exaggerate her generosity,
and of course you, señora . . ."

"I know, dear," said Señora Trejo. "And I'm not going to allow
that girl, if you call her that, to start getting involved with my little
boy. He's innocence itself, at sixteen, just imagine . . . But if it
were just him . . . And besides, she isn't satisfied with just one
flirtation. And not only that . . ."

"If she'd only concentrate on the teacher, it wouldn't seem to
me to be so bad," said Doña Pepa. "And that's not any good
either, because when one is married before God it isn't right to
look at another man. But Señor Lopez seems so decent . . . well,
maybe they're only talking."

"A vamp," said Doña Rosita. "Her husband may be very nice,
but if my Enzo saw me talking like that to another man, and it's
not that he's not a gentleman, but something would happen, believe me. Marriage is marriage and that's that."

Nora had lowered her eyes.

"I know what you're thinking," she said. "She's also tried to flirt
with my . . . with Lucio. But neither of us can actually take such
a thing seriously."

"Yes, child, but you have to be careful," said Doña Pepa, who
had the unpleasant sensation that the fish was slipping off the
hook. "It's all very well to say that you're not going to take it seriously, but don't forget a woman is always a woman and a man is
always a man, as they say."

"Oh, there's no need to exaggerate," said Nora. "As far as Lucio
is concerned, I don't worry in the slightest, but I'm aware that the
way that girl acts . . ."

"A tramp, that's what she is," said Doña Rosita. "To go out on deck in the middle of the night alone with a man, when the wife, poor angel, pardon the comparison, stays behind looking . . ."

"Come now, come now," said Señora Trejo. "You don't have to exaggerate, Doña Rosita. You can see that this girl is taking everything philosophically, and she's the one concerned."

"And how should I take it?" said Nora, feeling as if a tiny hand were beginning to squeeze her around the throat. "It won't happen again, that's all I can say."

"I should think not," said Señora Trejo. "And I don't intend to let her go on bothering the boy. I told my husband what I think, and if she oversteps again, that little lady will hear from me. The poor boy feels obliged to hang around because Señor Costa took care of him yesterday when he got ill, and even gave him a present. Imagine how embarrassed we were. But look who's coming over . . ."

"This sun is murderous," Don Galo declared, dismissing the chauffeur with both hands in a way which made him look like a magician. "Incredibly hot today, ladies! Well, here I am with my list almost completed now, and I'm ready to turn it over to you so you can go over it with me and give me any last-minute advice . . ."

XXXV

"*Tiens, tiens,* here comes Teach," said Paula.

Lopez sat down next to her at the edge of the pool.

"Give me a cigarette, I left mine in the cabin," he said, scarcely looking at her.

"But of course, with pleasure. This damn lighter will end up in the deepest oceanic trench there is. Well, and how's the morning been?"

"So-so," said Lopez, still pondering his dreams, which had left a bitter taste in his mouth. "And you?"

"Ping-pong," said Paula.

"Ping-pong?"

"Yes. I ask you how you are, you answer me, and then you ask

me how I am. I'm answering you: Fine, Jamaica John, fine in spite
of everything. The social ping-pong, always delightfully idiotic,
like encores at concerts, get-well cards, and three million other
things. The comfortable vaseline that keeps the wheels of the
world so well lubricated, as Spinoza said.'

"The only thing I like out of all that is that you called me by
my true name," said Lopez. "I'm sorry I can't add 'many thanks,'
after your peroration."

"Your real name? Well, Lopez is quite bad enough, we agree on
that. Just like Lavalle, although the latter . . . Yes, the hero was
behind the door and they shot him point blank; that's always an
illustrious historical event worth evoking."

"Well, if we get to that, Lopez was just as illustrious a tyrant,
darling."

"When one says 'darling' like you just finished saying it, it makes
you want to vomit, Jamaica John."

"Darling," he said in a much lower voice.

"Ah-hah. Much better. However, my dear gallant, allow me to
remind you that a lady—"

"Oh, for Christ's sake, enough, please," said Lopez. "Cut the
comedy. Either we talk straight or I'm leaving. Why do we have to
go on bugging one another? I got up this morning determined not
to look at you again, or to tell you to your face that your conduct
. . ." He burst into laughter. "Your conduct," he repeated. "That's
really great, I start talking about conduct. Get dressed, I'll wait for
you at the bar; we can't talk here."

"Are you going to lecture me?" said Paula, with the air of a
schoolgirl.

"Yes. Go get dressed."

"Are you very angry, but very, very angry, with poor little
Paula?"

Lopez started to laugh again. They looked at each other for a
moment, deeply. Paula took a breath. It had been a long time
since she had felt the desire to obey someone, and it seemed odd
to her, novel, almost pleasant. Lopez was waiting.

"All right," said Paula. "I'll go dress, Teach. Every time you act
like a boss I'll call you Teach. But we could stay here, too. Lucio

just got out of the water and nobody can hear us, and if you have to disclose important matters to me . . . why deprive ourselves of this warm sun?"

Why the devil should she obey him?

"Okay, the bar was a pretext," said Lopez, his voice still soft. "There are some things I can't say yet, Paula. Yesterday, when I touched your hand . . . Something like that . . . what's the use of talking about it?"

"But you talk very well, Jamaica John. I like to hear you say those things. I like when you're as mad as a bear, but I also like it when you laugh. Don't be mad at me, Jamaica John."

"Last night," he said, looking at her mouth, "I hated you. Let me lay some hideous dreams, a bad taste in the mouth, and an almost lost morning to your account. I didn't have any reason to go to the barber shop, I went because I had to do something."

"Last night," said Paula, "you acted like a fool."

"Was it absolutely essential to go out on deck with Lucio?"

"Why not? With Lucio or anyone else?"

"I'd like you to figure that one out yourself."

"Lucio's very nice," said Paula, crushing out her cigarette. "After all, I just wanted to see the stars, and I saw them. And so did he, I assure you."

Lopez said nothing but he looked at her in a way that made Paula lower her eyes a second. She was thinking (it was more of a feeling than a thought) how she would make him pay for that look, when she suddenly heard Jorge shout, and then Persio. They looked around. Jorge was jumping up and down on the deck, pointing at the bridge.

"A glucid, a glucid! I told you there was one!"

Medrano and Raul, who had been talking under the canvas awning, came running up. Lopez jumped to his feet and looked. In spite of the blinding sun, he recognized the silhouette of the thin officer on the bridge, the same thin officer with the short grey hair who had spoken to them the day before. Lopez cupped his hands around his mouth and shouted so loudly that the officer could not help but look. He motioned to him threateningly to come down to the deck. The officer went on looking at him, and

Lopez repeated the motion with such violence that he gave the impression of transmitting the message with flags. The officer disappeared.

"What's up with you, Jamaica John?" Paula asked, following him down to the deck. "Why did you call him?"

"I called him," said Lopez curtly, "because I damn well felt like it."

He went over to Medrano and Raul, who seemed to approve of his attitude, and signaled again. He was so excited that Raul looked at him with slightly amused surprise.

"Do you think he'll come down?"

"I don't know," said Lopez. "Maybe he won't, but I want to warn you beforehand that if he doesn't show up in a few minutes, I'm going to throw this lock-nut against the window."

"Perfect," said Medrano. "It's the least one can do."

But the officer did show up a few minutes later, looking neat and slightly withdrawn, as if he were still studying his script and his repertory of possible answers. He came down the starboard staircase, excusing himself as he passed Paula, who greeted him mockingly. Only at that point did Lopez remember that he was almost naked, and without knowing exactly why, this detail infuriated him more than ever.

"Good day, gentlemen," said the officer, nodding to each one of them.

Claudia and Persio were witnessing the scene from a distance, not wanting to interfere. Lucio and Nora had disappeared, and the women went on talking with Atilio and Don Galo, amid laughter and cackles.

"Good day," said Lopez. "Yesterday, if I'm not mistaken, you said the doctor on board would come see us. He hasn't been here."

"So sorry," said the officer, who, staring at his sleeve, seemed to want to remove a thread from his white linen jacket. "I hope all of you are in good health."

"Forget our health. Why didn't the doctor come?"

"I suppose he was busy with . . . our patients. Have you noticed some . . . any alarming symptom?"

"Yes," said Raul blandly. "There's a general atmosphere of the plague around here, straight out of an existentialist novel. Among other things, you shouldn't make promises without keeping them."

"The doctor will come, you can be sure. I don't like to say it, but for security reasons, which you can't help but understand, I think it's better that between you and . . . us, let's say, there be the least possible contact . . . at least during these first days."

"Ah, the typhus," said Medrano. "But if one of us were willing to risk it, I, for instance, why couldn't I go to the back of the boat with you to see the doctor?"

"But you would have to return, and then . . ."

"Here we go again," said Lopez, damning Medrano and Raul because they weren't letting him do what he felt like doing. "Listen, I've had enough, do you know what I mean when I say enough? I don't like this trip, I don't like you, yes, you, and all the other glucids, starting with Captain Smith. Now listen: there can be any kind of fuckup at all back there, I don't know, typhus, rats, anything, but I want to warn you that if the doors stay locked, I'm ready for anything to get through. And when I say anything, I mean it."

His lips were trembling with rage, and Raul felt slightly sorry for him, but Medrano seemed to agree with him, and the officer finally realized that Lopez wasn't speaking only for himself. He started to leave, bowing with cold amiability.

"I don't want to open a discussion on your threats, sir," he said, "but I will inform my superior officer. Personally, I'm deeply sorry that—"

"Okay, stop crying," said Medrano, stepping between him and Lopez, who was standing with clenched fists. "Better get the hell out of here, and as you put it so well, inform your superior officer. And as soon as possible."

The officer fixed his eyes on Medrano, and Raul had the impression that the glucid had gone pale. It was difficult to be sure because of the almost blinding light and the man's skin. He saluted rigidly and turned around. Paula scarcely let him pass, allowing him the least possible room for his shoe, and then she came up to the men, who were all looking a bit disconcerted.

"Mutiny on board," said Paula. "Well done, Lopez. We're all behind you a hundred per cent, madness is more contagious than typhus 224."

Lopez looked at her as if he were coming out of a bad dream. Claudia had come up to Medrano; she grazed his arm lightly.

"You are all the joy of my child's life. Look at the expression on his face."

"I'm going to change," Raul announced suddenly, as if the situation had lost all interest for him. But Paula kept smiling.

"I'm very obedient, Jamaica John. We'll meet in the bar."

They went up the staircase together, passing Beba Trejo, who was pretending to read a magazine. The darkness on the staircase was like veritable night to Lopez, a night with no dreams where someone who deserved nothing got the command. He felt elated and very tired at the same time. "It would have been better if I had socked him in the kisser and gotten it over with," he thought, but he almost didn't care.

When he got to the bar, Paula had already ordered two beers and was halfway through a cigarette.

"Extraordinary," said Lopez. "The first time a woman ever dressed faster than I did."

"You must have a Roman concept of the shower, to judge by the time you've taken."

"Maybe, I don't remember too well. I think I stayed in a while; the cold water felt good. I feel better now."

Señor Trejo interrupted his reading of an issue of *Life International* to greet them with a slightly glacial politeness, a relief from the heat, according to Paula. Seated on the corner bench, furthest from the door, they could see only Señor Trejo and the bartender, who was busy trying to get some gin and vermouth closer together. When Lopez lit his cigarette with Paula's, bringing his face close to hers, something which must have been happiness mixed with the smoke and the pitching of the ship. Right in the middle of it he felt a bitter drop fall, and he moved back, disconcerted.

She went on waiting, calm and light. The waiting lasted a long time.

"Do you still feel like killing the poor glucid?"

"Bah, what does that sonofabitch matter to me?"

"Of course he doesn't matter. The glucid would have paid for my crimes. It's me you really feel like killing. Metaphorically, of course."

Lopez stared at his beer.

"In other words, you go to your cabin in a bathing suit, get undressed as if it were nothing, take a bath, he comes and goes, and undresses too, and that's how it is, isn't it?"

"Jamaica John," said Paula, in a tone of comic reproach. "Manners, my dear."

"I don't understand," said Lopez. "I don't understand anything really. The ship, you, not even me; the whole thing's completely ridiculous."

"Dear heart, in Buenos Aires, one isn't so well informed about what goes on inside people's houses. How many girls whom you've admired *illo tempore* would undress in the presence of some surprising people . . . Don't you think you act like an old maid sometimes?"

"Don't be ridiculous."

"But that's how it is, Jamaica John. You're thinking the exact same thing that those poor fat ladies stuck under the awning would think if they knew Raul and I weren't married and had nothing to do with one another."

"That idea repels me because I don't think it's accurate," said Lopez, furious again. "I can't imagine that Costa . . . Then what *does* happen?"

"Use your head, as they say in detective novels."

"Paula, you can be as liberal as you like, I can understand, more than understand, but that you and Costa . . ."

"Why not? While bodies don't contaminate souls . . . That's what bothers you, the souls. The souls which, in their turn, contaminate the bodies and, as a consequence, one of the bodies goes to bed with another."

"Then you don't sleep with Costa?"

"No, Mr. Professor, I don't sleep with Costa. Now I'll tell you what you're going to say: 'I don't believe you.' See, I saved you four words. Ah, Jamaica John, how tiresome, how I'd like to say an evil word I have on the tip of my tongue. You wouldn't have any trouble accepting a situation like this in a novel . . . Raul insists that I tend to measure the world in terms of literature. Wouldn't it be far more intelligent if you did the same? Why are you so genteel, so Don-Lopez-of-Castile-and-Aragon? Why do

you let yourself be led around by atavisms? Right now I'm reading
your thoughts like the gypsies in Retiro Park. Now you shuffle the
hypothesis that Raul . . . well, let's say that a natural misfortune
deprives him of appreciating the thing in me which would exalt
other men. Well, you're mistaken, it's not that at all."

"I never thought that," said Lopez, a little embarrassed. "But
you'll admit it must seem strange that . . ."

"No, because I've been Raul's friend for ten years. There's no
reason for it to seem strange to me."

Lopez ordered two more beers. The bartender reminded them
that it was almost lunchtime and beer would spoil their appetites.
The order was repeated firmly. Gently, Lopez' hand touched
Paula's. They looked at one another.

"I admit, I don't have any right to act like a censor. You—yes,
let me use the familiar form, please . . ."

"Of course. And one up. I was about to use it myself. And that
would have got you depressed, because today you're all . . . well,
you started nine points down . . ."

"Darling," said Lopez. "Oh, sweetheart . . ."

Paula looked at him a moment, hesitating.

"It's easy to go from doubt to tenderness, and it's practically
fatal. I've noticed it more than once. But the pendulum swings
back, Jamaica John, and you're going to distrust me now more
than before because you feel closer to me. Don't kid yourself, I'm
far from everything. So far that it gets me sick."

"No, you're not far from me."

"The physical is illusory, sweetheart, it's one thing to be close to
me, and another . . . Tape measures break down when people
try to measure things like these. But a while ago . . . Yes, I should
tell you, for it's quite unusual for me to have an attack of sincerity
or honesty . . . Why do you look so shocked? You're not going to
pretend to know me better in two days than I know myself in all
my twenty-five years. A little while ago, I realized that you were
a delicious hunk of man, but, even more, that you're more honest than I had thought."

"How more honest?"

"Well, let's say more sincere. Come clean, till now you were in the same old play: boarding ship, sizing up the situation as it stands, electing candidates . . . Just like fiction, even if that does amuse Raul. You did exactly that, and if there had happened to be five or six Paulas aboard, instead of one (we'll leave Claudia out of it because she's not for you, and don't put on that outraged male face), at this moment I might not have the honor of drinking a well-chilled beer with Teach."

"Paula, what you're saying we call fate. You could have met six other men on board too, and it might have been my fate to adore you from afar."

"Jamaica John, every time I hear the word fate I feel like taking out the toothpaste. Have you noticed that Jamaica John doesn't sound so nice when I use the familiar form? Pirates require a more solemn form of address. Of course, if I call you Carlos, I'll be reminded of my Aunt Carmen Rosa's little dog. Charles . . . no, that's a hideous piece of snobbery. Well, we'll find something. For the moment, you must continue to be my favorite pirate. No, I'm not going."

"Who said anything?" Lopez murmured, startled.

"*Tes yeux, mon cheri*. I see the lower corridor, a door, and a number one on it clearly drawn in your eyes. I admit I've carefully noted the number of your cabin."

"Paula, please."

"Give me another cigarette. And don't think you've made progress just because I'm ready to admit you're more honest than I thought. To put it simply, I appreciate you, something new for me. I think you're a lovely man, and heaven help me if I've ever said this to many men before you. In general, I've a perfectly teratological idea of men. Necessary but regrettable, like sanitary napkins or Vicks Vaporub."

She kept making funny faces while she talked, as if she wanted to take some of the weight off her words.

"I think you're wrong," said Lopez, sullenly. "I'm not the lovely man you think I am, but I don't like treating a woman as if she were a pastime."

"But I am a pastime, Jamaica John."

"No."

"You can be sure. You can see it with your eyes, even though your good Christian education tries to fool you. Basically, I can't fool anyone, it's an advantage, believe me."

"Why the bitterness?"

"Why the invitation?"

"But I haven't invited you to anything," Lopez insisted, furious.

"Oh yes, oh yes, oh yes."

"I'd like to pull your hair," he said tenderly. "I feel like telling you to go to hell."

"You're so nice," said Paula, convinced. "Actually, we're both terrific."

Lopez began to laugh, he couldn't help it.

"I like to hear you talk," he said. "I like the fact that you're courageous. Yes, you're courageous, you're constantly exposing yourself to the possibility of being misunderstood, and that's the height of courage. Beginning with that business about Raul. No, I'm not pushing: I believe you. I told you before and I'm telling you again. I don't understand a thing, but that's another matter, unless . . . Last night it occurred to me . . ."

He told her about Raul's face when they came back from the expedition, and Paula listened to him in silence, leaning back on the bench, looking at the cigarette ash gradually growing longer between her fingers. The alternatives were so easy: to tell him or shut up. Basically, it was all the same to Raul, but this concerned her and not Raul. Confide in Jamaica John or shut up. She decided to tell him everything. There was no turning back; it was the morning of confidences.

XXXVI

News of the recent unpleasantness between the teacher and the ship's official traveled like a trail of gunpowder among the ladies. What strange behavior for the always gentlemanly and well-mannered Lopez! A really terribly disagreeable atmosphere was being created aboard this ship, and in Nelly's opinion (she was just returning from an agreeable chat with her fiancé near the reliable insurance of some high piles of cordage) the men, with all their whining, weren't doing anything but spoiling a good thing. Although Atilio made a manly effort to defend Lopez' conduct, Doña Pepa and Doña Rosita, who were indignant, overruled him, Señora Trejo turned purple with rage, and Nora took advantage of the general excitement by returning, at a run practically, to her cabin, where Lucio was still painfully trying to read a condensation of the experiences of a missionary in Indonesia. He didn't look up, but she approached his armchair and waited. Lucio finally closed the magazine, resignedly.

"There's been a very unpleasant argument out there," said Nora.

"What do I care?"

"An officer came down and Lopez treated him hideously. He threatened him, and told him he'd stone the windows of the bridge if that poop-deck business weren't cleared up."

"It's going to be tough to find stones," said Lucio.

"He said he'd throw an iron nut."

"They'll lock him up for being mad. I don't give two hoots."

"Sure, me neither," said Nora.

She began to brush her hair, glancing occasionally at Lucio in the mirror. Lucio tossed the magazine on the bed.

"I'm fed up. Damn the day I won that crummy raffle. To think that other people win a Chevrolet or a villa in Mar de Ajo."

"Yes, the atmosphere isn't the best," said Nora.

"You're so right, more than enough reasons to say that."

"I mean what's happening at the stern, and all that mess."

"I mean more than that," said Lucio.

"Let's not go back to that subject."

"Of course, I agree with you completely. It's so stupid, it's not worth mentioning."

"I don't know if it's stupid or not, but it's best we forget the whole thing."

"We'll forget it, but it really is stupid."

"If you say so," said Nora.

"If there's one thing I can't stand, it's a lack of frankness between husband and wife," Lucio said, virtuously.

"You know very well we're not husband and wife."

"And you happen to know very well I intend to marry you. I say
it for your *petit bourgeois* peace of mind, because as far as I'm concerned, we already are. And you can't deny that."

"Don't be rude," said Nora. "You seem to forget I have any
feelings."

With few exceptions, the travelers generously offered their talents to Don Galo and Dr. Restelli so that the soirée might be a
success and banish all traces of worry, which, as Dr. Restelli said,
only clouded over the magnificent sun, the long-standing pride of
the Patagonian coasts. Deeply offended by the morning's episode,
Dr. Restelli had gone in search of Lopez as soon as he found out
what had happened from the ladies and Don Galo. Since Lopez
was talking to Paula in the bar, Dr. Restelli restricted himself to
an Indian tonic with lemon at the counter, waiting for the opportune moment to intervene in the conversation, which more than
once caused him to turn his head and act as if he hadn't heard a
thing. Señor Trejo, whose issue of *Life International* seemed to turn
to stone between his fingers, threw more than one knowing look
at Dr. Restelli, but the Doctor thought too highly of his colleague
to act as if he understood the meaning of the glances. When Raul
Costa appeared, freshly bathed and dressed in an elegant shirt,
sat down next to Paula and Lopez with the most perfect ease,
and joined in the conversation as if it were the most natural thing
in the world, Dr. Restelli decided that he was authorized to cough
lightly and approach them. Hurt and annoyed at the same time, he
tried to get Lopez to promise not to throw an iron nut at the captain's window, but Lopez, who had seemed quite happy and not
at all belligerent up until then, suddenly turned serious and said
that his ultimatum was formal, and he was not about to have them
make fools out of everyone. As Raul and Paula kept silent, punc-
tuating the conversation with cigarette smoke, Dr. Restelli invoked
reasons of an aesthetic nature, and Lopez condescended almost
immediately to consider the soirée as a kind of sacred truce which
would expire at ten the following morning. Dr. Restelli declared
himself satisfied that Lopez, although rather regrettably excited
by a matter which hardly justified such violence, would carry out
his part of the agreement as the perfect gentleman he was, and

after accepting another Indian tonic he left to look for Don Galo, who was still recruiting participants on deck.

Laughing, Lopez shook his head like a drenched dog.

"Poor Black Cat, he's a great character. You should see him on Independence Day when he gets up to make his speech. His voice booms out from the very bottom of his shoes, his eyes roll back, and while the boys squirm with laughter or fall asleep with their eyes open, the glories of the revolution and the great men in white ties parade before their eyes like so many wax figures at some sidereal distance from the poor Argentina of the fifties. You know, one of my students asked me one day: 'Sir, if a century ago everyone was so noble and brave, what the hell's happening today?' "

"I remember the patriotic speeches when I was in school," said Raul. "I learned to hold them in exacting disgust at a very early age: the noble banner, the imperishable fatherland, the eternal laurels, the guardsman dies but surrenders? Never . . . no, I've already gotten it all mixed up, but it's the same thing. Is it possible they use this vocabulary as reins, or blinders? The fact is that, past a certain mental level, the absurd contrast between these words and those who use them kills any kind of illusion at all."

"Yes, but one needs faith when one is young," said Paula. "I can remember more than one decent and respected teacher saying these things in class or in speeches, and when I heard them, I promised myself to live up to a brilliant career, a martyrdom, a total deliverance of myself to the fatherland. It's a sweet thing, one's fatherland, Raulito. It doesn't exist, but it's sweet."

"It exists, but it isn't sweet," said Lopez.

"It doesn't exist, we exist it," said Raul. "Don't fall into simple phenomenology, you ignoramuses."

Paula felt that what he said wasn't exactly right, and the conversation suddenly acquired technical brightness which demanded Lopez' discreet and silent admiration. Listening to them, he again felt this lack which could hardly be given a name, he wasn't sure if you could call it noncommunication or simply individuality. Separated as they were by their differences and their lives, Paula and Raul meshed like a net; they recognized and judged one another continuously in allusions, the recollections of shared experiences, while he was outside of it all, listening in sadly—and at the same time he could be happy, so happy looking at Paula's nose, listening to Paula's laugh—to that alliance sealed by a time and space like cutting a finger and mixing blood and becoming one, forever and ever . . . Now he was going to become part of Paula's time and space, assiduously assimilating, during God-knows-how-long, the imponderable things that Raul already knew as if they were part of him: Paula's likes and dislikes, the exact meaning of a gesture or of a dress or a fit of anger, her system of ideas or simply the general disorder of her values and feelings, her yearnings and her hopes. "But she's going to be mine and that changes everything," he thought, tightening his mouth. "She's going to be born over again, for what he knows about her is what anyone who knows her a while can share. I . . ." But he had arrived late, and nothing would keep Paula and Raul from exchanging a glance at any given moment, and that glance could signify a concert at Wagner Hall, an afternoon in the Mar del Plata, a chapter from Faulkner, a visit to Aunt Matilda, a strike at the university, anything that had happened without Carlos Lopez, anything that had happened while Carlos Lopez was holding class in Room B, or walking down the Calle Florida, or making love with Rosalia; anything they had would be officially sealed in, like the motors of racing cars, like the envelopes that hold wills, something beyond his time and reach but still Paula, the same Paula who would sleep in his arms and make him happy. Then the jealousies of the past, which in Proust and Pirandello had always seemed too conventional and too impotent to bring the truth of the present to life, would begin to gnaw into the apple. His hands would know every moment of Paula's body, and life would deceive him with a minimal illusion of the present, with those few passing hours or days or months, until Raul would return or someone else, until a mother or brother or ex-schoolmate would turn up, or simply a page from a book, a note in an address book, or even worse, until Paula herself would make a gesture out of the past, a gesture quickened with meaning, yet incomprehensible, or would allude to something from another time as she passed in front of a house or saw a certain face or painting. If some day he really did fall in love with Paula, because he wasn't in love now ("I'm not in love with her now," he thought. "I only want to sleep with her and live with her and be with her now"), then time would show him its true blind face, and would proclaim the insurmountable space of the past, where hands and words have no meaning, where it would be useless to throw an iron nut at the captain's bridge because it wouldn't get there and it wouldn't hurt it, where every step would be stopped short by a wall of air, and every kiss would find an intolerable mocking mirror as an answer. Seated at the same table, Paula and Raul were all at once on the other side of the mirror; when his voice occasionally mingled with theirs, it was as if a foreign element intruded on the perfect sphere of their dancing voices, lightly enlaced, alternately meeting and parting in the air. To be Raul, to be Raul while continuing to be himself, to run so blindly and desperately against it that the invisible wall would shatter and let him through, to gather up all of Paula's past in a single embrace which would place him forever at her side, to possess her as a virgin, an adolescent, to play the first games of life with her, in that way to come closer to youth, to the present, to the mirrorless air which surrounded them, to go into the bar with her, to sit down with her at the table, to greet Raul like a friend, to talk about what they were talking about, to look at what they were looking at, to feel the other space behind him, the inconceivable future, but to know at the same time that all the rest was theirs, that this air of time which enveloped them now should not be the unreal bubble surrounded by nothingness of a yesterday where Paula belonged to another world, of a tomorrow in which life together would hold no force to draw her completely to him, to make her truly and forever his.

"Yes, it was admirable," said Paula, and she put her hand on Lopez' shoulder. "Ah, Jamaica John is waking up, his astral body was wandering through far-off regions."

"Whom were you calling the Volsung?" said Lopez.

"Gieseking. I don't know why we call him that; Raul is sad because he's dead. We used to go to listen to him. His Beethoven was so lovely."

"Yes, I went to hear him too sometimes," said Lopez. (But it wasn't the same, it wasn't the same. Each one to his own side, the mirror . . .) Furious, he shook his head and asked Paula for a cigarette. Paula leaned up against him lightly, not too much because Señor Trejo was looking at them from time to time, and she smiled at him.

"How far away you were, awfully far. Are you sad? Bored?"

"Don't be silly," said Lopez. "Don't you find her very silly?"

XXXVII

"I don't know, he hasn't got a fever, but there's something I don't like," said Claudia, looking at Jorge, who was tagging after Persio. "When my son doesn't manifest his wholesomeness by taking a second dessert, it's a sign his tongue is coated."

Medrano was listening as if the words were some kind of reproach. He shrugged his shoulders furiously.

"The best thing would be for him to see a doctor, but if we go on like this . . . No, it's really uncivilized. Lopez is absolutely right and this absurd business will have to end one way or another."

"I wonder why the devil we have those weapons in our cabins," he thought, understanding perfectly why Claudia fell silent, both disconcerted and skeptical.

"Probably they won't get anywhere," Claudia said after a while. "You can't open an iron door by pushing. But don't worry about Jorge, maybe it's just the tail end of yesterday's upset. Let's get some deck chairs and look for a little shade."

They sat down at a sufficient distance from Señora Trejo, not far enough to offend her, but far enough to be able to talk without her hearing them. It was cool in the shade at four in the afternoon. A breeze was blowing. Occasionally it hummed along the ship's rigging, and it ruffled Jorge's hair as he played a violently active game with the patient Persio. Claudia had the feeling that just under the surface of the conversation Medrano was mulling over his *idée fixe*, and that while he was commenting on Presutti's and Felipe's exercises, he was thinking about the officer and the doctor. She smiled, amused by so much masculine obsessiveness.

"It's strange, but we haven't even talked about our projected trip through the Pacific," she said. "I've noticed no one mentions

Japan, not even the modest Strait of Magellan or possible ports of call."

"The remote future," said Medrano. "Too remote for some people's imagination, and too improbable for you and me."

"There's no reason to suspect we won't get there."

"No reason at all. But it's a little like death. No reason to suspect we'll die, yet . . ."

"I detest allegories," said Claudia, "except those written in their own time, and I don't like all of those."

Felipe and Pelusa were practicing a series of acrobatic tricks which they would perform at the soirée. No one was visible on the bridge. Señora Trejo plunged her yellow knitting needles cruelly into the skein of yarn, wrapped up her knitting, and then after a polite nod, she amiably added up the number of people out of sight. Medrano stared off into space, his eyes on the beak of a bird of prey.

"Japan or no Japan, I'll never regret having gone on this damn *Malcolm.* Thanks to it, I've met you, I've had that bird, those soapy waves, and some bad moments, which I needed more than I would have admitted in Buenos Aires."

"And you've met Don Galo and Señora Trejo . . . not to mention other equally distinguished passengers."

"I'm talking seriously, Claudia. I'm not happy on this ship, and that surprises me because it didn't enter into my plans. Everything was set to make this trip something like the interval between the end of one book and the moment when one picks out a new one. A no man's land where we can lick our wounds, if that's possible, and replenish our carbohydrates, fats, and moral reserve, for the new plunge into the calendar. But it's turned out just the opposite: the no man's land was Buenos Aires for these last weeks."

"Any place at all is all right for clearing things up and making some sense out of them," said Claudia. "If only I felt the same, everything you told me last night, that still can happen to you . . . The life I lead doesn't worry me much, here or there. It's a kind of hibernation, a life on tiptoe in which I'm no more than Jorge's shadow, the hand that's always there when he stretches out his in the dark when he's afraid."

"Yes, but that's a lot."

"Seen from the outside, or measured in terms of maternal abnegation. The problem is that I'm something else besides Jorge's mother. I already told you this, my marriage was a mistake, but it's also a mistake to stay out too long in the sun. To make a mistake through an excess of beauty or happiness . . . what counts are the results. In any case, my past was full of lovely things, and it's no consolation to know I've sacrificed them for other things, just as lovely or necessary. Let me choose between a Braque and a Picasso, and I'll take the Braque, I know which one (if it's the painting I'm thinking of right now), but what a shame not to have that stunning Picasso hanging in my salon, too . . ."

She broke into a joyless laugh, and Medrano stretched out his hand and rested it on her arm.

"Nothing prevents you from being a good deal more than Jorge's mother," he said. "Why is it that when women are alone they nearly always lose their impetus, let themselves go? Do they only run when we take them by the hand, while we think we're running because they're showing us the way? You don't seem to buy the idea that maternity might be your only obligation, as so many other women do. I'm sure you'd be able to do anything you wanted to, satisfy all your desires."

"Oh, my desires," Claudia said. "I'd rather not have them, be finished with most of them. Maybe that way . . ."

"Then continuing to love your husband is enough for you to waste the rest of it?"

"I don't know if I love him," said Claudia. "Sometimes I think I never loved him. It was too easy for me to free myself. As it was for you with Bettina, for instance, and I don't think you were in love with her."

"And he? Didn't he ever try for a reconciliation? Did he let you go just like that?"

"Oh, he attended three neurology congresses a year," said Claudia, without a trace of resentment. "Even before the divorce was final he had already found a girlfriend in Montevideo. He told me about her so I wouldn't worry, because he must have suspected me of this . . . let's just call it a feeling of guilt."

They saw Felipe going up the starboard ladder, where he joined Raul. They went off down the corridor. Beba appeared and sat

down on the deck chair her mother had just left. They smiled at
her. Beba smiled at them. Poor girl, always alone.

"It's nice here," said Medrano.

"Oh yes," said Beba. "I couldn't stand any more sun, although I
do like getting a tan."

Medrano was about to ask her why she didn't go swimming, but
discreetly decided against it. "I'll probably put my foot in it," he
thought, irritated at the same time by the interruption of their
conversation. Claudia was asking something about a buckle Jorge
had found in the dining room. He lit a cigarette and sank a little
deeper into the deck chair. A feeling of guilt . . . words and more
words. A feeling of guilt . . . As if a woman like Claudia could
. . . He looked at her full in the face, he saw her smiling. Beba was
becoming more lively, more sure of herself, and she brought her
deck chair a little closer. At long last she was talking seriously with
adults. "No," thought Medrano, "this can't be a guilt feeling. Anyone who loses a woman like her is really the guilty one. He certainly couldn't have been in love with her; after all, I can only
judge him from my point of view. I really do admire her. The more
she talks to me, the more she confesses her weaknesses, the more
splendid and stronger I find her. And I don't think it's just the sea
air . . ." It was enough for him to recall for a second (but it was
scarcely recollection, it was earlier than all image, than all verbaliz-
ing, forming part of his way of being, of the monolithic block of
his life) the women he had known intimately, the strong ones,
the weak ones, those who forge ahead and those who merely follow the signs. He had more than enough reasons to admire Claudia, to hold out his hand to her, knowing that it was she who
would guide him. But the course and destination were uncertain,
everything was throbbing, inside and out, like the sea and the sun
and the wind humming along the rigging. A secret illumination, a
cry of meeting, a troubled certainty. As if later something terrible
and lovely too might occur, something final, a tremendous leap or
an irrevocable decision. Between this chaos, which was like music
somehow, and the everyday taste of his cigarette there was already
an incalculable rupture. Medrano measured this rupture as if it
were the frightening distance still there for him to clear.

·   ·   ·   ·

"Hold my wrist tight," Pelusa ordered. "Don't you see, if you slip now we'll get smashed to bits."

Raul, seated on the ladder, was attentively following the various stages of practice. "They've become good friends," he thought, admiring Pelusa's way of lifting Felipe, describing a semicircle in the air. He liked Pelusa's strength and agility, but his movements were somewhat impaired by his absurd bathing suit. Raul deliberately stared at his waist, at his forearms covered with freckles and reddish hair, refusing to look straight at Felipe, who, lips tight (he must have been a bit scared), held his head down while Pelusa, his legs spread apart to counteract the ship's movement, supported him solidly. "Hup!" Pelusa yelled, as he had heard guys in balancing acts do in the circus, and Felipe landed on his feet, breathing hard, but admiring his friend's strength.

"One thing," Pelusa advised, panting, "don't ever get stiff. The more relaxed you keep yourself the better it works. Now we'll do the pyramid, wait till I say hup, ready. Hup! No, kid, don't you see you'll pull your wrist out of joint like that? Look, I told you how a thousand times. If Rusito was here you'd really see what it is to train."

"Whaddya want, you can't learn it all at once," said Felipe, peevishly.

"Okay, okay, I didn't mean nothing, but you keep stiffening up. I'm the one who has to use the strength, you only have to jump, okay? And watch out for my neck, my skin's peeling."

They did the pyramid, fouled up the double Australian scissors, but acquitted themselves with a series of leaps and combined somersaults which Raul applauded emphatically. He was bored. Pelusa smiled modestly, and Felipe decided they had practiced long enough for the soirée.

"You're right, kid," Pelusa said. "If you go on too long your whole body'll kill you. Want to have a beer with me?"

"No, maybe later. Now I'm going to grab a shower; I'm all sweated up."

"No, that's good, kid," said Pelusa. "Sweat kills the germs. I'm going to have a Quilmes Cristal."

"Strange, for them a beer is almost always a Quilmes Cristal," Raul thought, but he was thinking that to mask the hope that perhaps Felipe had deliberately rejected the invitation. "Who knows, maybe he's still sore." Pelusa walked by him with a deep, sonorous "Excuse me, mister," and a pungent and almost visible halo of onion. Raul kept seated until Felipe started up the ladder with a red and green fringed towel over his shoulders.

"Every inch an athlete," said Raul. "You're going to look good tonight."

"Ecchh, it's nothing. I still don't feel too good, my head spins once in a while, but Atilio is going to do the hard part. Is it hot!"

"You'll feel like new after a shower."

"Sure, nothing like it. And what are you going to do tonight?"

"I don't really know. I have to talk to Paula and figure out something more or less funny. We usually improvise something at the last minute. It always turns out badly, but nobody pays too much attention. You're drenched."

"Natch, with all that exercise . . . Don't you really know what you're going to do?"

Raul had stood up, and they walked together down the starboard corridor. Felipe should have gone up the other staircase to reach his cabin directly. Of course it didn't matter, it was the same either way, just as easy to cross over the middle hall which joined the two corridors, but the logical thing would have been to go up the ladder on the port side. Since he had gone up the starboard one, it could be assumed that Felipe had wanted to talk to him. Not absolutely certain, but probable. And he wasn't angry, although he avoided looking directly at Raul. Following Felipe through the dark passageway, he could see the bright red fringe on his towel covering part of his back; he thought of a great wind coming up and making it float back like a charioteer's cape. Felipe's bare feet left a light, damp imprint on the linoleum floor. When they reached the connecting hallway, Felipe turned around, resting one hand on the wall partition. He had already struck this pose before, and again he was unsure about what he was going to say and how to say it.

"Well, I'm going to take a shower. What are you doing?"

"Oh, I'm going to rest a while, that is, if Paula doesn't snore too much."

"Snore? You mean a young girl like that snores?"

He blushed suddenly, realizing that the thought of Paula disturbed him in front of Raul, and that Raul was pulling his leg.
After all, women must snore just like other people, and to act
surprised in front of Raul was just like admitting he hadn't the
least idea of a woman asleep or of a woman in bed. But Raul was
watching him without smiling.

"Of course she snores," he said. "Not always, but sometimes during siesta. I can't read with someone snoring next to me."

"That's true," said Felipe. "Well, if you want to come and talk a
while in my cabin, I'll only be a minute in the shower. No one's
there, the old man spends his time reading at the bar."

"I'm with you," said Raul, who had picked up the expression in
Chile, and saying it brought back the memory of a few days of happiness in the mountains. "I'll fill my pipe with your tobacco. I left
mine in the cabin."

The door of his cabin was only a few steps from the hallway, but
Felipe seemed to accept the request as something almost necessary,
a gesture which rounded out the situation, something after which
he could go ahead with complete peace of mind.

"The steward's a card," said Felipe. "Did you ever notice him go
in or out of your cabin? I never have, but whenever I get back here
I find everything fixed up, the bed made . . . Wait, I'll get you
the tobacco."

He threw the towel in a corner and put the fan on. While he
was looking for the tobacco he explained how much he enjoyed
the electrical gadgets, and how he liked the bathroom and the
lighting, all of it so well planned. His back to Raul, he bent over
the lower dresser drawer, looking for the tobacco. He found it and
handed it to Raul, but Raul ignored the gesture.

"What's the matter?" asked Felipe, his arm outstretched.

"Nothing," said Raul, still not taking the tobacco. "I was looking at you."

"At me? Come on . . ."

"With a body like that I bet you've made a lot of chicks."

"Oh, come on," Felipe repeated, not knowing what to do with
the tobacco can in his hand. Raul took it and at the same time
grasped his hand, drawing Felipe toward him. Felipe freed himself
suddenly, but without stepping back. He seemed more discon-

certed than afraid, and when Raul stepped forward, he stood motionless, his eyes lowered. Raul rested his hand on his shoulder and then let it slide slowly down his arm.

"You're soaked," he said. "Go on, take your shower."

"Yeah, I better," said Felipe. "I'll be right out."

"Leave the door open, we can talk meanwhile."

"But . . . it's all the same to me, but if the old man comes in . . ."

"What do you think he'll say?"

"I don't know."

"If you don't know, then it doesn't matter."

"It isn't that, but . . ."

"Are you embarrassed?"

"Me! What should I be embarrassed about?"

"That's what I thought. If you're afraid of what your father will think, we can lock the cabin door."

Felipe was at a loss for words. He went up to the door hesitantly and locked it with the key. Raul was waiting, filling his pipe slowly. He saw Felipe glance at the wardrobe, and then at the bed, as if he were looking for something, a pretext to gain time, to decide. He took a pair of white socks and some shorts out of the dresser and put them on top of the bed; then he picked them up again, carried them to the bathroom, and left them next to the shower on a stool with nickel fittings. Raul had lit the pipe and was looking at him. Felipe turned on the shower and tested the temperature of the water. Then, with a rapid movement, facing Raul, he lowered his trunks and in an instant was under the shower, as if he were searching for some sort of shelter in the water. Whistling, he began to soap himself up energetically, without even glancing at the door.

"Really, you've got a terrific body," Raul said, leaning against the mirror. "A lot of boys your age don't look like men yet, but you . . . I must have seen boys like you in Buenos Aires."

"At the club?" Felipe said, incapable of thinking or saying anything else. He went on facing Raul, refusing out of modesty to turn his back. Something was buzzing deafeningly in his head; it was the water hitting against his ear and eyes, or something further inside, a whirlwind which deprived him of will and of any control

over his voice. He automatically continued to soap up his body
under the water, which kept washing away the foam. If Beba ever
found this out . . . In the back of his mind, at an infinite distance, he was thinking about Alfieri, that Alfieri could easily have
been this fellow standing there smoking, looking at him like
sergeants look at naked draftees, or doctors like the one on Char-
cas Street who made him walk around with his eyes closed and his
arms held out. He told himself that Alfieri (but no, this wasn't
Alfieri) would be making fun of his awkwardness, but suddenly it
made him angry to be such a fool, and he turned off the shower
abruptly and really began to soap himself up, with furious movements that left mountains of white foam on his stomach, armpits,
and neck. It almost didn't matter any longer that Raul was looking
at him, after all, between men . . . But he was lying to himself,
and as he spread the soap around he avoided certain movements,
and stood as straight as possible, always frontways, taking special
care to wash his arms, chest, neck, and ears. He rested one foot on
the edge of the green mosaic tub, leaned over a bit, and began to
soap up the ankle and calf of his leg. He had the feeling that he
had been washing for hours. The shower was no pleasure for him,
but it was still an effort to turn off the water, get out of the tub,
and begin to dry himself. When he straightened up, with water
pouring out of his hair into his eyes, Raul was handing him the
towel he had taken down from a hook, handing it to him from
afar, so as not to walk on the floor splashed with foam.

"Feel better now?"

"Sure. A shower feels good after exercising."

"Yes, especially after certain exercises. You didn't understand
me today when I said you have a handsome body. What I wanted
to ask was do you like women to tell you so."

"Well, sure, everyone likes that," Felipe said, saying the word
"everyone" after an imperceptible pause.

"Have you slept with many already, or only one?"

"What about you?" asked Felipe, putting on his undershorts.

"Answer me, don't be embarrassed."

"I'm still young," said Felipe. "Why should I brag about
women?"

"That's what I like. That means then you've still never slept with one."

"Not exactly. In whorehouses . . . Of course that isn't the same."

"Ah, you've gone to whorehouses. I thought there weren't any in the suburbs now."

"There are still two or three," said Felipe, combing his hair in the mirror. "I've got a friend in fifth year who gave me the addresses. A guy called Ordoñez."

"And they let you in?"

"Sure they let me in. Why not? I went with Ordoñez, he's of age. We went twice."

"Did you like it?"

"I sure did."

He turned off the light in the bathroom and brushed past Raul, who had not moved. Raul heard him open a drawer, looking for a shirt or shoes. He stood a second more in the damp shade, asking himself why . . . But it wasn't worth asking himself again. He went into the cabin and sat down in an armchair. Felipe had put on some white trousers; his top was still bare.

"If you don't like talking about women, just tell me and that's enough," said Raul. "I thought you were old enough already to be interested in those things."

"Who said I wasn't interested? What a character you are, sometimes you remind me of someone I know . . ."

"Does he talk to you about women, too?"

"Sometimes. But he's weird . . . There are weird types, you know? I didn't mean to say that you . . ."

"Don't worry about me, I suppose I must seem weird sometimes. So that guy you know . . . Tell me about him, we can smoke a pipe together."

"Sure," said Felipe, much more sure of himself inside his clothes. He put on a blue shirt, letting it hang over his pants, and took out his pipe. He sat down on the other armchair and waited until Raul passed him the tobacco. He felt as though he had escaped something, as if everything that had just happened might have gone very differently. Only now did he realize that he had been tense and nervous, withdrawn almost, waiting for Raul to do something he hadn't done, or to say something he hadn't said. He almost felt like laughing, and he filled his pipe clumsily and lit it, using two matches. He began to talk about Alfieri, the smart bastard, and how he had laid the lawyer's wife. He chose the things to tell accordingly; after all, Raul had talked about women, there was no reason to tell him about Viana and Freilich. He had more than enough stories about Alfieri and Ordoñez.

"But for all that you need a lot of loot, natch. Women want you to take them dancing, plus the taxi, and then to top it, you have to pay for the room . . ."

"If we were in Buenos Aires I could fix all that for you, you know. You'll see when we get back, I promise you."

"I bet you must have neat rooms, huh?"

"Yes. I'll lend them to you when you need them."

"Really?" said Felipe, almost frightened. "That would be terrific, that way you could take out a woman even if there wasn't much loot . . ." he turned red and coughed. "Well, someday we'd be able to share expenses. It wouldn't be right for you . . ."

Raul got up and came over to him. He began to caress his hair, which was soaked, almost sticky. Felipe made a movement, drawing away his head.

"Come on," he said. "You're going to mess up my hair. If the old man comes in . . ."

"You locked the door, I think."

"Yeah, but just the same. Leave me alone."

His cheeks were on fire. He tried to get out of his seat, but Raul put a hand on his shoulder and kept him down. He stroked his hair again, lightly.

"What do you think of me? Tell the truth, I don't care."

Felipe broke loose and stood up. Raul let his arms fall, as if he were going to let himself be beaten up. "If he hits me he's mine," he thought. But Felipe retreated a few steps, shaking his head as if deceived.

"Leave me alone," he said in a thread of a voice. "You . . . creep, you're all the same."

"All?" said Raul, smiling slightly.

"Yes, all of you creeps. Alfieri's the same, all of you are the same."

Raul was still smiling. He shrugged his shoulders and made a movement toward the door.

"You're too nervous, son. What's so wrong about a friend caressing another friend? What's the difference between shaking hands and stroking a friend's hair?"

"Difference . . . You know the difference."

"No, Felipe, you're very mistrustful of me because you find it strange that I want to be your friend. You don't trust me, you lied to me. You act like a woman, if you don't mind my telling you what's on my mind."

"Yeah, now you start picking on me," Felipe said, coming a little closer. "I lied to you?"

"Yes. I feel a little sorry for you; you lie badly, lying is something you don't learn overnight and you still don't know how to do it. I went back down below too, and I found out from one of the lipids. Why did you tell me you'd been with the younger one?"

Felipe waved his hand as if to brush the question aside.

"I can take a lot of disappointments from you," Raul said, talking softly. "I can understand your not liking me, or that you can't stand the idea of being my friend, or that you're afraid other people will misinterpret things . . . But don't lie to me, Felipe, not even over a stupid thing like that."

"But there wasn't anything wrong about that," said Felipe. In spite of himself, Raul's voice attracted him, and Raul kept watching as if he expected something else from him. "Really, what happened is that I was sore about you guys not taking me along yesterday, and I didn't want . . . Well, I went down on my own, and what I did down there is my own business. That's why I didn't tell the truth."

He turned around abruptly and went up to the porthole. His hand holding the pipe hung limp. He ran his other hand through his hair, flexed his shoulders a bit. For a moment he had been afraid that Raul might reproach him for something else, something he hadn't figured out: like wanting to flirt with Paula or something like that. He didn't want to look at him because Raul's eyes pained

him, they made him want to cry, to throw himself on the bed face
down and cry. He felt like a helpless baby in front of this man
who showed him the naked expression in his eyes. His back still to
him, he felt Raul approach slowly, and he knew that Raul would
wrap his arms around him with all his strength, and that his anxiety
would turn to fear, and yet, behind his fear there was a kind of
temptation to go on waiting, to find out what this embrace would
be like, an embrace in which Raul would have to renounce all his
superiority and become nothing more than a begging voice and a
pair of gentle dog eyes, conquered by Felipe, conquered in spite
of his embrace. He suddenly realized that the roles had shifted and
that now he was the one who could lay down the law. He turned
abruptly and saw Raul at the exact moment when his hands were
stretched out toward him, and he laughed in his face hysterically,
the laugh mixed with tears, laughing with sharp, broken sobs, his
face filled with grimaces and tears and mockery.

Raul grazed his face with his fingers, and waited once more for
Felipe to hit him. He saw the fist start toward him and he waited
for it, not moving. Felipe covered his face with both hands,
crouched, and jumped clear. It was almost inevitable he should go
to the door, open it, and stand there waiting. Raul passed in front
of him without a glance. The bang of the door sounded like a shot
in his back.

G

*Perhaps repose is necessary, perhaps at some point the blue guitar-
ist will let his arm fall and the sexual mouth will become silent,
sink inward, turning in upon itself as a glove left on a bed hideously
collapses inward, turning in upon itself. At this hour of disembodi-
ment and fatigue (because repose is only a euphemism for defeat,
and the dream is only a mask for the nothingness contained in
every pore of life), the scarcely anthropomorphic image, painted
disdainfully by Picasso on a canvas which belonged to Apollinaire,
more than ever stands for the comedy at its point of fusion, when
everything comes to a standstill before breaking into a chord which
will resolve the intolerable tension. But we're thinking in fixed
terms, terms set before us: the guitar, the music, the ship that sails
toward the south, the men and women whose steps cross and re-*

cross one another's like the trails of white rats in a cage. What un-looked-for reverse of plot can be born from a final suspicion which goes beyond what is happening and what isn't happening, which stations itself at that spot where the conjunction of the eye and chimera begins to operate, where legend rips the sheep's skin to shreds, where the third hand, barely seen by Persio in a flash of astral communication, grips for itself the bodyless, stringless guitar, and inscribes a music for other ears on a space hard as marble. It isn't easy to understand the anti-guitar as it isn't easy to understand the anti-matter, but anti-matter is already part and parcel of our newspapers and speeches given at congresses, the anti-uranium, the anti-silicon sparkling in the night. It isn't comfortable to imagine an anti-reading, an anti-being, an anti-ant, the third hand knocks off eyeglasses and classifications, pulls books out of bookcases, dis-covers the reason for the image in the mirror, its symmetrical and demoniacal revelation. The anti-I and the anti-you are there, and what then happens to us, what becomes of our satisfactory existence in which the disturbance never went beyond a meager German or French metaphysic, now that the shadow of the anti-star falls across our scalp, now that in the full embrace of love we feel a vertigo of anti-love, and not because this palindrome of the cosmos might be a negation of it (why should the anti-universe be the negation of the universe?) but rather because it is the truth of it, exposed by the third hand, the truth that awaits man's birth to join in the joy of it all!

Persio, in some way stretched out in the middle of the pampa, stuck in a dirty sack, perhaps just thrown from a bucking horse, watches the stars and feels the coming of the shapeless fulfillment. At this hour nothing can distinguish him from the clown who lifts his floured face to the black hole in the tent, contact with the sky. The clown doesn't know, Persio doesn't know what this yellow hail is bouncing off his wide-open eyes, and because he doesn't know, everything given to him he feels more violently, the shining crown of the night, the Southern Cross, turns slowly in its musical step, and the voice of the plains gradually penetrates his hearing, the rustle of grass growing, the fearful undulation of the snake which comes out into the dew, the light tap-tap of the rabbit quickened with a desire for the moon. Now he smells the dry and secret crack-

ling of the pampas, he touches with his wet eyeballs a new earth
which has scarcely anything to do with man, which rejects him, as
the wild horses of the pampas, its hurricanes, and its endless distances do. Little by little, his senses grow disembodied, and he is
hoisted and turned over on the black plains; he no longer sees nor
hears nor smells nor touches, he is gone, departed, let loose standing straight as a tree encompassing plurality in one single enormous
pain, which is chaos resolving itself, the shattered crystal fusing in
an orderly pattern, the primeval night in American time. What does
the secretive procession of shadows matter to him now, the revived
and then defeated creation which stands around him, the frightful
succession of abortions and armadillos and woolly horses and tigers
with fangs like horns, and sudden Indian attacks of stone and clay?
Immutable stone boundary, the indifferent witness to the revolution of bodies and eons, an eye posed like a condor with mountain
wings in the mad race of myriads, galaxies, infoldings, spectator of
monsters and deluges, of pastoral scenes or centennial fires, the
metamorphosis of magma, of sial, of the uncertain flotation of con-
tinent-whales, of island-tapirs, the austral catastrophes of stone, the
intolerable birth of the Andes opening into the sluice a shuddering
mountain range; Persio cannot rest a second and he cannot be sure
if the sensation in his left hand is a glacial age with all its deafening
sound, or only a nighttime slug crawling around in search of
warmth.

If it were difficult to renounce, perhaps he would renounce this
osmosis of cataclysms which plunges him into an intolerable den-
sity, but he stubbornly refuses the ease of opening or closing his
eyes, of getting up and going out to the edge of the road, of suddenly reinventing his body, the route, a night in the 1950s, the
help which will arrive with lanterns and exclamations and a trail of
dust. He grits his teeth (but maybe it's the birth of a mountain
chain, a crushing of clay and basalt) and yields to vertigo, to the
creeping of the slug or to the waterfall drenching his immersed and
confused body. All creation is a failure, the rocks fly through the
air, unnamed animals crumble and stumble about, their feet in the
air, giant pines burst into splinters, the joy of disorder crushes and
exalts and annihilates amid howls and mutations. And what remains of all these? Only an abandoned hut in the pampas, a cun-

ning tapster, a poor devil of a pursued gaucho, a pipsqueak of a
general in power? A diabolical operation in which colossal numbers
end up in a football championship, with the suicide of a poet, or a
bitter love affair on a street corner redolent with honeysuckle. Saturday night, résumé of glory: is this South America? Are we repeating in each gesture of each day this unresolved chaos? Are we
searching in an indefinitely delayed present, in a present of necro-
philic cult, in a tendency to loathing, to sleep without dreams, to
the simple nightmare which inevitably follows the mammoth in-
gestion of pumpkin and paprika sausage, are we searching for the
coexistence of destiny? Do we pretend to uphold both the sover-
eignty of the Indian and the last word in automobile racing? Are we
secretly preparing a renunciation of historical time as we lie
stretched out on the impermeable and idiotic plains, facing the
stars? We put on strange clothes, and in empty discussions which
glove the hands of the chief of state's greeting and from the glories
of national holidays and so much unexplored reality, we select the
antagonistic phantom, the anti-matter of the anti-spirit, of the anti-
Argentinity, for we stubbornly refuse to assume, as one must, a
destiny in time, a race which includes both conquerers and conquered. Less than Manichaeans, less than rotten hedonists, are we
the earthly representatives of the spectral side of becoming, its sarcastic larva crouching at the side of the road, the anti-time of both
body and soul, the cheap facility, the don't-get-involved-if-there-
isn't-something-in-it-for-you. The fate of not wanting a fate: don't
we spit with every highfalutin word, with every philosophical essay,
with every loud, clamoring championship match, the vital anti-
matter "elevated" to a table cover with tassels, to phony poetry
contests, to the patriotic plastic button on a lapel, to the social-
athletic club of every neighborhood in Buenos Aires or Rosario or
Tucuman?

XXXVIII

Furthermore the idea of a poetry contest always amused Medrano, the ever ironic spectator. He thought of it as he went down
to the deck, after having walked Claudia and Jorge, who had sud-

denly felt like having a siesta, to their cabin. Thinking it over, he
decided that Dr. Restelli should have proposed a poetry contest on
board; more a thing of the spirit, more educational than a simple
artistic soirée, and it would have provided an opportunity for the
perpetration of any number of enormous jokes. "But they couldn't
conceive of a poetry contest," he thought, stretching tiredly in a
deck chair, and slowly taking out a cigarette. He purposely delayed
the moment when he would no longer be interested in what he
saw around him, so he could yield deliciously to Claudia's image,
the meticulous reconstruction of her voice, the shape of her hands,
her manner, so simple and almost necessary, of keeping quiet or
talking. Carlos Lopez appeared at the portside ladder, looking dazzled by the four o'clock afternoon horizon. The other passengers
had left a while ago, the captain's bridge was still empty.

Medrano closed his eyes and wondered what was going to happen. The truce would be over the moment the last number on the
program ceded to the courteous applause and general dispersion
of the audience, and then the clock would begin to tick off the
third day. "The same old symbols, the boredom of a not-too-subtle
analogy," he thought. The third day, the showdown. The most
obvious facts could be predicted: the poop deck would simply
open by itself, after their visit, or Lopez would carry out his threat
with Raul's help, as well as his. The peace party would be formed
and led by the irate Don Galo; but from that point the future was
cloudy, the roads branched off and rebranched . . . "It's going to
be great," he thought, satisfied, without knowing why. Everything
was on such a ridiculous scale, so absolutely antidramatic, that his
satisfaction turned to impatience. He preferred thinking of Claudia, of reconstructing her face, which had seemed veiled with worry
when they said goodbye at the cabin door. But he hadn't com-
mented on it, had pretended not to notice it, although he would
have liked to be with her, watching over Jorge while he slept, talking softly about anything at all. Then a dark feeling of emptiness
overcame him, of disorder, of a need to put order into something
—but he didn't know what—to put together a puzzle lying in a
jumble of a thousand pieces on the table. Another easy analogy, to
think of life as a puzzle, each day a piece of wood with a green
daub, a little red, a nothing of grey, but all badly shuffled and

amorphous, topsy-turvy days, a part of the past stuck like a thorn in the future, the present perhaps free of what preceded it and what might follow it, but impoverished by too voluntary a division, a curt rejection of phantoms and projects. The present couldn't be this, but only now, when almost everything was already irreversibly lost, he was beginning to suspect, but not with too much conviction, that the greater part of his faults were due to a liberty based on a false hygiene of life, a selfish desire to dispose of himself during every moment of a day, a day constantly unique, without thinking of yesterday or tomorrow. Seen from this angle, the journey behind him suddenly seemed like an absolute failure. "A failure of what?" he thought, troubled. He had never thought of existence in terms of triumph, the notion of failure lacked sense. "Yes, logically," he thought. "Logically." He repeated the word, he made it slide along his tongue. Logically. Then Claudia, then the *Malcolm*. Logically. But the pit of his stomach, his startled dream, the feeling that something was approaching which would catch him off guard and unarmed, something he had to prepare himself for. "What the devil," he thought, "it's not that easy to throw habit overboard, this is too much like hard work. Like the time I thought I was going crazy and it turned out to be the beginnings of septicemia . . ." No, it wasn't easy. Claudia seemed to understand him, she hadn't once reproached him about Bettina, but strangely enough, Medrano was now thinking that Claudia should have reproached him for what Bettina represented in his life. Although she had no right to, of course, and she had even less right to think of herself as a possible successor to Bettina. The very idea of succession was insulting when he thought of a woman like Claudia. And for that reason alone, perhaps, she could have called him a base creature, she could have said it quietly, looking at him out of eyes in which her own unquietness shone, like a well-earned right, the right of an accomplice, the reproach of the reproachable, much more bitter, more just, and more profound than that of a judge or a saint.

But why did it have to be Claudia who suddenly opened the doors of time, turning him out naked into a weather that was beginning to lash him, causing him to light one cigarette after another, making him bite his lips and wish the puzzle might quickly be assembled, one way or another, and his uncertain hands, novices at these games, hesitatingly searched for the pieces, red, blue, and green, to construct out of all this jumble, a woman's profile, a cat curled up by the fire, a background of old storybook trees. And all that was stronger than the four-thirty sun, the cobalt-blue horizon, which he vaguely saw through his half-closed eyes, the horizon which rose and fell to the rhythm of the *Malcolm*, passenger/cargo ship of the Magenta Star Lines. Suddenly, there was Calle Avellaneda, the trees glowing with the rust colors of autumn, and his hands deep in his raincoat pockets as he walked along, fleeing from something obscurely menacing. Now there was an entranceway, similar to the one in Lola Romarino's house, but more cramped; he came out onto a patio—quickly, quickly, he hadn't a minute to lose—and he dashed up the stairs like those stairs in the Hotel Saint Michel in Paris, where he had spent a few weeks with Leonora (he had forgotten her last name). It was an ample room, and the walls were covered with draperies which must have concealed irregularities and deterioration, or windows which looked onto sordid black courtyards. He closed the door and felt enormously relieved. He took off his raincoat, his gloves, and carefully laid them on a bamboo table. He knew that the danger wasn't over, that the door only half-protected him; it was more of a respite which gave him time to think out a safer plan. But he didn't want to think, he didn't know what to think of; the threat was too uncertain, it was floating up above him, parting and returning like smoke-saturated air. He walked to the middle of the room. Only then did he see the bed, hidden behind a pink screen, a wretched hulk about to fall apart. An iron bed, unmade, an enameled washbasin and pitcher; yes, it could be the Hotel Saint Michel, though it wasn't, the room resembled the one in another hotel in Rio. Without knowing why, he didn't want to get too close to the disheveled, dirty bed, and so he stood motionless, his hands stuck in his pockets, waiting. It was almost natural, practically indispensable that Bettina should appear from behind one of the striped draperies and come up to him, as if gliding over the filthy rug, and that then she should stop at least a yard from him, gradually lifting her face, which was completely covered by her blond hair. The feeling of menace was dissolving, veering toward something else, even worse, which was going to happen. Bettina was slowly lifting her invisible face, her hair trembling and quivering, only the tip of her nose showing, then her mouth, which disappeared again, then her nose again, and sometimes the glitter of her eyes lost behind the mass of blond hair. Medrano felt like running, to at least feel his back against the door, but instead he was floating in a kind of pasty air in which every breath he took required an effort in his chest, in his whole body. He heard Bettina talking, for she had been talking all the time, but what she was saying was only a continuous, sharp sound, uninterrupted, like a parrot mechanically repeating a series of syllables and whistles. When she threw her head back and all her hair was flung back, falling over her ears and shoulders, her face was so close to him that by just leaning a bit he could have wet his lips in her tears. Her cheeks and chin were brilliant with tears, her half-open mouth from which the incomprehensible speech was still flowing was before him, the force of Bettina's face suddenly obliterated everything: the room, the draperies, the body that was still further down, the hands that he had at first seen pressed close to her thighs, and only her face remained, floating in the smoky room, bathed in tears, her wild eyes interrogating Medrano. And each eyelash, each hair of her eyebrows seemed to become isolated one from the other, he could see each one in itself and separately, Bettina's face was an infinite world, fixed and convulsed at the same time, before his eyes. He could not avoid her face, and her voice went on like a thick ribbon made of a sticky material whose sense was clarity itself, even though it was impossible to understand a thing, clear and definitive, an explosion of clarity and consummation, the menace finally concretized and resolved, the end of everything, the absolute presence of horror in that hour and place. Medrano, panting, saw Bettina's face, and although she moved no closer to him, it seemed more and more pressed to his; he recognized the features which he had learned to read with all his senses, the curve of her chin, the flight of her eyebrows, the delicious hollow between her nose and mouth, covered with soft down his lips knew so well; and at the same time he knew he was seeing something else, that this face was the opposite of Bettina's, a mask of inhuman suffering, a concentration of all the world's

suffering that trampled and took the place of the triviality of a
face he had sometimes kissed. But he also knew that this wasn't
true, that only what he was seeing now was true, that this was Bettina, a monstrous Bettina, in front of whom the woman who had
been his mistress was dissolving, as he himself was dissolving, and
he gradually recoiled toward the door, but without getting any
further away from the face floating at eye level in front of him. It
wasn't fear, this horror was beyond fear; it was rather like the privilege of feeling the most atrocious moment of torture without any
physical pain, the essence of torture without the twisting of flesh
and nerves. He was seeing the other side of things, for the first
time he was seeing what he was like, Bettina's face revealed a mirror of rushing tears, a convulsed mouth which had been frivolity
itself, a bottomless expression which had been caprice and gaiety.
But he didn't know this, because horror was canceling out all
knowledge, it was made of the same material as the passage to the
other side, previously inconceivable, and then when he awoke with
a cry, the entire blue ocean rushed into his eyes, and he saw the
ladder again and the silhouette of Raul Costa sitting on the top
step, only then, covering his face as if he feared someone else
might be able to see in him what he had just seen in Bettina's
mask, only then did he understand that he was reaching a solution,
that the pieces of the puzzle were finally falling into place. Panting as in the dream, he looked at his hands, the deck chair in
which he was seated, the floorboards of the deck, the iron of the
railing; he looked at them with curiosity, strange to everything
around him, strange even to himself. When he was capable of
thinking (painfully so, because everything in him was screaming
that to think would only be to falsify again), he knew that he
hadn't dreamed of Bettina, but of himself; the true horror had
been that, but now, under the sun and salt wind, the horror re-
ceded to forgetfulness, to finding himself safe again on the other
side, and it left him only with the feeling that each element in his
life, in his body, in his past, and in his present was false, and that
falsity was there within his grasp, waiting to be taken by the hand
and carried again to the bar, to the next day, to Claudia's love,
to Bettina's smiling, whimsical face, forever there in everlasting
Buenos Aires. The day he was living was falsity itself because it

was he who saw it; the falsity was outside because it was inside, because it had been invented piece by piece throughout his life. He had just seen the real face of frivolity, but fortunately, ah, fortunately it was only a nightmare. He returned to reason, the machine began to think again, the well-oiled rods and pistons were turning, receiving and exerting force, preparing satisfactory conclusions. "What a hideous dream," Gabriel Medrano decided, looking for his cigarettes, those cylinders of paper filled with black tobacco, at five pesos for a pack of twenty.

When it was impossible to stay out in the sun any longer, Raul went back to his cabin, where Paula was sleeping. He poured himself a little whisky and sat down in an armchair, making the least possible noise. Paula opened her eyes and smiled at him.

"I was dreaming of you, but you were taller and you had on a blue suit that wasn't right for you."

She sat up, folding the pillow over to use it as a backrest. Raul thought about the Etruscan tombs, perhaps because Paula was watching him with a subtle smile, which still seemed to be part of her dream.

"On the other hand, you were better-looking," said Paula. "Really, one might say you were on the verge of a sonnet or a couple of stanzas in rhyme royal. I've known certain bards to take on that air before their final burst of inspiration."

Raul sighed, slightly irritated as well as amused.

"What a senseless trip," he said. "I have the feeling we're going around in circles, and that includes the ship. But you're not, actually. I think your sun-tanned pirate is just right for you."

"That depends," said Paula, stretching. "If I could forget myself for a while, perhaps it would do me some good, but you're always around as if you were a witness."

"Oh, I'm no bother. Just give me the sign, any sign you like, for instance, crossing your fingers and tapping your left heel, and I'll vanish. Even from the cabin, if you need it, but I don't suppose you will. There are more than enough cabins here."

"This is what it's like to have a bad reputation," said Paula. "To listen to you, you'd think it only took me forty-eight hours to hop into bed with some character."

"That's about the right amount of time to hold off. It gives you time to examine your conscience, brush your teeth . . ."

"Resentful, that's what you are. You couldn't care less, but you're resentful just the same."

"Not at all. Don't confuse jealousy with envy, because it's pure envy as far as I'm concerned."

"Tell me about it," said Paula, settling back again. "Tell me why you envy me."

Raul told her. It was difficult for him to speak, even though he soaked each word in a careful bath of irony, avoiding any kind of self-pity.

"He's very young," said Paula. "You know, a baby."

"When it's not that it's because they're too grown up. But I'm not looking for excuses. The truth of the matter is I acted stupid, I went to pieces as if it were the first time. It's always the same, I imagine the whole thing before anything happens at all. The outcome is easy to predict."

"Yes, it's a bad system. A watched pot never, etcetera . . ."

"But just put yourself in my place," said Raul, without thinking that he could make Paula laugh. "I'm unarmed here, I haven't any of the possibilities at my disposal that I'd have in Buenos Aires. And at the same time, I'm closer to him here, hideously closer, because I meet him everywhere and I know a ship can be the best place in the world—later. It's the legend of Tantalus played out among corridors, showers, and acrobatic tricks."

"You're no great shakes as a corruptor of youth," said Paula. "I always suspected it and I'm happy to see it verified."

"Go to hell."

"But it's true, I'm happy. Now I think you deserve a little more than before, and maybe you'll be lucky."

"I'd rather have deserved it less and . . ."

"And what? I'm not going to start thinking about the details, but I suppose it isn't easy. If it were, there would be fewer characters in prison and fewer kids found dead in cornfields."

"Oh that," said Raul. "It's incredible what kinds of things women can dream up."

"I'm not dreaming things up, Raulito. And since I don't think you're a sadist, at least not as far as becoming a public menace, I can't see you making him an 'object of outrage,' as *La Prensa* would virtuously report the matter if they learned of it. On the other hand, I don't have any trouble visualizing you in more drawn-out tasks of seduction, and if you don't mind my saying so, achieving the 'outrage' by nonoutrageous means. But this time it seems the sea air has given you too much impetus, poor boy."

"I don't even feel like telling you to go to hell a second time."

"In any case," said Paula, putting a finger to her mouth, "in any case, there's something in your favor, and I suppose you're not too depressed to notice it. First, the trip promises to be long and you have no rivals on board. I mean, there aren't any women to encourage him. At his age, if he has any luck at all in the most innocent flirtation, a boy forms a very special idea of himself, and he's quite right. Perhaps I'm somewhat to blame myself, now that I think of it. I let him build up his hopes and talk to me as though he were a man."

"Oh, what does that matter?" said Raul.

"Maybe it doesn't matter, but I repeat, there are many things in your favor. Do I have to explain?"

"If it isn't too much trouble."

"But you must have figured it out by now, you dimwit. It's so simple. Look at him carefully and you'll see what he himself can't see, because he doesn't know it."

"He's too lovely for me to really see him," Raul said. "I don't know what I see when I look at him: a void, a terrible fear, an overflowing of honey, etcetera."

"Yes, considering that . . . What you must have noticed by now is that young Trejo is full of doubts, that he trembles and hesitates, and that basically, but very basically . . . Don't you feel he has something of an aura about him? What makes him gorgeous (because I think he's gorgeous too, but with one small difference: I feel like his grandmother) is that he's at the point of succumbing, he can't go on forever being what he is at this particular moment of his life. You *have* acted like an idiot, but perhaps, still . . . Well, it's not right for me to . . . honestly . . ."

"Do you really think so, Paula?"

"He's Dionysius as an adolescent, stupid. He hasn't the slightest stability, he attacks because he's scared to death, and at the same time he's full of desire, he feels love fluttering above him and he's a boy and a girl and both at once, or even much more than that. Nothing is very settled about him, he knows that the hour has struck, but he doesn't know for what, and then he puts on those ghastly shirts and comes to tell me how pretty I am and he looks at my legs, and at the same time, he panics . . . And you don't see any of this, you simply go around like a sleepwalker carrying a tray of meringue pastries . . . Give me a cigarette, then I think I'll take a swim."

Raul watched her smoking, and occasionally they exchanged a smile. He wasn't surprised by anything she had said to him, but now he felt it objectively, as presented by a second observer. The triangle was closing, the measurements were being established on more secure grounds. "The poor intellectual, always in need of proof," he thought, without bitterness. The whisky was beginning to lose its first bitter taste.

"And you," said Raul. "I want to know about you now. We'll end up fraternally prostituting ourselves, the shower is right over there. Talk, confess, Father Costa is all ears."

"We're delighted by the Doctor's and invalid gentleman's excellent idea," said the *maître*. "Take a hat, unless you prefer a mask."

Señora Trejo selected a violet hat, and the *maître* praised her choice. Beba decided that the least trashy item was a gilded cardboard diadem, sprinkled with a few red sequins. The *maître* went from table to table distributing party favors, commenting on the progressive (and so natural) fall in temperature, and taking orders. Nora and Lucio, who both looked tired, were at table number five along with Don Galo and Dr. Restelli, who were putting the finishing touches to the program. They had decided, after consulting the *maître*, to hold the soirée at the bar; even though it was smaller than the dining room, it was perfect for this type of fiesta (following the examples of previous trips, and there was even an album of comments and signatures of passengers with Nordic names). When coffee was served, Señor Trejo left his own table and solemnly completed the triumvirate of organizers. Cigar in hand, Don Galo went over the list of participants and submitted it to his companions.

"Ah, I see here that our friend Lopez is going to dazzle us with magic tricks," said Señor Trejo. "Very good, very good."

"Lopez is a young man of remarkable qualities," said Dr. Restelli. "As excellent a teacher as he is an amiable social companion."

"I'm happy to see he prefers to display his social side this evening, rather than some of his recent more exaggerated attitudes," said Señor Trejo, lowering his voice to a flutish piping so that Lopez would not hear him. "Really, these young fellows allow themselves to be carried away by a spirit of violence which is scarcely laudable, gentlemen, scarcely laudable."

"The man's peeved," said Don Galo, "and of course his blood is boiling. But you'll see how everyone's spirits will rise after our little fiesta. That's what's missing on this trip, a bit of boisterous fun. Innocent, of course."

"True, true," Dr. Restelli added. "We all agree that our friend Lopez has been too hasty in proffering threats that can lead nowhere."

Lucio looked occasionally at Nora, who was looking at the tablecloth or her hands. He coughed uncomfortably, and asked if it weren't time to go to the bar. But Dr. Restelli had it from a very good source that the busboy and *maître* were still arranging the lounge, hanging streamers, and creating an atmosphere propitious to the effusion of spirit and civility.

"Exactly, exactly," said Don Galo. "Effusions of spirit, that's what I say. To the frolic, friends! And as for these cocks of the walk, for you know it's not only young Lopez we're dealing with, we'll figure out how to put them in their place so that the trip runs smoothly. I remember an occasion in Pergamino, when the assistant manager of one of my subsidiaries . . ."

The *maître* announced that the passengers could move to the party room.

"Just like Luna Park at carnival time," Pelusa decided, admiring the colored lanterns and balloons.

"Oh Atilio, you scare me with that mask," Nelly complained. "Just like you to pick the gorilla one."

"Grab yourself a good chair and save one for me. I'm going to find out when we have to get ready for our number. Where's your brother, miss?"

"He must be around somewhere," said Beba.

"But he didn't come to eat, he's not here."

"No, he said his head was hurting. He always likes to seem special."

"What's he talking about, a headache," said Pelusa, authoritatively. "He's just got himself a cramp from our workout."

"I don't know," said Beba, disdainfully. "Mama has him so spoiled, I'm sure he's just putting on another act to get people to run after him."

It wasn't an act, and it wasn't a headache either. Felipe had not stirred from the cabin. It had gotten dark outside and he hadn't budged. His father came, satisfied at having won at cards, bathed, and went out again, and then Beba made a brief visit, presumably to look for some piano music which she couldn't find in her luggage. Stretched out on the bed, smoking listlessly, Felipe felt night descend in the blue of the porthole. Everything was like sliding down a declination—his fuzzy thoughts, the increasingly bitter, sticky taste of his cigarette, the pitching ship which gave him the feeling of sinking still further into the water. He had gone over a repertory of repeated injuries until the words had lost all sense, and then he felt an extreme malaise, cut in upon by sudden whiffs of malicious satisfaction, of personal pride, which made him jump off the bed and look in the mirror or think about putting on his red and yellow checked shirt and going out on deck, acting either indifferent or defiant. Then, almost immediately, he went back to the humiliating contemplation of his actions, of his hands stretched out on the bed, hands which hadn't been able to smash Raul's face to bits. Not once did he wonder if he had really wanted or needed to smash his face to bits; he preferred to recount the insults or to go off into a dream state, in which rash acts and explanations on the brink of tears would end in a voluptuousness which required his stretching out, or lighting another cigarette, or taking a vague walk around the cabin, wondering why he remained locked up here instead of joining the others, who must be eating by now. And then he was sure his mother was going to come in and bombard him with questions, impatient and frightened questions. On the bed again, he sullenly admitted he had come out ahead after all. "He must be desperate," he thought out loud. The idea of Raul desperate was almost inconceivable, but he must surely be desperate, he had left the cabin as if he were going to be killed on the spot, white as a sheet. "White as a sheet," Felipe repeated, satisfied. And now he would be alone, clenching his fists with rage. It wasn't easy to imagine Raul clenching his fists; every time Felipe tried to submit him to the worst of moral humiliations he could only visualize him with a calm, slightly ironic expression on his face; he was thinking of the gesture Raul had made when he offered him the pipe or the one he had used as he came up to him to stroke his hair. But maybe he was just lolling in bed, smoking away as if nothing had happened.

"The hell he is," he said, vengefully. "I bet it's the first time he's been given the boot like that." That would teach him to come on with a real man, the big creep. How could he have been fooled for so long into thinking that he was the only friend he could count on on board, this damned ship with no women to make out with, or parties, or even other fellows his own age to fool around with on deck. Now he was finished, it was almost better not to leave the cabin . . . A minute before, Paula's image had come to him, surprisingly, along with everything else—that is, if all the rest had actually come as a surprise. But Paula—where the devil was she in all this business? He shuffled around two or three hypotheses which occurred to him, all of them crude and unsatisfactory, and began to worry again—but exactly then, like a mist of contentment, triumphant moments were born and filled his chest with air and cigarette smoke, no longer pipe smoke, for the pipe was thrown on the floor near the door, and exactly above it, on the wall, was the mark of his shocked anger—why did it have to be him and not someone else? Why had Raul sought him out right off the bat, practically the same night they sailed, instead of fluttering around someone else? He almost didn't mind recognizing that there had been no other possibility, that the selection was limited, predestined, and in the fact that Raul had picked him he found the energy to smash the pipe against the wall and to breathe deeply with half-closed eyes, as if savoring a very special privilege. And he'd pay for it, Raul could be sure of that, he was going to pay for it piece by piece, until he learned once and for all not to make mistakes. "The prick, it's not as if I came on to him," he said, standing up straight. "I'm not Viana, not Freilich, fuck it." He was going to show him every hour on the hour that he was a real man, even if he did try to show off with his big-shot ways and his redheaded girlfriend who was all show. He had already given him too much leeway by letting him pretend to help and give him advice. He had gone too far, and Raul had gotten one thing mixed up with another. He heard a noise at the door and he shuddered. Damn it, he was nervous. He looked out of the corner of his eye and watched Beba, who was sniffing around the cabin with her nose wrinkled up.

"Just go on smoking like that and you'll see," said Beba, virtuously. "I'm going to tell Mama so she'll hide your cigarettes."

"Go to hell and stay awhile," said Felipe, almost affably.

"Didn't you hear the dinner bell? Thanks to the gentleman, I had to get up from the table and go down to fetch the little boy."

"Of course, since they're all hanging on you so."

"Papa says you should come and eat immediately."

Felipe took his time about answering.

"Tell him my head is hurting. Anyway, I'll come later for the party."

"Your head?" said Beba. "You could think up a better lie than that."

"What do you want me to say?" Felipe asked, sitting up. Again he felt as if his stomach were being squeezed. He heard the door bang, and he sat up on the edge of the bed. If he went to the dining room he'd have to pass table two and see Paula, Lopez, and Raul. He began to dress slowly, putting on a blue shirt and grey trousers. When he turned on the big light, he saw the pipe on the floor and picked it up. It wasn't broken. He thought it would be best to give it to Paula, together with the tobacco, so that she . . . And as he entered the dining room he'd have to pass in front of the table, see them . . . And if he took the pipe with him and left it on the table, without saying a word? It was idiotic, he was too nervous. Carry it in his pocket and later, if he saw him go out for a breath of air on deck, he could go up to him and say curtly: "This is yours," or something like that. Then Raul would look at him, as only he knew how to look, and would smile slowly.

No, maybe he wouldn't smile, maybe he'd try to take him by the arm, and then . . . He combed his hair slowly, looking at himself from all angles. He wouldn't go to supper, he'd only be waiting to watch him walk in and turn red walking past the table . . . "If only I wouldn't blush when I saw him," he thought, furious, but he couldn't help that. He'd be better off on deck or drinking a beer at the bar. He thought of the tiny staircase in the passageway, of Bob.

Doña Rosita and Doña Pepa were attentively escorted to their seats in the first row, and Señora Trejo joined them, looking very high and mighty, which could only be explained by her daughter's imminent artistic performance. The others began to take their places behind them, as they came in from the dining room. Jorge, very solemn, sat down between his mother and Persio, but Raul didn't feel like sitting down yet and leaned up against the bar waiting for the others to get settled. Don Galo's chair was placed in the presidential position, and the chauffeur hurriedly disappeared to the last row, where Medrano, smoking one cigarette after another and looking depressed, was sitting. Pelusa asked again about his fellow gymnast, and after leaving his mask in Doña Rosita's care, he announced that he was going to see how Felipe was doing. Paula, behind a vaguely Polynesian mask, was imitating Señora Trejo's voice for Lopez.

The *maître* gave the busboy an order, the lights were switched off, and two spotlights came on. The piano had been laboriously moved to a place between the bar and one of the walls. The *maître* solemnly opened the piano. There was a round of applause, and Dr. Restelli, blinking violently, walked up to the illuminated area. Naturally, he was not the proper person to open this evening's simple and spontaneous party, insofar as both the original idea and the leadership belonged to Don Galo Porriño, who was right there.

"Go on, old man, go on," said Don Galo, raising his voice above the friendly applause. "You can all see that I'm not about to become a master of ceremonies, and so fire ahead and long live the party."

In the slightly embarrassed silence that followed, Atilio's return was more noticeable and noisy than he liked. Sliding into his

place, and consequently creating a gigantic shadow on the wall
and ceiling, he informed Nelly in a soft voice that his acrobat pal
was nowhere to be found. Doña Rosita gave him back his mask
and angrily insisted he be quiet, but Pelusa was disconcerted and
went on complaining, squeaking his chair the whole time. Even
though Raul couldn't hear what was being said, he had an idea
of what might have happened. Yielding to an old habit, he turned
toward Paula, who had removed her mask and was taking in
the scene statistically. When her eyes met Raul's she raised her
brows questioningly, and Raul responded by shrugging his shoulders. Paula smiled before putting her mask on again and went
back to her conversation with Lopez, but her smile was something
like a passport to Raul, a seal stamped on a paper, a shot in the air
signaling the beginning of a race. But he would have left the bar
even if Paula hadn't looked at him.

"How they talk, my God, how they talk," said Paula. "Jamaica
John, do you really think that in the beginning was the word?"

"I love you," said Jamaica John, and for him, this was a conclu-
sive reply. "My God, it's wonderful to love you and to be able to
say it here without anyone hearing, from mask to mask, from pirate
to vahine."

"Maybe I am a vahine," said Paula, looking at his mask and adjusting her own, "but you look like something between Rocambole
and a provincial deputy, which doesn't suit you too well. You
should have taken Presutti's mask, though it's better when you
don't wear any and you're just Jamaica John."

Dr. Restelli was now eulogizing the remarkable musical talent of
Señorita Trejo, who was about to entertain them with a Clementi
composition and then a Czerny selection, both highly celebrated
composers. Lopez looked at Paula, who had to bite hard on her
finger. "Highly celebrated composers," she thought. "This soirée is
going to be a monument." She had seen Raul leave, and Lopez
had seen him too and looked at her in a joking, questioning way
which she decided to ignore. "Good luck, Raulito," she thought.
"I hope you get your nose busted, Raulito. Ah, I'll always be the
same, right to the end, I'll never be able to purge myself of the
Lavalle blood. Basically, I'll never forgive you for being my best

friend. The irreproachable friend of a Lavalle. That's it, the irreproachable friend. And there he goes, scurrying down an empty
corridor, trembling and excited, one more in a long line of those
who tremble deliciously, ruined before he starts . . . I'll never forgive him and he knows it, and the day he finds someone to follow
him (but he won't find anyone, Paulita is watching out for that,
and I suppose that in this particular instance it's not worth the
bother), on that day he'll leave me in the lurch forever, and goodbye concerts, goodbye *pâté* sandwiches at four A.M., goodbye long
walks around San Telmo, and goodbye Raul, goodbye poor little
Raul, and lots of luck and may things go well for you just this one
time."

Gurgling sounds floated out of the piano. Lopez slipped a
white handkerchief into Paula's hand. He thought she was crying
with laughter, but he wasn't sure. He saw her bring the handkerchief quickly to her face, and he caressed her shoulder, but just
scarcely, more of a slight grazing than a caress. Paula smiled at
him, not giving back the handkerchief, and when the audience
burst into applause she opened it wide and vigorously blew her
nose.

"Pig," Lopez said. "I didn't lend it to you for that."

"It doesn't matter," said Paula. "It's so coarse it will rub my
nose off."

"I play better than that," Jorge said. "Persio can tell you."

"I don't know anything about music," said Persio. "Outside of
pasadobles, it's all the same to me."

"Admit it, Mama, I play better than that girl. And with all my
fingers, not leaving half of them in the air."

Claudia sighed, recovering from the massacre. She put her hand
on Jorge's forehead.

"Do you really feel all right?"

"Of course," said Jorge, who was waiting for his turn. "Persio,
look what's coming."

At an amiable yet imperious signal from Don Galo, Nelly
went up and stood cornered between the back of the piano and
the wall. She had not counted on the bright spotlight glaring into
her eyes ("She's nervous, poor dear," Doña Pepa said, so that every-

one could hear), and she blinked violently and finally raised an arm to cover her eyes. The *maître* rushed up obsequiously and moved the spotlight a couple of yards further back. Everyone applauded to encourage the artist.

"I'm going to recite 'To Laugh While Crying' by Juan de Dios Peza," Nelly announced, placing her hands at her sides as if she were going to play castanets. "*When the public saw Mr. Garrick, an actor from England, and heartily applauded him, they said . . .*"

"I know that poem too," Jorge said. "Remember, I recited it in the café the other night? Now comes the part about the doctor."

"*The highest of the lords, all victims of melancholia,*" Nelly declaimed, "*Went to see the king of actors, and exchanged their melancholia for guffaws.*"

"Nelly's a born actress," Doña Pepa confided to Doña Rosita. "Ever since she was a little girl, you can believe me, she was reciting *Jack and Jill* like no one else."

"Not Atilio," said Doña Rosita, sighing. "The only thing he liked to do was crush cockroaches in the kitchen and play ball in the courtyard. And smashing all my potted hydrangeas, it's a constant battle with boys if you want to keep the house in one piece."

Leaning against the bar, alert to any wish on the part of the passengers, the *maître* and the bartender watched the spectacle. The bartender reached over and turned up the thermostat from two to four. The *maître* looked at him, they both smiled; they didn't understand very much of what was being recited. The bartender took out two bottles of beer and two glasses. Without making the slightest noise, he opened the bottles and filled the glasses. Medrano, half asleep at the back, envied them, but it was too complicated to make his way between the chairs to get to the bar. He noticed his cigarette butt had burned out between his lips, and he carefully took it out of his mouth. He was almost happy not to be sitting next to Claudia, to be able to look at her secretly from the shadows instead. "How lovely she is," he thought. He felt a kind of inner warmth and a slight anxiety, as if he were on a threshold he would not be able to cross for some reason, and the slight warmth and anxiety came from the fact that he was not going to cross it, and that it would be all right if he couldn't. "She'll never know how good she's been for me," he thought. Pained, confused, his papers all in disorder, his comb broken, no buttons on his shirt, shaken by a wind which tore off bits of time, of face, of dead life, he looked out again, more profoundly, at the half-opened, impenetrable door, a point from which, perhaps, something would be possible for him with more directness, something coming from himself which would be his work and his reason for being, once he had gotten all those things off his back which he had once thought acceptable, even necessary. But he was still far from that.

XXXIX

Halfway down the passage he realized he had the pipe in his hand, and he became infuriated all over again. Then he realized that if he took the tobacco with him he'd be able to offer some to Bob, and show him that he knew how to smoke. He went back to the cabin, collected the tobacco, put it into his pocket, and came out again, positive there wouldn't be anyone in the corridors at this hour. The main passage below was empty, as was the long passageway where the little violet lamp glowed, dimmer than ever. If he had any luck this time, and Bob helped him get through to the rear deck . . . The hope of vengeance made him run, helped him fight against his fear. "But just imagine, the youngest person has been the most courageous; he got to the poop deck all by himself . . ." Beba, for instance and even the old man, poor guy, wouldn't he look like a rat drowned in piss when the congratulations started pouring in. But that would be nothing next to Raul. "Really, Raul, didn't you know? Of course, Felipe went by himself and put his head in the lion's mouth . . ." The partitions of the passageway were narrower than on the previous visit; he stopped a couple of yards from the doors and looked back. The corridor really was narrower, it was suffocating. It was almost a relief to open the door on the right. The light from the hanging naked bulbs half-blinded him. There was no one in the cabin, and it looked as messy as before, strewn with bits of canvas, straps, tools on the workbench. Maybe that was why the door at the rear was silhouetted better, as if it were waiting for him. Felipe turned and slowly closed the door behind him, continuing on tiptoe. When he got as far as the workbench he stood still. "It's miserably hot down here," he thought. He could hear the motors working energetically, the noise came from all directions at once, adding to the heat and blinding light. He crossed the two yards that separated him from the door and gently tried the knob. Someone was coming. Felipe pressed up against the wall, so the door would hide him in case it was opened. "They weren't steps," he thought, anguished. Just noise. It was a relief to half-open the door and look out. But before doing so, he squatted down, as he had learned from mystery novels, so that his head wouldn't be at bullet level. He made out a narrow, dark passageway; when his eyes became adjusted to the darkness, he began to distinguish the steps of a ladder about six yards from where he stood. Only then did he remember what Bob had said. That is . . . If he went back to the bar immediately and brought Lopez or Medrano down, maybe between the two of them they could get there without any danger. But what danger? What danger could there be at the stern? Not counting the typhus, and besides he never caught anything, not even mumps.

He closed the door behind him and went forward. He was breathing hard in the thick air, which smelled of tar and rancid things. He saw a door to the left and he went toward the ladder steps. Suddenly his shadow surged before him, drawing itself for a brief moment on the floor, motionless, an arm raised over his head in a gesture of defense. When he managed to turn around, he saw Bob looking at him from the wide-open door. A greenish light came from the cabin.

"*Hasdala,* kid."

"Hi," Felipe answered, backing away a little. He took his pipe from his pocket and offered it toward the lighted area. He could find no words, the pipe was trembling between his fingers. "You see, I remembered that you . . . We were going to talk again, and then . . ."

"*Sa,*" said Bob. "Come on in, kid, come on in."

．　．　．

When his turn came, Medrano threw away his cigarette and went and sat down at the piano with a somewhat sleepy air. He began to sing *bagualas* and *zambas*, accompanying himself fairly well, shamelessly imitating Atahualpa Yupanqui's style. He received a long round of applause and was forced to sing some more. Persio, who followed him, was greeted with the usual distrust aroused by clairvoyants. He was introduced by Dr. Restelli as an investigator of remote secrets, and he began to read the palms of volunteers from the audience, giving them the usual list of trivialities, and among these trivialities, some phrase or other occasionally slipped out, which had meaning only for the person in question and which sufficed to stun and convince the interested party. Obviously bored, Persio ended his round of palmistry and approached the bar in order to exchange the future for a cooling drink. Dr. Restelli was compiling his most select vocabulary to introduce the youngest member of the gathering, the extraordinarily intelligent little Jorge Lewbaum, for whom the accumulation of only a few years was no hindrance to his many talents. This boy, a remarkable example of Argentine youth, would be the delight of the soirée, thanks to his very personal interpretation of various monologues, of which he was the author as well, and the first of them was titled: "The Story of an Octopat."

"I wrote it, but Persio helped me," Jorge said loyally, as he came up amid a round of reserved applause. He greeted everyone stiffly, coinciding for a brief moment with Dr. Restelli's description of him.

"'The Story of an Octopat,' by Persio and Jorge Lewbaum," he announced, and put out his hand as if to catch himself against the back of the piano. Jumping up, Pelusa reached him in time to seize his arm before he fell face down on the floor.

A glass of water, air, advice of all sorts, three chairs upon which to stretch out the boy who has just fainted, buttons which suddenly become recalcitrant and can't be loosened. Medrano looked at Claudia bent over her son and walked toward the bar.

"Telephone the doctor, quick. Now."

The *maître* was busy soaking a napkin. Medrano pulled him to attention, grabbing him by the arm.

"I said now."

The *maître* turned the towel over to the bartender and went up to the wall telephone. He dialed a number with two ciphers. He said something, and then repeated it in a louder voice. Medrano was waiting, not taking his eyes off him for a second. The *maître* hung up and nodded affirmatively to him.

"He's coming immediately, sir. I think that . . . perhaps it would be better to put the boy to bed."

Medrano wondered where the doctor would come from, and where the officer with the grey hair came from. The din caused by the ladies behind him was trying his patience. He opened a path toward Claudia, who was holding Jorge's hand.

"Ah, it seems we're getting better," he said, kneeling next to her.

Jorge smiled at him. He looked confused and was watching the faces floating over him as if they were clouds. He didn't really see anybody but Claudia and Persio, and perhaps Medrano, who unceremoniously put his arms under his neck and legs and lifted him up. The ladies made way for him, and Pelusa started to help, but Medrano was already leaving, carrying Jorge. Claudia followed him; Jorge's mask hung from her hand. The others exchanged apprehensive glances. It wasn't serious, of course, just dizziness brought on by the overly hot room, but no one felt much like going on with the fiesta.

"Well, let's carry on," Don Galo affirmed, moving from one side to another by jerking the steering mechanism of the wheelchair. "We won't get anywhere by getting depressed over a trifling incident."

"You'll see, the boy will recuperate in ten minutes," said Dr. Restelli. "We shouldn't be put off by a simple fainting fit."

"But *mamma mia*," Pelusa sympathized lugubriously. "First the big kid stands me up just when we have to do our act, and now the little kid falls apart in front of my eyes. This ship is really the end."

"At least let's sit down and drink something," Señor Trejo proposed. "We shouldn't dwell on sickness constantly, especially when there's . . . I mean, nothing's gained by adding to the alarmist rumors. My son also had a headache today, and you can all see that neither my wife nor I are worried. Of course, they've told us they've taken all the necessary precautions."

Señora Trejo, informed by Beba, signaled to her husband that Felipe wasn't in his cabin right now. Pelusa hit his head and said that he already knew that, but where in the world could the kid be.

"On deck, surely," said Señor Trejo. "A boyish mood."

"Some mood," said Pelusa. "Don't you know we already got a terrific acrobatic act going?"

Paula sighed, as she observed Lopez out of the corner of her eye. He had watched Jorge faint with an expression of growing anger.

"It could very well be," said Lopez, "that you'll find the door of your cabin locked."

"I wouldn't know what to do: to jump with joy or try to knock the door down," said Paula. "After all, it is *my* cabin."

"And if it is locked, what are you going to do?"

"I don't know," said Paula. "Spend the night on deck. Who cares."

"Come on, let's go," said Lopez.

"No, I'm going to stay a bit longer."

"Please."

"No. Probably the door is open and Raul is sleeping like a cow. You've no idea how these cultural affairs and good healthy entertainments tire him."

"Raul, Raul," said Lopez. "You're just dying to go back and strip down to the nude six feet away from him."

"Almost ten feet, Jamaica John."

"Come on," he said once more, but Paula looked directly at him, refusing, thinking that Raul deserved her refusal at this moment, and that she'd wait until she knew if he too had drawn a lucky card. It was completely useless, it was cruel for Jamaica John and for her: it was the last thing in the world she wanted, especially at that particular moment. But she did it precisely because of that, to pay a vague, obscure debt which was neither clear or meaningful. It was like an act of forgiveness, a hope of going back and finding one's roots, before she had become that woman who was now denying herself, encompassed in a wave of desire and tenderness. She did it for Raul but also for Jamaica John, so as to one day be able to give him something that wasn't anticipated ruin. She thought that perhaps the doors could be opened with gestures so incredibly stupid, the same doors that all the malice of intelligence was not capable of opening. And the worst thing was that she would have to borrow his handkerchief again and that he would refuse, furious and resentful, before going off to sleep by himself, his mouth bitter with the taste of tobacco which he would smoke against his will.

"Good thing I recognized you. A little further on and I'd have split your head. I already warned you, eh?"

Felipe squirmed uncomfortably on the bench where he had finally taken a seat.

"I told you I came to look for you. You weren't in the other room, and I saw the door open and I wanted to know if—"

"Oh, you didn't do anything wrong, kid. Here's to you."

"*Prosit*," Felipe said, gulping the rum down like a man. "Your cabin's pretty nice. I thought all the sailors slept together."

"Sometimes Orf comes when he gets tired of the two Chinks in his cabin. Hey, your tobacco isn't bad. A little mild maybe, but better than that junk you were puffing on yesterday. What'd you say we smoke another pipe?"

"Let's," said Felipe, without any great enthusiasm. He was glancing around the dirty walls of the cabin, looking at the photos of men and women tacked to the wall with straight pins. There was an almanac showing three birds carrying a golden thread through the air; two mattresses thrown in the corner, one on top of the other; an iron table whose successive coats of paint had dripped along the table legs, clotting together at several spots and looking as if it were still fresh and running. An open wardrobe closet revealed a clock hung on a nail, ripped shirts, a short whip, full bottles and empty bottles, dirty glasses, a purple pincushion. He loaded his pipe again with a shaky hand; the rum was devilishly strong, and Bob had already poured him another. He tried not to look at Bob's hands, which reminded him of hairy spiders, but he liked the blue serpent on his forearm. He asked if tattoos were painful.

No, not at all, but you had to have patience. And it depended on the part of the body to be tattooed. He once knew a sailor from Bremen who was brave enough to . . . Felipe was listening, shocked, wondering if there wasn't some sort of ventilation in the cabin, because the smoke and the rum smell were stifling; he was already beginning to see Bob as though there were a gauze curtain between the two of them. Bob, looking at him affectionately, was explaining that the best tattoos were done by the Japanese. The woman on his right shoulder had been tattooed by Kiro, a friend of his who also handled opium. He took off his undershirt with a slow, almost elegant gesture, so that Felipe could see the woman on his right shoulder, the two arrows and the guitar, the eagle whose enormous wingspread almost covered his thorax. To have the eagle tattooed he had had to get drunk, because the skin on some parts of the chest was very delicate, and the needle pricks hurt. Did Felipe have sensitive skin? Yes, I guess so, like everyone else. No, not like everyone else, because there were differences in different races and different jobs . . . This English tobacco really was good. Say, it was okay smoking and drinking. No matter how much he didn't much feel like it now, it was always the same halfway through, with a little perseverance he'd get back the taste for it. The rum was smooth, a very smooth, aromatic white rum. Another little drink and he was going to show him a photo album of their trips. It was Orf who took most of the photos on ship, but he also had many that women had given him at ports of call, women liked to give away photos, and some of the pictures were even . . . But first they were going to drink to their friendship. Sa. A good rum, very smooth and aromatic, perfect with English tobacco. It was hot, sure it was, they were near the engine room. He should do what he did, take off his shirt. No, why talk about opening the door, the smoke wouldn't blow out of the room anyway, and if someone found him here . . . It was just fine as it was, not a thing to do, just talking and drinking. Why did he have to worry, it was still early, unless his mama was looking for him . . . Okay, he didn't have to get mad, it was a joke, he knew perfectly well that he did what he pleased on board, just as it should be. The smoke? Well, maybe there was a little smoke, but when you're smoking such great tobacco, it's worth the trouble inhaling as much as possible. And just one more little swallow of rum to mix the flavors, they went so well together. Yes, it was a bit hot, he had already told him to take off his shirt. Like this, kid, don't get mad. He didn't have to run to the door, just keep quiet, because even if it wasn't on purpose, he could get hurt, really, and with such soft skin . . . Who would have thought that such a smart kid wouldn't be able to understand it was better to stay put and not fight to get loose. Running to the door like that, when he could be so well off in the cabin, right there in that cozy corner, especially if he didn't try to use force to break away, to get free of the hands finding the buttons and unloosening them, one by one, endlessly.

"It won't be anything," Medrano said. "It'll turn out to be nothing, Claudia."

Claudia was covering Jorge with the blankets. He had suddenly gone red and was shaking with fever. Señora Trejo had just left the cabin after assuring her that these children's sicknesses were nothing and that Jorge would be fine in the morning. Scarcely replying, Claudia had shaken down a thermometer while Medrano closed the porthole and adjusted the lights so there would be no glare in Jorge's eyes. Persio was pacing back and forth in the corridor with a long face, not daring to enter. The doctor came in five minutes later, and Medrano started to leave the cabin, but Claudia kept him there with a glance. The doctor was a fat man who looked bored and tired. He jabbered in French, examined Jorge without lifting his eyes, and suddenly demanded a spoon, took his pulse, and flexed his legs, all in an absent-minded fashion. He covered Jorge, who was groaning, and asked Medrano if he was the boy's father. When Medrano said no, he turned toward Claudia, surprised, as if he was noticing her for the first time.

"*Eh bien, madame, il faudra attendre,*" he said, shrugging his shoulders. "*Pour l'instant je ne peux pas me prononcer. C'est bizarre, quand même . . .*"

"Typhus?" Claudia asked.

"*Mais non, allons, c'est pas du tout ça!*"

"In any case, there's typhus on the ship, isn't there?" Medrano

asked. "Vous avez eu des cas de typhus chez vous, n'est-ce pas?"
"C'est à dire . . ." the doctor began. It wasn't absolutely certain they were dealing with typhus 224, at most it was a benign outbreak and no real cause for alarm. If the lady didn't mind, he was going to retire now, and he would send the maître with medicines for the boy. In his opinion, they were dealing with a pulmonary congestion. If his temperature went beyond 103 they should let the maître know, who would then . . .

Medrano dug his fingernails into the palms of his hands. He was on the point of going after the doctor and cornering him in the hall, but Claudia seemed aware of this and motioned him to return. He stopped at the door, indecisive and furious.

"Stay here, Gabriel, keep me company for a while. Please."

"Yes, of course," said Medrano, confused. He knew that this wasn't the moment to force the situation, but it was difficult for him to move away from the door, to admit defeat and near-mockery once more. Claudia was waiting, sitting on the edge of Jorge's bed. Jorge was delirious and was trying to pull the blankets off. There was a quiet knock at the door: the maître was carrying two boxes and a tube. He had an icebag in his cabin, and if there was any need for it, the doctor said they could use it. He would be at the bar an hour longer and would be at their disposal for anything at all. He would send the waiter with some hot coffee, if they liked.

Medrano helped Claudia give Jorge the first kind of medicine. He resisted it weakly and didn't seem to recognize them. A knock at the door: it was Lopez, a bit peevish and worried, coming for news. Medrano quietly told him about the conversation with the doctor.

"Damn it all, if I had known I would have grabbed him in the hall," Lopez said. "I just came from the bar and didn't know what had happened until Presutti told me that the doctor had been over here."

"He'll be back if we need him," Medrano said. "And then, if you think . . ."

"Right," Lopez said. "Let me know beforehand if you can; anyway, I'll be walking around here. I won't be able to sleep tonight. If that guy thinks Jorge has anything serious, then we

shouldn't wait another minute," he said, lowering his voice so
Claudia wouldn't hear. "I doubt if the doctor is any better than the
rest of the gang. They're likely to let the boy get worse just as
long as no one ever finds out. Look, the best thing to do is to call
him even if you don't need him, let's say in an hour. We'll wait
out here for him, and this time, no one will stop us from getting
to the stern."

"All right, but let's remember Jorge," said Medrano. "If we
don't handle it right and the doctor stays on the other side, it
might be very ugly."

"We've lost two days," said Lopez. "That's what we get with
courtesy and listening to the peaceful old fools. But do you think
the boy . . . ?"

"No, but it's more wishful thinking than anything else. Dentists don't know anything about typhus, you know. This delirium
and fever worry me. It could be nothing, too much chocolate, a
bit of sunstroke, anything. It could be the pulmonary congestion
the doctor talked about. What do you say we smoke a cigarette?
We'll talk to Presutti and Costa on the way, if they're around."

He went up to Claudia and smiled at her. Lopez also smiled.
Claudia felt his friendliness and thanked them, looking at them
simply.

"I'll be back in a while," said Medrano. "Lie down, Claudia,
try to rest."

Everything he said sounded to her a bit as if it had been said
before, useless but tranquilizing. The smiles, the tiptoes, the promise to be back, the assurance of knowing that friends were there.
She looked at Jorge, who was sleeping more quietly. The cabin
suddenly seemed to have grown, a vague perfume of black tobacco
floated in the air, as if Gabriel had not completely left. Claudia
rested her head in one hand and closed her eyes; she was going to sit watch next to Jorge again. Persio would be pacing
near by like a secretive cat, the night would advance interminably until the first rays of dawn. A ship, Juan Bautista Alberdi
Street, the world; Jorge was there, sick, among millions of other
sick Jorges everywhere on earth, but now the world had shrunk to
only one sick boy. If Leon had been with them, efficient and sure,
he would have immediately discovered the cause of the disturb-

ance, and nipped it in the bud without losing a minute. Poor
Gabriel, bending over Jorge with the face of a man who understands nothing; but it helped her to know that Gabriel was there,
smoking in the corridor, waiting with her. The door half-opened.
Paula leaned over, took off her shoes, and waited. Claudia motioned to her, but she walked in barely to the first armchair.

"He can't hear a thing," said Claudia. "Come, sit down here."

"I'll go immediately, too many people have already come in to
bother you. Everyone loves your little puppy very much."

"My little puppy with a hundred-and-two-degree fever."

"Medrano told me about the doctor, they're out there standing
guard. May I stay with you? Why don't you lie down for a
while? I'm not tired, and if Jorge wakes up I promise to call you
immediately."

"Stay, of course, but I'm not tired either. We can talk."

"Of the sensational things happening on board? I've the latest
news dispatch for you."

Bitch, damn bitch, she thought as she talked, *gloating about
what you're about to say, savoring what she's going to ask you
. . .* Claudia was looking at Paula's hands; Paula hid them suddenly, and began to laugh in a soft voice, and then put her hands
back on the arms of the chair. If only Claudia had been her mother,
but naturally, she would have hated her as she did her own. Too
late to think about a mother, or even a woman friend.

"Tell me," said Claudia. "It'll help us pass the time."

"Oh, nothing serious. The Trejos are on the verge of hysteria
because their son has disappeared. They're acting as if it's nothing,
but . . ."

"He wasn't at the bar, now that I think of it. I think Presutti
went out looking for him."

"First Presutti and then Raul."

Bitch.

"Well, he can't be too far off," said Claudia, indifferently.
"Boys are sometimes rather restless . . . Perhaps he felt like spend-
ing the night on deck."

"Perhaps," said Paula. "Fortunately, I'm not quite as hysterical
as the Trejos, but I can tell you that Raul, too, has disappeared off
the face of the earth."

Claudia looked at her. Paula had been waiting for her look
and she received it with a smooth, inexpressive face. Someone was
coming and going through the corridor, and in the silence, the
footsteps, deadened by the linoleum, sounded one after another,
nearer, further: Medrano, or Persio, or Lopez, or the despondent
Presutti, who was truly worried about Jorge.

Claudia lowered her eyes. All at once she was tired. The joy of
seeing Paula suddenly vanished, and in its place was a desire to not
know any more, to not accept this new contamination, still un-
formulated, but which a single question or a silence could explain
and confirm. Paula had closed her eyes and seemed indifferent to
what might follow, but she suddenly moved her fingers, tapping
noiselessly on the arm of the chair.

"This can't be jealousy," she said, as if to herself. "I feel so
sorry for them."

"Paula, go away."

"Yes, of course. Immediately," said Paula, getting up quickly.
"Forgive me. I came for another reason, I wanted to keep you
company. Pure selfishness, of course, because you do me so
much good. On the other hand . . ."

"On the other hand nothing," said Claudia. "We'll talk another day. Go to sleep now. Don't forget your shoes."

Paula obeyed and left without turning around.

He thought it was strange how a certain idea of method was capable of making you act in a predetermined fashion, even if you
knew perfectly well that it was a waste of time. He knew he
wouldn't find Felipe on deck, but just the same he walked around
slowly, first on the port side, then on starboard, stopping under
the awning to adjust his eyes to the dark, exploring the vague,
confused area of ventilators, cordage, and winches. When he
went back up, he heard the sound of applause coming from the
bar. He decided to knock on the door of cabin number five. An
almost disdainful indifference, the indifference of someone who
has all the time in the world, mingled with an unconfessed longing to hurry, and, at the same time, delay their meeting. He refused to believe that Felipe's absence (but he felt it, it was stronger
than he) was a sign of forgiveness or war. He was sure he wasn't

going to find him in his cabin, but he knocked twice and then
opened the door. The lights were on, the bathroom door was wide
open, no one inside. He left quickly, afraid Felipe's sister or father
would be coming back to look for him, and the thought of a cheap
scandal terrified him: the why-are-you-in-a-cabin-that's-not-yours,
the same old intolerable rundown. And suddenly he was spiteful,
and he had been even as he was walking along the deck, feeling
peevish, controlling his temper, because Felipe had made a fool
of him again, going off on his own to explore the ship, once more
avenging his offended rights. There was no sign, there was no
truce. War was declared, maybe contempt. "This time I'm going
to sock him in the eye," Raul thought. "He can go to hell, but at
least he'll be able to take a little souvenir with him, a souvenir
on his mug." He ran the distance that separated him from the
little ladder off the central corridor, and took the stairs down two
at a time. And yet he was such a kid, such a fool; who knows, perhaps all these insults would end in an embarrassed reconciliation,
maybe with conditions, with exact limitations, friends, yes, but
nothing more, don't confuse the issue . . . But it was stupid to
tell himself everything was lost; basically Paula was right. You
couldn't come to them with the truth on your tongue and in your
hands; you had to be devious, to corrupt (the word didn't have
its normal meaning here); and perhaps someday, long before the
end of the trip, perhaps like that . . . Paula was right, he had
known it from the first minute and yet he had made a tactical error.
How could he not have the advantage of Felipe's inherent misfortune, Felipe, who was his own worst enemy, ready to surrender
while he thought he was resisting? Everything about him was desire and longing; it was enough to gently rid him of his domestic
education and gang slogans, as well as the idea that certain things
were good and others bad, just to let him run rampant and then
smoothly draw in the reins, to tell him he's right and at the same
time to inject a note of doubt, opening a new vision of things for
him, more flexible and more passionate. To destroy and construct
in him, for he had a marvelous plasticity, to take the necessary
time, to suffer the delights of time, of waiting, and then one fine
day to reap his reward, exactly at the indicated and decided hour.

There was no one in the first cabin. Raul looked at the door

at the rear and hesitated. He wouldn't have had the nerve . . .
But yes, he might have. He jarred the door slightly and went into
the passageway. He saw the staircase. "He *has* made it to the
stern," he thought, amazed. "He's made it there before anybody
else." His heart was pounding like an escaped bat. He smelled
tobacco, he recognized it. A dull light filtered through the narrow chinks of the door on the left. He opened it slowly, he
looked. The bat burst into a thousand pieces in an explosion that
almost blinded him. Bob's snores pierced the silence rhythmically.
The blue eagle, fallen between Felipe and the wall, noisily raised
and lowered its wings at each snore. A hairy leg, crossed over
Felipe's, kept him prisoner in a ridiculous knot. The place
smelled of vomit, tobacco, and sweat. Felipe, his eyes wide open,
stared vacantly, sightlessly, at Raul standing at the door. Bob's
snoring grew louder, and he moved as if he were going to wake
up. Raul took two steps forward and rested his hand against the
table. Only then did Felipe recognize him. Stupidly, he put his
hands on his stomach and slowly tried to get out from under the
weight of the leg, which finally slipped down. Bob was babbling
something and his whole greasy body shook as if he were having a
nightmare. Sitting on the edge of the mattresses, Felipe stretched
out his hand to get his clothes, trying carefully to pick them up
from a floor splashed with his vomit. Raul walked around the table
and pushed the scattered clothes with his foot. He felt as if he
were going to vomit too, and went back as far as the corridor.
Leaning against the wall, he waited. The staircase to the poop
deck was no more than three yards away, but he didn't look at it,
not even once. He was waiting. He couldn't even cry.

He let Felipe go first and he followed him. They crossed
through the first cabin and the violet passageway. When they
reached the ladder, Felipe took hold of the banister, turned completely around, and gradually subsided onto one of the steps.

"Let me by," Raul said, motionless before him.

Felipe covered his face with his hands and began to sob. He
seemed much younger, a grown boy who has hurt himself and
can't fake it. Raul grabbed the banister and jumped over Felipe
to the upper stairs. He was thinking vaguely about the blue eagle
to keep from getting sick himself, to reach his cabin without vomit-

ing in the corridor. The blue eagle, a symbol. He no longer had a thought about the ladder to the stern. The blue eagle, of course, pure mythology delightfully concentrated into a digest worthy of our epoch, the eagle and Zeus, of course, it couldn't be clearer, a symbol, the blue eagle.

H

One time more, the last perhaps, but who could be sure; nothing is clear here, Persio has a feeling that the hour of conjunction has locked exactly the right house, dressed the dolls with exactly the right clothes. His eyes adrift, breathing with difficulty, alone in his cabin or on the bridge, he sees the dolls outlined against the night, adjusting their wigs, carrying on the interrupted soirée. Fulfillment, the goal attained: the obscurest words fall like drops from his eyes, they quiver a second on the edge of his lips. He thinks: "Jorge," and an enormous green tear slides slowly down his cheek, gets caught on a whisker, and turns at last into a bitter salt, which eternity itself could not obliterate. To see the stern no longer matters to him, whatever is further beyond opens onto another night, to other faces, to a willfulness of bulkhead doors. In a moment of warm vanity he thought himself universal, a prophet, his calling one of revelations, and he was overcome by the vague certainty that a central point existed from where one could see each discordant element like a spoke in a wheel . . .

Strangely, the enormous guitar has fallen silent up above, and the Malcolm sails over a sea of rubber, under an atmosphere of chalk. And as he can no longer see anything of the stern, and his will is manacled by Jorge's difficult breathing, by the desolation obliterating Claudia's face, he falls into an almost blind present, which is limited to a few yards of deck and a railing against a starless sea. Perhaps then, and because of that, Persio's conscience decides that the stern is (although it doesn't seem that way to anyone else) really his bitter vision, his twitching motionless advance, his most necessary and deplorable task. The monkey cages, the lions haunting the decks, the pampas stretched out face up, the vertiginous growth of South American pines, all explode and come back together again now in the dolls which have already adjusted their masks and wigs, the figures of the dance which repeat on any ship

the lines and circles of Picasso's man with the guitar (which belonged to Apollinaire), and then there are also the trains that arrive at and leave Portuguese stations, among so many other millions
of simultaneous things, among such a dreadful infinity of simultane-
ities and coincidences and crossings and ruptures, that everything,
unless submitted to one's intelligence, collapses in a cosmic death,
and everything, unless not submitted to one's intelligence, is called
absurd, is called concept, is called illusion, is called not being able
to see the woods for the trees, examining a drop of water with one's
back to the sea, preferring a woman instead of a flight to the absolute. But the dolls are ready and dancing in front of Persio; jauntily
dressed, dashing, some are functionaries who formerly unraveled
rolls of red tape, others have the same names as people on ship, and
Persio himself is among them, rigorously bald, server of the zig-
gurat, proof corrector at Kraft's, friend of a sick child. How can he
help but remember that this is the hour when everything seemed
to be coming violently to a head, when hands were already feeling
around a drawer for a revolver, when someone was crying face down
in a cabin, how can Persio the erudite help remembering the men
made of wood, that pitiful race of the first dolls? The dance on
deck is awkward, as if vegetables were dancing, or mechanical toys;
the meager wood of a grim and avaricious creation creaks and sways
in each movement of the dance; everything is made of wood, the
faces, the masks, the legs, the sexual parts, the heavy hearts where
nothing settles without immediately curdling and clotting, the entrails which voraciously accumulate the thickest substances, the
hands which seize other hands to keep the heavy body balanced, to
end the whirl. Crushed by fatigue and despair, satiated with a
clarity which has only brought him another return and another fall,
Persio watches the dance of the wooden dolls, the first act of the
American destiny. Now they'll be abandoned by the displeased
gods, now dogs and receptacles and even millstones will rise in rebellion against the stumbling, condemned golems, they'll fall on
them and smash them to bits, and the dance will turn to a dance
of death, the movements of the dance will be filled with teeth, hair,
and nails; the frustrated images will begin to succumb, one by one,
under the same indifferent sky, and right here in this present moment in which Persio also exists, thinking about a sick child and a

troubled dawn, the dance will continue its stylized movements, hands will have had manicures, the legs will have donned trousers, the entrails will have known the taste of foie gras and muscatel, and the supple, perfumed bodies will dance, without knowing that the dance of wood is still dancing and that everything is imminent rebellion and that the American world is a swindle, and that under it the ants are at work, the armadillos as well, the climate that spawns wet leeches, condors with rotted food scraps, political bosses whom the villagers acclaim and adore, women who weave in the doorways of the houses during their entire lifetimes, bank employees, football players, proud engineers, poets who stubbornly believe themselves important and tragic, sad writers of sad stories, and cities stained with indifference. Persio covers his eyes, but the stern pierces him like a thorn, and he feels the hopelessly contradicted and exalted past embracing the present, the now, which parodies it like the monkey parodies the men of wood, like men of flesh and blood parody the men of wood. Everything that will happen will be just as illusory, the immersion in an unchaining of destinies will resolve itself in a plethora of favored or contradicted sentiments, of defeats as dubious as the victories. An abysmal ambiguity, an incurable irresolution at the very center of all solutions: in a small world the same as all other worlds, the same as all trains, the same as all guitar players, the same as all prows and all sterns, in a world without gods and without men, the dolls dance in the light of the dawn. Why are you crying, Persio? Why are you crying? These are the things with which the fire is sometimes lit, from all that misery the song rises; when the dolls bite their last handful of dust, perhaps a man will be born. Perhaps he has already been born and you don't see him.

THIRD DAY

XL

"Five after three," said Lopez.

The bartender had gone to bed at midnight. The *maître*, seated behind the bar, yawned occasionally but kept his word. Medrano, his mouth bitter with tobacco and a bad night, rose once more to go look in on Claudia.

Alone at the end of the bar, Lopez wondered if Raul had gone to sleep. Strange that Raul should desert them on a night like this. He'd seen him shortly after they'd carried Jorge to the cabin; he was smoking, leaning up against the partition in the starboard corridor, a little pale and tired-looking; but he reacted immediately to the excitement the doctor's arrival had provoked, and joined the conversation until Paula came out of Claudia's cabin and they went off together. All these things were perversely ingrained in Lopez' memory, as he reconstructed all of it between swallows of coffee, or brandy. Raul leaning up against the partition, smoking; Paula, leaving the cabin, with an expression (but how to fathom Paula's expression, how fathom Paula?); and they both were looking at one another as if surprised to have met again—Paula surprised, Raul practically annoyed—and they went walking in the direction of the central corridor. Then Lopez had gone down to the deck and stood for more than an hour alone in the prow, looking up toward the captain's bridge where he saw no one, smoking and dreaming, lost in a vague, almost pleasant delirium of anger and humiliation, through which Paula passed like a figure on a merry-go-round, once, twice, and each time he stretched out his arm to strike her he let it fall and longed for her instead; as he stood there trembling with desire, he knew he wouldn't be able to go back to his cabin that night, that he'd have to keep vigil, to brutalize himself with drink or talk, to forget that she had refused him once more and that she was sleeping next to Raul or listening to the story Raul would tell her of what was going on while the soirée was going on, and then the merry-go-round turned once more and the image of a naked Paula passed close to him, or of a Paula in a red blouse, a different Paula at every turn: Paula in a bikini or in a pair of pajamas he had never seen, Paula naked again, her back to the stars, Paula singing *"Un jour tu verras,"* Paula saying no in a friendly fashion, scarcely moving her head from one side to the other, no, no. Then Lopez had gone back to the bar to drink, and had already spent two hours with Medrano, keeping watch.

"A brandy, please."

The *maître* took a bottle of Courvoisier from the shelf.

"You have one, too," Lopez added. Basically, the *maître* was okay, he was a little less poop than the other glucids. "And another one, here comes my friend."

Medrano motioned him not to order.

"We have to call the doctor again," he said. "The boy's fever's up to a hundred and four."

The *maître* went to the telephone and dialed the number.

"Take a drink anyway," said Lopez. "It's a little cold this time of the morning."

"No, old man, thanks."

The *maître* came back with a worried look on his face.

"He wants to know if he has been vomiting or has had convulsions."

"No. Tell him to come immediately."

The *maître* spoke, listened, spoke again. He hung up the receiver, disappointed.

"He's not going to be able to come until later. He says to double the dosage of the medicine that's in the tube, and to take his temperature again in an hour."

Medrano ran to the telephone. He knew the number was 5-6.

He dialed it while Lopez, elbows on the bar, waited, his eyes glued on the *maître*. Medrano dialed the number again.

"I'm so sorry, sir," said the *maître*. "It's always the same, they don't like to be bothered at these late hours. It's busy, isn't it?"

Medrano and Lopez looked at one another without answering him. They left together and each went to his own cabin. While he was loading his revolver and filling his pockets with bullets, Lopez saw himself in the mirror and thought he looked ridiculous. But anything was better than thinking about sleep. Just in case, he put on a dark leather jacket and took along an extra pack of cigarettes. Medrano was waiting for him outside, wearing a windbreaker, which made him look somewhat sporty. Beside him was Atilio Presutti, blinking with sleep, his hair tousled, and looking very bewildered.

"I called our friend Atilio because the more there are of us the better our chances of getting to the radio room," Medrano said. "Go get Raul and tell him to bring the Colt."

"And I left my shotgun home," Pelusa complained. "If I knew, I'd have brought it."

"Stay here and wait for the others," said Medrano. "I'll be right back."

He went into Claudia's cabin. Jorge was panting and a blue shadow encircled his mouth. There wasn't much to say. They prepared his medicine and succeeded in making him swallow it. As if he suddenly recognized her, Jorge hugged Claudia, crying and coughing. His chest hurt him, his legs hurt, there was something funny in his mouth.

"That'll all go away soon, little lion," said Medrano, kneeling next to the bed, stroking Jorge's head until the boy finally released Claudia and stretched out again in bed, moaning.

"It hurts, you know," he said to Medrano. "Why don't you give me something to get better right away?"

"You just finished taking it, son. Now, it's going to be like this: in a little while you'll sleep, you'll dream about the octopat or whatever you like most, and then at nine tomorrow you'll wake up much better, and I'll come and tell you stories."

Jorge closed his eyes, quieter. Only then did Medrano feel his right hand squeezing Claudia's hard. He did not move, but went on looking at Jorge so Jorge would feel his presence, which calmed him, and he kept holding Claudia's hand tightly. When Jorge's breathing was somewhat easier, he gradually stood up. He took Claudia as far as the door of the cabin.

"I have to go away for a while. I'll come back and keep you company as long as you need me."

"Stay now," Claudia said.

"I can't. It's ridiculous, but Lopez is waiting for me. Don't worry, I'll be right back."

Claudia sighed and suddenly leaned against him. Her head was very warm against his shoulder.

"Don't do anything silly, Gabriel. Please don't do anything silly."

"No, dear," Medrano said softly. "I promise."

He grazed her hair with a kiss. His finger sketched something on Claudia's tear-soaked cheek.

"I'll be right back," he said again, drawing away from her slowly. He opened the door and went out. The corridor seemed hazy to him, even Atilio, who was standing guard, seemed hazy. Without knowing why, he looked at his watch. It was three-twenty, the third day of the trip.

He saw Lopez and Raul coming down the hall, followed closely by Paula in a red robe. Raul and Lopez were walking as if they wanted to escape from her, but that wasn't easy.

"What is it that you're cooking up?" she asked, looking at Medrano.

"We're going to drag the doctor here by his ear and telegraph Buenos Aires," Medrano said, a little annoyed. "Why don't you go to sleep, Paulita?"

"Sleep, sleep, you all say the same thing. I'm not tired, I want to do what I can to help."

"Keep Claudia company, then."

But Paula didn't want to keep Claudia company. She turned to Raul and stared at him intently. Lopez had moved off a bit, as if he didn't want to get involved. It had been hard enough for him to go to the cabin, knock on the door, hear Raul say "Come in," and then find Raul and Paula half-buried under a mountain of cigarette butts and empty glasses, which gave him a good idea of the conversation. Raul had agreed immediately to join the expedition, but Paula seemed furious because Lopez was taking him away, because they were both leaving—and leaving her alone, relegated down to the status of the women and old men. She had ended up by asking angrily what new idiocies they were out to commit, but Lopez had only shrugged and waited till Raul had got his pullover on and his pistol in his pocket. Raul managed all this as if he were not even there, as if he were an image in a mirror; but again there was a mocking expression on his face, the expression of someone who had decided to risk everything in a game which, finally, meant nothing to him.

A cabin door flew open, and Señor Trejo made his appearance, his blue pajamas sticking incongruously out from under the grey raincoat in which he was wrapped.

"I was asleep already, but I heard voices and I thought the boy might be worse," said Señor Trejo.

"He's got a high fever and we're going to get the doctor," Lopez said.

"To get him? But doesn't it seem strange he doesn't come on his own?"

"To me too, but we'll have to go get him."

Señor Trejo lowered his eyes. "I hope there haven't been . . . that there's no new symptom that . . ."

"No, but we can't lose any time, either. Are we off?"

"Let's go," said Pelusa. The doctor's refusal had finally sunk in, and he was getting gloomier by the minute.

Señor Trejo was going to say something else, but they passed him and went on. Not very far, because the door of cabin nine was already open and Don Galo appeared, wrapped in an old dressing gown, his chauffeur beside him. Don Galo took the situation in at a glance and raised his hand menacingly. He counseled his dear friends not to lose their tempers at this hour of the morning. Informed of what had happened over the telephone, he tried to convince them that the doctor's prescriptions should be enough for the moment, and if they weren't, the doctor would come in person to see the boy, not to mention . . .

"We're losing time," said Medrano. "Let's go."

He started down the hall toward the connecting corridor, and Raul followed him. They could hear the loud conversation between Señor Trejo and Don Galo behind them.

"You're planning to go down through the bartender's cabin, right?"

"Yes, maybe we'll have better luck this time."

"I know a better way, more direct," said Raul. "You remember, Lopez? We'll go see Orf and his tattooed friend."

"Of course," said Lopez. "It's more direct, but I don't know if we'll come out at the stern that way. Well, let's try anyway."

They were entering the central corridor when they saw Dr. Restelli and Lucio coming over, attracted by the sound of voices. Dr. Restelli didn't need much to know what was happening. Raising his index finger in a gesture reserved for important occasions, he stopped them just a step from the door leading below. Señor Trejo and Don Galo joined him, still talking and excited. The situation was obviously unpleasant if, as young Presutti said, the doctor had refused to put in an appearance, but it was just as well that Medrano, Costa, and Lopez be made fully aware that they couldn't go exposing all the passengers to the logical consequences of an aggressive action, such as the one they were presumably about to perpetrate. If, unfortunately, as one surmised from certain symptoms, an outbreak of typhus 224 had just been declared on the passengers' deck, the only sensible thing to do would be to demand the intervention of the officers (and for that various recourses existed, such as the *maître* and the telephone), so that the dear sick boy could be transferred immediately to the dispensary at the stern, where Captain Smith and the others were being treated. But they would certainly not achieve that end with threats such as those they had made as early as this morning, and—

"Look, Doctor, shut your mouth," said Lopez. "I'm very sorry, but I've had enough hearts and flowers."

"My dear friend!"

"No violence!" Don Galo shrieked, supported by Señor Trejo's indignant exclamations. Lucio, very pale, stayed behind them and said nothing.

Medrano opened the door and began to go down. Raul and Lopez followed him.

"Cut the cackling, you hens," said Pelusa, looking back at the peace party with an air of supreme scorn. He walked down two steps, turned, and shut the door in their faces. "What a bunch of phonies, *mamma mia*. The kid in a bad way and these cats coming on with an armistice. I feel like cracking their skulls, I shit you not."

"I think you'll have your chance," said Lopez. "Look, Presutti, here you'll have to keep your eyes open. As soon as you see any sort of monkey wrench you can use as a club, grab ahold of it."

He glanced toward the cabin to the left, empty and dark. Pressing against the sides of the passage, they opened the door on the right with a single blow. Lopez recognized Orf, seated on a bench. The two Finns who had been busy scrubbing down the prow earlier were settled down next to the phonograph and were about to put on a record. Raul, right behind Lopez, ironically thought it must be the Ivor Novello record. One of the Finns stood up, surprised, and came toward them, his arms slightly open, as if he were about to ask for an explanation. Orf hadn't moved, but was watching them, shocked and stupefied.

In the silence that seemed to last forever, they saw the rear door open. Lopez was one step from the Finn, who still had his arms out as if he were about to embrace someone, but when Lopez saw the glucid outlined in the doorway looking at them in amazement, he took another step forward and waved the Finn out of his way. The Finn stepped lightly aside and at the same moment hit Lopez first in the jaw and then in the stomach. As Lopez was going down like a limp rag, the Finn hit him again full in the face. Raul's Colt appeared a second before Medrano's revolver, but there was no need to shoot. With a perfect sense of timing, Pelusa moved and in two steps landed next to the glucid and hauled him into the cabin with a slap, closing the door with a light kick. Orf and the two Finns raised their hands, as if they were ready to hang themselves from the ceiling.

Pelusa bent over Lopez, raised his head, and began to massage his neck with an unnerving violence. Then he loosened Lopez' belt and began a kind of artificial respiration on him.

"The sonofabitch, he hit him in the gut. I'll break your face, you dirty fuck! Wait till I get you alone, I'll split your fucking head open, you mother! What a way to go down, *mamma mia!*"

Medrano leaned over and took the revolver from Lopez' pocket as he began to come to.

"Hold it for a second," he said to Atilio. "How're you doing, old man?"

Lopez grunted something unintelligible, and vaguely felt around for a handkerchief.

"We're going to have to take all these guys across to our side," said Raul, who had sat down on a bench, enjoying the dubious pleasure of covering four tired men with their hands raised. When Lopez stood up, blood from his nose running down his neck, Raul thought of Paula and of the work she had cut out for her. "And she's the one who hates playing nurse," he thought, amused.

"Yes, the tough thing is we can't go ahead and leave them here," said Medrano. "What do you think of getting these birds back to the prow, Atilio, and locking them up in one of our cabins?"

"Leave 'em to me," said Pelusa, wielding the revolver. "You first, come over here, you prick . . . And then the rest of you. The first one to make a move gets a bullet in his skull. But wait here for me, eh? Don't go without me."

Medrano looked worriedly at Lopez, who had gotten up finally, very pale and staggering. He asked him if he wouldn't like to go with Atilio and rest a bit, but Lopez looked at him, infuriated.

"It's nothing," he mumbled, drawing his hand across his mouth. "I'm sticking, don't worry. I'm beginning to breathe better now. Shit, that's a bitch."

He went white and fell again, sliding against Pelusa, who grabbed and held him up. Medrano decided on a course of action. They took the glucid and lipids out to the corridor, leaving Pelusa to carry Lopez, who was cursing quietly, and then went quickly down the corridor. They'd probably find reinforcements and armed men once they got back, but there was nothing else to be done.

The appearance of a bleeding Lopez, followed by an officer and three of the *Malcolm*'s sailors with their hands up, was hardly an inspiring spectacle for Lucio and Señor Trejo, who were still talking outside the door. Dr. Restelli and Paula came running, re-

sponding to Señor Trejo's shrieks. Don Galo was close behind
them, pulling at his hair in a way which Raul had seen only in the
theater. Growing more amused by the minute, he lined the prisoners up against the wall and signaled Pelusa to take Lopez to his
cabin. Medrano turned a deaf ear to the blast of screams, questions,
and admonitions.

"Let's go, the bar," Raul said to the prisoners. He forced them
out to the starboard corridor, filing them between Don Galo's
chair and the wall, which wasn't easy. Medrano followed behind,
hurrying up the whole procedure as much as possible, and when
Don Galo, at his wit's end, seized him by the arm and shook him,
screaming that he-wasn't-going-to-consent-to, Medrano decided to
do the only thing possible.

"Everybody upstairs," he ordered. "If you don't like it, tough."

Delighted, Pelusa immediately grabbed Don Galo's chair and
shoved it forward, even though Don Galo seized hold of the spokes
with all his might and grabbed hold of the brake.

"Stop that, don't touch that chair!" cried Lucio. "Have you all
gone mad?"

Pelusa released the chair, took hold of Lucio right in the middle
of his pajama top, and tossed him heavily against the partition.
His revolver hung insolently from his other hand.

"Keep it moving, mushhead," Pelusa said. "I don't want to have
to mess up your waves."

Lucio opened his mouth and then closed it again. Dr. Restelli
and Señor Trejo were petrified, and it was somewhat difficult for
Pelusa to set them in motion. Raul and Medrano were waiting at
the foot of the staircase.

They lined them all up against the bar, locked the door which
led to the library, and Raul ripped the telephone out of the wall.
The maître, pale, twisting his hands in his most obliging manner,
had turned over the keys without the slightest resistance. They
whipped through the corridor and down the ladder again.

"The astronomer, Felipe, and the chauffeur aren't here," said
Pelusa, stopping short. "Shouldn't we lock them up, too?"

"Not necessary," said Medrano. "They won't give us any trouble."

Below again, they opened the door of the cabin; it was empty,

and suddenly it seemed much larger. Medrano looked at the rear
door.

"It leads to another passage," said Raul in an expressionless
voice. "The ladder that goes to the stern is at the back. We'll have
to be careful of the cabin on the left."

"But were you here already?" Pelusa asked, astonished.

"Umm."

"You were here and you didn't go to the stern?"

"No, I didn't go up," said Raul.

Pelusa looked at him distrustfully, but he liked Raul and decided that he was off his nut at the moment, considering everything that'd happened. Medrano turned off the lights without saying anything and carefully opened the door, going ahead blindly
into the darkness. They saw the shiny copper railings almost immediately.

"My poor, poor little pirate," Paula said. "Come and let Mama
put some cotton up your nose."

Lopez let himself fall to the edge of the bed. He felt air coming
into his lungs very slowly. Paula, who had stared at the revolver in
Pelusa's left hand with terror, watched him leave the cabin a little
more than relieved. Then she forced Lopez, who was still dead
white, to stretch out on the bed. She soaked a towel and began to
wash his face very carefully. Lopez was still cursing in a low voice,
but she went on cleaning him and scolding him at the same time.

"Now take off that jacket and get in bed all the way. You need
to rest for a while."

"No, I'm all right now," said Lopez. "You don't think I'm going to let them go on by themselves now, just when . . ."

But when he tried to stand up, everything started to spin again.
Paula held him, and finally persuaded him to lie down on his back.
There was a blanket in the wardrobe, and she covered him as
well as she could. She groped around blindly underneath the
blanket until she found his shoelaces, which she untied. Lopez was
watching her as if from a distance, his eyes half open. His nose
wasn't swollen yet, but he had a purple mark under one eye, and a
tremendous rise on his jaw.

"You're still beautiful," said Paula, kneeling to take off his shoes. "Now you're really my Jamaica John, my almost-invincible hero."

"Put something here," Lopez murmured, pointing at his stomach. "I can't breathe. Jesus, but I'm weak. Just a couple of punches . . ."

"But you must have gotten a couple in," said Paula, looking for another towel while she ran the hot water. "Didn't you bring alcohol? Ah, yes, here's the bottle. Loosen your trousers if you can . . . Wait, let me help you take off that jacket; it feels like it's made of asbestos. Can you sit up a little? If you can't, turn around, and we'll pull it off slowly."

Lopez let her do it, thinking at the same time about his friends. It didn't seem possible that he was out of action because of a lousy little lipid. Closing his eyes, he felt Paula's hand on his arms, getting the jacket off him, then loosening his belt, unbuttoning his shirt, and putting something warm on his skin. Once or twice he smiled because Paula's hair was tickling his face. She was going over his nose again, changing cotton wads. Without even thinking about it, Lopez lifted his lips to her. He felt Paula's mouth against his, light and fleeting, a nurse's kiss. He wrapped his arms around her hard, breathing with difficulty, and kissed her, bit her, until she moaned.

"Traitor," Paula said, when she was finally able to shake free. "Rogue. What kind of patient are you, I thought you were sick."

"Paula."

"Shut up. Don't come feeling me up just because they gave you the beating of your life. Half an hour ago you were the latest model in frigidaires."

"And you," Lopez murmured, trying to draw her toward him again. "And you, you devil, you should talk . . ."

"You're going to get blood all over me," Paula said heartlessly. "Be obedient, my black corsair. You're not dressed or undressed, not in bed or out of bed . . . I don't like ambiguous situations, you know. Are you my sick honey or what? Wait till I change the towel on your stomach. May I look without offending my natural modesty? Yes, I may. Where's the key to your precious cabin?"

She covered him up to the neck with the blanket and went to

soak the towels. Lopez, after fumbling around in his pants pockets, managed to find the key. Everything was a little blurred, but clear enough for him to realize that Paula was laughing.

"If you could only see yourself, Jamaica John . . . One eye is completely closed already, and the other one's looking at me with an expression . . . Oh well, this will help, wait . . ."

She locked the door and came back wringing a towel. Like this, you see. Everything was fine. Slower, a cotton wad in the nose that was still bleeding. Blood everywhere, the pillow was a mess, and the blanket, and Lopez' white shirt, which he was busy tearing off. "Oh God, the washing," she thought, and gave up. But a good nurse . . . she quietly fell into his arms, surrendering to the hands drawing her toward him, tightening her against his body, running over her, touching her. And she, her eyes wide open, felt the old fever rise in her, the same old fever that the same old lips would alternately inflame and assuage, through the hours which began like the old hours, under the old gods, to add to the same old past. And it was just as lovely and useless as ever.

XLI

"Let me go first, I know this part."

Crouching down, they kept against the wall to the left and advanced in single file as far as the cabin door. "He'll still be snoring in there with all that vomit," Raul thought. "If he's in there and attacks us, am I going to shoot? And am I going to shoot him because he attacks us?" He opened the door slowly and groped for the light switch. He flicked it on and off; only he could measure the bitter relief of not seeing anyone inside.

As if his command stopped exactly at this point, he let Medrano pass in front of him so as to be first on the ladder. Right behind him, almost creeping up the stairs, they reached the darkness of an open bridge. They could see no more than a yard ahead, there was scarcely any gradation between the darkness of the sky and the shadows of the poop rising in front of them. Medrano waited a moment.

"Can't see a thing, damn it. We'll have to hide somewhere until daylight. If we go while it's like this, they could burn us if they wanted to."

"There's a door over there," said Pelusa. "God help us, it's darker than a black cat in a coal cellar."

They slipped out of the hatchway and made a run for the door. It was locked, but Raul tapped Medrano on the shoulder to indicate another door a few yards away. Pelusa reached it first, opened it rapidly, and dropped to the deck. The others waited a second before joining him; the door closed behind them noiselessly. They listened, motionless. Not a breath was heard; a smell of polished wood reminded them of the cabins at the prow. Medrano went cautiously to the little window and drew the curtain. He lit a match and snuffed it out between his fingers; the cabin was empty.

The key to the door had been left on the inside. They locked it and sat on the floor to smoke and wait. Nothing could be done until dawn. Atilio was restless; he wanted to know if Medrano or Raul had a plan ready. But they didn't, they were just going to stay holed up until there was enough light to make the poop visible, and then they'd get through to the radio shack one way or another.

"Terrific," said Pelusa.

Medrano and Raul were smiling in the dark. They were silent, smoking, until Atilio's breathing became louder and more regular. Shoulder to shoulder, Medrano and Raul lit another cigarette.

"Our only worry is if one of the glucids should decide to go to the prow and find we've locked up his colleague and a couple of lipids."

"Not very likely," said Medrano. "If they haven't shown up by now, and we've been screaming to high heaven for them, I doubt they'll change their habits that quickly. Lopez is more of a worry, he might think he's honor bound to join us, and he's not armed."

"That would be a pity," said Raul. "But I doubt if he'll come."

"Ah."

"My dear Medrano, your discretion is delicious. A man capable of saying 'Ah' instead of asking reasons for my opinion . . ."

"Really, I think I can guess them."

"I suppose so," said Raul. "Anyway, I think I'd have preferred the question. It must be the hour, or the smell of ash wood in the

dark, or the prospect of having our heads bashed in before long
. . . It's not that I'm particularly sentimental or very enthusiastic
about exchanging confidences, but it wouldn't bother me at all
to tell you what Paula means to me."

"Well, tell me then. But keep your voice down."

Raul was silent for a while.

"I guess I'm looking for a witness, as usual. An anxiety, of
course; after all, it's possible something unpleasant might happen
to me, and if there were someone, a messenger, better, someone
who could tell Paula . . . That's the trouble: What's there to say?
Do you like Paula?"

"Yes, very much," said Medrano. "It makes me sad to think she's
not happy."

"Well, cheer up," said Raul. "It might seem strange coming
from me, but I'm sure that right now Paula is as happy as she can
possibly be in this life. And that's what the messenger would have
to relay to her: my best wishes. *To Lucasta, on going to the wars,*"
he added as if to himself.

Medrano did not say anything, and they sat quietly awhile listening to the thud of the engines and a far-off sound of splashing.

Raul sighed, tired.

"I'm happy to have known you," he said. "I don't think we have
much in common, except our taste for the *Malcolm* brandy. But
here we are together, not knowing exactly why."

"For Jorge, I suppose," said Medrano.

"Oh, Jorge . . . Jorge is the last in a whole series of things."

"That's true. Perhaps the only one who's really here for Jorge
is Atilio."

"Right."

Stretching out his hand, Medrano pushed the curtains a bit to
one side. The first pale light was beginning to appear in the sky.
He wondered if all that made any sense to Raul. Carefully crushing the cigarette butt against the floor, he stayed looking out at
the faintly greyish rent in the sky. He had to wake Atilio, to get
him ready to go. "Jorge is the last in a whole series of things," Raul
had said. So many things, but so vague, confused. Was it the same
for everyone as it was for him, suddenly subjected to an intricate
rush of memories and unexpected fantasies? The shape of Clau-

dia's hand, her voice, the search for a way out . . . It was gradually
getting lighter outside, and he would have liked to have his anxiety
evanesce into the dawning day at the same time, but there was
nothing certain, nothing was promised. He wanted to go back to
Claudia, to linger as he looked into her eyes, searching for an answer there. He was sure of one thing at least: Claudia had the answer, even if she wasn't aware of it, even if she too believed herself
condemned to question, to search. And so, even someone blem-
ished by an incomplete life could, at the right time, give abun-
dantly, point out the way. But she was not here beside him; the
darkness of the cabin and the smell of tobacco were the materials
of his confusion. How bring order back into everything, which
he had thought so orderly before embarking, how create a perspective in which Bettina's tear-streaked face would no longer be
possible, how achieve, one way or another, the central point where
each discordant element could be seen as a spoke in a wheel? To
see himself in the act of walking and to know that it made some
sense; to love, and to know that his affection had some meaning;
to run, and to know that his flight was not just one more betrayal.
He didn't know if he loved Claudia; he simply wanted to be near
her and near Jorge, to save Jorge so that Claudia might forgive
Leon. Yes, so she might forgive Leon, or stop loving him, or love
him even more. It was absurd, but it was true: so that Claudia
could forgive Leon before forgiving him, before Bettina even for-
gave him, before he'd be able to return to Claudia and Jorge again
to give them his hand and be happy.

Raul pressed his hand on Medrano's shoulder. They stood up
quickly, shaking Atilio. They could hear footsteps on deck. Medrano turned the key in the lock and opened the door halfway.
A corpulent glucid was crossing the deck, cap in hand. The cap
whipped back and forth against either side of his right leg; suddenly it stopped, began to go up to his head, then kept going up.

"Get in here fast and keep your trap shut," ordered Pelusa, who
had been given the job of bringing him into the cabin. "What a
fatso, *mamma mia*. Some chow you guys must get over here."

Raul fired questions at him in English, and the glucid answered
in a mixture of English and Spanish. His mouth was trembling;
he probably had never had three revolvers pointed so close to his

stomach. He understood immediately what they were talking about, and nodded his head. After having searched him for weapons, they let him bring his hands down.

"It's like this," Raul explained. "We have to go exactly where he was going, up the other ladder, and right to one side is the radio room. There's a guy there all night, but it looks like he isn't armed."

"Are you fellows joking? Is this some kind of bet, or something?" the glucid asked.

"Shut up or you'll be fish food," Pelusa threatened, shoving the revolver in his ribs.

"I'll go with him," said Medrano. "If we go quickly, maybe they won't see us. It will be better if you stay here. If you hear shooting, come on up."

"We'll all go," said Raul. "Why should we stay here?"

"Because four of us are too many; they'll spot us right away. Cover the rear, after all, I don't think these guys—" He stopped, without finishing the sentence, and looked at the glucid.

"You've all gone crazy," said the glucid.

Pelusa, puzzled but obedient, half-opened the door to make sure there was no one out there. A reddish-grey light bathed the whole deck. Medrano put his revolver back in his pocket, pointing it at the glucid's legs. Raul was going to say something else, but he kept quiet. They watched him climbing the ladder. Atilio, who was far from happy, started to gaze at Raul with the look of an obedient dog, which Raul found touching.

"Look, Medrano's right," he said. "We'll wait here, he may be coming right back, safe and sound."

"Well, it could've been me what went," Pelusa said.

"Let's wait," said Raul. "We'll wait just once more."

Everything felt as if it had happened before, right out of a cheap novel. The fat glucid was sitting next to the transmitter, his face covered with beads of sweat, his lips quivering. Leaning against the door, Medrano held the revolver in one hand and a cigarette in the other. The radio operator, his back to him, turned the dials and began to send a message. He was a skinny, freckled boy, who had gotten a good scare and couldn't calm down again. "As long as he doesn't trick me," Medrano thought. He was hoping that the language he had used and the solid presence of the revolver behind him would be enough to make the fellow think twice. He took an enjoyable drag on his cigarette, attentive to everything going on around him, but at the same time he felt far away, as if only his face were there for the proper edification of the fat glucid, who was watching him terrified. Little by little, light was beginning to enter through the window on the left, opening a path in the poor artificial lighting of the radio shack. A whistle could be heard in the distance, and a phrase in a language Medrano didn't understand. He heard the sputtering sound of the transmitter and the voice of the radio operator broken by a kind of hiccups. He thought of the ladder up which he had just dashed, his revolver pointing at the glucid's fat butt, the sudden perspective of the deserted poop deck, entering the cabin, the radio operator's leap as he was surprised over his magazine. It was true, now that he thought about it: the stern was completely deserted. An ashen-red horizon, a leaden sea, the curving rail, and all that had lasted a brief moment. The radio operator was finally making contact with Buenos Aires. He listened to the message transmitted word by word. Now the glucid begged permission with his eyes to take out a handkerchief from his pocket, now the operator repeated the message. But, man, the stern was deserted, a fact. But what did that matter? The freckled boy's words mingled with a dry, cutting sensation inside him, an almost painful fullness in this flashing comprehension that the stern was entirely deserted after all, and that it didn't matter, it hadn't the slightest importance, because what really mattered was something else, something inaccessible which he was trying to figure out, define in this sensation, an increasing exaltation which was pushing him toward *satori*. His back to the door, each drag of smoke was like a warm acquiescence, the beginning of a healing which was carrying off the remains of the long malaise of the last two days. He didn't feel happy, it was all beyond that or at least at the margin of ordinary sentiments. It was more like music being hummed, or simply like lighting and enjoying a cigarette. The rest—what did the rest matter now that he was beginning to make peace with himself, to feel that that "rest" would never again be organized in the same old selfish way.

"Maybe happiness does exist and it's something else," Medrano thought. He didn't know why, but to be there, the stern in view (and completely deserted) made him feel secure; it was something like a point of departure. Now that he was far from Claudia he felt her nearer to him, as if he was finally beginning to deserve her near him. Everything that had happened before counted for so little; the only thing really true had been this hour away from her, this interlude in the shadows while he waited with Raul and Atilio, a balancing of the books, which for the first time in his life left him in peace, without very clear reasons, without merits or demerits, simply because now he could reconcile himself to himself, and could boot the old Medrano out of his way like a clay doll, and accept Bettina's true face, even though the Bettina immersed in Buenos Aires would never have that face, poor girl, unless she sometime dreamt of a hotel room in which her old forgotten lover came forward, so she could see him, in her turn, as he had seen her, as frivolous things can be seen only in some hour they just don't have on clocks. And that's the way it was, and it hurt and it cleansed.

When he caught the shadow on the window and saw the face of the glucid, his eyes rolling in terror, he raised his revolver reluctantly, still hoping that a ploy wouldn't end up in a shooting match. The bullet whizzed past his head; he heard the radio operator scream, and Medrano dashed past him and made a parapet of the other end of the transmission table, yelling at the glucid not to move. He made out a face and the glitter of shiny nickel at the window; he shot, aiming low, and the face disappeared, while the noise of shouts and two or three different voices could be heard. "If I stay here, Raul and Atilio are going to come up and look for me, and the crew'll get them," he thought. He passed behind the glucid, forcing him to get to his feet and walk to the door at gun point. Leaning over the dials, the radio operator was shaking and muttering, and at the same time looking for something in a drawer. Medrano shouted an order and the glucid opened the door. "It wasn't that deserted, after all," he managed to think, amused, shoving the trembling fat fellow out. Though his hand was shaking, the radio operator found it easy to aim at the middle of Medrano's back and pull the trigger three times quickly, before throwing down the revolver and breaking into tears like the kid he was.

Raul and Pelusa had rushed out of the cabin at the sound of the first shot. Pelusa reached the ladder before Raul. At the level of the last stair, he straightened his arm and began to shoot. The three lipids pressed against the wall of the radio shack dropped to the deck; a bullet of Pelusa's had grazed one on the ear. At the cabin door, the plump glucid, hands raised, was screaming hideously in an unintelligible language. Raul covered them all with his pistol and, after disarming them, forced the lipids to stand. It was somewhat startling that Pelusa had been able to frighten them so easily; they hadn't even tried to return the fire. Raul shouted to Pelusa to line them up against the wall and then he went into the cabin, jumping over Medrano, who had fallen face down. The radio operator made a move toward the revolver again, but Raul kicked it away and began to slap the freckled boy's face from side to side, repeating the same question endlessly. When he heard the affirmative answer, he hit him once more, picked up the revolver, and went out on deck. Pelusa understood without a word: leaning over, he hoisted Medrano and began to walk toward the ladder. Raul covered their retreat, fearing a bullet at every step. They met no one on the lower bridge, but they heard shouting from another part of the ship. They negotiated the two ladders and managed to reach the room with maps on the wall. Raul pushed the table against the door; the shouts could no longer be heard; the lipids probably wouldn't dare attack without gathering sufficient reinforcements.

Atilio laid Medrano out on some canvases and looked wildly at Raul. Raul was kneeling on the blood-splashed canvases. He did what was necessary, but he knew from the start it was useless.

"Maybe we can save him yet," said Atilio. "Good God, what a mess of blood. We should call the doctor."

"In good time," Raul murmured, looking at Medrano's empty face. He had seen the three holes in his back; one of the bullets had come out near his throat and it was from there that the blood was gushing. There was a little foam on Medrano's lips.

"Let's go, pick him up again and we'll take him up. We have to get him to his cabin."

"Then he's really dead?" asked Pelusa.

"Yes, old man, he's dead. Wait, I'll help you."

"It's all right, he doesn't weigh anything. Maybe he'll come to in his cabin, maybe it's not so serious."

"Let's go," Raul repeated.

Atilio walked more slowly through the corridors, trying to keep the body from bumping against the partitions. Raul helped him on the climb. There was no one in the portside corridor, and Medrano had left his cabin open. They stretched him out on the bed, and Pelusa threw himself into a chair, wheezing. The heaving gradually turned to weeping; he was crying hoarsely, covering his face with both hands, and from time to time he took out a handkerchief and blew his nose with a kind of bellow. Raul was staring at Medrano's blank face, waiting, caught up in Atilio's already vanished hope. The hemorrhaging had stopped. He went to the lavatory and brought back a soaked towel and wet Medrano's lips, he raised the collar of the windbreaker to cover the wound. He remembered that in cases like this you couldn't waste time, that his hands had to be crossed over his chest; but not knowing why, he only stretched out Medrano's arms until the hands rested on the thighs.

"Sons of bitch motherfucking bastards," Pelusa was muttering, blowing his nose. "You realize? . . . What did he do to them, just tell me? We went there for the kid, and all we wanted to do was send a telegram. And now . . ."

"The telegram must be there by now, at least that can't be stopped. You have the key to the bar, I think. Go let all those guys out and tell them what happened. Be careful about the ship's crew. I'm going to stay here and guard this hallway."

Pelusa lowered his head, blew his nose again, and went out. It seemed incredible, but his clothes were barely stained at all by Medrano's blood. Raul lit a cigarette and sat down at the foot of the bed. He was looking at the partition which separated this cabin from the one next to it. He stood up and began to knock softly, then a little harder. He sat down again. It suddenly occurred to him that they had been at the stern, the famous poop deck. But what, after all, was there at the stern?

"And what do I care," he thought, shrugging his shoulders. He heard Lopez' cabin door open.

XLII

Pelusa met the ladies in the starboard corridor, all of them in states of hysteria that varied only in degree. For the past half hour they had done everything imaginable to open the door of the bar and free the vociferous prisoners, who were trying to break the door down with kicks and shoulder blows. Felipe and Don Galo's chauffeur were near the staircase to the deck, watching the scene indifferently.

When they saw Atilio, Doña Pepa and Doña Rosita rushed up, but he brushed them aside without changing his tight-lipped expression and continued. Señora Trejo, a monument of outraged virtue and dignity, blocked his path, her arms crossed, and gave him an explosive look, a look which until that moment had been reserved only for her husband.

"Monsters, murderers! What have you mutineers done! Throw away that revolver, immediately!"

"Let me by, lady," said Pelusa. "First you yell at me to let that mob out and then you block my way. Make up your mind, will you!"

Nelly freed herself from her mother's convulsive grip and flung herself on Pelusa.

"They're going to kill you, they're going to kill you! Why did you do it? Now the officers are going to come and put us all in prison!"

"Don't talk nonsense," said Pelusa. "It's nothing, if you knew what happened . . . Better I don't tell you."

"You've got blood on your shirt!" Nelly shouted. "Mama, Mama!"

"Are you going to let me by or not?" said Pelusa. "The blood is from when they hit Señor Lopez. Don't make a movie out of it, d'you mind?"

He pushed them away with his one free arm and went up the staircase. The ladies screamed louder than ever when they saw him raise his revolver before putting the key in the lock. Suddenly there was an overwhelming silence, and the door was flung wide.

"Easy does it," Atilio said. "Hey, you there, you come on out first, and just make one false move and I'll put some lead in your gut."

The glucid looked at him as if it were difficult to understand, and rushed down the stairs. They saw him head for the locked bulkhead doors, but everybody's attention was directed toward the appearance in quick order of Señor Trejo, Dr. Restelli, and Don Galo, who were received with howls, tears, and shrill complaints. Lucio came out last, looking at Atilio defiantly.

"Just don't be naughty," Pelusa told him. "I can't take care of you now, but later if you want I'll get rid of the gun and give you a real going over, I'll tromp you."

"Fat mouth," said Lucio, going down the stairs.

Nora was watching him without saying a word. He took her by the arm and almost dragged her off to the cabin.

Pelusa looked into the bar, where the *maître* was still quietly waiting, and then he went down the stairs, putting the revolver back in his pocket.

"Keep it down," he said stopping on the second stair. "Don't you know there's a sick boy here, and then you wonder why his fever goes up."

"Monster!" screeched Señora Trejo, as she marched off with Felipe and Señor Trejo. "This can't go on! To the hold with handcuffs and chains! They're no better than criminals, kidnappers, *mafiosos!*"

"Atilio, Atilio!" Nelly sobbed convulsively. "What's happened, why did you lock everybody up?"

Pelusa opened his mouth to say the first thing that crossed his mind and it was pure filth. So he kept quiet, squeezing his hand against the revolver, the muzzle pointed at the deck. Maybe it was because he hadn't moved off of the second stair, but he suddenly felt far away from the hysterical screams, questions, and demonstrations of hatred exploding around him in imprecations and reproaches. "I better go see the kid," he thought. "I have to tell his mama we sent the telegram."

He walked off without saying a word, passing among a cluster of extended hands and open mouths; at a distance it almost sounded as if these females were acclaiming him, accompanying him in some sort of triumph.

. . .

Persio had ended up by falling asleep on Claudia's bed. At dawn Claudia threw a blanket over his legs, looking at his lean, familiar figure with gratitude, and at his clothes, new but already wrinkled and slightly soiled. Then she went to Jorge's bed and listened to his breathing. He was sleeping quietly after the third dose of medicine. Just touching his forehead was enough to reassure her. Suddenly she felt weary, as if she had gone many nights without sleep; but she still did not want to lie down next to her son, for she knew someone would come soon with news or with a repetition of the same events, the same ridiculous labyrinths in which her friends had been roaming for the past forty-eight hours, not knowing exactly why.

Lopez, with a bruised, swollen face, appeared at the half-open door. Claudia wasn't surprised by his not knocking, nor was she surprised by the sound of female shrieks and babble in the starboard passageway. She waved her hand, inviting him to come in.

"Jorge's better, he has slept for two straight hours. But you . . ."

"Oh, it's nothing," Lopez said, touching his jaw. "It hurts a little when I talk, and I don't talk much because of it. I'm happy Jorge's better. Anyway, they managed to send a telegram to Buenos Aires."

"How ridiculous," said Claudia.

"Yes, now it seems ridiculous."

Claudia lowered her head.

"Well, what's done is done," said Lopez. "But there was shooting, because the people at the stern didn't want to let them through. It doesn't seem possible, we hardly knew one another, a two-day friendship, if it can be called friendship, and yet . . ."

"Something's happened to Gabriel?"

The affirmation was already in the question; Lopez had only to be silent and look at her. Claudia stood up, her mouth half-open. She was ugly, almost absurd. She stumbled and had to take hold of the back of an armchair.

"They've taken him to his cabin," Lopez said. "I'll stay here and watch Jorge, if you like."

Raul, who was standing guard in the hallway, let her pass and closed the door behind her. The pistol in his pocket was beginning to annoy him; it was ludicrous to think the glucids would retaliate. Be that as it may, it would have to end there; after all, they weren't at war. He felt like going to the starboard passageway, where Don Galo's yelling and Dr. Restelli's grandiose statements could be heard above the general background of feminine screams. "Poor animals," Raul thought. "Some trip we've given them . . ." He saw Atilio looking timidly into Claudia's cabin and he followed him. He felt the taste of dawn in his mouth. "Could it really have been an Ivor Novello record?" he thought, discarding Paula's image, which persistently returned. Resigned, he let it appear, his eyes closed, seeing her just as she had been when she appeared at Medrano's cabin, behind Lopez, wrapped in her red robe, her hair flowing beautifully over her shoulders, just as he liked to see her in the morning.

"Well, oh well . . ." Raul said.

He opened the door and went in. Atilio and Lopez were talking quietly, Persio was breathing with a whistling sound which suited him perfectly. Atilio came up to Raul, putting his finger to his lips.

"The kid's better," he murmured. "His mother told me his fever's gone. He slept great all night."

"Terrific," said Raul.

"Now I'm going to my cabin and explain things to my girl and the old ladies," Pelusa said. "What a state they're in, *mamma mia.* They really got themselves all steamed up."

Raul watched him leave, and went and sat down next to Lopez who offered him a cigarette. They pushed their chairs back from Jorge's bed and smoked a while in the silence. Raul suspected that his presence would please Lopez at this moment, an opportunity to square accounts and something else.

"Two things," Lopez said abruptly. "First, I feel I'm to blame for what happened. I know it's idiotic, because the same thing might have happened anyway, or might have happened to any of us, but I was wrong in staying behind while you—" He cut short his words, made an effort, and swallowed hard. "What happened is that I slept with Paula," he said, looking at Raul who was letting a cigarette roll between his fingers. "That's the second thing."

"The first thing is of no importance," said Raul. "You weren't in any condition to go on, besides it didn't seem so risky. And as for the other, I suppose Paula must have told you that you don't owe me any explanation."

"Explanation, no," said Lopez, confused. "Anyway . . ."

"Anyway, thanks. That was very cool of you."

"Mama," said Jorge. "Where are you, Mama?"

Persio leaped from sleep to the foot of Jorge's bed. Raul and Lopez did not move, waiting.

"Persio," said Jorge, sitting up. "Do you know what I dreamed? That snow was falling on our star. I swear, Persio, snow, snow-flakes like . . . like . . ."

"Do you feel better?" Persio asked, looking at him as if he were afraid of breaking the spell.

"I feel fine," said Jorge. "I'm hungry, you know. Go tell Mama to bring me some breakfast. Who's there? Hi, how are you? Why are you all here?"

"No reason," said Lopez. "We came to keep you company."

"What happened to your nose? Did you fall?"

"No," said Lopez, standing up. "I blew it too hard. It always happens. See you later."

Raul went out after him. It was certainly time to put away the damn pistol, which was getting heavier by the minute, but he wanted to look out on deck first, where the sun was shining. The prow was deserted and Raul sat down on the upper step of the ladder and looked at the sea and sky, blinking. He had gone so many hours without sleep and had drunk and smoked so much that the glitter of sea and the wind in his face were painful; he stayed until he got used to it, thinking that it was about time to return to reality, if this was returning to reality. "Forget the analysis, old boy," he thought. "A bath, a long bath in a cabin that will now be yours alone as long as the trip lasts, and that won't be too long unless I'm wrong all the way down the line." He hoped he was not, for then Medrano would have died for nothing. Personally, it no longer mattered very much to him: if they went on traveling or if they got involved in a still bigger mess; his tongue was too thick and coated for him to choose freely. Maybe when he woke up, after the bath, after a full glass of whisky, and a day's sleep, he'd be able to accept or reject; right now everything was the same: vomit on the floor, Jorge awake and well, three holes in a windbreaker. It was like shuffling poker cards, a total neutralization of forces; only when one should decide, if one decided, to pull out the joker, the ace, the queen, and the king, one by one . . . He took a deep breath. The sea was a mythological blue, the color he saw in certain dreams when he went flying in strange translucent machines. He covered his face with his hands and wondered if he were really alive. He must be, for he realized, among other things, that the *Malcolm*'s engines had just stopped.

Before leaving, Paula and Lopez had opened the porthole curtain, and the cabin was enveloped in a yellowish light, which seemed to empty Medrano's face of all expression. Motionless at the foot of the bed, her arm still extended toward the door, as if she would never finish closing it, Claudia looked at Gabriel. Muffled voices and footsteps could be heard in the corridor, but nothing seemed to change the total silence into which Claudia had just entered, the cottony substance which was the very air of the cabin, her own feet, the body stretched out on the bed, the scattered objects, the towels thrown into a corner.

Step by step, she approached the chair Raul had placed there. She sat down and looked at him more closely. She might have been able to speak effortlessly, to answer any question; she felt no constriction in her throat, there were no tears for Gabriel. Everything felt cottony inside her too, thick and cold like the world inside an aquarium or a crystal ball. It was like that: just—they had killed Gabriel. Gabriel was here in front of her, dead, this unknown person, this man with whom she had spoken a few times on a brief sea voyage. There was neither distance nor closeness, nothing to be measured or counted; death intervened on this stupid scene long before life, and the game was lost, stripped of the bit of sense that it had managed to achieve during these few hours at sea. This man had spent part of one night next to Jorge's sickbed, then something barely turned, a slight transformation (but the cabin was so similar, the set designer didn't have very many props at his disposal) and suddenly it was Claudia who was seated next to the bed of Gabriel, dead. All her lucidity and good sense hadn't prevented her from worrying about Jorge's dying dur-

ing the night, at an hour in which dying seemed an almost inevitable risk; and one of the things that had made her calm had
been the thought of Gabriel pacing back and forth, drinking coffee
at the bar, keeping watch in the passageway, or looking for the doctor hidden at the stern. Now something barely turned, and Jorge
was once again a living presence, once more her recognizable
son, as if nothing had happened; just another child's illness, the
gloomy thoughts in the middle of the night, and the fatigue; as if
nothing had happened, as if Gabriel had wearied of watching and
was sleeping awhile before coming back to look for her and play
with Jorge.

She could see the collar of the windbreaker covering his throat;
she was beginning to distinguish the blackish stains on the wool,
the almost imperceptible coagulation at the corner of his lips. All
that was for Jorge, that is to say, for her; this death was for her and
Jorge, this blood, this windbreaker which someone had pulled up
and arranged, these arms pressed close to his body, these legs covered with a traveling blanket, the mussed hair, the slightly raised
jaw and forehead which were pointed back, as if sliding back
along the low pillow. She couldn't cry for him, there wasn't any
sense in weeping for someone you scarcely knew, someone sympa-
thetic and polite and perhaps already slightly enamored, and in
any case, enough of a man not to tolerate the humiliation of this
trip, but who was no one to her, barely a few hours of conversation, a virtual closeness, a mere possibility of closeness, a firm and
affectionate hand on hers, a kiss on Jorge's forehead, an enormous
confidence, a cup of very hot coffee. Life was that too-slow operation, too secret to show itself at depth; they would have had to
go through many things together, or not to go through things,
which was what had happened; they would have had to find one
another gradually, with goodbyes and hesitations and misunderstandings and reconciliations, on all the levels in which she and
Gabriel resembled and needed one another. She gave him a
grudging, reproachful look; she had thought he needed her, and
this was more like a betrayal, a piece of cowardice to go off like
this, to give in to himself at the very hour of meeting. She chal-
lenged him, bending over him without fear, without pity; she refused him the right to die before being alive in her. He left her a

tender phantom, an image of summer, of a holiday, he left her hardly more than his appearance and a few moments in which the truth had tried to come forward, he left her the name of a woman who had been his, phrases he liked to repeat, episodes from his childhood, a bony, solid hand in hers, a reserved way of smiling, without questioning. He acted as if he were afraid, he chose the most vertiginous of flights, that of hopeless immobility, that of hypocritical silence. He refused to go on waiting for her, to deserve her, to discard the hours, one by one, that separated their meeting. What good would it be to kiss that cold forehead, to run her trembling fingers through that snarled, sticky hair, so that her own warmth should smooth that face, completely turned inward now, further away than any possible image of the past. She would never be able to forgive him; as long as she remembered him she would reproach him for having deprived her of the possibility of a new life, a new epoch, a time in which the certainty of being alive at the very center of life would be reborn in her, rescuing her, burning her, demanding of her what the moments of every day did not demand of her. She already felt that the time without him would unwind like an interminable path, she felt it as if it were a deafening grinding of gears in her temples, just as at an earlier time, the time without Leon, the time on Juan Bautista Alberdi Street, the time when Jorge was a pretext, the maternal lie *par excellence*, the alibi to justify stagnation, easy novels, afternoon radio programs, evening movies, telephoning at any hour, Februarys at Miramar. All that could have ended if he were not there, bearing the proofs of robbery and desertion, if he had not let himself be killed like a fool so as to prevent himself from really living in her and making her live her own life. Neither of them would have ever known who needed the other most, just like two digits do not know the number they form when combined. They could have derived from their uncertainty a force capable of transforming everything, of filling their lives with oceans, voyages, unexpected adventures, honey-sweet repose, foolishness, and catastrophes, and they would have come to a more worthy end, a less mediocre death. This forsaking before even having come together was infinitely awkward and more sordid than his way of deserting his past mistresses. What could Bettina complain of next to her complaint, what reproach could her lips weave in the face of this interminably repeated dispossession, which was not even born of an act of his own will, which wasn't even his own doing? They had killed him like a dog, choosing for him, finishing off his life, without his even being able to accept or reject. And that was the worst, the most unforgivable sin of all—since he was dead before her eyes—the sin of being dead against his will. A stranger to himself, a victim of other peoples' wills, the target for anybody's shot; his betrayal was like the inferno, an eternally present absence, a loss filling her heart and senses, an infinite emptiness into which she would fall with all the weight of her life. Now, yes, she could cry, but not for him. She could cry for his futile sacrifice, for his calm and blind goodness which had brought him to this disaster, for what he had tried to do and perhaps had done to save Jorge, but behind this weeping, when the weeping would end as all weeping did, she would again see so many things brought up in rebellion: the refusal, the flight, the image of a friend of two days who would not have the strength to be her dead one for the rest of her life. "Pardon me for telling you all this," she thought in despair, "but you were beginning to be somewhat mine, you were already going through my door with a step that I recognized from a distance. Now I'll be the one to flee, the one who will quickly forget the little she knew of your face, your voice, your confidence. You've betrayed me once and for all, eternally; and I'll perfect my betrayal each day, losing you little by little, until you'll be no more than a photograph, until Jorge doesn't even think of mentioning you, until Leon enters my soul again like a whirlwind of dry leaves, and I'll be dancing with your ghost, and I won't care."

XLIII

At seven-thirty some passengers responded to the sound of the gong and went up to the bar. That the *Malcolm* had come to a standstill did not surprise them much; it was obvious that after all the stupid goings-on of the previous night they'd have to pay the consequences. Don Galo announced this in his screechiest tone of voice, furiously buttering his toast, and the ladies who were present agreed with sighs and glances heavy with reproach and prophecy. The table of the damned came in occasionally for an allusion or a look of condemnation, stubbornly directed at Lopez' black and blue face, or at Paula's loose, disheveled hair, or at Raul's sleepy smile. The news of Medrano's death had caused Doña Pepa to faint and had provoked a hysterical crisis in Señora Trejo; they were trying to recuperate now with the help of a good cup of coffee. Lucio, still shaking with rage at the thought of the hours he had spent prisoner in the bar, narrowed his lips and abstained from any comment. Nora, who was sitting next to him, officiously affiliated herself with the peace party and quietly supported Doña Rosita's and Nelly's observations, but she could not keep herself from looking repeatedly at the table where Lopez and Raul were sitting, as if for her, at least, things were far from clear. The *maître*, the very image of outraged dignity, went from one table to another, taking orders, bowing without a word, and occasionally glancing wistfully at the yanked-out telephone wires and sighing.

Almost no one had asked about Jorge; fierceness carried more weight than charity. Under Señora Trejo's leadership, Doña Pepa, Nelly, and Doña Rosita had tried to enter the mortuary cabin at an early hour, so as to proceed with various operations in which feminine necrophilia excells. Atilio, who had had a howling battle with his family, guessed their pious intention and posted himself in front of the door like a hunk of iron. And when Señora Trejo invited him, in an icy tone of voice, to allow them to enter the cabin to fulfill their Christian duties, he answered with a "Go soak your head," which made everything absolutely clear. To Señora Trejo's attempt at slapping him, Pelusa responded with such a meaningful gesture that the worthy lady, most deeply vexed, flinched, her face turning purple as she demanded her husband's presence at the top of her lungs. But Señor Trejo did not appear, and the women retreated, Nelly bathed-in-tears, Doña Pepa and Doña Rosita terrified by the conduct of their respective son and future son-in-law, Señora Trejo in the throes of a nervous attack of hives. Breakfast was something of a strained truce in which everyone could observe the next person out of the corner of his eye,

with the disagreeable sensation that the *Malcolm* had stopped in
mid-sea; in other words, the trip was interrupted, and something,
God knows what, was going to happen.

Pelusa had just sat down at the table of the damned. Raul had
motioned to him the second he saw him appear at the doorway.
His face lit up with a happy smile, Pelusa ran and sat down among
his friends while Nelly lowered her eyes, almost falling into the
toast, and her mother blushed deeper and deeper. Turning his
back on them, Pelusa sat between Paula and Raul, who were enjoying themselves enormously. Lopez, who was very carefully
munching a toasted roll, winked his good eye at him.

"I don't think your family is overenthusiastic about your presence at this table of outcasts," Paula said.

"I'll eat where I want," said Atilio. "They can just stop bugging me, y'know?"

"Sure," said Paula, offering him bread and butter. "And now
we'll have the pleasure of witnessing the majestic arrival of Señor
Trejo and Dr. Restelli."

Don Galo's rasping voice burst forth like a champagne cork. He
was happy to see his friends had been able to sleep a couple of
hours at least, after the hideous night they had spent as prisoners.
As for him, it had been impossible to get any sleep in spite of
doubling his dose of sedatives. But there would be time to sleep
once they had cleared up certain responsibilities and had taken
measures against the unconscionable instigators of so great a bar-
barity.

"This is going to blow up any minute," Paula murmured. "Carlos, and you, Raul, keep still."

"Yeah, yeah," said Pelusa, involved in his coffee and rolls. "So
much bullshit about nothing."

Lopez was watching Dr. Restelli with curiosity, and Dr. Restelli
took care not to return his look. An "Osvaldo!" rang out imperi-
ously from the ladies' table, and Señor Trejo, who was on his way
to an empty place, seemed suddenly to remember an obligation
and, changing his course, approached the table of the damned and
faced Atilio, who was struggling with a slightly excessive mouthful
of bread and jam.

"Would you mind telling me, young man, what right you have to prevent my wife from going into the . . . the funeral parlor?"

Pelusa swallowed his mouthful of bread and jam with an extraordinary effort, and his Adam's apple looked as if it were about to break loose.

"All they wanted was to get their fangs under my skin," he said.

"What are you saying? Repeat that!"

In spite of Raul's motioning to him, Pelusa threw his chair back and stood up.

"Better get it over with," he said, as he clenched his left hand into a fist and shook it under Señor Trejo's nose. "You really want me to get mad? You didn't learn anything last night, eh? You didn't do enough penance, you and everybody else, you pack of shitheads?"

"Atilio!" Paula said virtuously, while Raul doubled over with laughter.

"Now that they come around looking for me they're going to hear it!" Pelusa screamed in a voice that would crack dishes. "A pack of dragasses, talk and more talk, now this and now that, and the kid was dying, that's what! What did you do, tell me about it? Did you and your pals go for the doctor? We went, now get that straight! Just us, this gentleman, and that gentleman over there who got his face pushed in! And the other one . . . yeah, the other . . . and then you think I'm going to let the first person who comes along in the cabin?"

He was choking, he was too upset to go on. Taking him by the arm Lopez tried to sit him down, but Pelusa resisted. Then Lopez stood up and looked Señor Trejo straight in the eye.

"*Vox populi, vox Dei,*" he said. "Go have breakfast, sir. And as for you, Señor Porriño, keep your comments to yourself. And that goes for the ladies too."

"Unbelievable!" Don Galo vociferated, to a background of feminine groans and exclamations. "It's an abuse of power!"

"They should have killed them all!" Señora Trejo shrieked, her flesh flowing over the back of her chair.

A wish as sincere as Señora Trejo's brought silence, for they suspected they had gone too far. They went on eating breakfast in an atmosphere of muffled murmurs and angry glances. Persio, who came in late, made his way between the tables like a hobgoblin and pulled up a chair next to Lopez.

"Everything is a paradox," Persio said, as he poured himself some coffee. "The lambs have turned into wolves, the peace party has become the war party."

"A little late," said Lopez. "They'd do better staying in their cabins and waiting . . . I wonder what for."

"Bad deal," said Raul yawning. "I tried to sleep, no good. It's better out in the sun. Should we go?"

"Let's go," Paula said, but she stopped short, as she was about to stand up. "Now look who's coming."

The thin, suspicious glucid with the short haircut was regarding them from the door. A number of spoons were put back on plates, some chairs were turned halfway around.

"Good day, ladies and gentlemen."

A weak "Good day, sir" was heard from Nelly.

The glucid ran his hand through his hair.

"First of all, I want you to know that the doctor has just visited the sick boy and has found him much improved."

"Terrific," Pelusa said.

"I want to inform you, in the name of the captain, that the security measures, with which you are all familiar, will be lifted at midday."

No one said anything, but Raul's gesture was too eloquent for the glucid to ignore.

"The captain regrets that a misunderstanding has caused a deplorable accident, but you'll understand that the Magenta Star declines all responsibility in this regard, especially since all of you knew we were dealing with an extremely contagious disease on board ship."

"Murderers," Lopez said clearly. "Yes, you heard right: murderers."

The glucid ran his hand through his hair.

"In circumstances like these, overwrought emotions and nerves can account for certain absurd accusations," he said, disposing of the question with a shrug of the shoulders. "One other thing: I didn't want to leave without telling you that perhaps it would be best if you packed your luggage."

At the center of the screams and questions hurled forth by the women, the glucid looked older and more tired. He said a few words to the *maître*, and left, running his hand through his hair more energetically this time.

Paula looked at Raul, who was diligently lighting his pipe.

"What a drag," Paula said. "You know, I've got my apartment sublet for two months."

"Maybe," said Raul, "you'll be able to get Medrano's, that is, if you make it there before Lucio and Nora. They must be dying to get a place."

"You have no respect for the dead, Raul."

"Death won't have any respect for me either, dear."

"Let's get out," Lopez said to Paula abruptly. "Let's go sit in the sun. I've had enough of all this."

"Let's go, Jamaica John," Paula said, looking at him out of the corner of her eye. She liked to see him angry. "No, sweetheart, you're not going to push me around so easy," she thought. "Proud male that you are, you're going to find out that behind those sweet kisses is always my mouth, that doesn't change so easily. Better try and understand me, not change me . . ." And the first thing he had to understand was that the old alliance was not broken, that Raul would always be Raul for her . . . No one would buy her freedom, no one would make her change unless she decided to on her own.

Persio drank a second cup of coffee and thought of going back. The streets around Chacarita paraded through his memory. He'd have to ask Claudia if it would be legal not to go back to work even though he was in Buenos Aires again. "Juridical details, delicate points," Persio thought. "If the boss sees me in the street and I've already told him that I was going to take an ocean trip . . ."

I

But what in hell does it matter if the boss does see him on the street, even if he has told him he was going to take an ocean trip. What in hell! Persio emphasizes this, as he stares at the dregs collected at the bottom of his second cup of coffee, and feels distracted and distant, as if bobbing like a cork on another even bigger cork in a vague area in the South Atlantic. He hasn't been able to stay awake all night, disconcerted by the odor of gunpowder, the running up and down, the hopeless palmistry with hands counterfeited with talc, by the steering wheels of automobiles and the handles on suitcases. He has seen death change its mind a few yards from Jorge's bed, but he knows that this was a metaphor. He has known that men who are his friends have broken the barrier and reached the stern, but he hasn't found the gap through which to renew contact with the night, to coincide with the precarious discovery these men have made. The only one to have known something about the stern can no longer speak. Did he go up the stairs of the initiation? Did he see the caged beasts, did he see the monkeys hung from cables, did he hear the primeval voices, did he find an explanation or a joy? Oh terror of our ancestors, oh night of our race, blind and gushing well, what was the dark and obscure treasure the dragons of the Nordic language were guarding, what reverse image was waiting there to show a dead man its true face? And everything else is lies, and the others, those who came back and those who haven't gone, know it equally well, the former by not looking or not wanting to look, the others through innocence or through the sweet mediocrity of time and habit. Lying the truths of explorers, lying the lies of cowards or the careful; lying the explanations, lying the contradictions of lies. Only Atilio's enraged glory is certain and useless, Atilio, the angel of the clumsy freckled hands, who doesn't know what he has been but who now stands erect, marked forever, separate in his perfect hour, until the inevitable conjuration of the Isle of Maciel brings him back to the state of satisfactory ignorance. And yet there were the Mothers—to give them a name, to believe in their vague configurations—who stand in the middle of the pampas, upon the land which is leaving its marks on the faces of their men, on their bearing and on their necks, and on the color of their eyes, and on the voice which impatiently insists on broiled chops and the latest tango; there were the archetypes, the hidden feet of history, which run madly through the official version, through the twenty-fifth-of-May-threatened-cold-and-rainy, through Liniers, mysteriously hero and traitor described between pages thirty and thirty-four, the fat feet of history awaiting the arrival of the first Argentine, thirsty with deliverance, metamorphosis, and birth. But once more Persio knows that the obscene rite has been fulfilled and that sinister ancestors have interposed themselves between the Mothers and their far-off sons, and that the ancestral fear will eventually kill off the image of God the creator, and will substitute a favorable commerce of phantoms for him, a menacing barrier of the city, an insatiable demand for religious offerings and appeasements. Cages of monkeys, wild beasts on the loose, glucids in uniform, national holidays, or only a deck washed down and grey with dawn, anything at all is enough to conceal what was tremulously waiting on the other side. The dead and the living have returned from below with troubled eyes, and once more Persio sees the image of the guitarist drawn before him, the painting of the guitarist which was once Apollinaire's, once more he sees that the music has no face, there is nothing but a vague black rectangle, a music without master, a blind and rootless event, a ship floating on its deviation, a novel which ends.

EPILOGUE

XLIV

At eleven-thirty it began to grow warm, and Lucio, tired of sitting in the sun and explaining many facts to Nora, facts which she didn't seem to consider irrefutable, decided to go up and take a shower. He'd had enough of talking, face up to the sun, damning those guys who'd ruined the trip; he'd had enough of wondering what was going to happen and why there was all this talk about packing up. The answer came to him as he was climbing up the starboard ladder: an imperceptible buzzing, a dot in the sky, and then a second dot. The two flying boats circled over the *Malcolm* a couple of times before they landed about a hundred yards away. Felipe, alone at the prow, looked on listlessly, lost in a half-dream which Beba attributed meanly to alcohol.

The siren on the *Malcolm* wailed three times, and a signaling device began to flicker on board one of the flying boats. Sprawled out on deck chairs, Lopez and Paula watched a fat glucid glide off on the prow of a launch. Time seemed to wind out indefinitely, the launch took what seemed an incredibly long time to reach the side of one of the flying boats. They saw the glucid finally crawl up along the wing and disappear.

"Help me pack," Paula asked. "I've everything strewn all over the floor."

"Okay, but it's so nice here."

"Then let's stay," Paula said, closing her eyes.

When they grew interested in what was happening around them again, they noticed that the launch, containing several men this time, had pushed off from the flying boat. Stretching his arms and legs, Lopez decided the moment had come to put his affairs in order, but before going up they leaned against the rail for a minute, near Felipe. They recognized the silhouette and dark blue suit of the man who was standing next to the fat glucid, talking excitedly. It was the Inspector from the Office of Municipal Affairs.

A half hour later the *maître* and busboy went from cabin to cabin and around the deck to gather the passengers together in the bar, where the Inspector was waiting for them, along with the grey-haired glucid. Dr. Restelli was the first one there, exuding an optimism which his forced smile denied. He had consulted with Señor Trejo, Lucio, and Don Galo in the interval, exchanging ideas as to the best way of presenting things (just in case they tried to deprive them of the cruise to which all of them, except for the rebels, were fully entitled). The women arrived in their smiles, greeting everyone affably, trying a few inane "What, you're here? What a surprise!" which the Inspector answered by tightening his lips slightly and raising his right hand, palm forward.

"We're all here, I think," he said, looking at the *maître*, who was checking the passenger list. There was a great silence, and the match Raul struck burst noisily into the middle of it.

"Good day, ladies and gentlemen," the Inspector said. "It would be impossible to tell you how deeply the Office of Municipal Affairs regrets the many inconveniences you have all undergone. The radiogram sent by the captain of the *Malcolm* was of such an urgent nature that, as you can well imagine, the Office did not hesitate in mobilizing its most efficient forces as quickly as possible."

"We sent the telegram," Raul said. "To be exact, the man who was murdered by these people sent it."

The Inspector was staring at the tip of the finger Raul was using to point out the glucid. The glucid ran his hand through his hair. The Inspector blew twice on a whistle he had taken out. Three young men in Buenos Aires police uniforms came in, looking definitely incongruous at this latitude and in this bar.

"I'd appreciate your allowing me to finish what I was saying," said the Inspector, as the police lined up behind the passengers. "It's regrettable in the extreme that an epidemic should have broken out once the ship had left Buenos Aires. But the officers of the *Malcolm* took all the necessary measures to protect the health of their passengers, going as far as to enforce a somewhat annoying discipline, which they had of necessity to impose."

"Exactly," said Don Galo. "All that's perfect. I said it from the very beginning. Now allow me, my dear sir—"

"Allow *me*," the Inspector said. "In spite of these precautions, there were two alarms, the second of which made it necessary for the captain to telegraph Buenos Aires. The first of the two cases fortunately did not go beyond the stage of false alarm, and the ship's doctor has already pronounced the little patient out of danger; but the second, provoked by the imprudence of the victim, who illegally crossed the precautionary sanitary barrier and reached the contaminated zone, has ended badly. The gentleman . . ." he consulted a little book, as the murmurs grew. "That would be Señor Medrano. Very regrettable, to be sure. Allow me, gentlemen. Silence! Allow me. Under these circumstances, and after having consulted with the captain and the doctor, we have reached the conclusion that your presence on board the *Malcolm* might endanger your health. The epidemic, although in the process of dissipating, could suddenly break out on this side, especially since the dead man has come to his end in one of the cabins at the prow. And because of all this, ladies and gentlemen, I beg you to prepare to board the flying boats within a quarter of an hour. Thank you very much."

"And why should we get on the airplanes?" Don Galo shrieked, pushing his chair forward toward the Inspector. "Then it's true about the epidemic?"

"My dear Don Galo, of course it is," said Dr. Restelli, quickly rushing forward. "You surprise me, my dear friend. No one has doubted it, not for a single moment; the ship's officials were fighting against an outbreak of typhus 224, you know that perfectly well. Inspector, it's not really a question of that, since we're all in agreement, rather that the measures you are taking seem, let's say, a trifle drastic. Far be it from me to try to secure profit from any privilege, which as beneficiary is rightfully mine, but at the same time, I urge that you reflect upon this measure, a bit precipitate, to be sure . . ."

"Look, Restelli, drop the nonsense," said Lopez, brusquely free-
ing himself from Paula's arm and her threatening pinches. "You
and everyone else know perfectly well that these guys from the
boat shot Medrano down in cold blood. It's not typhus or any
other goddamn thing. And just listen to me a minute. I'll be
damned if I mind going back to Buenos Aires after what we've
gone through here, but I have no intention of their getting out of
it by this kind of lying."

"Keep quiet, sir," said one of the policemen.

"I don't feel like it. I have witnesses and proof of what I'm saying. And the only thing I regret is not having been with Medrano
so as to have shot down a half dozen of those sonsofbitches myself."

The Inspector raised his hand.

"All right, then, gentlemen, I didn't want to see myself put in
the position of having to present an alternative to you, which will
be effected in case some of you lose a certain sense of reality, for
whatever reasons of friendship, and insist on falsifying the facts.
Believe me, it would be a pity to find myself in the position of
having to disembark you onto . . . let's say, some isolated area,
and keep you there until all of you calmed down and could take a
normal view of the information to be given."

"You can let me off wherever you damn well feel like," said
Lopez. "Medrano was murdered by these people. Take a look at
my face. Is that typhus, too?"

"You'll decide for yourselves," said the Inspector, turning to
address himself chiefly to Señor Trejo and Don Galo. "I wouldn't
want to have to intern you, but if you persist in falsifying facts
which have been verified by the most irreproachable witnesses . . ."

"Don't talk garbage," Raul said. "Why don't we go down together, you and I, and take a look at the dead man?"

"Oh, the body has already been removed from the ship," said
the Inspector. "It must be obvious to you that this is a matter of
elementary hygiene. Gentlemen, I implore you to reflect a minute.
We can all be back in Buenos Aires within four hours. Once there,
and the declarations signed, the contents of which we'll draw up
out of the common consensus, you need not worry, for our office

will take care of legally compensating you; it has not been forgotten that this trip corresponds to a prize, and the fact that it has not turned out well is no impediment."

"A pretty turn of phrase," Paula said.

Señor Trejo cleared his throat, looked at his wife, and decided to speak.

"I'd like to know, Inspector . . . since the body has been removed from the ship, as you've just told us, and the typhus outbreak is clearly over as well, wouldn't it be possible to . . . ?"

"But of course," said Don Galo. "What reason is there for those of us who might be of one mind . . . I say clearly, for those of us who might be of one mind not to go on with this trip?"

Everyone spoke at once; the women's voices rose above the clumsy attempts of the police to impose silence. Raul noticed that the Inspector was smiling with satisfaction and that he was making a sign to the police not to intervene. "Divide and rule," he thought as he leaned up against a partition and smoked. "Why not? What difference if they stayed or didn't stay. Poor Lopez, all that persistent in his attempt to make the truth shine through. But Medrano would be happy if he could see us here; what a hornet's nest he stirred up . . ." He smiled at Claudia, who was watching everything as if from a distance, far from the drama at hand, while Dr. Restelli explained that certain regrettable excesses should not threaten the well-earned holiday of the majority of passengers, and for that reason, he was confident that the Inspector . . . But the Inspector again raised his hand, palm forward, until a relative silence was achieved.

"I can well understand the point of view expressed by these gentlemen," he said. "However, the captain and other officials have decided that given the circumstances . . . In a word, gentlemen, we're all returning to Buenos Aires or I'll find myself forced, painfully so, to temporarily intern you until all misunderstandings are set at rest. You can see for yourselves that the typhus threat alone is enough to justify such an extreme measure."

"There it is," said Don Galo, turning to Lopez and Atilio like a basilisk. "That's the price of anarchy and the abuse of power. I said it from the beginning. And now the innocents will pay for the sinners, goddamn it. And those hydroplanes, are they safe or what?"

"Don't mention hydroplanes!" cried Señora Trejo, backed up by a predominantly feminine murmur. "Why can't we continue the trip, why not?"

"The trip is over, señora," the Inspector said.

"Osvaldo, are you going to stand for this?"

"My dear," said Señor Trejo, sighing.

"All right, all right," said Don Galo. "We'll all climb on the hydroplane and it's finished, and we won't go on jabbering any more about internments and other rubbish."

"Then," said Dr. Restelli, looking out of the corner of his eye at Lopez, "if we achieve the unanimity to which the Inspector refers, given the circumstances . . ."

Lopez felt both disgust and pity. He was so tired that pity won.

"Don't worry about me, hell," he said to Restelli. "I don't mind going back to Buenos Aires, and once there we'll do our own talking."

"Exactly," said the Inspector. "The Office of Municipal Affairs has to have the assurance that none of you will take advantage of your return to spread false rumors."

"Then," said Lopez, "the Office is dreaming."

"My dear sir, your insistence . . ." said the Inspector. "Believe me, if I don't have the assurance beforehand that you won't falsify —yes that, won't falsify the truth—I'll be forced to do what I spoke of before."

"All we need," said Don Galo. "First we spend three days hanging by a thread, and then God knows you figure it how much time up the asshole of creation. No, no, and no. To Buenos Aires, Buenos Aires!"

"But, of course," said Señor Trejo. "It's intolerable."

"Let's analyze the situation calmly," Dr. Restelli suggested.

"The situation is very simple," said Señor Trejo. "Since the Inspector believes it impossible to go on with the trip . . ." he looked at his wife, who was livid with rage, and made a gesture of impotence, ". . . the most logical and natural thing to do is return immediately to Buenos Aires and recover our . . ."

"*Our,*" said Raul, "recover *our* . . ."

"As far as I'm concerned, I don't see anything to impede that," said the Inspector, "once you sign the declaration, which will be drawn up."

"I'll draw up my own declaration, to the last comma," said Lopez.

"You won't be the only one," said Paula, feeling slightly ridiculous in her virtuousness.

"Of course not," said Raul. "There will be at least five of us. And that makes more than a quarter of the passengers, something not to be put down in a democracy."

"Don't start with politics, if you don't mind," said the Inspector.

The glucid ran his hand through his hair and began to speak softly, as the Inspector listened politely.

Raul turned toward Paula.

"Telepathy, dear. He's telling him that the Magenta Star is opposed on principle to the business of partial internment, because there will be more of a scandal in the long run. They won't take us to Ushuaia, you'll see, not even that. I'm glad, because I didn't bring any winter clothes along. Just watch, you'll see I'm right."

He was right, because the Inspector again raised his hand, with the usual gesture, which made him look incongruously like a penguin, and declared forcefully that if he didn't have unanimity, he would be forced to intern all the passengers, without exceptions. The flying boats could not be separated, for obvious technical reasons. He fell silent and waited for the results of the old maxim which had crossed Raul's mind shortly before. He did not have to wait long. Dr. Restelli looked at Don Galo, who looked at Señora Trejo, who looked at her husband. A polygon of glances, an instantaneous rebound. Orator, Don Galo Porriño.

"Look here, sir," said Don Galo, as he rocked his wheelchair back and forth. "Just because of the pigheadedness and stubbornness of these elegant young men, the rest of us, people of common sense and consideration, will find ourselves shipped off to God knows where, not to mention that we'll be slandered up and down later. I know this world only too well. If you tell us that the . . . that the accident was the outcome of that damn epidemic, then I personally think there's no reason to doubt your word as a public official. It wouldn't surprise me if this morning's wrangle turned out to be more smoke than fire, as they say. The truth is that none of us"—he emphasized the last word—"have been able to see . . .

the unfortunate gentleman, who nevertheless enjoyed our good graces in spite of his last-minute foolhardiness."

He turned his chair a quarter of a circle and looked triumphantly at Lopez and Raul.

"I repeat: no one has seen the body, because these gentlemen, aided by an outlaw, who dared lock us up in the bar last night— and just notice the significance of this unspeakable outrage when considered in the light of what we're saying—these gentlemen, I repeat, to give them a name they no longer deserve, prevented these ladies, who were inspired by Christian charity, a conviction which I respect even though I don't share their feeling, from entering the dead man's cabin. What conclusions, Inspector, can be drawn from all this?"

Raul grabbed Pelusa's arm, for Atilio had turned brick-color, but wasn't able to stop him from speaking out.

"What's that? What conclusions, you old idiot? I brought him back, I brought him back with this señor here! There was blood running out of his sweater!"

"A delirious alcoholic, no doubt," Señor Trejo muttered.

"And the bullet I shot on the stern that went through that guy's ear, what about that? He was bleeding like a stuck pig! If only I'd got him in the gut, dear God, we'd see if you'd come around here talking about typhus!"

"Don't knock yourself out, Atilio," said Raul. "They've got the story written already."

"What story?" said Pelusa.

Raul shrugged his shoulders.

The Inspector was waiting, knowing that the others would be more eloquent than he. Dr. Restelli spoke first, an absolute model of discretion and good sense; then Señor Trejo spoke, a vehement defender of the cause of law and order; Don Galo limited himself to lending support to his friends' speeches by turning some witty and opportune phrases. At first Lopez went to the trouble of answering, telling them that they were out-and-out cowards, and he was backed by Atilio's interjections and sudden fits of rage, as well as Raul's well-pointed digs. But Lopez finally found it all repulsive and no longer even felt like talking, and so he turned his back on them and sat down in a corner. The group of the damned gathered together in silence, discreetly patrolled by the police. The peace party rounded out their conclusions, encouraged by the women's approval and the Inspector's melancholy smile.

XLV

The *Malcolm*, seen from above, looked like a matchstick in a basin. After hurrying to get a seat by the window, Felipe looked indifferently at the spectacle around him. The sea was losing all volume, all texture, it was turning into a dark, opaque sheet. He lit a cigarette and glanced around him; the backs of the seats were unusually low. To the left, the other flying boat seemed suspended in a kind of perfect immobility. The passengers' luggage was being carried in that one and probably the . . . When he had gone aboard, Felipe had looked into all the empty spaces in the cabin, expecting to find a body wrapped in a sheet or a canvas, more likely a canvas. As he saw nothing, he suspected they had put it on the other plane.

"Well," said Beba, seated between her mother and Felipe. "We might have known it would turn out like this. I didn't like it from the beginning."

"It could have turned out perfectly," said Señora Trejo, "if it hadn't been for the typhus and . . . for the typhus."

"In any case, it's a fat laugh," said Beba. "I'll have to tell my girlfriends all about it, imagine."

"Well, darling, tell them about it and that's that. You know very well what has to be said."

"If you think Maria Luisa and Meche are going to swallow that . . ."

Señora Trejo looked at Beba for a second and then at her husband, seated on the opposite side, where there were only two places. Señor Trejo, who had heard the conversation, made a sign to his wife to stay calm. Once back in Buenos Aires they would gradually convince the children not to change the story; maybe it would be a good idea to send them to Cordoba for a month, to

Aunt Florita's place. Children forget quickly, and furthermore, as they weren't of age, their words carried no legal weight. It really wasn't worth a bother making a fuss over it.

Felipe continued to stare at the *Malcolm* until he saw it disappear beneath the plane; only an interminable boredom of water remained now, four hours of water until they reached Buenos Aires. The flight wasn't too bad; after all, it was the first time he'd been on a plane and it would be something to tell the guys. His mother's face before take-off, Beba's concealed terror . . . Women were incredible, they got frightened over the slightest . . . And by God, you'd never guess, a really fantastic thing happened, and in the end they had to pile us all into a Catalina and bring us back home. One guy was killed and everything, so . . . But they wouldn't believe him . . . Ordoñez would look at him with that superior expression. If that happened, we'd have heard all about it kid, what do you think newspapers are for? Yes, it was better not to talk about that part. But Ordoñez, and maybe Alfieri, would ask him how everything had gone on the trip. That was easier: the pool, a redhead in a bikini, he comes on very strong, the girl coming on all square, looking to see if anyone was digging the scene, I'm embarrassed, cool it, baby, no one's going to find out nothing, come on, push that at me a little. At first she didn't want to, she was scared, but you know how it is, I hardly had begun to maul her before she shut her eyes and let me push her on the bed and undress her. What a piece, baby, just remembering it . . .

He slid down a little in the seat, his eyes half-closed. Look, if I told you what happened . . . The whole day, you know, and she didn't want me to leave? One of those put-it-in-deep-and-leave-it-there types who can't get enough, you know, until you don't know what else to do . . . Redhead, yeah, but she was more blond in the . . . Sure, I wondered about that too, but I'm telling you, more on the blond side.

The pilot's cabin door opened and the Inspector looked out, with a satisfied, almost youthful air.

"Marvelous weather, ladies and gentlemen. We'll be at Puerto Nuevo in three and a half hours. The Office thought that after filling in the forms, the ones that we've already discussed, you'd probably rather go back home at once. To avoid a loss of time, there will be taxis for everyone, and you will receive your luggage as soon as we disembark."

He sat down on the first seat, next to Don Galo's chauffeur, who was reading an issue of *True Detective*.

Nora, sitting deep in a seat by the window, sighed.

"I can't make up my mind," she said. "Believe me, it's more than I can figure out. Yesterday everything was fine, and now . . ."

"You're telling me," Lucio murmured.

"I don't understand. At the beginning, you were very worried too about the poop-deck business . . . Why did they get so worked up? I don't know, they seemed like such nice refined men."

"A bunch of ruffians," Lucio said. "I didn't know the others, but I swear Medrano left me cold. Just watch, the way things'll go in Buenos Aires, a mess like this can do us all damage. Figure it out, if someone hands this information over to my bosses, it could mean my not getting a raise or something worse. After all, they were *official* prizes, no one paid any attention to that. They only thought about making trouble so they'd look good."

"I don't know," said Nora, looking at him and then immediately lowering her eyes. "You're right, of course, but when the little boy got sick . . ."

"So what? Don't you see him sitting over there eating candy? Now what kind of sickness was that, do you mind telling me? All those Counts of Monte Cristo wanted to do was to make trouble so they could come off heroes. You think I didn't realize it from the start and that I didn't try to slow down their wagon for them? A lot of guns and a big parade . . . I'm telling you, Nora, if this gets around Buenos Aires . . ."

"But it's not going to get around," said Nora, timidly.

"Let's hope not. Fortunately, there are some of us who think as I do, and we're in the majority."

"You'll have to sign that declaration."

"Naturally, I'll have to sign it. The Inspector will arrange everything. Maybe I'm worried about nothing; after all, who's going to believe that story anyway."

"Yes, but Señor Lopez and Presutti were so furious . . ."

"They wanted to save face up till the end," said Lucio, "but you'll see, in Buenos Aires, you won't hear any more out of them. Why are you looking at me like that?"

"Me?"

"Yes, you."

"But Lucio, I was only looking at you."

"You were looking at me as if I was lying, or something like that."

"No, Lucio."

"Yes, you were looking at me funny. But don't you see I'm right?"

"Of course I do," said Nora, avoiding his eyes. Of course Lucio was right. He was too angry not to be right. Lucio who was always so cheerful . . . she'd have to do everything possible to make him forget these days and make him happy again. It would be awful if he went on being ill-tempered once they got to Buenos Aires, and then, if he decided to do something, what thing, she didn't know what, any thing, stop loving her or leave her, though it was ridiculous to think Lucio might leave her just when she had given him the greatest proof of love, now that she had committed sin for him. It seemed incredible that in three hours they'd be downtown, and now she'd have to ask Lucio what he was thinking of doing, if she should go back to her house, or what. Her sister Mocha would understand, but her mother . . . She could see herself going into the dining room, and her mother glaring at her, getting paler by the minute. Where had she been for three days? "Tramp," her mother would say. "So that's the education you got from the nuns, tramp, whore, no-good." And Mocha would try to protect her, but how *could* she explain those three days? It was impossible to go back home, she would call Mocha and have her meet them somewhere. But if Lucio, who was angry . . . And if he didn't want to get married right away, if he began to put off the wedding, and went back to work, to the girls in the office, especially that Betty, if he started going out again with his friends . . .

Lucio was looking at the sea over Nora's shoulder. He seemed to be waiting for her to say something. Nora turned to him and kissed him on the cheek, the nose, the mouth. Lucio didn't return the kisses, but she felt him smiling when she kissed him again on the cheek.

"Darling," Nora said, putting her soul into it so that what she was saying would be as it had to be, "I love you so much. And I'm so happy with you, I feel so safe, you know, protected."

She caught a glimpse of his face as she kissed him, and she saw that Lucio was still smiling. She pulled herself together to talk about Buenos Aires.

"No, no, enough candies. Last night you were dying and now you want to get a good stomach-ache."

"I've only had two," said Jorge, looking martyred, as he let himself be wrapped in a traveling blanket. "What a smooth trip. Persio, don't you think that we could get to the star on a plane like this?"

"Impossible," said Persio. "We'd blow up the minute we hit the stratosphere."

Closing her eyes, Claudia rested her head on the back of the uncomfortable seat. It irritated her to have to get worked up at Jorge. *Last night you were dying . . .* She shouldn't have said that to him, but she knew that she wasn't really talking to him. What Jorge was guilty of went far beyond him. Poor kid, it was stupid of her to dump on him something so distinct, so apart from all that. She wrapped him up again, felt his forehead, and looked for cigarettes. Across the aisle Lopez and Paula were playing at interlacing their fingers, hand wrestling. Raul, enveloped in a cloud of smoke, was dozing against the window. Some images out of his fitful sleep floated briefly before him and then disappeared, suddenly waking him. Dr. Restelli's head and Señor Trejo's thick neck were only a few inches from his face. He could have reconstructed their conversation, almost word for word, though the roar of the motors prevented his hearing a syllable. They were exchanging calling cards, determined to meet very soon, and they were assuring one another that everything would turn out well and that none of the hotheads (who were now well in line, thanks to the Inspector and their own heavyhandedness) wouldn't dare start a press campaign in the left-wing papers, publicity which might drag all their names through the mud. At this altitude, and to judge by the vehemence of Dr. Restelli's gestures, he must be insisting on the fact there was no proof of anything these disorderly malcontents could possibly advance as testimony. "At least a good lawyer would have no trouble," Raul thought, amused. "Who would believe there were firearms within hand's reach on a ship like that, or that the lipids, after we fired at them on the bridge, didn't make mincemeat of us within five minutes? Where's our proof? Medrano, of course. But all there'll be left of Medrano is a three-line obit, carefully edited."

"Hey, Carlos . . ."

"Hold it a second," said Lopez. "She's getting my arm down, the bitch, look."

"Pinch her, that's the best way to win at hand wrestling. Listen, I was just thinking, by way of amusement, that maybe the old bucks are right. Did you bring your revolver?"

"No, Atilio must have it," said Lopez, surprised.

"I doubt it. When I went to pack my bags, the Colt had disappeared, along with all the ammunition. It wasn't mine, so it seemed fair enough. Let's ask Atilio, but I'm pretty sure they robbed his shootin' iron too. Something else that occurred to me: you and Medrano went to the barber shop, right?"

"The barber shop? Wait a minute, that was yesterday. Is it possible it was only yesterday? It seems so long ago. Yes, sure we went."

"I wonder," said Raul, "why you didn't ask the barber about the stern. I'm positive you didn't ask him a thing."

"As a matter of fact we didn't," said Lopez, puzzled. "We were only talking, amusing ourselves. Medrano was so . . . first-rate, so . . . But you know, these cynics act as if things happened altogether differently . . ."

"Let's get back to the barber," said Raul. "Doesn't it strike you as odd that when we were looking for any way at all to get to the stern . . . ?"

Almost without listening, Paula was looking from one to the other, wondering how long they'd go on tossing that business back and forth. Men were the true inventors of the past; what worried her was what was going to happen—that is, if she worried at all. What would Jamaica John be like in Buenos Aires? Not like on ship, not like he was at this moment; the city was waiting to transform them, to turn them all back into what they had been before leaving, along with the necktie and the little black book of telephone numbers. And suddenly Lopez was just a teacher, what did they call it . . . a member of the faculty, someone who had to get up at seven-thirty to go and teach gerunds at nine forty-five or at eleven-fifteen. "How hideous can you get?" Paula thought. "And it'll be even worse when he sees what I'm like in Buenos Aires; that's going to be much, much worse." But what did it matter? They felt perfectly wonderful right now, their hands interlaced like idiots, looking at one another or sticking out their tongues or asking Raul didn't they make the ideal couple.

Atilio was the first to notice the chimney stacks, the towers, the skyscrapers, and he ran through the plane with extraordinary enthusiasm. He had been bored during the whole trip, sitting between Nelly and Doña Rosita and attending to Nelly's mother who was airsick, which brought on crying fits and confused suggestions duly credited to relatives and friends.

"Look, look, we're at the river already, if you look hard you'll see the Avellaneda bridge! Wow, think it took us more than three days getting there and now we're back in two shakes!"

"That's progress," said Doña Rosita, who was watching her son with a mixture of fear and mistrust. "Now, when we get there we'll call your father for him to come and pick us up with the truck."

"We won't have to, señora, the Inspector told us they'd have taxis for all of us," Nelly said. "Atilio, please sit down, you're making me nervous jumping around like that. It feels as if the plane's going to tip, I swear."

"Just like in the movie where everybody dies," Doña Rosita said.

Pelusa let loose a disrespectful guffaw, but he sat down just the same. It was difficult for him to keep quiet and he couldn't stop feeling that there was something he had to do. He didn't know what, he was busting with energy, and was ready for anything if Lopez or Raul would ask him. But Lopez and Raul were sitting quietly smoking, and Atilio felt vaguely disappointed. It looked like the oldsters and the fuzz were going to win out, it was a shame. If Medrano had been there it wouldn't have turned out like this.

"You're so jittery," said Doña Rosita. "Yesterday's bungling around wasn't enough for you? Look at Nelly, look at her. You should hang your head in shame to have made her suffer so much, the poor dear. I never saw so much crying, I swear. Oh, Doña Pepa, sons are a cross, believe me. And it was so nice in that cabin, with all that beautiful woodwork, with that funny Señor Porriño, and then these maniacs go and get us into a mess."

"Knock it off, Mama," said Pelusa, pulling a bit of skin off one finger.

"Your mother's right," Nelly added weakly. "Can't you see they fooled you? The Inspector told you so. And they made you believe everything they said, and you, of course . . ."

Pelusa straightened up as if he had been jabbed with a knife.

"Look, do you want me to take you as far as the altar or not?" he yelled. "How many times do I have to tell you what happened, you ninny?"

Nelly burst into tears, protected by the noise of the motors and the tiredness of the passengers. Furious and full of remorse, Pelusa preferred looking at Buenos Aires. They were already close, tilting a little, you could already see the chimney stacks of the electricity company and the port, everything came up, went past, and disappeared behind them, pulsating in a cloud of smoke and midday heat. "What a pizza I'm going to down with Humberto and Rusito," Pelusa thought. "That was the one thing they didn't have on the boat, I got to admit it."

"Here you are, señora," said the impeccable police officer.

Señora Trejo took the fountain pen with an amiable smile and signed the bottom of the page, where there were already ten or twelve signatures.

"You, señor," said the officer.

"I'm not signing that," said Lopez.

"Nor I," said Raul.

"Very well, gentlemen. You, señora?"

"No, I won't sign," said Claudia.

"Nor I," said Paula, bestowing upon him a very special smile.

The officer turned toward the Inspector and said something. The Inspector handed him a list which included the names, professions, and addresses of all the travelers. The officer took out a red pencil and underlined some of the names.

"Ladies and gentlemen, you may leave the dock at your convenience," he said, clicking his heels. "The taxis and luggage are outside."

Claudia and Persio left, taking Jorge by the hand. The thick, damp heat from the river and the port odors were disgusting to Claudia, who ran her hand across her forehead. Please, Juan Bautista Alberdi, the seven-hundredth block. She said goodbye to Paula, Lopez, and Raul beside the taxi. Yes, her number was in the phone book: Lewbaum.

Lopez promised to visit one day, armed with a kaleidoscope, over which Jorge had grand illusions. The taxi left, carrying Persio too. He seemed half asleep.

"Well, you see they're going to let us go," said Raul. "They'll keep an eye on us for a while, but then . . . They know perfectly well what they're doing. I assume they're counting on us. I, for instance, I'll be the first to ask myself what I should do and when I should do it. I'll ask myself so many times that in the end . . . Should we take the same taxi, you lovely couple?"

"Of course," said Paula. "Put the bags up here."

Atilio came running over, sweat pouring down his face. He shook Paula's hand until it felt crushed, gave Lopez a loud crack on the back, and tried to break a few of Raul's fingers. His brick-colored jacket returned him completely to everything that was waiting for him.

"We'll have to see you," said Pelusa enthusiastically. "Look, lend me a pencil and I'll give you my address. Come out one Sunday and we'll have a barbecue. My old man'll be happy to meet you."

"Sure, sure," said Raul, sure that they'd never see one another again.

Pelusa was looking at them, radiant with emotion. He slapped Lopez on the back again and wrote down his address and telephone number. Nelly was screaming for him, and he went off downcast, perhaps understanding or sensing something he could not understand.

From the taxi, the three of them could see the peace party dispersing, and the chauffeur installing Don Galo in a big blue automobile. Several onlookers were taking in the scene, but there were more police than spectators.

Squeezed between Lopez and Raul, Paula asked where they were going. Lopez kept silent, but Raul said nothing either, as he watched them in an amused, mocking fashion.

"Well, to start things off, we could have a drink," Lopez said finally.

"Extremely sane idea," said Paula, who was thirsty.

The driver, a smiling young fellow, turned around for his orders.

"Oh, well . . ." said Lopez. "We're going to the London—Peru and Avenida."

ABOUT THE AUTHOR

Julio Cortázar, an Argentine who was born in Brussels in 1914, has lived and worked in Paris since 1952. He is a poet, translator, and amateur jazz musician as well as the author of several volumes of short stories and novels. He has had nine books published in English: *The Winners, Hopscotch, End of the Game, Cronopios and Famas, 62: A Model Kit, All Fires the Fire and Other Stories, A Manual for Manuel, A Change of Light,* and *We Love Glenda So Much.*

Pantheon Modern Writers Series

WHEN THINGS OF THE SPIRIT COME FIRST
Five Early Tales
by Simone de Beauvoir, translated by Patrick O'Brian

The first paperback edition of the marvelous early fiction of Simone de Beauvoir. These five short stories illuminate the climate in which de Beauvoir grew up, the origins of her thought, and the fascinating young mind of the woman who was to become one of the cultural giants of her day.

"An event for celebration."—*The New York Times Book Review*

0-394-72235-3 $5.95

THE BLOOD OF OTHERS
by Simone de Beauvoir, translated by Roger Senhouse and Yvonne Moyse

In this vivid and disturbing story about the French Resistance, Jean Blomart, patriot leader against the German forces of occupation, waits throughout an endless night for his lover, Hélène, to die. He is the one who sent her on the mission that led to her death, and before morning he must decide how many others to send to a similar fate. A brilliant existentialist novel.

"A novel with a remarkably sustained note of suspense and mounting excitement due to the sheer vitality and force of de Beauvoir's ideas."—*Saturday Review*

0394-72411-9 $6.95

THE OGRE
by Michel Tournier, translated by Barbara Bray

The Ogre is the bizarre story of a gentle giant who enters World War II as a Parisian garage mechanic but becomes, as a German prisoner of war, gamekeeper to Hermann Goering and then "recruiter" of children for the Nazi school at the castle of Kaltenborn. A gripping tale of innocence, perversion, and obsession.

"The most important novel to come out of France since Proust."—Janet Flanner

"Quite simply, a great novel."—*The New Yorker*

0-394-72407-0 $8.95

THE WINNERS
by Julio Cortázar, translated by Elaine Kerrigan

A luxury ship sets sail from Buenos Aires, filled with passengers who have won their tickets in a national lottery. At first the mood is festive...but a looming sense of menace gradually builds to an explosion.

"This formidable novel...introduces a dazzling writer....[*The Winners*] is irresistibly readable."—William Goyen, *The New York Times Book Review*

0-394-72301-5 $8.95

Pantheon Modern Classics

MEMED, MY HAWK
by Yashar Kemal

The most important novel to come out of modern Turkey, this vital and exciting story of a latter-day Robin Hood is set against the beauty and brutality of Turkish peasant life. "Exciting, rushing, lyrical, a complete and subtle emotional experience."—*The Chicago Sun-Times*

0-394-71016-9 $6.95

THE LEOPARD
by Giuseppe di Lampedusa

This powerful novel of a Sicilian prince perched on the brink of great historic change is widely acknowledged as a masterpiece of European literature. "The finest historical novel I have read in years."—*Saturday Review*

0-394-74949-9 $5.95

YOUNG TÖRLESS
by Robert Musil

Taut, compelling, pitiless first novel by the author of *The Man Without Qualities*. A meticulous account, set in an Austrian military academy, of the discovery and abuse of power—physical, emotional, and sexual. "An illumination of the dark places of the heart everywhere."—*The Washington Post*

0-394-71015-0 $5.95

THE STORY OF A LIFE
by Konstantin Paustovsky

Universally acclaimed memoir of Russian boyhood coming of age amidst war and revolution. A startlingly vivid, deeply personal yet panoramic view of Russia during the tumultuous first two decades of the twentieth century. "A work of astonishing beauty...a masterpiece."—Isaac Bashevis Singer

0-394-71014-2 $8.95

WITHDRAWN

Gramley Library
Salem College
Winston-Salem, NC 27108